NEW STORIES
FROM THE SOUTH

The Year's Best, 1987

edited by
Shannon Ravenel

NEW STORIES
FROM THE SOUTH

The Year's Best, 1987

Algonquin Books of Chapel Hill
1987

published by
Algonquin Books of Chapel Hill
Post Office Box 2225, Chapel Hill, North Carolina 27515-2225
in association with Taylor Publishing Company
1550 West Mockingbird Lane, Dallas, Texas 75235

Library of Congress Cataloging-in-Publication Data

New stories from the South.

 1. Short stories, American—Southern States.   2. American fiction—20th century.
3. Southern States—Fiction.   I. Ravenel, Shannon.
PS551.N49 1987   813'.01'08975   87-1356
ISBN 0-912697-66-0
ISBN 0-912697-73-3 (pbk.)

CONTENTS

PREFACE

"Mom worries about dumb stuff," Corey told the counselor. "During tornado season she writes our names on our legs in Magic Marker."
(from Mary Hood's "After Moore")

He is a pastor. Not a prophet. Not a radio evangelist. He does not believe in Gods that quote the King James Version out of bushes and trees.
(from Peggy Payne's "The Pure in Heart")

. . . here came Billy of Billy's Martinizing himself, out of his office and over to me. You should see Billy—he is real fat and wears a blond toupee which comes right down to his eyebrows and open neck shirts with gold chains.
(from Lee Smith's "Life on the Moon")

From Gram's screened-in porch we can see straight into their front yard, where amongst corroded junk and clumps of weeds a Harley hangs, chained ten feet up to an old oak branch . . . it's their banner, their heraldic arms: Here live the Motoheads.
(from Luke Whisnant's "Across from the Motoheads")

These are four of the voices that tell the fifteen stories in this second annual volume of *New Stories From The South*. For a Southerner, a short story lover, and a tireless maker of judgements, the opportunity to edit such an anthology is a wonderful one. For each annual volume, I choose my favorite Southern stories from American stories published first-serially in magazines, reviews, journals, and quarterlies over the preceding year. This plan insures that the stories collected each year are indeed new. I am also intent upon seeing to it that the best of the new approaches to Southern fiction are represented, along with any new twists on traditional

Southern themes. Certainly, the four voices I've quoted come from a Southern experience that is unmistakably contemporary. I say all this to indicate that I am serious about the term "new" in the series title.

I'm just as serious about the term "stories." It is my intention that all the stories really be stories—that is, that they stand on their own and are not enticements for larger or, I should say, longer, works.

But the biggest challenge for me is to keep the promise of the words, "from the South." Sometimes it's not so hard. Nine of these fifteen stories were first published in periodicals issued from Southern locations (*The Crescent Review,* Winston-Salem, N.C.; *The Southern Review,* Baton Rouge, La.; *The Greensboro Review,* Greensboro, N.C.; *The Georgia Review,* Athens, Ga.; *Sewanee Review,* Sewanee, Tenn.; *Virginia Quarterly Review,* Charlottesville, Va.). All of these magazines include biographical notes about their authors and often I can be sure of the technical truth of "from the South." The other six stories were in decidedly un-Southern magazines—*The New Yorker, Esquire, Redbook, The Hudson Review,* and *Grand Street* are all published in New York City. And then there is *Playgirl.* A California publiciation, it is an unlikely but nevertheless excellent source of new fiction.

In order to meet various printers' deadlines, the stories must sometimes be selected without knowledge of their authors' origins. When a story appears in *The New Yorker,* for instance, there isn't a contributor's note with biographical information. I can't, therefore, always be sure that an author is a born Southerner. It's not really the technical truth of "from the South" that matters. Vicki Covington, author of the beautiful *New Yorker* story, "Magnolia," is "from the South," one way or the other. My choice of her story for this collection didn't depend as much on her regional details or on the title as it did on my response to a narrative immediacy that I consider characteristic of the best short stories, Southern, or not—a voice that cannot be ignored because of the fullness of characterization behind it.

Listen:

I was Lila's project, her charity work. She felt that being married to a drunk had tainted and scarred my character. Oh, my older two hated that. The desire to both thank her and forgive her daily is a blessing I don't take lightly.

I had the same sort of confidence in Marly Swick when I heard:

My daddy'd run off with my teacher and now my mama was crazy. I felt real special.
(from "Heart")

Is it worthwhile trying to pin down what, if anything, sets Southern fiction apart? If you read all the stories in this book, you'll notice at least several themes that might come up in such a discussion. For one, there's always been a lot of experienced drinking in Southern fiction:

. . . his body was relaxed, his hands resting on either side of his drink on the bar. Now his body tautened out of its slump, and he lifted his glass and drank till only the lime wedge and ice touched his teeth; he swung the glass down hard on the bar and said: "Do it again, Al."
(from Andre Dubus's "Dressed Like Summer Leaves")

He finished the second whiskey and curled a finger at the bartender for a third. This would do it. He was cooler now and feeling better than all right. Whatever they told him, he would just listen and say nothing. He would not mention the old scruffy stuffed animals that lay in a heap on the daybed on the back porch of the house he still occupied, where Doreen had grown up, where he had once been married. The puppy was named Jiggs, the snake Olaf, the frog Feed.
(from John William Corrington's "Heroic Measures/Vital Signs")

He lifted the first shot in his hand and checked the mirror. Mama looked a hundred years old in her love for him. He drained the whiskey from the glass and set it back on the counter. He chased the drink with Coca-Cola. He looked into the mirror again. He was handsome and manly and tragic and fine. He was the Marlboro Man of alcoholism.
(from Lewis Nordan's "Sugar, the Eunuchs, and Big G.B.")

For another, visions—religious and otherwise—occur with some regularity and vividness in Southern fiction. *New Stories From The South 1987* has its share. Here's an example:

He was wearing a blue suit. Not like the ones they wear in the Bible, but a furry one. Kind of like winter pajamas, with zippers up the front of the coat and the front of the legs of the pants. It was neat.

(from Rosanne Coggeshall's "Peter the Rock")

Strong women abound—we all know that. There's no dearth of them here. To quote just one:

I forgave Edward his trespasses.

(from Robert Boswell's "Edward and Jill")

And a child's narrative viewpoint is a Southern favorite:

Last summer and fall there had been a whole batch of child molestations, at least that was what her mother said, and so Debra just had to be sure to check in, that was all. When Debra thought about it, though, she wondered if it didn't have more to do with her leukemia. Maybe her mother was afraid she would collapse somewhere between the bus and the kitchen phone and crash into the stone flowerpots . . .

(from Trudy Lewis's "Vincristine")

Have I said that my mother was a beautiful woman? She was. I found this somewhat of an embarrassment, another instance of how my family was not right.

(from Robert Taylor, Jr.'s "Lady of Spain")

The only other officer's kid is Evelyn Pallas who no one sits next to. Cora says it's because she "wears the old man's rank on her sleeve." Col. Pallas is CO. Still, I believe Evelyn is in love with me even though we've never sat next to each other on the bus.

(from James Gordon Bennett's "Dependents")

But as common as those themes, characters, and literary devices are to Southern fiction, of course they are neither restricted to it nor essential to it. I'll go out on a limb, however, and suggest that there is one element that is nearly always present in the stories I like best (I'm already equivocating!)—an insistent, idiosyncratic, and undeniable voice. It can be heard in first or third (and even in the flashy new second) person narrative, from young or old or middle-aged viewpoints, reliable or unreliable, single or multiple. What is always true is that it's at once urgent and familiar—a voice that takes me by the scruff of the neck and holds tight until it is finished telling. Here is one last example of that voice:

To Colonel Coates's eye, President Trass looked like an old salamander in
bib overalls, a slick, lymphatic edgelessness to the black man's features.
President Trass thought that the colonel, removed of the hat squashed onto
his skull like a bottle cap, resembled a newly hatched chicken hawk, hot-
skinned, old-ugly, and fierce at birth.

(from Bob Shacochis's "Where Pelham Fell")

If a story appears to be technically "from the South" and is told
in that undeniable voice, I want it for my Southern anthology. In
this Preface, you've heard one voice from each of the fifteen *New
Stories from the South*. Let them finish the telling.

Shannon Ravenel

NEW STORIES
FROM THE SOUTH

The Year's Best, 1987

Luke Whisnant

ACROSS FROM THE MOTOHEADS

(from *Grand Street*)

They're at it again. From Gran's screened-in porch we can see straight into their front yard, where amongst corroded junk and clumps of weeds a Harley hangs, chained ten feet up to an old oak branch. Rust-pitted, skeletal, like some strange carcass swinging dry in the wind, it's their banner, their heraldic arms: here live the Motoheads. They stand outside in full view, large and hairy, troglodyte, popping beers and burning red meat over an open-pit fire—a brick-lined hole dug with much cursing in the early afternoon. Their chests are bare under sleeveless jeans jackets. They roar at each other not to park their bikes on the lawn. They park their bikes on the lawn.

Gran says she's not afraid of dopers and that she's seen them worse. We believe her. Like everywhere else, the neighborhood has gone downhill. Even the cops lock their car doors. "They ain't gonna do a thing to me but maybe burn my house down with me inside it," Gran says. She won't move, though. She's lived here for twenty-two years, ever since she got back from Manila. "I wish you could have seen the yards there—pretty as a golf course. And every blade in place. You can't get help like that here, I hope to tell you. Those Filipinos. They cut the grass with a scissors, one piece at a time, down on their knees."

My uncle Bubba laughs because he's heard all this so many times before and because Gran's been after him for two days now to mow the lawn. But Pop's old push mower's too dull to cut, he says; it just smashes the grass flat.

Gran snorts. "Looks like my own son could do some yard work once in a while instead of me paying good money to those little black boys," she says. "What do you think, Jake?"

"Pretty damn slack," I say, winking at Bubba.

We've been looking at TV. Most nights Gran does up the supper dishes, I put the food away while Bubba sits; then we watch the news. It's still too hot to stay inside, though, and so we move out to the porch as soon as we can. Bubba and my mother bought Gran an air conditioner last summer, but she doesn't like to run it much; "Gives me the arthritis," she says. Tonight Newsroom Five from Savannah showed a segment about a handgun crackdown, and that reminded Gran of something: she herself had once bought a gun, without a license.

It's been a while since I heard her tell it, so I ask. And Bubba shakes his head, laughing.

"You can laugh now," Gran says. "I don't remember as you laughed then."

He hadn't been in Korea a week, she says, speaking directly to me and ignoring him, before a letter came: Dear Mom, sell anything you got, get me a .38 and send it airmail. All the guys say if your rifle jams, and the gooks are charging . . . Gran shivered just to think of it, she says. "I went out that afternoon and sold our radio—and it was brand new, a new Philco, I think—and where I sold it they showed me two little guns, I don't remember what kind now, and so I got one, the biggest one, and with bullets too, because who could say if Bubba could of got the kind he needed there in Korea? And it burnt a hole in my bag all the way back on the streetcar; the conductor was looking at me funny, asked me was I okay, and all the people were looking at me like they could see through my clothes. All those men . . . When I got that gun home I closed all the drapes and put it dead center of the kitchen table and then I set down and just looked at it. I was shaking like a pudding."

"Where was Pop?" Bubba says.

"He wasn't here."

She bought a big fruitcake. She hollowed it out and set the gun inside and wrapped the whole thing in wax paper and then in newspaper, in the *Weekly Gazette* social page with a photo of one of Bubba's prom dates announcing her engagement—

"Which I never even noticed and never heard you say something about till now," says Bubba,

"—and yet it was, don't contradict me, Ellen Louise that married what's-his-name, you know the one I mean, divorced just a few years ago and never did have a single child."

"Maybe I ought to look her up," Bubba says. Gran tells him he's broken enough poor girls' hearts in this town, and Bubba just blows her a kiss off the ends of his fingers. I forgot to mention that he separated from his second wife two weeks ago and has been up here from north Florida eating Gran's home cooking ever since and lying around in his T-shirt and army fatigues full of holes like they'd been hit with buckshot or like he'd spilled battery acid on them.

Across the street the Motoheads are dancing weird sixties dances and laughing at themselves. Their arms make swimming motions in the air, their torsos·bend and jerk, their heavy feet hardly move. Two shaggy Moto women dance with each other. They toss their heads like dirty horses.

"What happened to the gun?" I ask.

"You know what happened to it," Bubba says.

She sent it to Korea. She stood in line at the post office and hefted it in her hands and wondered how to stop her voice from shaking. And she told the counter clerk it was a fruitcake.

"I was sick for months about that thing. I thought that I had bought something for my only boy to help him kill somebody and it like to made me crazy. I couldn't stop thinking about it, nights, couldn't sleep, couldn't eat, 'cause here was Bubba off in that God-awful faraway place and maybe he was shooting at people with a gun I had bought. I don't know why the army don't give enough guns to its soldiers, you'd think they would, wouldn't you? But he just had to have it, and so I went out and broke every law in America for that gun, and it got so I couldn't pass a police on the corner without ducking my head. Every night I prayed. And for a solid year I hid whenever the mailman come to the door."

And Bubba laughs and laughs and says, "She was afraid they were gonna return to sender, and she'd have to find something to do with it, find some way to get rid of the damn thing."

"I worried about it every blessed minute till Bubba come home from that awful place. And he didn't have a single gun on him. Not his rifle or even a bayo-net or the pistol or anything. Just his uniform, khakis, they called them. And do you know what he had the nerve to tell me about that pistol," Gran says, "that I had broken every law in America for and could go to jail for and maybe even the electric chair?"

"No," I lie.

"Lost it in a poker game," Bubba says.

Gran says he had to go to Korea to stay out of trouble. And Bubba, gray-haired, grinning, laughs.

"You laugh," he tells me, "can't nothing touch you. That's all I learnt over there."

It's early still. The sidewalk puddles are still pink from holding the sun all day. A kid at the stop sign burns rubber, the Motoheads cheer derisively, and I know that the story I've heard ten thousand times, as regular as moonrise, is coming up again:

"Most everybody'd pulled back," Bubba says, "running like be-jesus—"

But he was cut off. He knew to run south, since they were fighting the North Koreans, but somehow he'd gotten turned around in a snowstorm. Hugging the ground, circling back through a scree-clotted valley, he'd lost his wits and his rifle and he almost ran smack into a tank. He stood there, muzzle to muzzle, you might say, and the turret swung and stopped and lowered itself and drew a bead on his heart, two feet away, and Bubba laughed. He could smell the barrel—powder, oil, and heat rising off it in waves—and he could have reached out and touched it—that's how close he was. Fish or cut bait, you slant-eyed sons of bitches, Bubba says he said, and then he sat down in the snow and laughed.

Probably inside the tank the Chinese were laughing too, since there wasn't anything else they could do. Something about my uncle appealed to them, I guess, sitting cross-legged there, scratching himself and grinning, or maybe they just couldn't see such a waste of heavy ordnance, overkill, blowing a hole the size of a football into a man at such close range, blood and tissue flying everywhere. Maybe somebody made a joke about how it would ruin the shine on their brand-new nice clean tank, and then they got tickled and couldn't machine-gun him.

He walked away. Inside of half a minute the blizzard had covered him from view and he came to his senses and began to run. For the rest of the war he tried not to shoot anyone unless he had to. "I even gave Gran's gun away," he says, "lost it in that poker game."

What I say is what I always say: "That's a good story, Bubba."

The phone rings and Gran comes back a minute later to tell Bubba that his mother-in-law wants to talk with him. "There sure is no love lost between the two of you," Bubba says, rolling out of the hammock and heading indoors.

"Well, she's been calling every blessed night," Gran tells me. "Set your clock by it. I don't know what's wrong with that boy, Jake, that he'd leave Bonnie. She's just as sweet to him as she can be."

"Maybe he's just restless."

"Huh. Just no account, you mean."

I ask if Bubba really used to be wild.

"Lord, yes. Hot rodding up and down the street, running with a fast crowd, drinking. I don't guess they had all those drugs back then, but he'd of done 'em if they had. Pop had to bail him out of jail one time too many, and finally the judge said Bubba could join the army or else get sent up to the penitentiary."

When Bubba comes back out, his face is set like maybe he's decided something. He takes his time reloading himself into the hammock. Gran won't look at him. "Well?" I ask finally.

"Same as yesterday. Had I called Bonnie? Had Bonnie called me? Could she give Bonnie a message from me? I wish you two would kiss and make up, I'm so upset, I just don't understand it. Etcetera, etcetera."

"What did you tell her?"

"I told her I was tired."

Gran makes a disgusted little sound under her breath.

Across the street a Motohead pisses into the fire. Two Motoheads crawl on all fours, barking like dogs. A cop car pulls up, blue light flashing, and then two more. "Look at that," I say.

The cops are all out of their cars and most of them start walking up through the yard, slow and real steady. One Motohead raises his empty hands above his tangled hair. All the other Motoheads raise their hands, grinning. "Hello, officers," they chant. The cops leave their guns sheathed. The 'heads ask them in.

"Looks like a powwow," Bubba says. "Gran, why don't you go in the kitchen and get this boy and me a Co-Cola?"

"I'm not your Gran," she says.

Robert Taylor, Jr.

LADY OF SPAIN

(from *The Hudson Review*)

When the Lady of Spain revealed herself to me, I was fourteen years old, the owner of an Allstate motorscooter and a large and shining Polina accordion. The accordion lessons had begun several years earlier with a tiny rented instrument and were held in the Sunday school room of the Britton Baptist Church. My teacher, a red-cheeked, dark-haired woman named Lorena Harris, wore little makeup and pinned her soft dark hair atop her head in a circle capped by a delicate net. I thought her the member of a strict religious sect, perhaps a Nazarene. The Nazarenes, my father once told me, had founded the town of Bethany, then a few miles away from Oklahoma City instead of surrounded by it, and to this day Bethany permitted neither the sale of tobacco nor the showing of movies. I also had the notion that the Nazarenes had no musical instruments in their church—that they only sang their hymns, and therefore would surely scorn Miss Harris's beautiful accordion, so lavishly trimmed in chrome and pearl. I entertained the idea that she might keep it a secret from them, lead two lives or more, like the spies on television who, throughout that innocent decade, kept track of communists, and this was a pleasant notion that bore much embellishment. Late at night when I grew bored with the radio broadcasts of the latest humiliation of the Oklahoma City Indians, I saw her take her accordion from its plush velvet case, strap it effortlessly to her chest, and begin to play, somewhere in smokeless, movieless Bethany, secret melodies, intricate versions of "Lady of Spain," "Dark Eyes," "La Golondrina." I always imagined her alone, by herself in a room, a version of myself, doomed to solitude but redeemed by strong feeling.

Closed up in my room with bunk beds, an old desk of my father's, and plastic model airplanes dangling above me from the ceiling, I played my accordion for Lorena Harris and for my mother. For Miss Harris I played "Blue Moon," "Sentimental Journey," "Are You Lonesome Tonight"; for my mother, "Whispering Hope," "Nearer My God to Thee," "Sweet Hour of Prayer." The accordion was costly, paid for in large part by money that my mother had managed to put aside from her grocery allowance. It had ten shifts on the treble, so that a single note might be made to sound at one moment rich and deep like an organ and in the next shrill and high like a piccolo. Three shifts lined the bass, and a marvelous black and white zig-zag design decorated the front of the bellows. Its weight alone bespoke a vast and intricate interior, a secret realm of lever and wheel. What made the sound? A system of trembling reeds, Miss Harris told me. In my mind the word *reed* was highly significant. It was Biblical. I remembered that among the reeds of the Nile the baby Moses had been hidden from the Pharaoh.

My father had to travel days at a time from one end of Oklahoma to the other, selling class rings and diplomas and band uniforms to reluctant school districts. I had heard stories of his tribulations. It was all politics, he said. His competitors were expert at politicking a superintendent. They did not permit their products to stand on merit. They sold their souls and robbed him of his rightful customers. I imagined smooth-talking, pallid men, plump in pinstriped suits and black and white wing-tipped oxfords. They drove big somber Buicks and their daughters were cheerleaders, their sons quarterbacks.

Such children I had nothing to do with. Anyway, they did not seek me out. My best friend Steve, who had only recently given up his accordion lessons in order to devote more time to baseball, was a quiet, nice church-going boy like myself. I knew he had betrayed something important when he quit his accordion lessons. His mother, I remember, attended all his lessons and had a small beginner's accordion of her own that she practiced on, using Steve's music. I heard her play on several occasions, late afternoons when, out of a need for companionship, I played catch with Steve. The songs floated forth from her bedroom as if from a phonograph record, distant and dreamy. Even the bright polkas sounded plaintive and sweet. Several years older than my mother, Steve's mother wore dresses rich with eyelets and lace. Her husband scowled a lot, though he was cheerful enough when spoken to. He was a U. S. Marshal. Once I saw his picture in the *Daily Oklahoman*. He was handcuffed to the notorious murderer of entire families, Billy Cook, and although considerably shorter than the killer he looked like he meant business.

My father was surely cut out for better things than measuring the breadth of the fingers of high school juniors for their class rings, the length of their legs for band uniforms. I knew that given the opportunity he would do nothing at all, or else be an artist. A high school teacher of his had urged him to pursue a career in commercial art, but he had graduated from high school in 1932 and had to take what he could get. Selling, he once told me, was the backbone of the country. But there was no conviction in his voice.

During this time his was a quiet presence in the house. He enjoyed a cigar with his evening paper. Then he went out to the office that he had built a few summers ago adjoining our garage, where he worked evenings and sometimes well into the night on his designs for class rings. I liked going out there and was always pleased when asked to deliver a telephone message from a customer, usually some superintendent or principal cancelling an appointment. After relaying the message, I sat on a small sofa just behind the desk, lingering amidst an amazing clutter of papers—what could they have been—orders, bills, magazines, unfinished designs. I remember liking to find copies of the newsletter put out by the company that he worked for, Star Engraving Company of Houston, Texas, a mimeographed pamphlet really, printed on a dozen or so pastel sheets stapled together, its chief function to report on the volume of business done by the sales force, ranking the top salesmen in various categories (rings, caps and gowns, diplomas, invitations, and the like). Finding my father's name most often near the top of each list, I was proud. Sometimes there were notes written by the sales manager or even the president of the company congratulating selected men, the week's leaders.

My father worked diligently at his broad desk, a cigar gone out in the ashtray, a crooked-neck fluorescent lamp glowing and humming softly above his head. Frequently he used a magnifying glass, holding it steady a few inches from the sketch, which might have been a representation of a lion's head or the entranceway to a high school, an Indian's profile or a crouching tiger, or a coiled rattler. Once he had drawn (not for a ring design, of course) a picture of my mother, a pencil sketch of her head in profile, a good likeness and life-size, her long hair upswept in front and cascading into tiny curls on the side and in the back. It was done, I had been told by her, when she was pregnant with me. She looked stern, even a little angry, but a certain serenity also came through. The picture hung in a white frame above their bed and I thought it a very romantic thing to have drawn and wished that I had such a gift.

What do you think of this, he said, pausing to show me what he worked on. Pretty good, eh. There's nothing in McDowell's line to compete with this.

I believed him an excellent artist, but except for these moments of pride in a new design he spoke disparagingly of his talent. It had been compromised, he said, spoiled before it could properly be developed.

The Allstate motorscooter was the cheapest offered by Sears, its engine only slightly larger than the one on my father's power mower. It had a foot brake and tires the diameter of hubcaps. On it I was nonetheless enabled to crisscross Oklahoma City, circle it, ride out Western Avenue until on either side of me the plains stretched endless, the trees disappeared, and the strong wind in my face smelled of hay and occasionally of cattle or horses. Back in town, I paid visits to girls and took them for rides. They had to ride behind me on the tractor-style seat, their legs straddling my hips, their arms wrapped tightly around my chest. Often I could feel their hair brush against the back of my neck, and I shivered and wished, as we crept up a slight rise, the throttle wide open, for more speed, more power.

That summer I worked as a carhop at the Orange Julius stand on May Avenue, near the Lakewood and Lakeside Shopping Centers. Sometimes carloads of teenaged girls came in. These girls, mightily rouged and perfumed, their dark mascaraed eyes flashing, hinted in no uncertain terms of the wonderful pleasures one might have in the back seat of their father's Pontiac or Olds Eighty-Eight. I flirted mercilessly and cultivated a swagger, a nonchalant wink, a rakish grin. They told me I was cute, oh so much cuter than the boys their own age, and I began to fancy that I would always have a taste for older women. It did not surprise me that the girls seldom left a tip. Wasn't the feeling that we had so briefly shared beyond the realm of appetite and commerce?

Steve, who also worked at the Orange Julius stand, said that if he ever had the chance, he would be in that back seat in a jiffy. I feared for his soul, but suspected that he wasn't as likely as I was to be put to the test. My attraction, I believed, was somehow connected to playing the accordion, and Steve had left his accordion playing to his mother.

What would you do, I asked him, if you were in the back seat of one of those cars with girls in them?

We were picking up trash on the lot during a lull in customers, stabbing at paper cups and wadded napkins with our spears, as we called the broomsticks with nails in the end.

I would know, Steve said. I'd know what to do all right.

What?

It all depends.

If they let you kiss them then, what would you do?

It still all depends.

On what?

It was not the ethics of the situation that concerned me. I was after reliable information, and suspected that Steve might have known something that I didn't. I knew precious little, it seemed to me. My two sisters were younger than I was and no help. My curiosity was not just academic. Having kissed a girl before, I was keen on repeating the experience. Was it as pleasant for the girl though? That's what I couldn't imagine. A memory that I cherished was of a party given by my cousin and a few of her girlfriends at which kissing was the object of several games. These girls were a year older than I was, dazzling in their promise, with such smooth red lips and soft warm cheeks, the air surrounding them thick with the scent of a variety of perfumes. A boy was mysteriously chosen and led into a darkened room where one of the girls awaited him, kissed him before he could properly see her, and then he was sent back out to the lighted room, to be greeted by giggles and jeers. I wanted to stay in that darkened room. Let them laugh—in there I wouldn't hear a thing.

That night on the lot of the Orange Julius stand, Steve seemed annoyed by my question, but at last said that what you did after a girl let you kiss her depended on whether she let you kiss her on the cheek or on the mouth.

On the mouth, I said.

Then you just keep kissing her until she says quit it.

What if she doesn't say quit?

They always say quit.

A car came in then—my customer. The girl in this car sat very close to her date, and her hand rested on his thigh. I was the one she looked at—there was no mistaking it—and in that look I suddenly seemed to see all I needed to know. I vowed to memorize her eyes, and also the shape of that hand resting securely on her date's thigh. It was a small hand, the fingernails long and red. Her scent, I told myself, was like fresh almonds, her voice like a love song. She said, I could drink a pint. And her date said, Two pints, thick, no straws. When I picked up their tray after they were finished, she winked at me. Her boyfriend, a big guy in a letter jacket, left no tip. He sprayed gravel getting out of the lot and laid down rubber on May Avenue. Wherever he was taking her, he was in a big hurry. Too big a hurry, I concluded. I knew now that I would treat her different. I'd take my time.

This was the summer that my accordion teacher got married. I saw the man briefly one day as I was leaving my lesson. Leaning against the fender of her car, he smoked a cigarette and seemed on the verge of sleep. Tall and lanky, long-necked and tightly jeaned, he had a head shaped like the grill of an Edsel, with hair congealing into dark ribbonlike strands that curved over his head and curled at the upper reaches of his neck. I could not imagine him with a regular job, or even with one such as my father had. He would stand around like that all day, smoking, contemplating the trees, leaning on some fender. The money from my lessons—I saw it in a flash—would make possible his squalid languor.

Have a good lesson? my mother asked.

It was okay, I said, keeping my eye on the new husband as Mother pulled the car onto Britton Road.

I hope you did, she said. I certainly hope you had a good lesson. It means a lot to have a good lesson.

That was Mr. Cox back there, wasn't it?

Mr. Cox?

Miss Harris's husband.

I didn't see anyone.

He was right there. Leaning against her car.

I must not have noticed.

I'm sure it was him.

Well, maybe it was.

It was him all right.

Maybe it was. I wouldn't know the man if I saw him. I've got other things on my mind.

What could she see in a man like that?

I said I didn't see him.

Where are we going?

Home.

We don't usually go this way.

We had passed Western Avenue and now were in Britton, which was like a small town, though really part of Oklahoma City, on the very edge of it. There was a Main Street with a T. G. & Y. store, a C. R. Anthony Department Store, a Western Auto, and a drugstore that had a good soda fountain. Western Avenue connected it to the city, to supermarkets and shopping centers and subdivisions such as Nichols Hills, where we lived. I rode here often on my motorscooter and liked to imagine that I had come to a town far away from Oklahoma City, perhaps in Texas or New Mexico. In the drugstore I purchased cherry Cokes and then examined the rack of paperback books near the cash register to see if there were any new titles among the westerns and detective thrillers and to read the covers avidly. I picked up a copy of *Playboy,* then a bold new magazine, and discreetly flipped to the centerfold photograph, careful not to linger too long on it before putting it down and then feigning interest in *Field and Stream* or, even duller, *Sports Illustrated.*

At the drugstore my mother pulled into a parking place.

You drive, she said.

Since I had never driven a car before—aside from backing and pulling forward on the driveway—this command came as a surprise.

You've got to learn sometime, she said. She took a deep breath and opened the door. I realized that I was to trade places with her, and I managed to do as she did, get out and cross to the other side, the driver's side.

Have I said that my mother was a beautiful woman? She was. I found this somewhat of an embarrassment, another instance of how my family was not right. Mothers were supposed to be plump and gray, slightly younger versions of grandmothers, but mine was trim and dark, with auburn hair and hazel eyes that flashed brilliantly. Around the house during the summer she wore shorts and high-heeled wedge sandals, usually with a halter top. When she picked me up at my accordion lesson she was on her way home from the volunteer work that she did every Thursday at the big Veterans' Hospital on N. E. 13th Street, and so she always wore what she called her Gray Lady uniform, in fact a gray dress rather like a nurse's uniform except for the gray color. But on this Thursday she wore a scoop-necked blouse, white with bright red and green trim around the neckline, and a flowing full skirt, also white, trimmed with the same bright colors as the blouse. So preoccupied with scorn of my music teacher's husband, I had not even noticed this bold departure from her usual Thursday style of dress until, seated at the wheel of her DeSoto, I watched her get in beside me, the engine running smoothly, air conditioner humming.

Push the lever to *R,* she said. You know how to back up. Just watch where you're going.

Where are we going?

I don't know. For God's sake, I don't know. Nowhere. Anywhere. Will you just go, please.

But I had been struck by two unnerving realizations: first, that I was scared to death to back into the traffic that was steadily coursing through Britton, and, second, that my mother was upset. Tears were in her eyes, and she began to rummage through her purse, at last pulling forth a crumpled tissue. It did not seem the right time for a driving lesson. The car loomed large and lethal, but at the same time was dangerously vulnerable. I kicked at the brake pedal and pretended to have trouble finding *R* on the gear-shift column.

I don't know, I said. Maybe there's too much traffic.

You just have to watch where you're going, she said, wiping at her eyes with the tattered, lipstick-stained tissue. It will be all right. Just go.

And so I backed the big DeSoto out onto Britton Road ever so slowly, looking from one side to the other. Sure enough, a car had to stop in order to allow me onto the street. Mortified, I pressed the accelerator. The immediate surge forward took my breath away. I gripped the wheel firmly and vowed to remain calm. One only had to concentrate, watch the road ahead, glance now and then into the rearview mirror. Would I have to stop? No, I had traveled this route often on my motorscooter and knew that there was no stoplight or sign between us and the open highway. Once outside Britton—a matter of only several blocks—traffic would fall off, the wide flat prairie land on either side of us, the highway stretching straight ahead as far as the eye could see. The knowledge of this ahead was comforting, and as we crept past the last of the storefronts, and then at last the frame houses on their small treeless lawns gave way to the full breadth of the sky and the land leveled out into immensity, I was certain that I could drive this DeSoto to the end of the continent if need be.

My mother began to sob, softly at first, so that I could easily enough pretend not to notice, and in fact I succeeded quite well in not noticing, such fun it was to see the highway ahead, to feel the power of the big engine, a hundred times greater than that of my motorscooter, that strange sense of limitlessness, as if this were my life itself opening up before me, a straight line to eternity.

I glanced at the speedometer. We were going sixty-five miles per hour, yet scarcely seemed to move, so vast was the land that we moved across. The sobbing had grown louder, and, in the quickest of glances, I saw that she covered her face in her hands. The crumpled tissue had fallen to her lap.

It's no good, she said. Everything's all wrong. Every time you think things are getting better, they only get worse.

I didn't know what to say. Really she didn't seem to be addressing me, but rather talking to herself. Perhaps she didn't mean for me to have heard. The road was smooth. Soon we would come to the Edmond turnoff. A few distant trees bent to the strong wind and now and then a red sworl of dust whipped across the highway. The sky was pale blue, cloudless. I was absolutely confident.

Keep going, my mother said. I can't go back yet. I don't care if we end up in Tulsa. I'll tell you when to stop.

I drove and drove. We skirted the city, staying always on the edge of it, away from the traffic, making an almost complete circle by the end. It is one of the most dreamlike memories that I have, those dizzying plains all around, the red soil badly eroded, the tufts of sharply pointed weeds bordering the highway, now and then the skyline of the city appearing, those twin bank buildings rising like grand gray monuments tall and eternal from the sealike vastness, now to the west, now to the north, at last again to the south, and then windmills in the middle of nowhere or oil derricks thumping steadily into the depths of a land that looked as dry as the dust ever blowing across it. The car rolled along, heavy and smooth and quiet. My mother's tears subsided. She told me about the sorrow of her life, and her voice might have been the very sound of the landscape. I cannot imagine that place, that straight highway, those gullies and the red flat land, without hearing again her voice as it came to me across the car, the grief in it as pure as any I have ever known.

The reason for my mother's not wearing her Gray Lady uniform on that particular afternoon was that there had been a special party on the ward. The veterans had seemed to languish of late, and the women who gave their own time to cheer up the men had agreed that something extraordinary had to be done. Thus the party. It was to be, my mother said, a *real* party. Everyone was to dress up for the occasion in his best clothes. There was to be music, dancing, entertainment, refreshments, the ward decorated with bright-colored streamers and balloons. The balloons would contain messages and the veterans were to be encouraged to puncture those balloons and find the messages, which would be cheerful, optimistic phrases from *The Prophet* and *The Power of Positive Thinking*. My mother did not care for this last idea. It was treating them like children, she argued, when what they needed was to be treated as responsible adults. How else were they to regain their pride and dignity. She was overruled. The men of the ward were *not* like other men. In many ways they were like little boys—boys who had been asked to assume the responsibilities of manhood before they were ready. They needed to find their lost childhoods. My mother saw that there was no arguing with the other women. At least they had accepted her suggestion that uniforms be put aside in favor of nicer clothes, even though one of them said quite vehemently that to do so was to invite trouble. Wasn't that silly, my mother said to me, and of course I agreed, having no idea what such trouble would mean.

I was never to find out exactly what did happen at that Thursday's party to make her so unhappy, though she talked to me often of her work with the veterans, of how much that work meant to her and at last of the one veteran that she took a very special interest in. Sometimes we went for long drives similar to that first one, drives that she spoke of to my sisters and my father as instruction, but increasingly that instruction occurred late at night in my room, when I lay in the top bunk of my bed only half awake. Sometimes she actually slept in the bottom bunk—other times she returned to her own bed before dawn. I confess that sometimes, tired from a particularly busy night carhopping at the Orange Julius stand, I fell asleep as she talked. Nonetheless, I remember with absolute clarity the underlying sorrow, the sense of lamentation and attendant relief, the strange feeling of shared grief, the notion that I had become for her a confidante, as much sister as son.

I constructed in my own mind a version of the Thursday party, seemed at last to see it as though I had been there. I put this version together as I rode out the highways that crossed wheat fields and prairies, rutted soil and pasture, the same territory we covered in the DeSoto for my instruction. The special veteran would have been waiting for her. He was a lot like me, she had told me, not in looks of course, but in temperament. *Sensitive* was the word she used. Shy. Kept to himself and thought a lot. Liked to read, and read everything he could get his hands on. She brought him books, paperbacks that she purchased at Rector's downtown, and he received them eagerly, gratefully.

He never had a chance, she said. His father mistreated him and then he was drafted and sent to Korea. Something bad happened to him over there. Maybe something bad happens to them all, but some can't forget it. Some are haunted by what they had to go through. Can you imagine? It's hard for us to imagine.

I could imagine.

She would have had a book for him on that Thursday, a mystery novel with a lurid cover, carried in her large straw handbag. He would stand to one side of a group of talkative men, somewhat taller than most of them, his face in shadow. Music comes from a portable record player, one similar to my sisters', the size of one of my father's suitcases, with the speaker across the front. It is lively music, music to jitterbug to, to rhumba or samba to. Xavier Cugat, Tommy Dorsey, Bob Crosby. Occasionally a ballad sung by Jo Stafford or Margaret Whiting, a love song, not too sad. Records the women would have brought from home, records such as my parents had, in booklike albums, six big 78s per album, each in its own slot within. Some of the men bat at the balloons. Others dance—this part was harder to imagine. I was no dancer myself, and I concluded that neither would her veteran be. But the others—I had little to go on, junior high school formals, to which the girls wore stiff gauzy dresses.

She would encourage him to dance, for she was a good dancer herself. I had heard my father say so, and even remember seeing him dance with her in our living room. They reminded me of Fred Astaire and Ginger Rogers, whose movies my sisters loved to watch on television, my father spinning her and twirling her, drawing her close, dancing cheek-to-cheek, twirling again so that her full skirt fanned outward and she began to laugh, saying, That's enough now. You'll knock something over. This room is too small, the way you dance! Oh, my father said, you always spoil the fun. Just like your mother! Come on. Let's show the kids what real dancing is like.

But she had had enough, and so the best I could do was picture something like that, incomplete but lovely while it lasted. For the others though, not for my mother and the veteran whom she wished to help. Off to the side the two of them stand. She looks pretty in her white dress, so pretty that the other women are envious.

You should dance, she says. Dancing is good for you.

No, he says, I don't feel like dancing.

Well, would you like a cup of punch then?

No, thanks.

I've brought you a book.

I'm tired of reading.

And with that he turns and leaves her, making his way across the crowded dance floor, through the crepe paper streamers and the floating balloons and at last down a long narrow hallway and into the tiny room where she would not be permitted to follow him. The room would have bunk beds—made of black metal though, not varnished maple like mine—and a single curtainless window with bars on the outside. He would throw himself upon the bottom bunk and glower at the mattress springs above him, his jaw clenched tightly. Then his terrible memories overcome him and he closes his eyes, sinks into the nightmare of war, bombs flashing and exploding all around him, friends shrieking and dying everywhere.

My mother makes her apologies to the other women.

I have to take my son to his music lesson, she says. He can't carry that heavy accordion on his motorscooter.

She sought understanding from me. While I pretended to understand, much in fact escaped me. I believe I learned to become a good listener, and perhaps, after all, that is a kind of understanding. Coming home late from the Orange Julius stand, my lungs filled with the sweet night air, I sat on the living room floor of the silent house and counted my earnings, then went to bed and awaited my mother's arrival in the bunk beneath me. Sometimes I heard a sound from my parents' bedroom first, the raised voice of my father, and then their door opening, shutting, and her soft footsteps in the hall. I imagine her pausing to look into my sisters' bedroom, seeing them deep in their own dreams, motionless in their twin beds. Why had she not chosen one of them to confide in? One was too young surely, only seven at this time, but the other was just a year younger than I was. This one, however, Carolyn, the elder of the two, was considerably more spirited than I, even scrappy, and often argued long and hard with her mother over issues that I would have let pass as trivial. She seemed to me in fact to go out of her way to pick a fight, and both girls got along better with their daddy, though even he could become the focus of their tempers. There is something with mothers and daughters, finally and significantly, that does not exist with mothers and sons: fundamental antagonism, no doubt a rivalry. Whatever, I was chosen and not one of my sisters.

She came to my doorway and I heard her breathing, even now hear it, and smell again the scent of her perfume, a smell in memory more carnal than floral. Are you asleep? she asks. I know that an answer is not required. She enters my room, and I hear her pull back the bedspread, the sheets, and then feel the bedframe move slightly as she eases herself into the bunk beneath mine. Are you awake? she asks. This time I say yes.

Once she said this: I knew nothing about men, not the first thing about love. My mother told me nothing. I was married to another man before your father. I was too young and though I cared deeply for him and he loved me that marriage failed. I thought that I would never marry again.

All my life, she said another time, has been a sacrifice for others. I didn't finish high school because my father needed me to bring in an extra paycheck to help support the family. I was the oldest, and happy to help. I know that he was grateful. I worked in Baker's Shoe Store downtown, selling hosiery, and then at the jewelry counter of John A. Brown's. That's where I met your father, and when we were married another long sacrifice began. I learned what it meant to be a mother as well as a wife, to be responsible for a home. Please understand. I don't resent what I've been given. I love my children, all of you. But I have to ask—do you understand this—when my own time will come, when I can begin to live for myself. Is that so much to ask for, a life of my own?

I said no, that it certainly was not, but I really had no idea what it would mean for her to lead a life of her own. I responded on an abstract level, guided only by a sense of fairness. Life was short, she said, and was one's own. You could kill the life within you if you neglected it. The life within—that's what mattered, that's what must not be allowed to die. It had to be kept alive.

From their hidden homes in the big elm outside my window, the crickets whirred, and above the branches that I loved so much to climb upon in the daytime, the stars no doubt held their own

in the broad night sky. Everywhere an eloquence that would not—
no matter how much it insist—be comprehended.

I did not practice my accordion often in the summer, but some
mornings before the heat grew deadly I strapped the heavy instrument to my chest and labored mightily to perfect "Claire de Lune"
or "Santa Lucia" or "*The Washington Post* March." My own favorite
was something called "Sweet Sugar," a fox-trot in the key, if I remember correctly, of B-flat. Dutifully, to please Lorena Harris
(now Mrs. Cox), I worked on chromatic scales, on arpeggios, on
bass runs. In the afternoons I rode my motorscooter or had my
instruction in the DeSoto.

Before I knew it, August came. In that month heat was general,
day and night. My father purchased a small air conditioner, still
somewhat of a novelty in those days, and had it installed in a living
room window. This room, shut off from the others in order to
keep the chilled air effective, became a cool refuge. When the air
conditioner was turned on in midmorning, we all sat around it,
watching "Queen for a Day" or reruns of "My Little Margie" or
the old movie musicals tht my sisters were so fond of. Summer
was my father's off-season, since the high schools that he called on
were not in session, and so he often sat there in his big green chair,
sometimes with a *Daily Oklahoman,* the cigar smoke puffing out
from behind it. Mother kept busy in the kitchen or in the back of
the house, claiming that the heat did not bother her, though frequently joining us by midafternoon—the heat of the day, as she
called this time. On milder mornings she might be found stretched
out on a towel in the backyard, tanning her legs.

In our talks she came to speak less of her youth—of her overly
stern mother and sweetly indulgent father—and more of her dis-
satisfaction with my father. They argued fiercely all during those
years. This had become simply a fact of our family life. Why don't
they get divorced? Carolyn wondered. How can two people live
together and fight all the time? It made no sense to me either, but
mine was not an inquiring mind in those days—if it *ever* has been!
Maybe they still love each other, I said to Carolyn. In my heart I
knew that this could not be true. Hadn't I heard her say as much?

She began to urge me to visit the ward with her.

I've told the men about you, she said. It would mean so much
if you came to visit them.

She wanted me to play my accordion for them. "Lady of Spain," she kept saying. Wouldn't I play "Lady of Spain" for the men on the ward.

It was the last thing I would have chosen to do to end the summer, but there was no resisting her. She wanted "Lady of Spain." She would have it. I thought that she might have wanted "Whispering Hope" or perhaps my last recital piece, a complicated arrangement of "The Stars and Stripes Forever" that she had praised fervently, even though I'd made several mistakes and left out an entire section. But it made no difference to me. I'd played "Lady of Spain" almost from the start of my lessons—in increasingly difficult arrangements—and was fond enough of its quick pace and rollicking rhythm. In the sixth grade I'd played it for my girlfriend, who did a dance to it with castanets, on a program for the entire school. Perhaps it was that triumph that my mother remembered. Or perhaps the melody was a favorite of one of the men. Whatever, she had got it into her head that I would play "Lady of Spain."

All right, I said. When?

Thursday, she said.

This gave me five days to prepare myself. Once I had agreed, and the date was set, I began to feel intensely nervous, the way I always felt before those yearly recitals in the Baptist churches that Lorena Harris found for her students to perform in. The more recitals I played in, the more nervous I became beforehand. What got me through was the thought that it would soon be over.

The dynamics of "Lady of Spain" were crucial. So Lorena Harris had taught me, and as I took out the accordion and slid my shoulders into its cushioned straps I seemed to see her clearly before me. She wore a sky blue blouse of thin gauzy material and a tiered skirt that made a soft swish when she crossed her legs. A strand of her dark hair had come loose from her hair net and the top button of her blouse was undone. Soft here, she says, raising a finger to her lips. Now *crescendo!*

Sometimes the student who had his lesson after me did not come, and my lesson continued overtime. We were surrounded by tiny folding chairs and back of us hung a large bulletin board filled with color pictures of Jesus at the important stages of his life, from manger to cross. On a desk to one side of Lorena Harris the Sunday school lesson books were stacked in three even ranks. A banner across one wall displayed in large black letters John 3:16, For God so loved the world that he gave his only begotten son. . . .

My mother would be waiting in the car, of course, but so would the new husband of Lorena Harris. It was pleasant to think that he was kept waiting. I imagined it while unsnapping the bellows of the accordion, saw him as I listened to the air flow through the mysterious corridors of that strange instrument. He wore pink-soled suede shoes and leaned on the fender of her little Plymouth, his palms pressed against the clean and shining metal. He would have to wait. "Lady of Spain," I played. *Lady of Spain I adore you*. And when I was finished, I played it again.

I practiced hard for the men. As I have said, I was scared to death. There was an edge to this fright that made it worse by far than the usual recital nervousness. Who, after all, were these men that were so eager to hear me play? What did a veteran look like? They have feelings, my mother had told me, just the same as you and me, only they've never been given a chance. But what would they look like?

At the Orange Julius stand, the lights that encircled the lot bobbed back and forth in the strong wind, and I fancied them eyes, the eyes of the veterans. With the girls who drove up in their fathers' big cars, I flirted as usual, but my heart was not in it.

I asked my father if sometime in the fall I might go along with him on one of his sales trips. I must have been feeling guilty for having agreed to play on the ward. Unlike those veterans, he had never been to war. When the Japanese bombed Pearl Harbor, he had gone down to enlist, but was turned away because he had recently become a father—I was the child, of course.

Yes, he would take me along with him sometime. He did not look up from the book he was reading—I think it must have been Sandburg's *Young Abe Lincoln*—and did not remove the cigar from his mouth. The floor lamp shone brightly on his head, through his thinning hair and onto his pink scalp. When my mother and I left for the Veterans' Hospital, he was not home. I thought it just as well. He prided himself on her not having to work outside of the house and did not even approve of her volunteer work. Perhaps also he was suspicious, a little jealous. He had good reason to be. Years later, when my mother at last went through with her divorce, she told him she planned to marry one of these veterans. And she did. I could not have foretold such an event, but I sensed the reason in my father's fear of her work.

I hope you know how much this means to me, she said to me in the car.

I assured her I did.

It did not matter how well I played, she said. It was the gesture itself that counted.

I told her I understood.

I did not. Otherwise why would I be shaking so? When at last it came time to strap on the instrument, I felt faint. The great black thing was impossibly heavy.

The men milled about, tall and short, young and old. Some wore blue pajamas with white trim at the sleeve and pantscuff. Others dressed as if for a formal ball, white shirts and bow ties, gleaming black shoes. Still others wore T-shirts and blue jeans. I thought there were hundreds of them, but surely there could not have been more than thirty. The room itself was small. Couches and chairs had been pushed back against the walls, and some of the older men, their mouths hanging open and eyelids half shut, slumped in the big cushions, clutched the arms of the chairs as if they expected sudden movement. Through the high oblong windows above the seated men, the glass so thick it was almost opaque, I saw the bars that I had imagined.

Gray Ladies circulated among the men, carrying trays of paper cups and paper napkins. One of the women I had met before—she had come to our house on several occasions—but the others, perhaps there were six of them altogether, I had never seen. Yet they looked familiar. The gray dresses, of course, were identical, the same stiff uniform my mother wore. They smiled pleasantly, handing out the punch with ease. They might have been, I realized, the mothers of my friends.

My mother led me from group to group. *This is my son.* I shook innumerable hands, gripping firmly as my father had taught me. No, they invariably said, you couldn't have a son this big! They were all well-mannered, soft-spoken, polite. One man kissed my mother's hand.

I must have been brought there to meet the man my mother would later marry, though I remember no such meeting. The man

I've come to know as my stepfather must have been one of the inconspicuous ones. He would have preferred watching me from a distance. My mother has explained to me that he cannot work because he refuses to be bossed around. They live on a government pension in an apartment complex near Will Rogers Field. Fearing robbery, they seldom go out. It is not an unfounded fear. Apartments all around them have been hit. He recently screwed shut their windows and during my last visit sat up all one night, his recliner turned to face the window, watching to be sure that no mischief was done to my poor, shabby car.

My father remarried—twice, but the first marriage was brief. She was a schoolteacher, a widow, and must have known right away that she had made a mistake. By then he had become a little wild, spending a lot of time in singles bars and not keeping track of where the money went. He lost his job—also more than once. Took to representing several companies, no longer handling profitable class rings and diplomas but textbooks, which he lugged around to the adopting school districts all over Oklahoma and the Texas panhandle. He no longer worked on his designs for class rings, of course. The house where he'd had his office was sold when he went into bankruptcy, not long after I started college. In the end he achieved a degree of stability. His last marriage lasted four years, until his death by heart failure quite suddenly last year. He was sixty-nine. He had begun to draw and paint again and was tolerably solvent.

That afternoon in the ward I played "Lady of Spain," and as I played, my fear passed away. In its place came a strange elation. The men listened, and their listening was of a different order from what I felt at recitals. They too might have played the tune, the sentimental quality of it giving way to a passion that went into the depths of all music and included my mother in it, drew her into it. *Lady of Spain!* When I saw her, that Gray Lady, that dark-eyed Nazarene atremble in the shadows of shades of men, it was as if I saw all the women I would love. This was music, this was the life within, this was the love I would sell my soul to possess. The air that set the reeds to quaver, God help me, might have been my own breath.

Marly Swick

HEART

(from *Playgirl*)

Mama was smoking a cigarette and talking on Cody's toy telephone when Aunt Lucette and Uncle Bob came for us. We had
our suitcases packed. I'd packed Cody's for him because he was
too little to know what he'd need. Cody and I sat out on the front
stoop while Aunt Lucette and Uncle Bob went inside to see
Mama. Cody dug a tunnel in the dirt with an old spoon and I
twisted my birthstone ring this way and that to catch the sunlight
and make it sparkle. It was an aquamarine and my daddy gave it
to me right before he ran off with my teacher, Miss Baker. After a
few minutes, Cody got bored and went inside. I could hear them
all fighting in there. Uncle Bob was shouting at Mama and then
the screen door banged open and he threw Cody's toy phone out
into the yard where it landed in the tall grass with a little jingle.
Then Aunt Lucette swished out carrying Cody and hurried me
into the car. Cody sat in her lap in the front seat and I sat in the
backseat with my suitcase. Cody let loose with his tears, like a
cloudburst. Aunt Lucette reached over and beeped the horn until
Uncle Bob marched out and slid in behind the wheel.

"She's C-R-A-Z-Y," he said. "Breaks my heart."

He mopped the back of his neck with a handkerchief and started
up the engine. I traced the letters on the side of my blue suitcase.
I felt a little thrill. My daddy'd run off with my teacher and now
my mama was crazy. I felt real special.

"She's skunk drunk," Aunt Lucette said. "She'd have to sober up to be crazy."

"We can't just leave her." Uncle Bob crossed his arms over the steering wheel and rested his head on them like he was about to take a nap. "She's liable to burn the place down with one of them fancy cigarillos of hers."

Ever since my daddy'd left, she'd been smoking these cigarettes that came in a flat box like crayons—pink and turquoise and purple. Sometimes she'd light one up and stand in front of the medicine chest mirror, watching herself smoke it down to a stub and then she'd flush it down the toilet.

Uncle Bob shifted the car into reverse. "Maybe we should call a doctor," he said.

"She's heartsick and there's no medicine for that," Aunt Lucette sighed, "except time. We ought to know that."

Uncle Bob nodded and squeezed her hand. "Don't let's start," he said. There were tears shining in his eyes. I figured he was thinking about Little Bob.

As we pulled out of our driveway onto the paved road, I turned around and looked back at our house. Mama was kneeling in the tall grass that hadn't been mowed since Daddy left, clutching Cody's pink plastic phone to her chest. She saw me looking at her and put the receiver to her mouth like she was trying to tell me something.

Once we were onto the highway we stopped for gas at a Sinclair station. I pointed out the green dinosaur to Cody who was only half crying now. Uncle Bob told the man to fill her up, then turned to us and said, "Come on outta there. I wanna buy you kids a root beer."

We climbed out of the car and followed him over to the soda machine. I held Cody while Aunt Lucette went to the ladies' room. Uncle Bob dropped some change into the machine and handed me a root beer.

"You kids," he said, "is going to come live with us. Your mama's sick."

"How long for?" I asked, passing the root beer can to Cody.

"No telling," he shrugged. "Till your mama's her old self again."

"You poor kids." Aunt Lucette reached down and gave Cody and me a bear hug. "It's gonna be all right."

She took a pink Kleenex out of her skirt pocket and dabbed at her eyes. We climbed back in the car and I started whistling "You Are My Sunshine, My Only Sunshine." Daddy showed me how to whistle before he ran off and I'd been practicing up on some of the songs he used to like to whistle. Aunt Lucette swiveled her head around like Mama's old lazy Susan and looked at me like I was something real odd.

"Don't she beat all?" she asked Uncle Bob. "Not one little bitty tear drop. You suppose that's normal?"

"I expect it's the shock," Uncle Bob said.

I was whistling and watching the fields roll by. Some of them smelled real bad. I'd hold my nose and breathe through my mouth. I saw a sign that said WELCOME TO INDIANA.

"You know what, Cody?" I jiggled him on my lap.

"What?" He was half asleep.

"We're in a new state." I pointed over my shoulder. "That back there's Kentucky." I pointed over the front seat. "And that up there's Indiana."

"I wanna go home," Cody whined.

"Look at my ring," I said, holding it eye level so it sparkled right in front of his face. "See how pretty?"

He took his hand out of his mouth and tugged at my ring with his wet fingers.

Cody and I slept in the same bed at their house. At home we slept in the same room but in separate beds. We slept in Little Bob's room. In bed the first night I whispered to Cody about how Little Bob got run over by a bulldozer before Cody was even born. That made him remember his red dump truck my daddy gave him before he ran off, same day he gave me my ring. I'd set it out on the porch to take along, but at the last minute I forgot. Soon as he remembered it, I knew I wasn't going to get any sleep. Cody threw a fit and kept it up even when I lied and said we could go get it first thing in the morning.

The first week we stayed at home. I didn't go to school. Aunt Lucette was always asking me if I felt sad and telling me how it was good to cry.

"Cody cries enough for both of us," I said. "So does my mama. She cried for a solid week when my daddy ran off."

I polished up my ring with the hem of the tablecloth.

"Well, life can be real sad sometimes," Aunt Lucette said, her eyes filling with water. "There's no shame in crying." She looked at me like she was waiting for me to join in, but I just slid off my stool and went out the back door.

I liked sitting in the sun on the old aluminum milk box outside the back door. I'd sit out there with my eyes squeezed shut, pointing my face at the sun, whistling and rocking back and forth on the tin box. Sometimes, if no one bothered me, I could rock myself right into this trance. I felt like I just turned into pure sunlight.

The following Monday Aunt Lucette walked me to the school down the road from their house. She dropped Cody off at the neighbor lady's and we could hear him wailing for most of two blocks. We found the principal's office and I shook the principal's hand and told her my name was Heart Patterson and I was in the fifth grade. Then I sat on a bench and waited in the hall while Aunt Lucette told her all about me.

My new teacher, Mrs. Mitchell, was old and had a jelly belly. While she was writing spelling words on the board, I thought about how if I'd had Mrs. Mitchell back home instead of Miss Baker, my daddy'd still be at home and my mama wouldn't be crazy. He met Miss Baker when my mama was down with the flu and he went to a parents' conference by himself. They brought in a substitute after Miss Baker and Daddy left town, but my mama kept me home from school. She said all the kids would be talking and making fun.

After Daddy left, Mama sat around in her bathrobe all day, not even combing her hair. She cried and watched the TV and drank Daddy's liquor. But one morning she took a bath, set her hair on hot rollers, then put on a fancy dress and painted herself up. She walked out onto the front porch where I was painting my nails. To keep Cody happy, I'd paint the nails on my one hand and let him blow on them. Then I'd do the same with the other hand. I was just starting in on my toenails when Mama sat down on the glider, smelling of perfume.

"Heart," she said. "Do you think I look as pretty as Miss Baker?" She patted at her hair. "I want your honest opinion."

I looked at her for a minute, squinting and tilting my head. "No," I said. "But you smell real nice."

She slammed the screen door and locked herself in the bathroom. When she came back out, she was wearing her old bathrobe and no makeup. She didn't talk to me for two days. She'd say, "Cody, you tell your sister to bring me a beer," or "Cody, you tell that sister of yours she better run on down to the store and buy us some hamburger for dinner." Then Cody'd turn to me real serious and say, "Buy hamburger."

I was the one who found the note my daddy left. My mama was at the hairdresser down the road when I came back home from school and found it under the salt shaker on the kitchen table. He wrote:

Dear Coral,

I won't be home for supper tonight or ever again. I never meant to hurt you or the kids, but I just can't help it. Fourteen years is a long time for two people like us to be married for. Maybe it's just too long. I don't want that you should be the last to know I'm taking Jean (Miss Baker) with me. She says Heart is a smart girl and she hopes Heart won't hate her now. We both feel sick about this. The money in the bank is yours and I'll send more on a regular basis. I got no intention of letting you starve. It's nothing personal against you, Coral. I never knew I was the type to do something like this.

I sat in the kitchen chair shaking out little ant hills of salt and pushing them around the flowered tablecloth till Mama came home. She set a bag of groceries down on the counter and took off her kerchief.

"Hi, Sunshine, you have a nice day?" She put some Half-and-Half in the refrigerator.

I shrugged.

Mama took some meat out of the bag. "You want pork chops or chicken for dinner?"

"I don't care." I turned my ring backward so that you couldn't see the stone and made a fist around it.

"You feel OK?" Mama studied me and rested her palm against my forehead like a cool rag.

"I'm OK," I said.

"Well, you look like you got a fever." She began stacking some fruit cocktail cans in the cupboard. "How was school?" she asked. "You like my new haircut?"

"Looks real nice," I said. "We had a substitute 'cause Daddy ran off with Miss Baker."

Mama looked at me like she was going to haul off and smack me. I handed her the note and ran outside. I started to skip rope as fast as I could. My feet barely touched the dirt. As I skipped rope, I sang as loud as I could: "'A' my name is Alice, my husband's name is Albert, I come from Alabama, and I sell applejack." Whenever I had to stop to catch my breath, I could hear Mama inside cursing and crying up a storm. Once, when I was on 'Q,' she called me to the porch and asked me had I ever seen my daddy with Miss Baker. I said no and she went back inside and I picked up where I left off.

Once a week in my new school, Mrs. Mitchell would let me out of class for an hour so I could go talk to the school psychologist. He told me he traveled around from school to school, he was 27 and I should call him Jack. His office was the prettiest room in the school. The walls were bright yellow, there was a hooked rug like Grandma Patterson used to make before she went blind, and there were framed posters on the walls. Jack liked for us, him and me, to sit on big pillows on the floor, but I liked the wood chair. The first time I went to his office we sat on the big pillows and he explained to me that a psychologist was like a special friend. He told me I should feel free to say whatever popped into my mind. He said everything I told him would be a secret. I said OK, but I didn't have anything to say to him really. I'd just sit on the wood chair and look around at the animal posters till it was time to go back to class. Some days Jack would move my chair over by the window where there was this sandbox on legs filled with little toys—tiny plastic adults and babies and animals and furniture and cars. He was always trying to get me to play with the toys and make up stories, but I didn't want to. I thought how my mama would like all those little toys, but I didn't say it out loud. I figured Aunt Lucette and Uncle Bob wanted to find out if I was C-R-A-Z-Y like my mama. That's why I was there. He even had a toy telephone hidden in a box of junk in the corner. There was a tambourine and an Etch-A-Sketch on top, but I spied the receiver dangling down the side of the box.

One night I had a dream our mama was lying in her bed with the house burning down around her. The firemen rescued her and took her to the hospital in an ambulance. When Cody and I visited her there, she was sitting all by herself in her yellow nightgown. The next morning at breakfast I asked Uncle Bob if Mama was in the hospital.

"Now, where'd you go and get an idea like that?" he said. "Your mama's at home like she always was. She's just resting up."

"It's been a month," I said. "We gonna stay here forever?"

"Don't you like it here?" Aunt Lucette slid a pancake onto my plate. She looked like she was about to cry.

"I like it fine," I said. "I just like to know."

"Maybe this Sunday we could call your mama and you and Cody could talk to her. I bet she'd like that," Uncle Bob said.

Cody knocked over his milk and Aunt Lucette sponged it up.

"I don't want to talk to her," I said. I felt cold inside like I'd swallowed an ice cube. I jumped up and ran outside. I sat on my milk box and rocked real fast. I did this whenever I felt like crying and it worked real well. I never cried. I thought about my dream. Jack wanted me to tell him my dreams. Every time he asked me about them I said I couldn't remember. Sometimes I'd tell them to Cody when I woke up in the morning. Cody was always whimpering in his sleep like a dog. I was always shaking him awake. "Bad dream," I'd say. "Wake up." Once he bit me in the shoulder during a bad dream—broke the skin. When I snapped on the light, he looked like one of them werewolves lying there sound asleep with my blood on his baby teeth.

We got two postcards from our daddy in the same week. One had a crocodile and the other was a map of Florida. He said he was missing us and hoping we were taking good care of our mama. He said he would send for us to visit him on holidays just as soon as they found them a permanent place. The postcards arrived in a white envelope with a letter from our mama, but Aunt Lucette wouldn't let me see the letter even though it had Cody's and my name on it. She folded it into squares and slipped it into her brassiere.

"I'll tell Jack if you don't give me that letter." I looked her straight in the eye.

Aunt Lucette flushed and looked all flustered. "Maybe I'll just

discuss the matter with him myself," she said. "If he says to give it
to you, then I will."

"Hmmmph," I snorted and stormed up to my room. I stared at
the ceiling and suddenly hoped that Jack would tell her not to
show me the letter. I'd seen this TV show where a crazy person
sent a letter that was pasted-up words cut out of the newspaper.
The words were all different sizes—some in tiny, thin print and
some in fat black print. The envelope my mama sent had her fancy
writing on it. Before my daddy ran off, my mama prided herself
on her round, curlicued handwriting. I thought maybe my heart
would stop beating if I opened up that envelope and saw those
paste-up words.

While I was lying on the bed, Aunt Lucette knocked on the
door. She put a plate of home-baked gingersnaps and a glass of
milk on the bureau.

"I didn't mean to be mean to you, Heart," she said. "I'm just
trying to do what's best." Cody was dragging on her skirt and she
reached down and brushed his yellow hair out of his eyes. "I know
you miss your mama, but that's not your mama talking in that
letter."

"Then who is it?" I reached over and took a cookie, still lying
down.

Aunt Lucette was halfway out the door. "It's the fury of hell,"
she said. She put her hands over Cody's ears. "You ever hear that
expression 'Hell hath no fury like a woman scorned'?"

"What's 'scorned'?" I was sitting up now. I had the feeling Aunt
Lucette was talking to herself and once she remembered I was
there, she'd hush up.

"'Scorned' is like when you get tired of something and throw it
away," she said. "You understand?"

"You take it to the dump," Cody piped up. Uncle Bob had
bought him a new truck like the one we'd left at home.

"I understand," I said. I sort of did.

Aunt Lucette walked over and took the empty plate from the
bureau. "You drink your milk up." She started out the door.

"Aunt Lucette?"

She turned around and smiled at me.

"You keep the letter," I said. "I don't want it."

*   *   *

The next day I was sitting in Jack's office and he put the plastic dogs facing each other in the sand tray. "What do you think the dogs are doing?" he said.

I studied them for a while. "That dog there—the big one—is scorning that little dog," I said.

Jack looked surprised. Usually I didn't answer him when he asked me questions.

"Why's he scorning him?"

"It's not a him—it's a her." I pointed to the small white dog.

"Well, why's he scorning her?"

I shrugged.

"Those dogs remind you of anyone in particular?" He moved his chair closer to mine.

"No," I said.

"Maybe this big dog's sort of like your daddy?" He accidentally bumped his chair against the table and knocked the dogs over in the sand.

"Maybe," I said. I picked up the white dog and set it on its four legs.

"Are you angry with your daddy?"

"No." I moved my chair back a little.

"Then why'd you leave him lying there in the sand?" He pointed to the black dog.

I just looked at him. "My daddy's in Florida," I said. I squeezed up a handful of sand, then let it sift out through my fingers. "In Florida the sand is hotter than this. It's like walking on fire."

"Actually it's not," Jack said. "It's white sand and it stays quite cool."

A bell rang. I could hear the chairs scraping and everyone's loud footsteps racing downstairs to the cafeteria. In a minute it was all quiet again, like a storm had passed us by. Jack patted my hand and smiled at me.

"When I say 'Florida' what's the first word pops into your mind?" he asked.

"Sunglasses," I said. I could see Daddy and Miss Baker driving in a convertible car wearing big sunglasses.

"What are you feeling right now, Heart?" His voice was soft and sneaky.

I looked out the window at the empty playground. One of the students had left his lunch sack by the jungle gym and some brown birds were pecking at it, pecking right through the paper.

"I'm hungry," I said.

After supper, Cody and I were watching TV on the floor in the den when Uncle Bob came in and said, "There's someone on the phone wants to talk with you."

I went into the kitchen and Aunt Lucette kissed me on the cheek as she handed me the receiver. "Hello?" I said.

"Hello, Sunbeam, that you?"

"Daddy?" I put my hand over the receiver and whispered to Cody that it was our daddy.

"You get my postcards? I sent three so far," he said.

"We got them. You still in Florida?"

Cody was yanking on the phone cord. I shooed him away.

"We're in Tallahassee. I just found out this minute you been staying with Uncle Bob. You seen your mama at all?"

"No," I said. "She's crazy."

"That's no way to talk about your mama." He didn't say anything for a minute. "I know your mama. She'll snap out of it. You get your uncle to take you back home for a visit, you hear? Ain't nothing wrong with your mama that seeing you kids won't cure."

Cody was climbing on the kitchen chair trying to grab at the receiver. "Cody wants to talk," I said. "He's talking real grown up now."

"OK. You tell your Uncle Bob I said to take you home," he said. "You kids don't never forget your mama and I love you."

"Here's Cody." I sat Cody down on the chair and handed him the phone. Then I walked out into the living room where Uncle Bob and Aunt Lucette were talking. They'd turned the volume on the TV down low. Aunt Lucette was twisting her Kleenex.

"Daddy says to tell you to take us home for a visit," I said. Then I turned the volume on the TV back up loud and lay down on my pillow in front of the set.

Saturday morning we woke up early, while it was still dark out, and threw our pajamas and toothbrushes in our suitcases we'd packed the night before. I was making up our bed when Aunt Lucette came in to check on us.

"You got Cody's toothbrush in there?" She walked around to the other side of the bed and helped me with the quilt.

"Yes."

"You excited?" she asked. "You glad we're going?"

"Guess so," I shrugged.

Aunt Lucette reached out and held my chin with her hand so I had to look right at her. "It worries me, honey, the way you act like nothing bothers you. You don't cry, you don't laugh. Dr. Jack says you're just 'repressing' everything—you got all your feelings squashed way down inside you like a jack-in-the-box and if you don't let them out bit by bit like a normal little girl, they're just going to pop out all at once some day."

Uncle Bob walked up behind her, pressing a little wad of bloody Kleenex to his chin where he'd cut himself shaving. "Everybody all set?" he asked, winking at Cody and me. "Don't fill her head up with all that psychiatrist talk," he said to Aunt Lucette. "She got troubles enough already."

Riding in the car I thought about what Aunt Lucette told me Jack told her. Cody and Aunt Lucette were snoozing. Uncle Bob was listening to the ball game on the radio. It was drizzling out and the car windows kept fogging up. I tried to picture my feelings all repressed together inside me—tears and laughs and frowns— trying to come out. I went limp and opened my mouth and closed my eyes and waited. I kept trying to coax them up, calling to them in my mind like you'd call a scared kitty. I pictured them flying up and out like a swarm of mad hornets. Then I pictured them float- ing up and out, nice and easy, like a row of bubbles. But nothing happened. I didn't feel a thing except a little carsick. I wondered if Dr. Jack had actually said that about me. I figured Aunt Lucette must've got it all wrong.

I bunched my pillow up so I could lean my head against the window. I hadn't thought much about seeing Mama again. Uncle Bob said she was still sick, but he didn't want no one accusing him of keeping our mama from her kids. My birthday was next week. I was going to be eleven. This thought floated into my mind like a bubble that maybe this was my birthday surprise and when we drove up in front of our old house, Mama and Daddy would be standing out on the porch waving to us. Balloons would be tied to the porch railing, fluttering like butterflies in the wind, and inside there'd be a chocolate cake with pink marshmallow icing like I had last year, only with eleven candles instead of ten. Daddy'd be standing there with the camera while Mama lighted each candle with a match, trying not to burn her fingers. He'd be all ready to snap my picture as I blew out the candles and I wouldn't be able to think of anything to wish for.

Everyone was wide awake by the time we turned off the highway into Spottsville. Cody was standing on the seat looking out the window kind of puzzled. I think it was the first time in his life he was old enough to come back to a place he recognized. Aunt Lucette got her comb out of her purse and began yanking it through her hair. Then she handed it to me to do the same. When we turned down our street, we saw Farrah Hodge and Rusty Miller riding their bikes. They stared at us like they seen a ghost. Uncle Bob reached back and gave us two sticks of gum, the kind with sugar that Mama never let us chew. I put mine in my pocket. I didn't want to start off on the wrong foot with Mama.

Even from a distance, I could see there were no balloons. The grass still wasn't mowed and my daddy's red Chevy wasn't parked in the driveway. As we pulled up to the house, Uncle Bob cleared his throat and said, "Remember what I said, now. Your mama's still feeling puny. Don't take anything personal."

"Your mama loves you," Aunt Lucette said. "You just remember that."

We got out of the car and headed up the steps behind Uncle Bob. Cody's dump truck was lying right where I left it on the porch all rusted up.

"It's broke," he said like he was about to throw a fit.

"No it's not," I said. "That's just rust. Looks like a *real* dump truck now."

He brightened up and began playing with his truck. He'd forgot all about Mama and he hadn't even seen her yet.

"Anybody home?" Uncle Bob shouted and knocked on the screen door.

Mama walked out of the bedroom fastening her belt. She had on her good red dress and high heels. She unlatched the screen

door and we walked into the living room. Her dress was half unzipped in the back. Aunt Lucette walked over and zipped it up.
Mama said hello to everyone and sat down in the rocker. We sat
across from her on the sofa. No one said anything for a minute.
Then Uncle Bob said, "You're looking good, Coral."

"Am I?" Mama said.

"Real pretty," Aunt Lucette said. "Don't you think so, Heart?"
Aunt Lucette jabbed me in the ribs.

"Real pretty," I said. "Prettier than Miss Baker."

Uncle Bob coughed and lit a cigarette. Mama started to cry.

"You seen Frank?" she asked Uncle Bob.

"You know I haven't," he said. "I told you that on the phone."

Mama got up and went to the kitchen. We heard the refrigerator
door open. I saw Aunt Lucette looking around the living room.
It didn't look like Mama'd done much cleaning since we left. There
were piles of dishes and magazines everywhere. I remembered how
Mama used to yell at us for leaving a dirty glass or pair of socks in
the living room and how she was always wiping this or polishing
that, smelling of pine or lemon. She walked back in with a six-pack
of beer which she set down on the floor next to her rocker. She
peeled off three beers and handed one to each of us. Aunt Lucette
reached over and grabbed mine away from me before I had a
chance to open it.

"Really, Coral," she said. "Where's your mind at?"

Mama opened her beer and took a long sip. No one said anything. Outside on the porch we could hear Cody yelling,
"VVrrroomm, vroom! VVVrroommm, vrooooomm!"

"It's Heart's birthday next week, Coral," Aunt Lucette said.

Mama didn't say anything. She took another sip of beer and
spilled some down the front of her good dress. I got up and walked
outside. Cody looked up from his truck.

"Mama's in there," I said.

He steered his truck across the porch to the door. He could just
barely reach the door handle now on tiptoe. I reached over and
held the door open for him while he vroomm-vvroommed over to
Mama's rocker. I saw Mama reach down. I thought she was going
to pat his head, but she just moved her beer out of his way. "Don't
spill that," she said.

I stood on the porch watching the rain drip off the roof. I heard Mama say, "I saw Frank yesterday. He brought me some candy. He says he's tired of that woman." I heard Uncle Bob say, "You know you didn't see Frank, Coral. You know he's in Florida. You gotta snap yourself out of this. You ain't the only woman whose husband ever run off." I heard Cody making his truck noises. The metal wheels made a real racket on the wood floor. Mama yelled at him to watch where he was going. Then I heard Aunt Lucette say, "You've got to think of your children, Coral. The school psychologist says Heart is too 'withdrawn', she's like some walking zombie. He says she could end up real warped from all this."

I never heard what Mama said 'cause I went out into the yard. I held my arms straight out in front of me and stared straight ahead like my eyeballs were frozen. I walked back and forth across the yard with my arms and legs stiff as boards like the zombies I'd seen on TV. The tall grass wet my knee socks. I felt my hair frizzing in the rain. From inside I heard Uncle Bob shouting and Cody howling. I got in the car and curled up on the backseat with my head on the pillow. The rain sounded loud beating on the tin roof of the car. I remembered my stick of gum in my pocket and unwrapped it. I had just popped it in my mouth when the car door flew open and Uncle Bob dumped Cody in the backseat. Cody's pants were soaked with beer and he smelled like a brewery, which was what my mama used to tell my daddy when he came home late. Cody was crying and Aunt Lucette was crying, but she looked mad, too.

"What happened?" I said, my mouth full of gum.

"She hit me," Cody said.

"Why?" I asked.

"She's crazy," Uncle Bob said and threw the car into reverse.

Uncle Bob backed up so fast we ended up on the lawn and heard a soft crack.

"Hope that wasn't a glass bottle," Aunt Lucette said.

"Jesus." Uncle Bob pounded the steering wheel with his fist. "Don't it never end?"

He got out and looked underneath the car. I noticed how my finger was turning green underneath my ring.

"Look at this." Uncle Bob held Cody's toy telephone up to the window for us to see. It was squashed like a pink pancake. Just as he was about to toss it back into the weeds, I rolled down my window and reached out my arm.

"Give it to me," I said.

Uncle Bob handed it to me. "What you want with that old piece of junk?" He got back in the car.

"I just like it," I said. "It's all repressed."

Uncle Bob shook his head and looked at Aunt Lucette. She reached over with her crumpled Kleenex and touched the little spot of dried blood from this morning still on his chin. Suddenly everyone seemed nice and calm, even Cody. Once we were out onto the paved road, I sat there staring at the telephone in my lap. It reminded me of those dead animals, skunks and squirrels, you see flattened on the highway. I picked up the receiver and tried to dial our home number on the mashed dial. "Hello, Mama?" I said. "This is Heart."

Uncle Bob turned the radio down. It was so quiet I could hear her breathing on the other end.

"I know you're there, Mama," I shouted. "You hear me?"

Cody looked at me like he'd never seen me before in his life. "Don't cry," he said. He reached over and touched me on the arm. "Don't cry."

Aunt Lucette handed me her Kleenex. Cody put his ear up against the receiver and listened, real puzzled, like maybe there was something he didn't understand.

Lee Smith

LIFE ON THE MOON

(from *Redbook*)

This story starts at the National Air and Space Museum in our nation's capital, with me and Lucie taking the Beginner Space Quiz and Richie and Tommy (her little boy) running wild all over the place while Darnell held on tight to my hand. I guess I ought to say something about the Air and Space Museum, I don't know if you've been there or not. It is a huge beautiful building, all glass and concrete, with real planes hanging from its high ceiling and rockets and things all over the place. Then you can go in any of the exhibits and learn about something in particular—hot-air balloons, World War I, you name it. Wilbur and Orville Wright's plane, the first one, hangs right up at the front where you go in, and it is so tiny you can't imagine how it ever got off of the ground. It's the littlest thing in the whole museum. But anyway, this museum is like the biggest room you ever saw, full of color and noise and flight. It made Richie and Tommy crazy like they wanted to fly themselves; they wouldn't stay with us or watch any of those programs all the way through. "Let them go," Lucie said, which I did because there wasn't anything else to do, no point to try to keep them if they wouldn't stay.

Now this museum had another effect on Darnell, more like it had on me. It made her hunch her shoulders and press real hard against my side. And me? It made me want to shrink too, pull in my feet and arms for fear they would touch something foreign and cold and made of some material you never would find on this earth, something slimy you didn't know what it was. At the same time it made my head sort of float up off of my body—the way I get in malls ever since Lonnie left me—like I was talking and hearing myself talk at the same time, or walking and watching myself walk, or taking the Space Quiz with Lucie and watching myself do it while I did.

First thing we did was press the button that said MINIMUM DIFFICULTY.

The square green letters came out on the screen like on a computer.

WHAT PLANET, we read, MOST CLOSELY RESEMBLES THE EARTH?

"Venus," Lucie said right away.

CORRECT, the machine spelled out. NUMBER TWO. WHAT PLANET IS FARTHEST FROM THE SUN?

"Mama, I have to go to the bathroom." Darnell pulled at my hand.

"Mercury," I said, but we missed whether that was right or not because Richie and Tommy came up right then with their faces looking like Christmas, to tell us that the Lunar Module was at the other end of the building, the real thing, they said, and we had to come right away.

"I have to go to the bathroom," Darnell said again but Richie punched her.

"Listen," he said. "The astronauts peed in their suits."

"You quit that," I told Richie from my mouth which floated away up high in my face above us all. I could look down and see us and see all the tourists from foreign lands.

WHAT PLANET IS CHARACTERIZED BY RINGS? the machine spelled out, and Richie and Tommy together hollered out, "Saturn!"

Darnell was crying.

"Come on then," Lucie said.

She moved off easily through the saris, the backpacks and blue jeans and car coats, looking like a foreigner herself with her jeans and those running shoes. I think you should dress for a trip myself, but I have to say that by then my feet were hurting from my heels.

After the bathroom, where we had to stand in line with French people and I had to put toilet paper all around the seat for Darnell, you can't be too careful, we finally made it to the other end of the Museum where Lucie stood reading the sign by the Lunar Module and Richie and Tommy jumped all around.

Lucie turned her face to me then, that same dark quick fairy-tale face she had as a little child, and took my hand.

"Oh, June," she said. "Oh, June, don't you remember? Oh, June, aren't you glad you came?"

Well, I was. I still am. But it was a bigger trip than you can imagine by a long shot.

When Lonnie left me, all I did for two weeks was throw up and cry. Oh, I was plenty mad too. Everything that happened made me sick or mad or sometimes all of it, like when I went down to the mall to get some pantyhose at Belks and when they were out of my size I had to get a paper bag from the salesgirl and breathe in it right there in the middle of the Hosiery Department to keep from passing out. Then I went into the Ladies' and threw up. Another time I was walking through the Montgomery Ward TV section, about two hundred of those TVs were on and there was a bowl game with Bear Bryant in full color on every one, wearing his hat. Lonnie loved TV football, he loved the Bear. I used to get mad at him for watching and try to make him look at educational things on Channel 6. I wanted to expand his horizons, as Lucie said when she ran off with the disc jockey. But Lord it made me cry, I had to run out of Montgomery Ward and over to the Green Thumb and hide behind the ferns to collect myself. I lost eleven pounds the first two weeks.

Meanwhile Richie and Darnell were shooting down spaceships on the Atari that Lonnie had given them for Christmas, shooting down ship after ship. Lonnie just spoiled them to death, he always did, gave them everything they wanted and then some. They did that for one week solid, while they were out of school for Christmas, then they started skating their new skateboards straight through the family room where Lonnie had taken the rug and the E-Z Boy recliner, and I never said one word. This was not like me you can be sure. It's not the way I am about a house.

Lonnie took the rug and the E-Z Boy and his clothes and six pieces of Tupperware, that's all, and moved in with a nurse from the hospital, Sharon Ledbetter, into her one-bedroom apartment at Colony Courts. He met her at the hospital, I found out later, last year when Richie had his tonsils out. So I guess it had gone on since then, and I never knew a thing.

Sharon Ledbetter is twenty-three years old. *It is trite,* I thought of saying, but Lonnie would not have even known what that meant, so why bother? *Why bother?* I asked myself. You can subscribe to the *National Geographic* for ten years straight but there are some people who won't do a thing except look at the naked pictures.

Richie and Darnell went over to visit the apartment at Colony Courts and came back saying that Sharon Ledbetter had a cat named Ms. Pacman and a whole lot of terrific rock albums which she was going to tape for them. They had a real good time. Now right after this was when my first cousin Lucie called from Alexandria where she lives and said why didn't I and the children come up to Washington and sightsee, it would be good for all of us to get away. She knew what a hard time I was having, Lucie said.

"Thanks but no thanks," I told her. "I'm too busy trying to put my life in order again," I said, and Lucie said she knew I was good at *that,* she wished me the best, but I ought to remember that sometimes it just isn't possible to do it right away. At this point I started to cry. I have never approved of Lucie and the way she left her own little boy down here with her mama to raise, in fact for years Lucie has made me real nervous.

"Come on, Mama, let's go to Washington," Richie said. Richie is always right there at your elbow when you think he's not, he never misses a trick. He's a redhead like his daddy, into something every minute of the day.

"I want to go to Washington," Darnell whined. She says everything Richie does. "Come on, Mama, we never go anywhere."

"Sharon has a sky blue LTD," Richie said, "with a tape deck."

"Lucie," I said into the phone, "thank you so much for asking, I really can't tell you how much I appreciate it, but I just have too much to contend with here. Why, there's not even a recliner in the TV room. I have so much to do, and the children of course are in school."

"Well just take them out for a couple of days." This is exactly the kind of thing you'd expect Lucie to say.

"Children need a routine," I told her, "and thank you so much for calling."

"But how are *you?*" Lucie simply refused to get off the phone. Her voice, sweet and serious, came clear as a bell across West Virginia and down through all these years. "Listen, June," she said, "you need to think of *yourself* now, you need to do something for you."

"Lucie," I said, "I'm just fine."

Then I hung up and went in the bathroom to vomit.

When I came out, Richie had busted one of the joysticks on the Atari, and Darnell had gone to her room to cry. I looked down at the list in my hand.

Every day of my life I have made a list, and every day I do everything on it. I looked down at the list and I looked around the family room which echoed with Atari beeps and Darnell crying. I knew I ought to go in her room and hug her but I just didn't have it in me at that time, I knew I'd start crying myself. *Pick up cleaning,* the list said. This cleaning had been at Billy's Martinizing for three weeks by then, ever since Lonnie left.

"I'll be back in a minute," I told the kids, and I went out and got in the car. We have a new car and a new house—we hadn't been in the house five months when all of this happened. "I can't stay here," Lonnie said and then he left. He said he was real sorry. "Real sorry, ha!" I said. But I do have to say he never wanted to build the house in the first place, he wouldn't take a bit of interest. They would have put cheaper tile in the downstairs bathroom and charged us the same, for instance, if I hadn't been right there. So now the house was built and still so new that the red dirt showed in patches through the new grass all over the yard, and the patio wasn't even poured yet, just blocked out with two-by-fours, and Lonnie was over in Colony Courts Apartments with Sharon Ledbetter, who nobody nice in this town had ever heard of, listening to rock records.

"I'll just pick up the cleaning," I said to myself, but when I got down to Billy's Martinizing, I could hardly get out of the car.

"Cleaning for Lonnie Russell," I said to the girl behind the counter. She had bright green eyelids, sitting there reading a magazine.

"*Lonnie Russell,*" I said louder, and then she stood up and walked over and pressed the button which made all the clothes on the line go around and around.

"Ticket?" she said, and when I said "what?"—I couldn't hear her over the sound of that machine, the clothes went around and around—she said "ticket" again.

I went through everything in my billfold, then everything in my purse. I make them, needlepoint purses, which everyone loves.

"I'm sorry," I said. "I can't find it." This was not like me to lose the ticket. I started to cry.

"Now that's all right, honey, we'll find those clothes," the girl said, looking scared, batting her bright green eyelids at me. "Don't you worry, Mrs. Russell," she said, and I guess she must have pushed a button or something because here came Billy of Billy's Martinizing himself, out of his office and over to me. You should see Billy—he is real fat and wears a blond toupee which comes right down to his eyebrows and open-neck shirts with gold chains.

"What seems to be the trouble here?" he said. He has a voice with oil in it.

"Why just nothing at all," I said. I was crying, and the clothes went around and around, but then the girl found the cleaning and stopped the machine. It was a lot of cleaning, thirty-four dollars to be exact, and half of it Lonnie's. I saw his tan corduroy jacket and his good blue suit he bought in Charleston, all wrapped up nice in the cellophane beside my red wool dress.

"Now, now," Billy said.

"Listen," I said. "My husband has left me and I am not about to pay for his cleaning."

The girl backed all the way to the office door and disappeared.

"Why of course not," Billy said. His voice just ran all over me. "Why I wouldn't think of such a thing," he said, and he ripped off the cellophane and started separating the clothes. He acted like all of this was exactly nothing, like it happened every day.

Lonnie's gray jacket on the right hook, my car coat on the left. I couldn't even see.

"I don't think I can stand it," I said.

"There now," said Billy, who wore a big diamond ring on his right hand. "That'll be eighteen seventy-five."

I wrote the check and crossed *cleaning* off my list and just stood there because I had crossed off everything on my list for that day, cleaning was the last thing.

"I can't think what to do next," I said.

Billy cleared his throat. "Well, Mrs. Russell," he said, "how about a beer?"

He looked me up and down, I used to be Miss Welch High. His toupee had slid down lower over his eyes and I could see where the little hairs were stitched together in the part. "No thanks," I finally said, but it was all I could do to get my cleaning out to the car where I started hyperventilating like crazy the minute I got inside.

A beer! I drove home and went into Darnell's room and gave her a big, big kiss. "Get up," I said. "We're going to Pizza Hut," and when the kids got all excited I said, "and we're going to Washington too. Next weekend we're really going."

"Who's going to drive?" Richie had a point, since Lonnie always drove on trips.

I hadn't thought of that.

"I guess I am," I said, and so we went.

I'll get to the Moon Landing in a minute, but Lucie and I we go way back beyond that. After Daddy got killed in the wreck, Mama and I moved over here to Welch, West Virginia, to be near her sister—that's Lucie's mother, my Aunt Adele—since Mama had asthma and me to raise. We moved when I was thirteen years old. "Now this is home, June," I recall Mama said when she opened the screen door. "We're going to stay here." This made me so happy. Our house was nothing much—five rooms and a porch that had coal dust all over it and a fat-bellied woodstove standing up like a little man in the front room, for heat. All the other houses in that holler were just like ours—they used to be company houses before the company mined out the coal and moved on to the other side of the mountain.

I loved that house, because Mama had said we would stay there. And I loved the mountains too—they rose all around our holler, straight up and rocky and too rough for roads or settling, closing us in. Lucie hated them. She had a nice brick house in the bottom about a mile from where we were, with a grass yard and a patio as well as everything else I wanted in the world—a fat father with glasses who ran the Rexall Drug Store and wore a red bow tie, two cute little baby brothers to play with, a cocker spaniel, air-conditioning, patent leather shoes for Easter, a transistor radio when they first came out. Still we were best friends. We spent all day together every day and saw every movie that came to town at least five or six times. We were so close in those days that sometimes I'd be thinking something and Lucie would say it out loud. I don't know what it was that turned her different unless maybe it was heredity from her mother, my aunt Adele.

Aunt Adele was as different from Mama as night and day. Aunt Adele taught piano and had pretensions, Lord knows where she got them. When we ate over at my house, for instance, you knew what you'd have—meat and potatoes, green beans in summer and big red slices of the tomatoes that Mama grew in her garden right by the back door. But when we ate at Lucie's house it was no telling. You might get chicken cacciatore, for instance, or even pizza which Lucie's family found out about when they took the trip to Myrtle Beach. Lucie's daddy, my uncle Earl, sent Aunt Adele a dozen yellow roses for her anniversary, her birthday, Christmas and Valentine's Day, any excuse you can think of. He was just crazy about Aunt Adele.

"Why couldn't Daddy have been like that?" I used to ask Mama, but she'd smile and look off down the road. Mama's mouth turned down when she smiled.

"Your daddy had his good points," was all she'd say.

Maybe so, but I was too young when he died to remember many of them, or even to remember him very well since he was a traveling man and mostly always gone. We lived in eleven different towns before Mama and I moved to Welch. According to Daddy there was a sure thing right around the corner every time. Mama never said a word. She'd haul out the cardboard boxes which she never threw away and sometimes never even had time to unpack, and we'd put them in the car and off we'd go. We traveled light. You can't get much of anything together with a life like that. Still Daddy was sweet. He could really whistle, is the main thing I remember—he could whistle anything. He used to whistle, "How much is that doggie in the window?" the year it was big, and then he'd bark. He still looked like a boy when he died, so that's how he has stayed in my mind, as a boy getting out of a car and whistling.

Anyway Daddy's car ran off the mountain while he was working

for the Jewel Tea Company door to door, and then we moved to
Welch where we stayed put and Lucie was my best friend in the
world. I think the piano recital in sixth grade was the first time I
caught on to any difference between us.

Now Aunt Adele's piano recitals were always a very big deal.
She'd rent the banquet room of the Draper Hotel and borrow
folding chairs from the funeral home. Then she'd have yellow roses
in big containers standing on either side of the piano, and colored
spotlights rigged up by Uncle Earl. You had to wear a semiformal
and gloves. Mama always made my dress and Uncle Earl paid for
the material, and of course I got the piano lessons for free too. I
didn't know that then, and ever since I found out it has made a
difference. That's one reason I have tried to make something of
myself and Lonnie, since I realized how hard Aunt Adele and
Uncle Earl tried to expose me to culture. I wanted to let them and
Mama and everybody else in town know that it *took*.

I had piano lessons for four years and practiced a half an hour a
day over at Lucie's house before I found out I was tone-deaf. But
Lucie played like an angel. On the night of the recital when we
were in sixth grade, Lucie played ahead of me, "Rustle of Spring,"
a flowery runny piece, and she was so good that all the parents in
the folding chairs sat absolutely still for a second before they burst
into applause. Lucie curtsied, cool as a cucumber, like it was nothing at all. Aunt Adele had taught us all to curtsy.

Then it was my turn. I wore a pale blue dress with spaghetti
straps and a ruffle around the bottom and white shoes with Cuban
heels. My piece was the "Trish-Trash Polka." I could see my mama
in the audience, and Uncle Earl and Aunt Adele, and everybody
who was anybody in town. I started my piece. Now this was a
piece with a refrain between each section and a great big finale at
the end. Only when I was almost through I realized I couldn't
remember how to begin the ending. So I played the refrain again,
and when that didn't work I played the part before the refrain,
and then I played the refrain again. I could feel the spotlight shining hotter and hotter on my face, I could see Aunt Adele in her
blue sequined evening dress lean forward in her chair. I heard
somebody clear their throat and Susie Milligan, who I hated, start
to giggle. I played the refrain four more times and then I just stood

up and said, "I'm sorry, I forgot my piece." Then I locked myself in the bathroom for the rest of the recital and wouldn't go over to Lucie's for two whole days.

We grew apart a little, after that. I quit taking piano. Lucie got interested in boys. But we still went to the movies every weekend, same as always, and sat together in church and in school, and read *Teen* magazine swinging in the swing on her front porch. The big break didn't come until 1956, I can tell you exactly because of Elvis Presley. That was the year when "Heartbreak Hotel" hit so big.

Now I had never heard of Elvis Presley until Lucie called me on the phone one day after school—it was winter—and said I had better come over right away. "I'm busy," I said, which I was, doing I think it was math. "Come on over here anyway," Lucie said. "It's real important." So I did, and when I got there she was jumping all around the record player in the living room saying, "June, you've just got to listen to this." Nobody else seemed to be at home right then, I remember wondering where her little brothers were. So I sat down in Uncle Earl's chair and she put one of those little red plastic things on the record, it was a forty-five, to make it work on their record player. "Just wait," Lucie said. She held onto the edge of the record player so hard that her fingers were white and her eyes shone out from her white face in a dark liquid way, which seemed to me somehow scary. She pushed a button, the forty-five dropped. Elvis came on.

I had never heard anything like it, the way his voice went way down and trembly on "I'm so lonely baby, I'm just so lonely I could die." Elvis's voice seemed to fill up Lucie's whole darkening living room with something hot and crazy and full of pain. It made me think about things I didn't want to, such as Uncle Earl sending Aunt Adele all those roses and my own mama carrying cardboard boxes around after Daddy or just standing on the back porch and staring at nothing, which I had found her doing only a couple of days before Lucie played Elvis for me, standing on the back porch staring at an old photograph of her and Daddy they had made one time at a fair, dressed up in sailor suits. She said they rented the sailor suits from the photographer. When I came out on the porch, she put the picture in her apron pocket but I saw. "It's down at the end of Lonely Street," Elvis sang. I stood up to go. Lucie's face shone out white in the darkness of her living room. "Don't you just love it?" she said. I didn't say a thing.

I left, followed by the shaking, wanting voice of Elvis across the freezing grass. So this is how I remember it—the end of Lucie and me. Of course it wasn't truly the end, I know that, just like I know it must not have been longer than a half hour after that when Aunt Adele came in from wherever she was, probably the grocery store, rustling her paper bags, and Uncle Earl came in from the Rexall puffing on his cigar, and the boys came back from wherever they were and started kidding Lucie about Elvis. Which they did for the next two years. I know Lucie didn't sit there in the rocking dark forever, nobody does that, the same way I know I didn't play the refrain of the "Trish-Trash Polka" over and over forever either, but still it seems like it.

Lucie got her hair cut in a pixie, painted her fingernails purple, started smoking Winston cigarettes and cutting school, and ran off in our senior year with a disc jockey named Horace Bean. She broke Uncle Earl's heart and gave Aunt Adele migraine headaches. I stayed home working part-time at the dime store and taking care of Mama, who got worse and worse. I was Miss Welch High School as I said. In the fall of my senior year I got engaged to Lonnie Russell, the quarterback.

Whole years went by after that when I didn't see Lucie, although I kept up with her through Aunt Adele and Uncle Earl. Horace Bean didn't last long—Uncle Earl had him annulled right away. Then Lucie went to college, then she taught school in Richmond and led the life of a gay divorcée. I didn't care much one way or the other. I was working two jobs to put Lonnie through school at the community college, trying to keep a decent house and take care of Mama, who was living with us then. Twice while Lonnie was working for Grassy Creek Coal—this was his first job after college—they tried to send him off to other places. One time to Texas and one time to north Alabama. "Count me out!" I said. I didn't want to try to move Mama and besides I think you ought to stay in a place where people know you, and know who you are. I just couldn't see Texas, all that wind and sand, or north Alabama, or even Bluefield, where Lonnie wanted to buy into a mine explo-

sives company and would have made a lot of money, as it turned
out, if he had. But I just couldn't see it. We stayed in Welch, and
eventually Lonnie started his own mine explosives company which
has done so well and I always kept the books for him. We were
renting Mrs. Bradshaw's house in town and I was pregnant the
summer Lucie came back and ran into Richard Young.

Ran into is exactly right! But actually he ran into us. Lucie and
I were sitting out in my front yard on the lawn chairs getting some
sun and trying to talk, which was hard to do, our lives were so
different by then, when here came a VISTA jogging up the road,
sweat pouring down all over him. This was during the Poverty
Program, we had VISTAs all over the place then.

He ran right up to the gate and stopped dead in his tracks,
looking at Lucie. Lucie was twenty-two or twenty-three by then I
guess, and so was I, but I had been married for years. I was as big
as a house, I still have these stretch marks I got from Richie. Lucie
stood up and went over to the gate to say hello and that was it.
You couldn't have pried them apart with a crowbar the rest of that
summer long. Aunt Adele and Uncle Earl were just beside themselves too—at last Lucie was going with somebody worth his salt,
Uncle Earl said. Lonnie and I thought he was weird though, which
he was. In addition to the jogging, he used to climb the mountains
for fun, which nobody around here has ever done. Or maybe he
was just ahead of his time. Now we have all this ecology and phys-
ical fitness but nobody had it then. Lucie climbed with him. He
used to spend hours testing children's eyes away up in the hollers,
things like that. That stuff was part of his job. Lucie helped him.
In fact she never went back to Richmond at all, just moved into
his trailer on Guesses' Fork, and Uncle Earl and Aunt Adele never
said a word because he had gone to Princeton.

I tried to steer clear of Lucie, she made me nervous as I said.
She had this way of squinting her eyes when she looked at things,
you never could tell what she thought or what she might take it
into her head to do next. Such as live in a trailer with a VISTA
when everyone knew it. I was so embarrassed. But Lonnie surprised me too, he said it was none of my business. I couldn't get
over it—there was none of that between *us,* you can be sure, until
we got married. Lonnie said I drove him crazy and especially my

breasts, but I said no handling the merchandise! So it made me uneasy that summer the way they carried on.

And then the night of the Moon Landing they asked to come over to watch it on our TV, Richard naturally not having one in that trailer. It was so hot. It must have been ninety degrees that day, and the heat never slacked off at all as night came on. I had fixed a big dinner for everybody—fried chicken and potato salad, even Lonnie would have to tell you I'm a good cook—but then after all that I got so hot I had to lay in the bathtub in the cold water for awhile I felt so tired. My stomach stuck up round and white above the water where I lay, I could see the baby moving around in there. I could hear them all in the living room—Lucie and Richard and Lonnie—talking and laughing, I could hear the TV. I felt like I was miles and miles away. By the time I got out there I could see they had all had several drinks of bourbon, which Richard had brought over. Lonnie fixed me one too and I sipped along to be sociable, but it was ten o'clock before we ate and eleven o'clock before the astronauts reached the moon. Right before that, when I was in the kitchen straightening up, Lucie came in and splashed cold water all over her face. I had noticed she didn't eat much, so I asked her how she felt.

"Well," she said, "June, I might as well tell you." Lucie's eyes were dark and shining even with all the makeup washed off.

"Tell me what?" I was not so sure I wanted to know.

"I'm pregnant," Lucie said. "Me too." She looked absolutely delighted.

"Are you sure?" I asked. "Did you take a rabbit test yet?"

"No, but I'm *sure*," Lucie said. "I can just tell. Isn't it wonderful?"

"Well"—I had to sit down in a chair—"I guess it is, if you're going to get married, I mean."

Lucie looked fifteen years old with her dark hair curling around her face.

"I haven't decided," she said.

She didn't get married either, as it turned out, at least not to Richard Young. She had Tommy all by herself in Washington, then sent him home for a year for Aunt Adele to raise while she got some other degree, and then she sent for him and after a while she married the professor she's still married to now. Aunt Adele kept on teaching piano that year and hired a high school girl to look after Tommy. Aunt Adele was fine except for the occasional migraine.

But you could have knocked me over with a feather the night of the Moon Landing when Lucie said *that*. I didn't even have time to answer because here was Lonnie at the kitchen door saying, "Come on girls, they made it!" and grabbing me up with a big kiss so we had to go watch. *One small step for man, one large step for mankind*. It reminded me of that game Lucie and I used to play, giant step. It didn't seem any realer than that, them in their space suits like snowmen, walking around on the moon.

And then of course the next morning you found out that Teddy Kennedy was driving around with Mary Jo Kopechne at exactly the same time, but it was the day after that before it really hit the news. Now I wonder, did Mary Jo Kopechne think she was in love, too? Anyway it seems so strange to me now that it happened that night, all of it, and all of us sitting there burning up in that rented house drinking bourbon and watching the TV news. Lonnie put a lampshade on his head and started walking around stiff-legged like a moon man, I got to giggling and Lucie did too. I laughed so hard I thought I would go into labor right then and there but I did not. We all laughed some more, and drank some more bourbon, and I can't even remember when they left.

I remember being in the bed with Lonnie though later, him and me with no sheet and the light over Dawson's Store shining in the window where I'd forgotten to pull the drapes. I got up to do it then but Lonnie said, "Leave it, I like to look at you," even as big as I was. We couldn't do anything then of course because I was too far along but I remember we went to sleep like that, me lying on my side and Lonnie's arms tight around me, him breathing through my hair into my ear, the streetlight shining white across the bed.

Lucie and I stood there looking at the Lunar Module which was a whole lot bigger than I had thought, maybe because we had watched it on that little old black-and-white TV so long ago. "Don't you remember?" Lucie said and I said yes.

But the Lunar Module itself was so pretty in a weird kind of way—all shiny, like a combination of lace and tinfoil, like Cinderella's coach on its spidery legs. It looked magic to me right then, and I could feel my face floating up again over the crowd.

Lucie was giving advice. "You know, June," she said, "even if Lonnie is giving you plenty of money—" which he was, he's always been so generous to a fault—"the first thing you need to do now is get a job." I have always thought a woman should stay at home if humanly possible, so this went against my grain. "You need to get out, get a job," Lucie went on.

"What would I do?" I asked from my face which was floating way up there above us all.

"Well," Lucie said, looking at my needlepoint purse, "what about a craft shop or something? You always were creative."

"A craft shop!" my voice said, and then it said, "Creative! I guess I am. I guess I'm real creative, as a matter of fact. I think I made it all up, Lucie, all of it, my marriage and Lonnie too. You remember Lonnie? Well let me tell you, I just made him up."

As soon as I said this, I knew it was true.

Lucie looked real surprised. But then she laughed, a tinkling laugh as silver as the Lunar Module before us or maybe I mixed it all up in my head, I was mixing up the way things looked with how they sounded because my head was so far away.

"It was finished a long time ago," I said. "I was just dragging it out. Lonnie was so unhappy and I wouldn't listen or even let on that I noticed. I thought if he didn't say it, then maybe it would all go away. It was my fault too, Lucie"—I could see this for the first time, being in Outer Space—"I tell you, I made Lonnie up."

"That's all right," Lucie said. "People do that." And then all of a sudden I forgave her being so wild and leaving Tommy that year with Aunt Adele and playing "The Rustle of Spring" so well. But Lucie didn't even need it, my forgiveness. All of a sudden I knew that too.

"You'll be okay," Lucie said. "*Hey!*" She reached out to grab Tommy and Richie who came running past like the wind. "Listen," she told them, "when this thing landed on the moon, your mom and I were right together in the same room watching it. We saw it land together, and we were both pregnant, so that means you were both in our stomachs right then, that long ago, and we were together watching. And now you're twelve years old. Isn't that amazing?" I could tell by Lucie's voice that she really did think it was amazing, just like I did.

"Huh," Tommy said. You could tell he was not impressed. Some Japanese people came up all around us and started taking pictures.

"Richie," I said, "isn't that something?" but Richie grinned just like Tommy and said, "So what?"

Bob Shacochis

WHERE PELHAM FELL

(from *Esquire*)

Less than a year after Colonel Taylor Coates had been told not to drive he was behind the wheel again, smoking Chesterfields, another habit he had been warned not to pursue, clear-headed and precise in his own opinion, holding to the patriotic speed limit north on Route 29 away from Culpeper in a flow of armies and horses and artillery across the battlefields of Virginia. On one flank the landscape pitched toward a fence of blue mountains, on the other it receded through the bogs and level fields of Tidewater, and as far as Colonel Coates was concerned, there was no better frame for a gentleman's life. There never had been, there never would be, which wasn't just a guess, because the Corps of Engineers had made him world-sore, a forty-year migrant before they discharged him in the direction of the Piedmont.

The Confederate John Mosby came onto the road at the Remington turnoff and galloped alongside the car for a mile or two, spurring his Appaloosa stallion. The Colonel decelerated to keep in pace. Mosby pointed to a field map clutched in the same hand that held the reins. His boots were smeared with red clay, the tails of his longcoat flapped, and he held his head erect, his beard divided by the wind. Colonel Coates rolled down the car window and shouted over into the passing lane. *You!* Mosby arched an eyebrow and tapped an ear with his map, leaning to hear the Colonel's voice in the thunder of a diesel truck poised to overtake them. The breeze flipped the Colonel's walking hat into the passenger seat, exposing the white brambles of his hair, blew cigarette ash into his eyes. *That coat you're wearing,* he said, pointing. *Your grandson honored me with a button from the cuff.* The Gray Ghost, as Mosby was known to those who loved or feared him, saluted and rode off onto the shoulder of the pike. The truck rumbled past between them, followed by a long stream of gun caissons pulled by teams of quarter horses showering froth into the air.

Well now, in the presence of consecrated ground even the imaginations of simple men are stirred to hazy visions, and Colonel Coates wasn't simple, only old, recuperating from the shingles and a number of years of puzzling spiritual fatigue, having been given too many years on earth. Brandy Station, two miles south of Elkwood, was where Colonel Coates really headed when he deserted his slumbering wife to replenish the supply of dog food at home, a legitimate errand that he automatically forgot in favor of cruising Fleetwood Hill. The hill was the field of war that engaged him most thoroughly, for there was fought the greatest cavalry battle ever on American soil. The site, virtually unchanged since the mayhem of 1863, had the smell of clover and apple blossoms at this time of year, a nostalgic blend that floated a man's thoughts through the decades of Aprils he'd survived. The Colonel studied accounts of the conflict, knew its opposing strategies, its advances and countercharges, flankings and retreats. He preferred to sit atop a granite outcropping on the knob of the rise and, with an exhilarating rush of details, play out the twelve-hour struggle for himself, the harsh sputtering rake of the enfilades, the agonizing percussion of hooves, swords, musketry. Here the sons of America had devoured one another as if they were Moors and Christians. Here slaughter within the family was an exquisite legend. History could be scratched by the imagination and made to bleed on a few hundred acres of greensward and farmland fouled magnificently by violence.

Almost a year without independence had made Colonel Coates lust for a prowl at Brandy Station. After the war between North and South, that was all the aristocracy had left, the right to remembrance. Taylor had claimed this right and felt obliged to it; his vigil registered in the bloody heart of the land as if he himself—his existence—were the true outcome of the fray: a florid, half-bald man alone in a rolling pasture, hitching his loose pants up repeatedly to keep them above the horns of his failing hips, stricken by the deep blue plunge of loss for those things he wanted but now knew he would not have; for those things he possessed and loved but whose time was past; for myth and time itself, for what was, for the impossibility of ever being there.

And yet he would return from the battlefield uplifted.

Out on the road, however, the Colonel was distracted by the withdrawal of federal troops back across the Rappahannock, and he bypassed Brandy Station, not realizing his mistake until he spotted the marker post commemorating Pelham on the east side of the highway. Major John Pelham commanded Stuart's Horse Artillery until he fell at the battle of Kelly's Ford, mortally wounded by shrapnel that ribboned his flesh and broke the forelegs of his sorrel mount. The skirmish was between cavalry charging blindly through a terrain of deep woods and dense scrub along the banks of the river, the riders cantering through trackless forest, squads of men blundering into tangled thickets, the legs of their coarse pants cut by lead and briar thorns. Down went Pelham as he inspired his men forward, and the event was memorialized many years later by a roadside marker at a junction on Route 29, erected near Elkwood by the United Daughters of the Confederacy, informing the curious that four miles to the southeast the young major had been martyred to the rebel cause.

Abruptly and without signaling, the Colonel veered to the shoulder and turned on the country road, grim but unrepentant of the nuisance he made for the traffic behind him. Before the privilege of mobility had been taken from him, he had spent the afternoons in aggravated search for the location of Pelham's slaying. The direction of the marker was vague—four miles to the southeast—and the road that supposedly went there split, forked, crossed, and looped through pine and hayfields without bringing Taylor to the ford of the river. Sixteen miles later he threw up his hands and jogged west, eventually arriving at a surfaced pike that returned him to Route 29.

It was now or never again, the Colonel rationalized. From the diaries of the generals he had learned that an opportunity renewed by destiny could not be prevented. The soldiers themselves often hastened forth under the influence of such patterns through the same geography, wandering here and there until suddenly foes met and clashed. The paths they followed were subject to mortifying change. What was right yesterday might be wrong today. But that was the nature of rebel territory—a free-for-all. The Colonel, in slow reconnaissance, took the road to a T intersection, craning to see the houses at the end of their lanes, under guard of oaks, evergreens, rail fences. Virginia, he thought, was the abattoir of the South, mother of the destruction. These were the estates that sent their young men to war, the houses were the lucky wounded returned to expire, where the enemy plundered, where the secessionist ladies wept through the night as the armies marched by. What did people in the North know of the residue of terror that had settled in the stones and beams of these estates? Where in America were there such noble structures, one after another after another, league after league, each a silent record of strife and defeat? It was not an exaggeration to say that the Colonel adored these houses.

At the intersection the pavement ended and an orangeish gravel lane ran left and right. Taylor calculated a southeast direction by examining the sun. The odometer had advanced three miles. He swung left, pleased that the road soon curved, auspiciously by his reckoning, to the south, over swampy ground created, he was sure, by its proximity to the river. For four miles more the road wormed through this low, wet countryside reeking of bog rot, switched its designation twice, and then ascended to higher land, no river in sight, no water crossing, no defunct mill-house, no aura of hostility, nothing but the warm hum of springtime.

By God, I'm missing in action, the Colonel thought, confused as to his whereabouts. And that was how he met President Trass and ended up in possession of the bones.

Cresting a ridge, he sighted the glint of running water a half mile in the distance. The road he was on went off away from it, but there was a narrower track burrowing through a strand of hardwood that appeared as though it might drop in the right direction. On the opposite fringe of the grove, the Colonel saw he had blundered onto private property—and a trash haven at that. The track wasn't a road at all but a drive dead-ending in ruts around an unpainted frame house, the center of a cluster of shantylike outbuildings and rusted junk. An ancient pink refrigerator stood sentry on a swayback porch, the only color in the monotony of gray and weather-hammered boards. A hound scrambled from under the foundation and barked an alarm. Colonel Coates tried to reverse back through the woods, but he wasn't up to such a maneuver. The rear wheels went off the packed dirt into a spongy muck at the same time the front fender debarked the trunk of a hickory tree. The station wagon lodged across the track, the Colonel demoralized and flustered.

It must be understood that the Colonel was not a man who was unaware, who had no insight into his behavior. He knew full well that he was becoming more spellbound by both the sacred and profane than ever before. Contact with the world at hand was lost or revived on an inscrutable schedule. So distressed was he by this condition, he had devised a plan for its rougher moments: If you get confused, sit down. If you sit down, stay put until the mind brightens.

He remained where he was, smoking Chesterfields with pointless determination, the ashes collecting in his lap. Picket lines formed in the underbrush beneath the skirt of trees. Then the guns played on him, and an ineffective hail of grapeshot bounced across the hood of the wagon. The Colonel withstood the onslaught, battling against the failure of the vision. Then came his capture and subsequent imprisonment at Fort Delaware, the parole, and at last the shameful journey home.

President Trass was a tolerant man but eventually he became annoyed that his bird dog was baying itself hoarse. When Trass came out on the porch of the house he was born into, the Colonel noticed his advance and ducked down onto the car seat, felt immediately foolish in doing so, and rose back into view. He cranked open the window, shouting out with as much vigor as was left in his voice.

"I'm unarmed."

President Trass halted in front of the station wagon, wary of tricks. No telling what was up when a white man blockaded your drive. "Yeah?" he said suspiciously. "That's good news. What y'all want 'round here?"

The Colonel admitted his mission. "I'm looking for Kelly's Ford, where Pelham fell."

"That a fact," President Trass said. He slowly pointed in the direction the Colonel had come from. "You way off. You about two miles east of the crossing."

"Is that so," said the Colonel. "Much obliged." He stepped on the gas. A volley of mud kicked into the air over President Trass's head. The rear wheels spun in place.

Colonel Coates was invited into the house to wait for President Trass's neighbor to bring a tractor over for the car. They sat in the parlor, the Colonel on a threadbare sofa, President Trass in an overstuffed wingback chair. Neatly framed pictures were tacked in a well-sighted line across one wall: four tintypes of nineteenth-century Negroes. A sepia-toned group portrait with a Twenties look, an array of black-and-white snapshots, some of the subjects in the caps and gowns of graduation—presumably President Trass's ancestors and offspring.

To Colonel Coates's eye, President Trass looked like an old salamander in bib overalls, a slick, lymphatic edgelessness to the black man's features. President Trass thought that the Colonel, removed of the hat squashed onto his skull like a bottle cap, resembled a newly hatched chicken hawk, hot-skinned, old-ugly, and fierce at birth. They faced each other without exchanging a word. The longer President Trass considered the Colonel's *there*ness in the room, the more he began to believe that it was no coincidence, that something providential had happened, that Jesus had sent him a chicken hawk to relieve the Trass clan of the macabre burden they had accepted as their own for more than a hundred years, the remains of the soldiers President's granddaddy had plowed up on the first piece of land he cleared as a free man, a sharecropper in the year 1867. President Trass licked the dry swell of his lips, looked down at his own cracked hands as if they were a miracle he was beginning to understand.

"What you 'spect to see at ol' Kelly's Ford anyway? Ain't nuthin' there worth even a quick look."

"Eh?" said the Colonel.

"Say there ain't much there."

"That so."

President Trass kept his head bowed and prayed himself clean: Shared a lot of jokes, Jesus, me and You. First white man I ever *invite* through my door and You lettin' me think he some kinda damn cracker angel. Why's that, Lord? Well, I ain't afraid no more somebody goin' take this all wrong, leastwise this ol' chicken hawk.

"What's worth seein', I got," said President Trass.

The Colonel coughed abruptly and squinted. "I'm not the man who would know," he said.

"You come lookin' for soldiers, you must be the man. They's yo' boys, ain't they?" said President, and he led the Colonel out back to one of the cold sheds and gave him the bones that four generations of Trass family couldn't quite decide what to do with.

So the Colonel had defied Dippy, his wife, sneaked out onto the road ostensibly to buy dog food, and was returning home with two dirty burlap sacks full of what President Trass had described to him as noisy bones. Bones they were, laced with rotted scraps of wool and leather, too sacred for canine bellies and tasteless anyway. But no noise to them the Colonel could detect, other than the dull rattle and chalky shift they made when he and the old black fellow carried them out of the shed and hoisted them into the rear of the station wagon. President Trass had what he and the Colonel agreed was accurately called a nigger notion: the bones talked too much, jabbered like drunk men in an overcrowded rowboat; the men whose flesh had once hung on these disjointed skeletons were still in them, like tone in a tuning fork, refusing the peace of afterlife in favor of their military quarrels. "That's a voodoo I never had use for," the Colonel said. "Men our age find queer ways to pass the time." "I ain't yo' age as yet," President answered back, "and I never said I had trouble fillin' a day like some folks I know."

Colonel Coates wasn't a man to heed mere telling, nor to concede to age what age had not yet earned or taken. "All right," he said to the black man. "With all respect for your habits, I am duty bound to recover the remains of these brave boys."

"That's right. Take 'em," President said. "You might just be gettin' some nigger notions yo'self. Prob'ly do you some good."

"I've been waiting half my life for a younger fellow to set me straight," the Colonel said, "and I don't reckon you're him."

"Well, Colonel," President Trass said with a tight smile, winking at the sacks of bones in the car. "You finally get in with the right crowd to tell you a thing or two."

*   *   *

Since turning eighty, Dippy Barrington Coates slept more during the day, catnaps on the sofa in the den, a quilt pulled over her legs, not because she was tired but because her dreams were more vivid and interesting than they had ever been before, and nothing she witnessed in them frightened her. She hadn't slept so much in daylight since 1942, when she was always tired. Awaking from those naps back then she had been miserable. The extreme loneliness of the dead seemed in her, as if she had been spinning in solitude through the blackness beyond the planets. That ended, though, when she left the house to become a nurse. After the war Taylor came home from Europe. It took some time for him to become her friend again, to settle to his own mind that he wasn't going anywhere without her the rest of his life. The migrations began again, so many places, so many homes she created only to dismantle them a year or two later.

But none of the early years were as hard to endure as the three before the last. Taylor, infirm but alert, first his prostate and then the shingles, which left extensive scars across his shoulders and chest, issuing orders from bed: I want this, I want that. Goddamn the pain, let it off for sixty blasted seconds. You're a nurse, do something. Dippy, have you fed the dogs? Has the *Post* been delivered yet? Did you hire a boy to pick the apples? Dippy, come up here and tell me what's happened to your ability to fix simple egg and toast.

The house and lands were too much for her to manage alone. She had secretly put herself and the Colonel on the waiting list at Vincent Hall up in Fairfax. There were days when she wished to God that He would make Taylor vanish into history, which was what the man had always wanted anyway. Just as she became acclimated to the regimen of his illness and moods, he popped out of bed one day fifteen months ago, announcing he would occupy his last days touring the fields of battle in the area. He recharged the battery in the Ford pickup and motored down the cedar-lined drive on his excursions, to be grounded semivoluntarily three months later after what seemed like, but wasn't, a premeditated string of collisions, mad acts against authority. He plowed into a Prince George County sheriff's patrol car, a state-park maintenance vehicle, a welded pyramid of cannonballs at New Market.

None of these accidents injured more than vanity and metal. Each occurred during a low-speed drift, the Colonel mesmerized by the oblique and mystical harmonies played for him by Fredericksburg, by Bull Run, by New Market, where the cadets had fought.

She had made him sell the truck rather than repair it. Taylor sulked and groused for several weeks, the pace of his recuperation slackening to a plateau. He entered a year of book reading, map gazing, talking back to the anchormen on the television news, typing letters to the editors of papers in Washington, Richmond, and Charlottesville, disavowing the new conservatism because its steam was religious jumpabout, lacking in dignity and too hot-blooded for an Episcopalian whose virtue had never faltered to begin with. *Are we cowards?* one letter inquired about a terrorist attack on an embassy. *Many Americans today seem to think so. We are afraid we are but I tell you we are not. What the true citizens and families of this nation have learned is not to abide by courage wasted.*

Writing in his study on the second story of the antebellum brick farmhouse, Taylor could look out across hayfields and orchards to the Blue Ridge. He found the gentility of the view very satisfying. On stormy days the mountains were purple. Dramatic shafts of light would pierce the clouds, and the Colonel was reminded of the colors of the Passion and Golgotha. For his grandchildren he penned accounts of the clan, the Coateses and the Barringtons and Tylers and Holts and Hucksteps, hoping to seduce them into a fascination with their heritage, the precious ancestral silt deposited throughout the land. *My grandpa,* he wrote, *was Major Theodore Coates of the Army of Northern Virginia. He was assigned to General Early's staff and fought valiantly for the Confederate cause until the Battle of Antietam where within an hour's carnage he was struck directly in the ear by a cleaner bullet. The wound itself was not fatal but it destroyed the Major's inner ear, denying him his equilibrium and orientation and causing him to ride in front of his own artillery as they discharged a salvo over the lines. The charge lifted horse and rider far into the air, so witnesses said.*

When one of the grandchildren, a boy at college in New England, wrote back that the rebellion, not to mention the family's participation in it, was too disgraceful and produced in him a guilt by association, Taylor responded, *You might reasonably suppose that your forefathers were on the wrong side in this conflict, but I assure you they were not wrong-minded, no more so than the nation itself was. White men weren't slaughtering each other because of black men, that was clear from the start. Read about the City of New York during those years. When you go into Boston on your weekends, what is it that you see? Do you really mean to tell me that Northerners died to save the Negro from us?*

What do you think of communism? he had asked a married granddaughter last Christmas. It's foo foo, she answered, and afterward the Colonel decided he had communicated enough with the newest generation. Altogether it was a serene year they had passed in each other's company, and neither Dippy nor Taylor had much desire to go beyond their own land. When once a week she took the station wagon into Culpeper to shop, Taylor would occasionally come along, and he did not protest being demoted to the status of a passenger.

She knew last night had been a restless one for him, though. Troubled by a vague insomnia, the Colonel had slipped out of bed three or four times to listen to the radio, stare out the window at the silhouettes of the outbuildings in the Appalachian moonshine. When he urinated he said he felt as though the wrong stuff was streaming out, not liquid waste but vital fluid. Nights such as this he felt were nothing more than waiting to kick off into eternity, to blink and gasp and be a corpse. At breakfast his shingles burned again and his breathing was more constricted. He had difficulty concentrating on the morning paper. He complained that his tongue seemed coated with an aftertaste of medicine that even her coffee couldn't penetrate.

After lunch Dippy snoozed on the couch, the afghan she was knitting bunched on her chest. When she awoke she went right to the kitchen door, knowing he was gone. It was wrong of Taylor to do this to her. Trusting him had never been much of an issue in the course of their marriage except when the children were growing up, and only then because he played too rough with them, wanted them to learn reckless skills, and showed no patience for the slow art of child rearing. He had once knocked out Grover when the boy was twelve years old, demonstrating how to defend yourself. Throughout his life the Colonel had been a good enough man to admit to his shortcomings, by and by, but now he had survived even his ability to do that.

She walked nervously around the house, emptying the smelly nubs of tobacco he had crammed into ashtrays, thinking about what she might do. Nothing. Phone the sheriff and have the old mule arrested before he banged into someone and hurt them. That would serve him right and placate the annoyance she felt at Taylor's dwindling competence, three-quarters self-indulgence and willful whimsy anyway, she thought, the man trespassing everywhere, scattering his mind over too much ground. It was as though the Colonel had decided to refuse to pay attention. If he hadn't returned within the hour she would call Taylor's nephew in Warrenton for advice. In the meantime she couldn't stay in the house alone, marking his absence.

She put on her black rubber boots, cotton work gloves from out of a kitchen drawer, a blue serge coat over her housedress, wrapped a red chiffon scarf around her tidy hair and knotted it under her chin. On her way out she turned the heat to low beneath the tea kettle. In the yard the dogs ran up to her and she shooed them away, afraid their clumsy affection would knock her down.

Behind the house the pasture was sprayed with wild flowers for the first time she could remember, the result of a Christmas gift called Meadow in a Can from one of the grandchildren. She walked out into it and the air smelled like sun-hot fresh linen. She went as far as the swale, sniffed at its cool stone dampness, and headed back, the dogs leaping in front of her, whirlybirds for tails. She went to the tool shed and found the rake and garden scissors, thinking she'd pull what remained of last autumn's leaves out of the ivy beds, and cut jonquils to take inside. Below the front veranda, where the boxwoods swelled with an aroma that Dippy associated with what was colonial and southern, she tugged at the ivy with the tines of her rake, accomplishing little. Then the Colonel came home.

The station wagon bounced over the cattle bars sunk into the entrance of the drive and lurched ahead, slicing gravel. She looked back toward the road, wondering if Taylor was being chased, but certainly he wasn't. Dippy reached the turnaround as he pulled in, swerving and skidding, making white dust. One of the front fenders was puckered from the headlight to the wheel well. She stamped over and rapped with the handle of the rake on this new damage Taylor dared to bring home.

He remained in the car, veiled behind the glare on the windshield, his hands clawed to the steering wheel, reluctant to drop them shaking onto his lap while he suffered his pride. The dogs barked and hopped into the air outside his door as if they sprang off trampolines. Dippy kept rapping on the fender with the rake, harder and harder, drumming shame. His jaw slackened and his shoulders seemed no longer able to sustain the gravity of the world in its orbit. He prayed for composure, for the muscle of his feckless heart to beat furiously against their damn devilish luck, the fate that had made them two living fossils, clinging to the earth with no more strength than moths in a rising breeze.

The Colonel rolled down his window. "Stop that," he ordered.

"You are a hazard, old man."

"Stop that. I won't stand for this Baptist behavior."

"Come out of there."

"Here now, stop that and I will."

Well, Dippy did cease her banging on the fender but she didn't know what to do next to emancipate the sickness that came when she realized Taylor had launched himself back onto the highways where he was likely to murder himself. She jabbed at the fender with the rake once more.

"What was so important you had to sneak off like a hoodlum?"

"Bones," he said too loudly, "bones," followed by a sigh. He had jumped ahead and had to backtrack his explanation.

"Dog food," he corrected himself. She knew better and he had to tell the truth. "I wanted to see where Major Pelham fell, that's all."

She wanted to cry at this irony—an old man's irrepressible desire to see where a young man had died—but she could only shake her head. Taylor coaxed his limbs out of the car and she listened skeptically to him tell the story of what he had been up to. "Noisy bones?" she repeated after him, becoming alarmed. This was not the sort of information she took lightly. He brushed past her to open the tailgate on the wagon. She frowned because inside she felt herself straining to hear the muddled end of an echo ringing across the boundlessness. Was a message being delivered here or not? Her longevity had made her comfortable with the patterns of coincidence and happenstance that life enjoyed stitching, cosmic embroidery on the simple cloth of flesh. She tried to make herself extrareceptive to this peculiar sensation of contrivance, but nothing came through.

"I think you've finally gone cuckoo, Taylor Coates," she said.

"None of that. These are heroes." He patted the sacks. "Gallant boys."

Dippy was bewildered. Goodness, she thought, what sort of intrusion is this? Who's to say how she knew, or what sense was to be made out of it? A bridge formed between somewhere and somewhere else and Dippy understood that the man who had given the Colonel the bones was absolutely right—they were *noisy* bones, not the first she had met either. Oh, you could call those invisible designs by so many names: intuition, spirit and ether, witchery and limbo. Don't think she didn't reflect endlessly about the meaning of each word that could be attached to the force of the unknown. Even as a child her life had been visited by startling moments of clairvoyance and fusion. Each instance felt as if she had just awakened at night to someone calling through a door.

"Look," the Colonel invited, and peeled back the lip of the burlap to reveal the clean dome of a skull.

She had dreamed and redreamed such a thing. There were occasions in Dippy's life, each with its own pitch and resonance, chilling seconds when she attracted information from the atmosphere that translated into impulsive behavior: refusing to allow children out of the house, once persuading Taylor not to buy a horse because she sensed evil in the presence of the animal, sending money to a Buddhist temple she had entered briefly when they lived in Indonesia. She avoided riding in cars with Connecticut license plates if she could. As a nurse at Bethesda Naval Hospital during the war, she watched a sailor die on the operating table after hearing her son's voice say, *He's a goner, Ma.* What about you, she thought. You're dead too, aren't you? and then held her tears while still another dying patient was wheeled in.

There are a few things you don't know about me, she said to the Colonel in February when he saw her mailing a letter to a scientist she had read about in the paper, a man at Duke University who researched these phenomena.

That's not right. After all this time.

Yes it is, she said. Secrets are what crones and children thrive on.

The Colonel pawed through the bones, exhibiting a look of sanctified pleasure. Warriors in a sack, seasoned messengers of glory. Conscripts from the republic of death. Dippy cursed them like any mother or wife. Dog food indeed. Why else were the bones here but to tantalize the Colonel with their chatter.

"I suppose we better call the police."

"The police!" the Colonel said. "Never. I'm going to find where these poor boys belong."

"There's only one place bones belong," she said.

"They'll take their seat in history first," Taylor insisted, shuffling the bones he had pulled out back into their sacks. He straightened up, frail and indignant.

"God wants those souls placed to rest."

"No, He don't, Dippy. Not yet He don't. Not till I find out who they were."

Rally them, Colonel, rally the boys.

As Dippy expected he would, given his interests, the Colonel became obsessed with the bones, the necroscopic opportunities they presented, and she readjusted her daily life to accept the company of both the living and the dead. Because she had forbidden Taylor to bring the two burlap sacks inside the house, he spent his time in the workshop that adjoined the garage, paying little attention to much else than his mounds of dusty relics. Every two hours she brought the Colonel his medication. At noon she brought him lunch and tea, and at 4:00 each afternoon for the full five days he spent in the workshop, she took him a shot of brandy to tire him out so he'd come willingly back to the house, complaining of the heaviness in his arms. Between trips to the workshop she'd fuss with needless cleaning, cook, or nap, instantly dreaming. She dreamed of her first daughter's elopement in 1939 with a German immigrant who later abandoned her. Once she dreamed of the good-looking doctor who plunged his hand into her drawers when she worked at Bethesda—she woke up smoothing her skirt, saying, *Wooh,* that's enough of that. And she dreamed of the two of her children in their graves, a little girl from influenza, the boy who died during the liberation of France. They would stay in her mind all day after she dreamed them. Not so great a distance seemed to separate them now, and she took comfort in the sensation of a togetherness restored. Even a long life was daunted by its feeling of brevity and compression.

And Taylor out there in the garage, history's vulture, pecking through the artifacts. She dreamed him, too, atop a horse, leading his skeletons toward the fray into which they cheered. They cheered, and the extent of her sadness awakened her.

"How do we teach our souls to love death?" he asked her in bed the evening of the second day, the fumes of wintergreen ointment rising off his skin.

"Who says you have to bother," she said. "Leave those bones alone."

"They'll be placed with their own," he answered. "I'm working on it."

What do you remember of your life, the Colonel had asked President Trass in the shed. It ain't over yet, President said. But I remember everything—the gals, the dances, the weather. What about white men? the Colonel was eager to know. President answered, They was around. Then he told the Colonel about his nigger notion and said take the bones because there wasn't a Trass alive or dead who was willing to put them to rest. Not on Trass property anyway.

The Colonel cleared his worktable of underused tools and spread the contents of the sacks across the length of its gummy surface. He turned on the radio, lit a Chesterfield, and surveyed what he had. He counted twelve pelvic cradles but only ten skulls and nine jawbones. One of the jaws had gold fillings in several of the bare teeth, evidence attesting to the integrity of hate passing through generations of Trass caretakers.

Well, twelve men then, a squad, a lost patrol, eighteen complete though fractured legs between them sharing twenty feet, one still in its boot. The first and second day the Colonel reconstructed what he could of twenty-three hands from two hundred and sixteen finger joints. He divided the ribs up, thirteen to a soldier.

Something curious happened, but he didn't speak of it to Dippy. Metal objects in the workshop began to spark him, fluttering his heart when he touched them so he put on sheepskin gloves and wore them whenever he was out there. His hands became inept and the pace of his work slowed. He started the third day aligning vertebrae into spines but gave it up by lunch. His interest transferred to those material objects that fell from the sacks: the boot with its rattle of tiny bones, a cartridge box with miniballs intact, a flattened canteen, six belt buckles (five stamped CSA), a coffee can he filled the first day with copper and fragile tin buttons, indeterminate fragments of leather and scraps of delicate gray wool.

On the fourth day he brought to the workshop a wheelbarrow-load of books and reprinted documents from his study in the house, prepared to concentrate on the forensic clues that would send the boys home. The weather changed, bringing a frost, and his legs cramped violently. Dippy helped him carry a space heater up from the cellar to supplement the one already glowing in the shop. When she delivered his lunch on the fifth day, she found him on a stool bent over the table, his reading glasses off-balance on his nose, a book opened across his thighs, lost in abstraction as he regarded the buttons arranged in groups of threes. He appeared not to notice when she set down the tray. The radio was louder than usual. Easter was a week away and the announcer preached irritatingly about the sacrifices Christ had made. Dippy turned the sound off. Taylor looked up at her as if she had somehow thwarted his right to sovereignty.

"I'm close, damn it all," he said, scowling, and yet with a fatigued look, the remoteness quickly returning. "These are General Extra Billy Smith's Boys." His voice became unsure. "The Warren Blues, maybe."

"You don't have to tell me how close you are," she said. "I can hear the racket they're making."

The Colonel waved her away and she left. Dippy did not think his devotion to the bones morbid or absurd, only unnecessary, wasted time for a man with nothing more to spend. She could have told Taylor, if he believed in what could not be properly understood, the nature of the noise the bones were making. The bones were preparing to march. She loathed the clamor they made, a frightening, crazed exuberance. She returned to the house and suffered the grief of its emptiness.

That night a thunderstorm moved in from the west, blowing

down the eastern slope of the mountains. The Colonel couldn't sleep. He stood at the bedroom window and peered out, seeing atomic sabers strike the land. He slid back under the covers with his wife and felt himself growing backward. His muscles surged, youth and confidence trembling once again in the tissue. Here too was Dippy, ripe in motherhood, squirting milk at his touch. And here were his school chums, the roster of names so familiar, Extra Billy's Boys one and all. *Company D. Company K.* Fellows he grew up with. Well I'll be, he said to himself in wonder. I went to school with them damn bones.

On the sixth day Dippy went to the workshop shortly after Taylor, disturbed by the extreme volume of the radio music coming across the drive. Pushing open the door she was assaulted by a duet from Handel's *Messiah,* the words and music distorted by loudness. The Colonel was on his feet, at attention, singing with abandon although his lyrics were out of sequence with the broadcast of the performance for Holy Week:

O death, where is thy sting? O grave, where is thy victory?

His face turned red and waxy as she watched in anguish. His shirttails flagged out between his sweater and belt, the laces of one shoe were untied. His gloved hands quivered at his side. The Colonel seemed trapped between euphoria and turmoil, singing to his audience of skulls propped along the table. His voice became cracked and tormented as he repeated the lines, faster each time and with increasing passion. Dippy, thinking the Colonel had gone mad, was scared to death. She hurried to the radio and pulled its plug from the wall. Taylor gradually became aware that his wife had joined him. He felt a funny pressure throughout his body, funny because its effect was a joyous feeling of weightlessness—he could levitate if he chose to. He tried to smile lovingly but knew he failed in his expression. Dippy stared back at him, mournful, one hand to her mouth, as if he were insane. Then a calmness came to him.

"Dippy," he bargained feebly. "I don't wish to be buried in my blue suit."

She helped him back to the house, insisted he take a sleeping pill, undressed his dissipating body, and put him to bed. She couldn't raise him for his supper, nor did he stir when she herself retired later in the evening. She woke the following morning startled by the sound of the station wagon leaving the garage. By the time she reached the window there was nothing to see. She telephoned the police to bring him back, covered herself with a house robe, and went to the kitchen to wait.

Two hours later the curator at the Warren Rifles Confederate Museum in Front Royal observed an old man enter the building and perform a stiff-legged inspection of the display cases. Afterward, the same man approached the curator with a request to view the muster rolls of the 49th Regiment. There was nothing unusual about the old man's desire, and the curator agreed. He offered the gentleman a seat while he excused himself and went into the archives, but when he returned to the public area with the lists, the old man had left.

As he waited for the curator the Colonel was overwhelmed by a sense of severe desolation. The room seemed all at once to be crowded beyond capacity. He felt claustrophobic and began to choke. The noise was deafening, unintelligible, and he was stunned to think how Dippy and President Trass could tolerate it.

In the car again he felt better, yet when the road ascended out of the valley to crest the Blue Ridge, suddenly the Colonel couldn't breathe the air for all the souls that thickened it. He died at the wheel, his hands grasping toward his heart, the station wagon sailing off the road into a meadow bright with black-eyed Susans, crashing just enough for Dippy to justify a closed coffin. The undertaker was a childhood friend of Taylor's, loyal to the military caste and the dignity of southern families, understanding of the privacy they required when burying their own. With discretion he gave her the large coffin she asked for, assisted her in carrying the two heavy satchels into the mourning parlor, and then left, closing the doors behind him without so much as a glance over his shoulder to witness her final act as a wife, the act of sealing the Colonel's coffin after she had heaped the bones in there with him.

She was dry-eyed and efficient throughout the service and burial in the Coates's family plot outside Warrenton. Children and grandchildren worried that she was holding up too well, that she had separated from the reality of the event, that when the impact arrived she would die, too. She could have told them not to concern themselves. She could have told them how relieved she was to be the last southern woman, the last of the last to lower the men who had broken from the Union into their graves, how relieved she was to hear the Colonel exhorting the bones, *Keep in ranks, boys, be brave,* until the terrible cheering grew more and more distant and their voices diminished and she was finally alone, free of glory.

Peggy Payne

THE PURE IN HEART

(from *The Crescent Review*)

He would not have said that he was ever 'called' to the ministry. It wasn't like that. Instead, he grew up knowing that it would be so. The church was Swain Hammond's future—unofficially. He got his doctorate at Yale. Then, after one brief stint as an associate minister, he became the pastor at Westside, a good choice for—as he had become—a man of rational, ethical orientation.

The church, in Chapel Hill, North Carolina, is Presbyterian. It is fairly conventional, though influenced, certainly, by the university community. Swain is happy here. Westside suits him. But it is clearly not the best place to hold the pastorate if you're the sort who's inclined to hear the actual voice of God. Up until recently, this would not have been a problem for Swain. But about eight weeks ago, the situation changed. At that time, Swain did indeed hear God.

He and his wife Julie were grilling skewers of pork and green peppers on the back patio of the stone house they chose themselves as the manse. They have no children. Julie works. She is a medical librarian at the hospital, though if you met her you would never think of libraries. You might think of Hayley Mills in some of those movies from her teenage years. She has the same full features and thick red hair. On this particular night, Julie is turning a shish ke-bab, which seems to be falling apart. Swain, bare-footed—it is June—is drinking a beer and squinting up the slight hill of their backyard, which they have kept wooded.

"Isn't that a lady slipper?" he says. "Was that out yesterday?" But Julie is busy; she doesn't look. Swain, his long white feet still bare, carefully picks his way up the hill to examine the flower. It is then, as he stops yards away from the plant—clearly not a lady slipper—that he hears God for the first time.

The sound comes up and over the hill. One quick cut. Like a hugely amplified PA system, blocks away, switched on for a moment by mistake. "Know that there is truth. Know this." The last vowel, the 'i' of this, lies quivering on the air like a note struck on a wineglass.

The voice is unmistakable. At the first intonation, the first rolling syllable, Swain wakes, feeling the murmuring life of each of a million cells. Each of them all at once. He feels the line where his two lips touch, the fingers of his left hand pressed against his leg, the spears of wet grass against the flat soles of his feet, the gleaming half-circles of tears that stand in his eyes. His own bone marrow hums inside him like colonies of bees. He feels the breath pouring in and out of him, through the damp red passages of his skull. Then in the slow way that fireworks die, the knowledge fades. He is left again with his surfaces and the usual vague darkness within. He turns back around to see if Julie has heard.

She has not. Her back turned to him, she is serving the two plates that he has set on the patio table. A breeze is moving the edge of the outdoor tablecloth. She turns back around toward him, looking up the hill. "Soup's on," she says, smiling. "Come eat." She stands and waits for him, as he walks, careful still of his feet and the nettles, back down to her. Straight to her. He takes her in his arms, ignoring her surprise, the half-second of her resistance. He pulls her close, tight against him, one hand laced now in her hair, one arm around her hips. He is as close as he can get. He has gathered all of her to him that he can hold.

He puts the side of his face against her cheek, so he will not have to see her eyes when he says: "Julie, over there on the grass, I heard something. A voice."

She pulls back from him, forcing him to see her. She raises her eyebrows, half-smiling, searching his face for the signs of a joke. "A voice?" she says. There is laughter ready in her tone.

"God," he says. His mouth is dry. "God's voice."

She watches him carefully now, her eyes scanning his eyes, ever-so-slightly moving. The trace of a smile is gone. "What do you mean?"

"Standing up there on the hill," he says, almost irritably. "I heard God. That's what I mean." He watches her, his own face blank. Hers is struggling. Let her question it if she wants to. He doesn't know how to explain.

"So what happened?" she says. "Tell me some more." She pauses. "What did it—what did the voice sound like?"

Swain repeats the words he heard. He does not say then what happened to him: that hearing the voice, he had felt the mortality of his every cell.

They stand apart from each other now. She reaches over and touches his hair, strokes it. If one of us was to hear God, it should have been Julie, he thinks. But a different God—the one he has believed in until today.

She is looking at him steadily. "I don't think you're crazy, if that's what you're worried about." Her uncertainty has left her. "It's all right," she says. "It is."

"For you it would be," he says. He means it as a compliment. He has envied her her imaginings, felt left behind sometimes by the unfocused look of her eyes. Though she will tell him where she is: that she goes back, years back, to particular days with particular weathers. That she plays in the backyard of her grandparents' house, shirtless, in seersucker shorts, breathing the heavy summer air, near the blue hydrangeas. Swain wants to be with her then. He wants to go: "Except ye become as little children, ye shall not enter. . . ." He wants, and yet he doesn't want.

She glances at the food on the plates. They move toward the table. The sweat that soaked his shirt has started to chill him.

"I'm going to get a sweater," he says. "Do you want anything?" She shakes her head 'no.' She sits, begins to eat her cooling dinner.

There are no lights on inside the house, only the yellowish glow of the patio light through the window, shining on one patch of floor in the hall. He goes to the hall closet, looking for something to put on. He finds a light windbreaker. He has his hand in the closet, reaching for the jacket, when he hears the voice again. One syllable. "Son." The sound unfurls down the long hall toward him. He feels the sound and its thousand echoes hit him all at once. He holds onto the wooden bar where the coat hangs, while the shock washes over his back.

He stays where he is, his back and neck bent, his hand bracing him, waiting. Nothing else happens. Again, it is over. Again he is wet with sweat. He straightens, painfully, as if he had held the position for hours. He walks again out onto the patio. Julie, at the table, squints to see his face against the light beside the door.

"Are you all right?" she says.

He sits, looks down at his plate. He holds the jacket, lays it across his lap like a napkin. He shakes his head. A sob is starting low in his chest, dry like a cough. He feels it coming, without tears. He has not cried since he tore a ligament playing school soccer. He has had no reason. Now he is crying, his own voice tearing and breaking through him. Inside him, walls are falling. Interior walls cave like old plaster, fall away to dust. He feels it like the breaking of living bones. In the last cool retreat of his reason, he thinks: I am seeing my own destruction. Then that cool place is invaded too. He feels the violent tide of whatever is in him flooding his last safe ground. He holds himself with both arms; Julie, on her knees beside his chair, holds him. God has done this to him. This is God. Tears drip from his face and trickle down his neck.

Two days later Swain sits alone in his office at the church. He has a sermon to write. Should he tell the congregation what happened to him? His note pad is blank. He has put down his pen. It is an afternoon with all the qualities of a sleepless night: hot, restless, unending. There are no distractions from what he is unable to do. The secretary is holding his calls. The couple who were to come in with marital difficulties cancelled. The window behind his desk is open; he stares out into the shimmery heat and listens to the churning of a lawn mower. He has already been through the literature and found nothing to reassure him.

Son. He keeps coming back to that one word in his mind. It was not Swain's own father talking. That was clear. His father would never have been so definite, so terse. The elder Dr. Hammond would have interspersed his words, and there would have been more of them, with long moments of musing and probably the discreet small noises of his dyspepsia. He would have asked Swain to consider whether there was indeed 'a truth.' Swain would have considered this, as he was asked. And possibly at some later time they would have discussed it, without conclusion.

Swain, twisting in his chair, resetting his legs, knows he did not create the voice. He did not broadcast that sound out through the pines of his own backyard. He sees again the reddish gold light of the late sun on the bark of those backyard trees. He did not imagine it. His mind does not play tricks.

Though the whole thing seems like a bad trick, a bad dream— divine revelation, coming now. He imagines himself in the pulpit, staring out at the congregation, telling them. He sees the horror waking on their faces, as they understand him. He sees them exchanging glances, glances that cut diagonally across the pews. He would be out. It would cost him the church. Leaders of the congregation would gradually, lovingly ease him out, help him make 'other arrangements.' He tries to imagine those other arrangements: churches with marquees that tally up the number saved on a Sunday, churches with buses and all-white congregations. Appalling. It makes him shudder.

He turns his chair away from the window, back to his desk. It is too soon. He has nothing to say. Know that there is truth? A half-sentence? He at least needs time to think about it. Then perhaps he can make some sense out of it. Of course he will make public confession finally. He will witness. He has to. "Whoever shall confess me before men, him shall the Son of Man also confess before the angels of God." There is no question. " . . . He that denieth me before men . . ." It is his mission—to speak. A man could not remain a minister with such a secret.

On Saturday, he has a wedding. He has already put on his robe. His black shoes gleam. He sits at his desk, ready early, signing letters left here in his box by the secretary. Routine business. His sermon for Sunday is written, typed in capital letters. It makes no direct reference to hearing the voice of God.

He does like marrying couples, thinks of it, in fact, as an important part of his ministry. When a couple gets together within the church, it always seems to him a sort of personal victory. As the

boy said two weeks ago at the junior high retreat, "Human relations is where it's at."

The pair this afternoon is interesting to him in a more particular
way. He has been counseling them since Louise, the bride-to-be,
found out she was pregnant. She is thirty-eight, roughly his own
age. She and Alphonse, a Colombian, have lived together for
about three years. They have planned for today a fairly traditional,
almost formal ceremony. She is not yet showing. He remembers
her when she was alone. He could see her on Sunday mornings
canvassing the congregation with her eyes, picking out the occasional male visitor holding his hymnbook alone. Watching her in
those years, he wondered what his own life would be like, without
Julie. Whether he would show that same hunger so plainly on his
face. He is glad for Louise, pregnant as she is. He caps his pen and
stands. It's time to go in.

The feel is different now in the sanctuary, more relaxed than the
eleven o'clock. Maybe it's only the afternoon light, filtered as it is
by stained glass. He stands at the chancel steps, the ceremony begins. Alphonse comes to stand beside him. They face the aisle
where Louise is to enter on the arm of her sister's husband. Swain
tests the sound of their names, rehearses them in silence—Louise
Elizabeth Berryman, Alphonse Martinez Vasconcellos. The twang
and the beat of the Spanish—he has resolved to get it right, not
to anglicize. He runs through the name again—and a scene un-
winds like a scroll inside him. Gerona.

Louise, coming down the aisle now, slowly, slowly, moves in her
long pale dress behind the clear shapes of his sudden unsought
memory. He is twenty years old, standing in a stone-walled room
in Spain. The straps of his backpack pull at his shoulders. It is
quiet here, blocks away from the narrow river and the arched
bridges. In this room—he read it in his guidebook—there was a
revelation. He stands, with his two friends, in a medieval landmark
of the kabbalah. It is the moment, unplanned, when all three become quiet, when he can only hear the muted traffic from the
street. He is looking for something in this room. He lays his hand
on the grainy stone of the wall. Standing now in the sanctuary, he
feels the damp grit of rock against the flat of his palm. He can't
escape it, he can't shake it off. He wears it—this slight tingling

pressure—like a glove. A wet glove that clings to his skin. Louise is now at the front before him.

The couple turns to him. They wait. "Dearly beloved," he hears himself say. Faces stretch in a blur to the back of the church. He hears his voice—it must be his—float out to those faces, saying, "We are gathered here today. . . ."

He has told Julie everything, about hearing the voice. Not just the words, but how it felt. He has told her about the intrusion of the scene from Spain at the wedding this afternoon. "That was the last thing I needed," he says. "For that to happen while I'm actually standing at the front." They are sitting at the kitchen table. It's late.

She shrugs. The look on her face is the one he tries to cultivate in counseling. She is not shocked. Yet she does not diminish what happened to him. The look is one of sympathy and respect at once. She does it, he knows, without thinking.

She nods toward the typewriter, his old one, standing in its case near the bookshelves. They both use it for letters, neither one of them has a legible handwriting. "You've always set the margins so narrow," she says. "On yourself, on what's real. You don't give yourself much room."

She waits. He thinks about it.

"True," he says, nodding, looking away from her. "And you give yourself that kind of—'room' you're talking about." He looks at her, her chin propped on one hand, her face pushed slightly out of shape. "But do you actually believe in it," he says, "in what you see and hear, in the things you imagine? You don't. Of course you don't."

She puts her hand down, on the table, away from her face. She takes a breath and holds it a second before she speaks. The look she has had, of authority, is gone. "In a way," she says. She searches his face. "I don't think too much about it. But—yes, in a way, I do."

There is no joy in it. That's what bothers him. He is lying on the living room floor, still thinking about it, though he hasn't mentioned any of it, even to Julie, for almost a week. Maybe silence will make the whole thing go away. Julie is in the armchair reading, her feet in old white tennis shoes, her ankles crossed near his head. He watches her feet move, very slightly, in a rhythm, as if she were listening to music instead of reading. Maybe she hears music and never mentions it. She likes music. Maybe she's hearing Smetana's *Moldau,* close enough to the orchestra to hear between the movements the creakings of musicians' chairs. She would do this and think nothing of it. She has been patient with his days of silent turmoil.

As a kid, he wanted something like this to happen. Some sign. He did imagine though that it would bring with it pleasure—great happiness, in fact. He had a daydream of how it would be, set in the halls and classrooms of his elementary school, where he first imagined it. A column of warm pink light would pour over him, overpowering him with a sensation so intensely sweet it was unimaginable. He tried and tried to feel how it would feel. The warmth would wrap around his heart inside his chest, like two hands cradling him there. He would be full of happiness, completely at peace. The notion stayed with him past childhood, though, certainly in his earlier years, he didn't talk about it.

But he did what he could to have that experience. Divine revelation. He wanted it. He lay on the floor of his bedroom at home, later his dorm room at Brown, and waited. He stared at rippling creeks and wind-blown leaves and the deep chalky green of blackboards until his mind was lulled into receptive quiet. The quietness always passed, though, without interruption, at least by anything divine.

The search must have ended finally. Only now does he realize it, lying here with the front door standing open and moths batting against the screen. He doesn't recall any such preoccupation during divinity school, though there was that one thing that happened in his last year. It hardly qualified him as a mystic, though it was reassuring at the time.

He was sitting out on the balcony of his apartment, a second-floor place he shared with two other students. He and Julie, not married then, were in one of their off times. He was feeling bad. The concordance, the notepad had slid off his lap. His legs were sprawled, completely motionless, in front of him, hanging off the end of the butt-sagged recliner. He had lost Julie; he was bone-tired of school, he wouldn't have cared if he died.

He was staring at the scrubby woods behind the apartment complex, behind the parking lot and a weedy patch of mud and three dumpsters. Nothing mattered. Nothing at all. Then while he watched, everything—without motion or shift of light—everything he saw changed. He stared at the painted stripes on the asphalt, at water standing on the yellowish mud. It was all alive. Alive and sharing one life. The parking lot, the bare ground had become the varied skin of one living being. In the stillness, he waited for the huge creature to move, to take a breath. Nothing stirred. Yet he felt the benevolence of the animal, its power, rising off the surface before him like waves of heat.

What he felt then was a lightness, a sort of happiness. This was so important. It was at least a hint of what he had once imagined.

That afternoon he was buoyed. He finished the work he had sat with the whole afternoon. He fried himself a hamburger and ate it and was still hungry. He watched a few minutes of the news. He did not die or think further of dying that day, other than for the purposes of sermons, counseling, and facing the inevitable facts.

Facts. He is lying on the floor of his living room. Julie is reading in the chair. God has spoken to him, in English, clearly, in an unmistakable voice. He is not glad.

"What would you do, Julie?" he says. He is looking at the ceiling, he does not turn his head. "Would you stand up in that pulpit and tell them, 'I have heard the voice of God'? Would you do it?" He rolls over on his side and looks at her. Her foot has stopped moving. She has put her book down.

"I've been thinking about that," she says.

"What did you decide?"

"Probably," she says. "I think I would." She is not smiling. She looks at him steadily. Her eyes are tired.

"Oh?" he says. There is an edge in his voice. "What else would you say? How would you explain it? Explain to me, if you understand so well." He pauses, waits.

"Say as much as you know," she says.

"What is that? One piece of a sentence: know that there is truth. It isn't enough. I have nothing to say."

"It's your job, isn't it?" she says. "To tell them. Isn't it?" He sees the fear flickering across her face now. She needs to say it, but she's scared. It's the way he would be, standing before his incredulous congregation. Fearing the cost. What could it cost her to say this?

"You're afraid to tell me," he says. His voice is weary, dull.

She nods.

"Why?"

She swallows, looks away from him. "Because I'm saying you need to do something that may turn out bad. It would be the most incredible irony—but it could happen. They might decide you're losing your marbles. They might call it that, when really they don't want a minister who says this kind of stuff—about hearing God. It's not that kind of church. You know?"

He ignores the question. "We could have to move," he says. "We could wind up somewhere we would hate. Is that what you're worried about?"

"Some," she says. "But mostly that you would blame me, if it happened—that you would always feel like I pushed you into it."

"And then the marriage would fall apart," he says.

"Yeah," she says. Her voice shakes. Her mouth has the soft forgotten look it gets when all of her is concentrated elsewhere. In this case, on fear. He is not in the mood to reassure her.

"And what if I don't do it?" he says. "What if I never say a word and you spend the rest of your life thinking I'm a shit—a minister who denies God? What happens to us then?"

She shakes her head. She is close to tears. "I don't think that will happen," she says. It comes out in an uneven whisper.

Swain stands, straightens his pants legs. He looks at her once without sympathy, but her face is averted, she doesn't see. He leaves the room, goes into the kitchen. He gets out a small tub of Haagen-Dazs and a spoon, stands near the fridge, eating from the container. There is no sound from her in the other room. Pink light—what a joke. "Suppose ye that I am come to give peace on earth? I tell you, Nay; but rather division." The voice didn't warn him, didn't remind him. He shakes his head. He digs and scrapes at the ice cream.

He is turning his car into the church parking lot when it happens again. He hears God. His window is open. The car is lurched upward onto the incline of the pavement. The radio is on, but low.

From the hedge, a few feet from his elbow on the window frame, a sound emerges. It clearly comes from there: a burst, a jumble of phrases, scripture, distortions of scripture: "He that heareth and doeth not . . . for there is nothing hid . . . the word is sown on stony ground . . . why reason ye . . . seeketh his own glory . . . he that hath ears . . . he that hath. . . ." A nightmare. A nightmare after a night of too much reading. A spilling of accusation, reproach. Swain is staring straight ahead. A hot weight presses into him, into the soft vee beneath the joining of his ribs. It hurts, it pins him to the seat. It passes like cramp, leaving only a shadow, a distrust of those muscles.

Another car is waiting behind him, easing toward his fender. He pulls into the parking lot, into a space. He does it automatically. His face feels as hot as the sun-baked plastic car seat. He looks at the hedge, running between the sidewalk and the street. Tear it out—that's what he wants to do. Pull it up, plant by plant, with his hands. He is a pastor. Not a prophet. Not a radio evangelist. He does not believe in gods that quote the King James version out of bushes and trees.

He gets out of the car, goes into the church, into his office. He kicks the door shut behind him. He tosses a new yellow legal pad onto the bare center of his desk. There has to be something in this room to smash. He looks around: at the small panes of the window; at the veneer on the side of his desk; at the cluster of family pictures, framed; at the bud vase Julie gave him, that now holds two wilting daisies and a home-grown rose. Something to break. He grabs the vase by the neck and slings it, overarm, dingy water spilling, into a pillow of the sofa. A soft thump, and the stain of water spreads on the dark upholstery. He looks away from it, looks at the yellow pad on his desk. His career. That's what he'll smash. That ought to be enough. He walks around behind the desk, sits, red-faced, breathing audibly through parted lips. He stares at the lined paper with the pen in his hand. Say as much as you know. He begins to write. Beyond writing it down, he tells himself, he has made no decision.

On the following Sunday, he walks forward into the pulpit. He has received the offering. He has performed the preliminary duties with a detached methodical calm. Now he stands with his hands on the wooden rail, his fingers finding their familiar places along the tiered wood. "Friends," he says. He looks at no one in particular. "I have struggled with what I have to say to you today." They are waiting, with no more than their routine interest. "I have come to say to you that I have heard the voice of God." He says it to the rosette of stained glass at the back of the sanctuary. He cannot look at Julie in the third row. He cannot look at the McDougalls or Sam Bagdikian or Mary Elgar, as he says it. In the ensuing silence, his eyes sweep forward again, from the window back across three hundred faces. They are blank, waiting still, mildly interested. No one is alarmed. They have not understood.

He begins again. As much as he knows. "I think you know that I believe in an immanent God. I think you know that I believe in the presence and power of God in all our lives. I have come to tell you today that something has happened to me in recent days which I do not understand.

"A voice has spoken to me. I know that it is God. A voice has spoken to me that was a chorus of voices. I know that they are God." He pauses. "My wife Julie and I were cooking dinner on the grill on our back patio. . . ." The faces grow taut with attention. Sudden stillness falls over the church to the back pews of the balcony. There is no flutter of church bulletins. There are no averted faces. It is not a metaphor, not a parable he is telling. His wife Julie, the back patio—they are listening. He proceeds, with a trembling deep in his gut. He begins with the lady slipper and voice that came over the hill.

He tells them about the word "son" and the windbreaker and his own tears. "I asked myself whether I should bring this to you on a Sunday morning," he says. He looks from face to face in the rows in front of him. What are they thinking? It's impossible to tell. The shaking inside him has moved outward, to his hands. He feels them damp against the wood of the pulpit rail. He does not trust his voice.

"I asked myself how you, the members of this congregation, would react. Would you think that I've—" he tries to say this lightly, with a wry laugh—"that maybe I've been under too much stress lately." The laugh is not convincing. He himself hears its false ring. "But I will tell you," he says, "that that is not what has happened. I have not taken leave of my senses."

He looks at Julie. He can see her wrists, before the back of the pew breaks his vision. He knows her hands are knotted together, moving one against the other. He pulls his eyes away.

"I asked myself whether you would want a pastor who hears voices. Or even whether some of you might come to expect wisdom from me, because of what has happened, that I do not have." He pauses. "I don't know what to expect," he says, "from you or—" he hesitates—"from God. But I will tell you that my heart is now open. I will listen." He steps back, hearing as he does so the first note of the organ; reliable Miss Bateman is playing. The congregation stands, hymnbooks in hands. The service ends without incident. Swain stands as usual at the front steps afterwards to shake hands and greet people. Three of all those who file past tell him that the Lord works in wondrous ways, or something to that effect. Miss Frances Eastwood squeezes his elbow and tells him to trust. Ed Fitzgerald lays one hand on his shoulder, close to his collar, and says, "I like what you did here today." The rest make no mention of what has occurred. The line moves quickly past him, handshakes, heartiness, veiled eyes.

It is not over, of course. Julie keeps her hand on his knee as he drives home, though they say little. During the afternoon, he receives several phone calls at home, of an encouraging and congratulatory nature. Coming back into the kitchen, where Julie is cleaning out drawers to keep busy, he says, "It's the ones who don't call, who are calling each other. . . ."

What does occur happens gradually. Swain is given no answer, no sense of having-got-it-over on that Sunday afternoon. First, as he surmises, conversations buzz back and forth, on the telephone, at get-togethers, in chance meetings on the street. People inside and outside the church talk about what happened, about Swain Hammond's sermon.

The night the church operations committee meets, Swain and Julie stay home and play Scrabble. Swain can't concentrate, but Julie protests every time he wants to quit. The call comes at 11:15. It's Joe Morris. "Between you and me," Joe reminds him, "this is an unofficial. . . ."

The upshot of it is that the committee voted five-to-four to privately recommend that Swain get professional help. The chairman, Bill Bartholomew, who made the motion, comes to Swain's office to tell him. "Of course," he says, "this is something which is not easy to say. But we all go through times when we need. . . ."

"Thank you for your prayers and concern," Swain says. He is accustomed to assuming a look of gratitude when it is called for. It only fails him in the last minutes of the conversation.

"Are you so sure I'm crazy, Bill?" he says. The two of them are standing now in the office doorway, there is no one in the hall. "Doesn't it seem contradictory?" Swain says. Bill is watching him carefully. "It's okay to believe in God, but only if God is distant. A presence in history. Is that the idea?"

"I'm sure I don't want to debate this with you," Bill says. "It's only the will of the committee—"

"I understand your position," Swain says. He does not seek counseling.

When news of the committee's action leaks, a petition circulates and the members take sides. This time the vote is with Swain. The letter, signed by the majority of the members, affirms that Dr. Swain Hammond is in his right mind and will continue to be welcome as minister. These are not the exact words, but this is the meaning.

Swain mentions this decision from the pulpit, but only as a brief comment among the day's other announcements. "Thank you for your love and support," he says. Unexpectedly, as he says it, he feels a tightness in this throat. He looks from face to face. He won't be leaving. If he thinks about it, he'll lose his composure. He summons a bit of the anger that has sustained him through the last few weeks. It works, he manages to keep the wave of love at bay.

"Besides," he tells Julie later that day, "I don't completely trust it." They are taking a late afternoon walk through the neighborhood around their house. "I feel like all this could change, if the balance shifted just a little. I'm reasonably secure for the moment," he says. "I suppose that will have to do."

She doesn't say anything. She has said her part several times already: that she is proud of him, that she is proud of what he did.

"I'm also disappointed," he says. They stop for a moment to avoid the arc of spray from a sprinkler cutting across the sidewalk. "I thought maybe a few people would be curious about what actually happened. Would want to hear more." He shakes his head. "They don't." It makes him mad to think about it. They've decided to put up with him—that's what they've made of all this. They're being broad-minded and tolerant, that's all.

Swain does hear the voice of God again. This time—last Tuesday morning—it is as a note of music, as he is just waking up. Julie lies beside him asleep. It is early, still twenty minutes before the alarm is set to go off. He knows before it happens that it's coming. He does not move. He waits, while the note emerges from a sound too deep to be heard. Then it is audible, filling the room, humming against his bare stomach, like the live warm touch of a hand. In the same moment, it begins to diminish, a dwindling vibration on piano strings.

Swain lies still. He does not cry this time, or soak the sheets with his sweat. He does not wake Julie, whose breath he can feel on the curve of his shoulder. He looks at the morning light on the far wall, shifting with the shadows of tree branches. He watches the triangles and splinters of light, forming and re-forming, and feels the slow rise and fall of his own chest. Everything is quiet: the room, the yard beneath the window, the street out front. He can see it all in his mind now, one surface, connected, breathing with his same slow breath. What he feels then, flooding the whole space of his being, is joy, undeniably joy, though it has not come as he would have expected. It is not what he looked for at all.

Lewis Nordan

SUGAR, THE EUNUCHS, AND BIG G.B.

(from *The Southern Review*)

One time when I was eleven—this was fifteen years ago, soon after my daddy first told me that wild bands of eunuchs run amuck in the Mississippi Delta—I spent the night with a friend named G.B. Junior. His daddy's name was Big G.B. and his mama was Sweet Runa, rhymed with tuna. Big G.B. had a house full of guns, all kinds, pistols and rifles and muzzle-loaders and shotguns, even a blunderbuss with a bell-shaped barrel, and an illegal thing or two, grenade launchers and automatic rifles. He loved to show them to G.B. Junior's friends.

In fact, the guns were about the only reason G.B. Junior had any friends. He was fat and had a round, snoutish nose with prominent nostrils. He would wrestle you to the ground and hold you with his fat and put his face into your neck or bare belly. He would make a grunting, rooting sound with his mouth and nose against your skin. He called this "giving pig." G.B. Junior was a mess.

Big G.B. would show us boys his guns and treat us grown-up. He'd say, "I wouldn't show you men these here firearms if I didn't know I could trust you." Sometimes he would tell us, "Always remember, it's the *un*-loaded gun that kills." He would look me and G.B. Junior in the eye and say, "Now do each and every one of you men get my meaning?" Sweet Runa, his wife, might holler

out from the kitchen, "Explain your meaning to them, Big G.B."
He'd give us a manly wink.

So it was a bunking party and I was in a big bed with G.B.
Junior. I don't know why I couldn't sleep. I felt lonely all the time,
that's one reason. I wanted to be home where I could hear my
mama and daddy in the kitchen. I could stand anything I could
hear—that's what I thought. Anyway, I couldn't sleep.

I lifted the comforter and sheet off me and slid my legs from
under the covers. It was January and cold in the room. I sat on the
edge of the bed and pulled on blue jeans and a T-shirt, no shoes.

I eased out of the room and down the hall toward the bathroom
to take a leak. When I was finished I stopped outside the bedroom
where Big G.B. and Sweet Runa were sleeping. There were no
lights on in the house, but the moonlight was bright and I could
see the two of them beneath the covers sweet as whales.

I went into the room and prowled a little. I poked through some
bureau drawers and didn't find much. I found a box of rubbers in
Big G.B.'s bedside table and took one to keep; it couldn't hurt.

There wasn't much else to do. I walked out of the bedroom and
down the hall.

I started to go back to bed, but on second thought walked down
to Big G.B.'s gun room and snapped on the light at the wall switch.

Guns were on every wall, most of them behind glass locked up.
The dark bright oiled woods of the stocks and butts made me love
Big G.B. and Sweet Runa. The room seemed orderly and under
control and full of love. There were deer heads and goat heads and
a bearskin on the walls. The face of Jesus was made out of Indian
arrowheads and spear points. There were boxes of dueling pistols
on a low table and a great gray papery hornets' nest hanging on a
hook from a ceiling beam.

I went to a chestlike table topped with rose-veined marble and
opened the drawer. I knew what was in it. There were two green
felt bags, heavy with their contents. I took out the first and loos-
ened the drawstring and put my hand inside and ran my fingers
through the bullets like a pirate through coins in a treasure chest.

I set it on the marble top. The second bag was heavier, the pistol
Big G.B. called his three-fifty-seven.

I took it out of its bag and held it in my right hand and measured
its weight. It was nickel plated and had a handcarved grip with a

nickel ring at the bottom. I pressed the release near the trigger guard, the way I had seen Big G.B. do a hundred times, and the cylinder swung out with a soft metallic sound.

It was loaded with six cartridges. Daddy said one time Tex Ritter performed live and in person right here in Arrow Catcher, Mississippi, on the stage of the Strand Theater. Tex Ritter would sign your program. Daddy said he was just a little boy at the time and he asked Tex Ritter if he had any advice for somebody who wanted to break into show business. (I wondered why Daddy would ask a question like that.)

I snapped shut the cylinder of the pistol with one hand, like a policeman, and it clicked into place. I used both thumbs to cock the hammer. I pointed the barrel at the bearskin on the wall and said, "Blammo," and then eased the hammer back down. (I don't know what Tex Ritter answered.)

I stuck the big revolver inside the front of my pants and walked out the gun room door. I walked down the hallway and into the kitchen and right out the kitchen door and let the screen door slap shut behind me. It was freezing cold. Before I could get down the splintery frosty steps and out of the stiff grass of the backyard, my feet were numb.

Nobody was on the streets. I felt invisibility grow in my freezing bones.

I walked past the gin and past Runt Ramsey's house. I walked past the light plant and past the firehouse where Hydro Chisolm, the marshall's grown son, shot stray dogs and blew the fire whistle, fire or no fire, and sometimes chased cars. I walked beneath the legs of the water tower and past a blind man's house, Mr. O'Kelly, who was sitting on his porch in the middle of the freezing night carving soap. A ventriloquist's dummy was sleeping in his lap. I crossed the railroad tracks at Scott Butane and from there I could see my house. The lights were on, as I knew they would be, no matter how late.

I walked into the side yard, outside the kitchen window, and stood beside a line of fig trees. I was out of sight of the midgets, in case they were awake. They lived in a trailer on the other side of the house and worked construction on the pipeline. Mavis Mitchum, a lady who sucked her skirt, lived on this side. My bare feet were numb, and I could scarcely feel the frozen dirt beneath them.

I could see Mama and Daddy in the kitchen. Mama was wearing a quilted robe and looked like a witch, the way she looked when Daddy was drinking. Daddy wore white painters' overalls and a billed cap all day and then got dressed up to drink. He was wearing his salt-and-pepper suit and a fresh starched shirt and his favorite tie, with a horse head painted on it, which he got long years ago when he was a boy and visited the summer circus in Sarasota, Florida, and fell in love with a woman who swallowed things, swords and fire.

Daddy had propped a square mirror in the kitchen window. On the counter were four half-pints of Early Times and four shot-glasses. (He called this "shooting fours.") Mama was saying something to him, I knew what. She was saying to him that he was an artist, that he was special and perfect and magic, that his pain was special. She was telling him she wanted to carry his pain for him. I had heard it a hundred times; she meant every word. In front of the bare fig trees I grieved and celebrated my invisibility.

Daddy was looking into the mirror. Sometimes he would cut his eyes to it, quick, and glimpse himself there by surprise. Then he would stare at himself full face and turn his head, real slow, to catch another angle. He was tragic and handsome. He was dreaming of the woman who swallowed things. Mama was telling him that if his heart had to break she wanted it to break inside her own chest.

Daddy filled one shotglass from one bottle and then the next from the next bottle, and on to the end, until four drinks had been poured from four bottles into four glasses. He filled a larger glass with Coca-Cola from a quart and put it on the sink too.

He lifted the first shot in his hand and checked the mirror. Mama looked a hundred years old in her love for him. He drained the whiskey from the glass and set it back on the counter. He chased the drink with Coca-Cola. He looked into the mirror again. He was handsome and manly and tragic and fine. He was the Marlboro Man of alcoholism. He drank each of the four shots of whiskey in the same way.

I took Big G.B.'s three-fifty-seven out of my pants and pulled back the hammer with my aching cold thumbs and held the pistol in both hands.

The sound of the gun might as well have been Niagara Falls, it was so permanent and loud and useless.

A column of fire a foot long jumped out of the pistol's muzzle. The window I had shot through disappeared in one piece, glass and wood. Even the screen dropped straight down in front of me. When I fired the second shot I looked at my mama and believed that she was all women in the world, beauty and grief, and at the same time nobody at all, as shadowless and invisible as myself beside the white bare limbs of the fig trees. Then the lights were out and I was alone in my invisibility.

I walked out of the yard with the pistol still in my hand, swinging at my side, and went back to Big G.B.'s the same way I had come. The blind man was still carving soap, the dummy was awake now, had opened his eyes. Joseph of Arimathea was the dummy's name.

Neither of the shots had hit my daddy. I had missed him both times. I heard the siren of Big'un Chisolm's car just as I stepped inside Big G.B.'s back door and felt my feet start to thaw out. I put up the pistol and the cartridges and I slipped back into bed beside G.B. Junior. My body and my heart were saying, crying, *I want I want I want I want.*

Joseph of Arimathea told the marshall I was the one fired the shots. The soap-carving blind man agreed with him. I heard this from the men talking at the Arrow Cafe. They were big talkers and big laughers and they acted like it was a joke and told me what a fine boy I was and don't worry about a thing, they all knew better than to believe a word those two dummies said, but it was nothing funny about it to me. I'll tell you why. Mavis Mitchum—the neighbor who sucked her skirt—she told on me too. She said she was up late watching for eunuchs and saw me. (She agreed with Daddy about the eunuchs. She said they sing and dance at Episcopal baptizings. Mavis Mitchum was a mess her own self.) Hydro saw me too, said he did. Hydro had a big head and wanted to be believed. He swore to his daddy he would never chase another car if somebody would please believe him. It was Sugar Mecklin who did the shooting, he said, he saw me.

Big'un didn't believe any of them, the marshall, least of all his own poor son Hydro. Big'un apologized to Daddy, and even to me. He made Hydro apologize. Big'un said it was bad enough to live in a town full of freaks—oh, he was hard on Hydro—let alone be accused by them. Daddy said, "It don't matter, Big'un." Big'un said, "I just wouldn't want you to think a whole townful of freaks has turned on your boy." Daddy said, "I know that, Big'un, it ain't everybody who's against us." Big'un was relieved. He said, "You so right, Gilbert. The midgets, for example, ain't said a word."

I was sick with grief. I cried all the next day and Mama held me and told me Daddy was fine, just fine, you hush, Sugar, he's not hurt one bit. It didn't help. I still couldn't stop. I lay on my bed in my room, but I couldn't lie still. I walked out in the yard and threw corn to the chickens. Nothing helped.

I wanted to confess to Daddy. I walked through our house and looked at all the things that told me he was alive. I looked at the closet full of empty whiskey bottles, I stirred them with my hand and made them rattle and clank. I read their labels and fondled their shapes. I held them up to the light, one and then another, and looked at the small drops of amber fluid that collected in the corners when I tilted a bottle to one side. I unscrewed the caps and tasted the fluid on my tongue and knew that this was the only magic that kept him alive and in love with the sorry likes of me.

People were in the kitchen. A party started that day around the bullet holes and lasted a month. People loved Daddy for being shot at. The Communists did it, somebody said, the Klan did it, jealous husbands and heartbroken women and politicians and "the money men" did it—the law, the church, the blacks, the Indians, even the Iranians—no suggestion was too outlandish—and Daddy and Mama didn't deny one possibility. There were a million good reasons a man as fine as my daddy might be shot at.

I went in Daddy's bedroom and opened the drawers of his chest. I looked in his shirt drawer and picked up a shirt and held it to my face and breathed in the smell, the fragrance of Daddy's flesh that could never be washed out. It was whiskey and paint and Aqua Velva and leather and shoe polish and wool and peppermint. I closed that drawer and opened others. In the deepest drawer I reached in and searched with my hand, behind the underwear and the rolled socks—I knew what I was looking for—until I found

the candy, the peppermint puffs that he hid there, the light, un-
believable airy candy that melted on the tongue, as if it had never
been there, and left only the taste, the sweet aroma that was always
with Daddy. I don't know why he hoarded peppermint.

I looked between his mattress and box springs and found the
cracked leather folder with the brass zipper. I opened it and took
out the old Tex Ritter program with the faded-ink autograph.
There was a full-face picture of Tex on the front, a black-and-white
drawing of him wearing his big hat and smiling his big smile. "For
Gilbert Mecklin, your friend, Tex Ritter," the autograph said.
There was also a ticket in the folder, faded, torn across the center,
with the words Ringling Brothers Circus on the stub. And there
was a picture of Elvis Presley, an 8 × 10 glossy with Elvis's signature
in the corner. There was a triangular tip of steel—it might have
been a sword point. I believed that it was; I believed it had belonged to the woman who swallowed things. I put the sword point
in my pocket and stuck everything else back in the folder.

I went to Daddy's closet and knew where to look for the suit.
Not even Mama knew about the suit. I had found it by accident a
year before.

Deep in the closet, back behind his shotgun, behind the rubber
hipwaders and the canvas jackets, behind the croquet set with its
wire wickets and slender-handled mallets and wooden balls with
bright stripes, which he had bought drunk and had never taken
out of the box or allowed Mama to set up, behind the box of
souvenirs from the junior high school he had dropped out of—a
script from a play called "The Beauty and the Beef," a boutonniere
he had worn to a dance—lay the suitbox I was looking for.

I lifted the box out of the closet—white sturdy cardboard—and
put it on the floor of Daddy's bedroom. The house was full of
people, more and more of them, looking at the bullet holes and
congratulating Daddy. People were laughing and happy, whiskey
bottles and ice and glasses were clinking. I lifted the top off the
large rectangular box and laid it aside. I knelt on the floor in front
of the box and lifted out the airy tissue paper, a piece at a time,
away from the cloth of the suit.

The suit was cheap—thin and shiny, almost brittle, and there
was no lining. There were a million loose threads in the seams. It
was a suit jacket studded with rhinestones. The pants had a double

row of rhinestones down either leg. I lifted the jacket from the box and held it in my fingers to test its incredible light weight.

I learned to cry with no sound. I could hear Daddy in the kitchen, with Mama and their friends. I could tell by the way he talked and laughed that he was dressed in his Sarasota tie with the painted horse's head. I knew that Mama was glowing with pride and joy and grief.

I put on the jacket and stood looking at myself in the door-length mirror on the closet. I thought of the woman who swallowed things. I thought of trapeze dancers and jugglers and freak shows. I thought of Tex Ritter and of lariats and spurs and chaps. I thought of a man my daddy had known when he was a boy, who carried with him a saddlebag full of knives and another saddlebag full of harmonicas. He told me, "Sugar, I would die to play 'Orange Blossom Special' on one of those harmonicas on stage." He said his favorite musicians were a group called the Harmonicats, which featured a dwarf with a harmonica three feet long. He said, "I would live forever if I could throw those knives." He said, "If I could throw those knives, I would name them, each one. I would name one Boo Kay Jack, I would name one Django. I would throw them and I would watch the bright brave frightened face of a beautiful woman as it sailed end over end towards her— one knife and then the next and the next—until every knife was quivering in the board next to her sweet bare body and her perfect figure was outlined in steel." I was wearing the rhinestone-studded coat of my daddy, which was too big for me, and I was looking at myself in the mirror. The coattail hung down to my thighs, the sleeves covered my hands. Rhinestones ran the length of the sleeves, they outlined the lapels. I turned my back to the mirror and looked over my shoulder. I read the words spelled out in rhinestones on my back: *Rock 'n' Roll Music*. I thought—dreamed, somehow, although I was awake—that knives were being thrown at me, that harmonica music was being played. I thought I was riding horseback, behind somebody else, a man, that I was holding onto him, my arms around his waist, and that the horseman was insane and smelled of peppermint and whiskey and that he dug the horse's bloodless sides with silver spurs and was Death made flesh and was somehow also my Daddy and Mama and Tex Ritter and everybody else in Arrow Catcher, Mississippi, and that there was a voice in the wind and in the horse's hooves and it told me that we lived, all of us, in a terrible circus geography where freaks grow like magic from the buckshot and gumbo, where eunuchs roam the Delta flatscape looking for Episcopalians. I didn't know why I had shot at Daddy. I only knew I wanted to confess to him, to have him know that I knew he was magic and that I loved him, that I wanted to drink whiskey and be like him, to find a woman who swallowed swords and fire, to marry a woman like my mama, who could grow ugly with love. I wanted to confess my betrayal of Daddy to the midgets, so the last freaks in town might know and not think well of me. Nobody caught me that day, nobody came into the bedroom from the kitchen. I took off the jacket and replaced the tissue paper and folded the suit and hid it away again in the box, far back in the closet.

I was insane until April, when the eunuchs came to Arrow Catcher looking for St. George. I poached pigeons in the belfry of the Baptist Church—it was Daddy's favorite kind of hunting—and with a tennis shoe swatted down the warm fat feathery ovals, with amazed eyes and all their bustle and clutter and complaint, purple and gray and brown and white and with glittery heads. I peeled off their feathers and took out their insides and spread them in front of me. I wanted to live in my Daddy's skin, behind his rib cage, to share his heart and lungs and liver and spleen. I wanted to confess to Daddy, but I could not. I cooked the pigeons over fires in the woods near Roebuck Lake, and ate them, mostly raw. I chanted *I want I want I want I want*. I squatted on the lake bank, or in the pigeon-fragrant dark of the church loft, and imagined wild bands of roving eunuchs galloping the Mississippi roads and flatwoods, clattering across bridges and through pastures, skirting the edges of small towns. I thought of farmers with rifles on the lookout for them like wild dogs among the livestock. I looked for my own face among the eunuchs.

I ran a low fever every day for months, and frightened my mama with my crying, which I could not stop. She was afraid for me, and Daddy drank, and I spent the night almost every night with friends, and finally with only one friend, G. B. Junior—and not really with G.B. Junior, with his daddy. I spent as many nights as I could with Big G.B. It may have been Mama's idea, to get me away from the drinking and the loud bullet-hole parties—I don't know whose idea it was. Big G.B. invited me to go places with him, especially out to his farm, which he called Scratch-Ankle. He let me drive his pickup through the cattlegaps, we shot a .22 pistol at dead tree stumps. I was not afraid of the pistol. I shot accurately and he congratulated me on my aim. G.B. Junior was never invited to go with us.

Sometimes Sweet Runa would make Big G.B. take him with us, but it never worked out. G.B. Junior said he hated the stupid farm, he said the pistol shots hurt his ears, he said the pickup made him carsick. Big G.B. said, "Well, Runa, if he don't *want* to go . . ." So it was always the two of us. Sometimes we would check the horses, sometimes Jabbo Deeber, the black man who ran the farm, would take us to a honey tree and we would scoop out honey in the comb and suck it off our fingers and dodge the angry bees. Sometimes the three of us—Jabbo and Big G.B. and me—would pinch Red Man out of a foil pouch and I would end each day dizzy with joy.

Big G.B. knew who shot at my daddy. He didn't tell Sweet Runa, he didn't even tell me—I just knew he knew. He started keeping me, like I was his child. I wished I was his child.

On the first day of turkey season, in April, I was spending Saturday night with Big G.B. to go hunting early the next morning. Even Mama believed I was getting better in Big G.B.'s care. I had stopped crying and running fever and poaching pigeons. I had put back some of the weight I had lost after the shooting. Daddy was still the town hero for getting shot at. People bought him drinks, gave him tickets to football games, asked his advice on things he knew nothing about. He dressed up more and went to work less. He drank whiskey in front of the mirror and spoke of taking a trip to see the summer circus, which he said had been moved to Venice, Florida. I held onto the sword point, I ate from his stash of peppermint, I wore his Rock 'n' Roll suit.

And then, on that Sunday morning, the first day of the season, when the rain was lashing the windows and the abelia hedges and I was awake at four o'clock and sitting at Big G.B.'s kitchen table eating Rice Krispies and milk while Sweet Runa and G.B. Junior slept, I brought out Daddy's sword point and laid it on the table. I laid out a few peppermint puffs. I told him about the Tex Ritter program and the Rock 'n' Roll suit. I told him about Django and Boo Kay Jack and the saddlebag full of knives and the one full of harmonicas. I told him about the woman who swallowed things and about shooting fours and Mama's housecoat and the pigeons. I told him Daddy was magic.

Big G.B. said, "Your daddy ain't magic."

I said, "He ain't?"

He said, "Naw, there ain't any magic."

I said, "What about the blind man's dummy? Is Joseph of Arimathea magic?"

He said, "Get your shotgun, Sugar."

I went to the corner near the stove and took my shotgun by the barrel. I got my shell bag and looked at Big G.B. to see what he was thinking. His face didn't tell me. I stood by the kitchen door holding the shotgun and shells. I said, "Is Joseph of Arimathea magic, Big G.B.?"

He said, "There ain't no magic. Magic is the same as sentimental. Scratch the surface of sentimental and you know what you find?—Nazis and the Ku Klux Klan. Magic is German in nature and evil and not real. Scratch magic, Sugar, and you're looking for death."

I said, "You already know, don't you?"

He said, "No man is going to get mad at his boy for taking a shot at him, Sugar."

This was the first time the shooting had been spoken between us. He said, "Shooting to kill is what a boy is supposed to do to his daddy, Sugar-man."

We went out the kitchen door together into the morning darkness, both of us carrying unloaded shotguns and the shell bag clicking between us. The rain was whipping through the porch screens and the floor was slick. We ducked out the screened door and down the steps and into the pickup. We slammed the doors and wiped rainwater off our faces. Sweet Runa and G.B. Junior were awake, trying to get G.B. Junior dressed to go with us.

Big G.B. didn't want to take him. He started up the engine. He said, "Sweet Runa is not a bad woman, Sugar. I want you to know that." Sweet Runa was shouting something to us from the back door, but we couldn't hear. Big G.B. shifted into first gear and we pulled out of the yard. I didn't say anything. He said, "And your

daddy is not a bad man. He truly ain't." He was going through
the gears of the truck now and his feet in the big boots covered
his whole side of the cab floor. I looked back through the rear
window and saw Sweet Runa and G.B. Junior standing in the yard
in the rain. I said, "Big G.B., sometimes I hate myself so much."
He slowed the truck and pulled to a stop. He started turning
around to go back to the house. He said, "I just try to keep an
open mind about Joseph of Arimathea."

So now G.B. Junior was in the front seat of the pickup too,
surly and sleepy and unhappy and silent. Big G.B. and I were
wearing the two camouflage ponchos and G.B. Junior was wearing
a Day-Glo yellow slicker his mama had put on him. Big G.B. told
him he couldn't wear a yellow raincoat in the woods, he would
look like a fool. G.B. Junior said don't worry, he wouldn't wear it
to a fucking dog fight and said he hadn't brought his shotgun, he
wasn't going hunting. Big G.B. said don't use that word and what
did he mean he wasn't going hunting, what was he doing in the
truck if he wasn't going hunting. When we parked near the Arrow
Cafe, G.B. Junior opened the truck door and stepped out into the
rain and took off the Day-Glo raincoat and threw it into the bed
of the pickup. Big G.B. said what did he want to do that for. I
knew none of us would see the turkey woods that morning.
Hunters from all around Arrow Catcher were in the Arrow
Cafe. Everybody was in camouflage and hip waders and rain gear,
a dozen or more men. The lineoleum was slick with rain that had
blown in and had been tracked in, and Miss Josie, who ran the
cafe, had thrown a couple of blue towels on the floor to soak up
the water. Some of the men were at the counter and others were
at tables or in booths, eating sausages and eggs and biscuits. Miss
Josie was bringing extra gravy. A couple of men were having shots
of whiskey with their coffee. The rain was lashing the streets and
blowing like sheets on the line across the streetlights. G.B. Junior
was soaked through, because he had taken off the raincoat. It was
hard to think of a child as lonely and unhappy as G.B. Junior, or
one as happy as I was. There were guns and ammunition belts
everywhere, propped against the counter, leaned in corners,
draped across tables and bar stools. I thought of Tex Ritter on the
little stage of the Strand Theater in Arrow Catcher, the way he

looked on the program and the way Daddy had described him. I thought of my daddy as a boy in that audience, sitting on a hard chair down front and looking up at the big horse and the lariat and Tex Ritter's six-guns and boots and spurs and hat. I believed that my daddy and I were somehow the same person, that I had visited Florida and loved the woman who swallowed things. I believed that when I cried in my heart *I want I want I want I want* that I was speaking, crying, in my daddy's voice, saying what he meant to say when he dressed in secret in his Rock 'n' Roll suit and watched himself drink whiskey in the mirror.

We looked for a place for three people to sit in the Arrow Cafe. Big G.B. made Runt Ramsey change to another seat at the counter so there were two empty stools together near the rear. I sat on one of the stools and could see through the low window into the kitchen. A large black woman in an apron was flipping hotcakes and cracking eggs into a bowl. I loved the turkey hunters in the Arrow Cafe. I loved Miss Josie, who owned it. I loved Big G.B., who gave me love without pain. Big G.B. told G.B. Junior to sit on the other stool at the counter with me, but G.B. Junior wouldn't do it. He said he wanted to sit on the floor next to the jukebox. Big G.B. said, "Oh, got-dog, son," and went over and tried to talk him into sitting at the counter. He still wouldn't. He wouldn't even look at his daddy. He was fat as lard and shivering and drenched and angry and cold but he would not come up to the counter. I knew how much he hated me. I didn't care. I was glad he wouldn't sit at the counter. Some people in a booth told G.B. Junior come on over here, they had plenty of room if he wanted to sit with them. He wouldn't do that either. Big G.B. said, "Well, don't meddle with the jukebox." G.B. Junior said, "I ain't studying no fucking jukebox." Big G.B. pretended not to hear.

Big G.B. came to the counter and sat beside me—this was why I was glad for the empty seat. He put his hand on my left shoulder and squeezed it. Miss Josie poured me a cup of coffee, because I was with Big G.B., and then looked in the direction of G.B. Junior on the floor and decided against asking if he wanted a cup, it was too much trouble. I felt like a king. In the midst of these men and their camouflage and, in my nostrils, the smell of coffee cooking and breakfast and whiskey and the fragrance of wet rubber rain gear and canvas and in this room full of breached firearms and the click click of ammunition in the pockets of these men—in my own pockets—and the fine low sound of manly laughter and good southern whiskey voices, I felt for the first time free of my daddy, of his magic if there was magic. I felt it even now, when it was hardest to know which was Daddy and which was me, when I wasn't sure just who had sat in the Strand Theater and heard a whiskey-voiced cowboy sing, "Rye whiskey rye whiskey rye whiskey I cry if I don't get rye whiskey well I think I will die." Even when it was hardest to believe that it was my daddy and not myself who remembered Sarasota and longed for Django and Boo Kay Jack and loved the music of Spike Jones and the Harmoni-cats and the dwarf with the three-foot harmonica, and Daddy who dressed in secret (as I did now myself) in a rhinestone suit and ate peppermint puffs—I felt free of him, free to feel hatred if that came to me, and resentment and pure anger where I thought there should be acceptance and awe and love. I was free of Daddy's shooting fours, would never have to aim a pistol at anyone ever again, never have to know or care why I shot at him in the first place, never have to confess to him those evil seconds and know the pain it would inflict in his heart and in mine.

I was sitting beside Big G.B. and he was pouring milk into my coffee and a drop of whiskey from a flat bottle into his. I looked out the big window and saw the rain lashing at everything, at the steel awning in front of the Arrow Cafe, the sidewalks gleaming with reflected light, the pickups with gun racks and STP stickers and water standing in the beds, and the alley, its slick brick street where somebody had piled mattress boxes, and I saw the van drive up. I could see it out the window, blue and extra-long, with lots of seats in it. It was filled with grown-up men in suits—I could see them already—eight or nine of them lined up in rows in their seats. The lights of the van shone through the sheeting rain, yellow and wonderful and unexpected in the dark morning. I watched the van park and sit with its motor running and the lights still on. Nobody got out. Nobody was looking at it but me. I kept watching, felt strange and frightened. I leaned on my stool far to the side so that my shoulder touched Big G.B.'s sleeve and allowed my heart to fill up with love for this big man, and for all these men who were not my daddy.

G.B. Junior had gotten up from his place on the floor and had pulled the jukebox out from the wall. He was groping around in the oily dust behind it for the cord, he wanted to plug it in. Miss Josie saw him and walked from behind the counter to where he stood. I could tell she didn't want to scold him in front of everybody, especially not in front of his daddy, or in front of me. I could almost feel sorry for G.B. Junior. He was trying to stick the plug into the wall socket.

A spray of rainwater and cold April wind caused Miss Josie and everybody else to look at the front door, which had opened. G.B. Junior went ahead with what he was doing and plugged in the jukebox. He started going through his pockets for a quarter, but he didn't have one. I looked at the door too. I expected to see whoever had been out in the van, the men in suits, but it was not them.

It was Daddy who came in the door. He was a little out of breath, not from running. His face was streaming with rainwater. He was wearing a plastic raincoat and a billed cap, so wet it stuck to his head. The men in the cafe cheered when they saw him, Runt Ramsey and Red Raby and Grease Foley and Billy Corley and Jimmy Scallion, everybody. He was still the town hero for getting shot at.

He was looking around the room, looking for me. I made myself small so he might not see me. Men slapped him on the back, offered him coffee and whiskey, which he didn't notice just now. G.B. Junior stopped meddling with the jukebox and looked at Daddy, with love I thought. I wondered why G.B. Junior and I couldn't swap daddies.

Only Big G.B. didn't look up. He seemed to know it was Daddy and that Daddy knew something or had something or disproved something that might change everything. Miss Josie's smile lighted up the room when she saw Daddy. He didn't notice. He walked across the blue towels on the floor and stopped and looked around until he found me.

I could see through the cheap plastic raincoat, of course, to the paint-stained overalls and the flannel shirt. And yet I half expected to see that Daddy was wearing the Rock 'n' Roll suit. He looked handsome and certain and hopeful, the way I thought he might look in the rhinestones. I looked at his face and saw that he was not drunk yet, maybe still sick with a hangover, it was hard to tell. We faced each other and I felt emotions come into my heart that I didn't want. I saw myself with Daddy when I was six years old. I was sitting in a low tree in our yard, maybe six feet off the ground, and Daddy was painting the tree blue. He dipped carefully into the paint can with a brush and then spread the bright enamel evenly over the bark, trunk and branches. There was sweet magic in the combined fragrances of enamel paint and mimosa blossoms. The limb I sat on swayed and threatened to give way. I loved the danger and the blue tree. Daddy said, "I hope this don't kill it. The yard needs the color, though." I had believed in the Arrow Cafe that I had become another man's child, that because I had fired his .22 pistol into tree stumps and had driven his truck through the cattlegaps and fished his ponds and lain on his floor in his den in front of his television set and fallen asleep and been carried in his arms to a warm bed and had loved him that all my terrible past had not really happened, that I had never been born into the family of a drunkard, handsome and tragic and fine as any man who ever walked across a movie screen, and that I had never learned from mama that Daddy was magic and should be worshipped until she and I and everyone else who loved him grew ugly and pure and mad with love, and that the only control we could expect in our lives was exactly what we needed most, blue trees and pigeon suppers and lonely secrets in the backs of drawers and closets.

I turned on the bar stool and held Big G.B.'s arm with both my hands. I knew Daddy had come for me. I didn't want to go. I was afraid to love him again, and yet I already did love him, I had never stopped loving him, even when I hated him. I held on tight to Big G.B. I cut my eyes toward G.B. Junior and read his hatred of me. No one else in the Arrow Cafe cared about hatred, everyone else was in love with my daddy. They loved him—not, as I had thought, simply because he had been shot at, but because he truly was in some way pure, in some way perfect, as they knew they would never be—as I knew I would never be—in some way special, as Mama had known he was and had given up her life and beauty in wonder of, and that nothing he had ever done—his drunken violence and self-pity, his pettiness and bullying and meanness—was unforgivable, nothing too terrible to embrace. I had no words for any of this at age eleven, I hardly have them now, fifteen years later.

All the men wanted Daddy's attention. All asked about him, asked to do things for him. He did not ignore them, but he was not interested either. I was still clinging to Big G.B., and Big G.B. had laid his big hand over both of mine.

Daddy came squishing and squelching and squeaking across the lineoleum in his rubber boots. He stood beside me at the bar stool. He said, "Sugar, those men out in the van—do you know who they are?" He might have been giving me a gift, might have been afraid I was too young to know its value, too small to accept it. I shook my head to say no. He said, "It's the eunuchs. I called Sweet Runa and she told me y'all were down here. I wanted to let you know."

I let go of Big G.B.'s arm. I didn't know what to do with my hands. I put my face in them and put my head down on the counter, the way Daddy put his on the kitchen table sometimes after he had been shooting fours. I didn't know whether I would faint or cry or become invisible or explode, anything seemed more likely than that I would feel this chaos of strange love well up in my blood. I felt as if Daddy had shot me from ambush and that I was mortally wounded and that the gaping great bloody hole in my chest and heart was the dearest prick of pain and forgiveness and loss of hope that ever touched the purest part of man or child.

I said, "Daddy, I shot at you through the window. It was me."

He said, "You'll never guess who told me."

I said, "About me shooting at you?"

He said, "No, about the eunuchs."

I said, "Mavis Mitchum?"

He said, "Nope."

I said, "The midgets?"

He said, "No, of course not the midgets, that's silly."

I said, "I know who it was then. I know exactly who it was."

He was proud of me for guessing. He said, "He's a smart little bugger, ain't he?"

I said, "How does he do it, Daddy? Is it really Mr. O'Kelly who knows these things?—Is it really the blind man?"

He looked surprised that I would say such a thing. He said, "Mr. O'Kelly?—that pore thing?" He said, "Mr. O'Kelly don't know much of nothing, Sugar. Pore Mr. O'Kelly wouldn't last the night, if he didn't have Joseph of Arimathea to wait on him hand and foot."

I said, "Did you talk to them—the eunuchs?"

He said, "Let's go outside, I'll introduce you."

I left Big G.B.'s side without really even a thought. I don't know what he felt, or what G.B. Junior felt or did, whether he moved onto the stool where I had been sitting and took the place he should have had all along, or whether he found a quarter and played the jukebox against everybody's wishes. I just don't know, didn't think to look, didn't think to ask, even later.

Daddy held the door and we went out into the lashing rain. Daddy said, "They are looking for St. George By The Lake, the little Episcopal chapel Dr. Hightower built out of the old Swiftown depot. We'll ride out and show them where it is."

I said, "Is it a baptizing this morning?"

He said, "The Barlow child."

The eunuch who was driving the van wore a short haircut and no moustache or sideburns. He rolled down his window and said, "I sure appreciate your help in locating the place, Mr. Mecklin. It's some kind of weather we're having this morning."

Daddy said, "This is my boy Sugar. Y'all just get behind us, we'll lead you out to the church."

The rain slacked up some, though it didn't quit yet. The turkey hunters—one or two of them—had already started out to their trucks. The woods were flooded, there would be no hunt today. Me and Daddy led the eunuchs out of town toward St. George, the old converted depot down by Roebuck Lake.

Trudy Lewis

VINCRISTINE

(from *The Greensboro Review*)

Before the needle was even settled in her arm, Debra could already taste the vincristine taking effect. Bitter salt crystals from nowhere pickled up on the bed of her tongue. When she swallowed, they got stronger. When she sniffled, they seeped stinging up into her nose. But that was how it happened with vincristine.

Ever since Debra started leukemia treatment last summer, her mother had insisted she learn the name of everything the doctors put into her body. Everything they took out of her body and everything wrong with her body. There were so many names, after a while, that Debra had to think up sneaky ways of learning them. She fit some of the long rhyming kind to the rock songs she heard on her stepfather's truck radio, or on Stephanie's Sony Walkman at school. That was all right, but she felt stupid hearing different words than everyone else when she was in the cereal aisle at the grocery store and they started playing the fizzy instrumental version of a song that had been alive and blooming behind Stephanie's ears just the month before. Then Debra figured out how some of the medical names sounded like comfortable ones she already knew. She could remember "thorazine," for example, by the way it resembled the last name of her best friend, Stephanie Thorpe. And "lymphocyclic"—the kind of leukemia she had—reminded her of her music teacher, Lindley Cybert.

Actually, Debra knew Ms. Cybert's first name only because of a program she had passed around class when she first started teaching in the middle of the year. It was from the opera in Dallas, Texas, and "Lindley Cybert" was listed under the soprano chorus. After everyone was finished looking at it, Ms. Cybert picked up the program and started to use it as a fan, then curved it up against her chest instead, where the top corner nudged at the opening of her blouse. "Opera," she said, "has got to be the most vivid experience of the human voice. You just can't imagine the subtle crevices of sound until you sing them for yourself." Then she had started to sing something that wriggled all over her face before it finally worked into the high note and slithered down shimmering. Debra couldn't get over how ugly Ms. Cybert was when her voice was climbing, how beautiful she turned out when it fell. And for some reason, she wanted to stop the giggles percolating in the back row, not because she felt sorry for the new teacher, but because she sensed whatever was making people laugh now was the same thing that made them twitch their voices around and look pitiful when they found out about her own disease. It just sounded different, was all.

The nurse slowed her breath and Debra felt the needle change its position in her arm. Now it was almost over. Now there were just a couple of minutes to go. Debra was so used to the routine that the nurse didn't even bother to explain the different pains and pressures, the reasons they were necessary.

"Debra, tighten up your fist there. You're not concentrating, child." Debra's mother had stopped right in the middle of her most famous gesture, sliding the charm on her necklace back and forth across her chin. Today the charm was an enamel daisy, white and gold. Though no one said so, Debra knew that the habit had to do with luck, and that her mother had chosen the daisy on purpose, hoping it would somehow influence the results on Debra's remission.

"Don't cut your eyes at me that way. I'm not going to be the one crying about some big ugly bruise, come Friday."

"Me neither," Debra said.

"Well good, because I decided you need a new dress for that spring program you're so worked up over. And I don't want to see any tears spilling down the front of it."

"May Fête, Mama. Ms. Cybert says it's like a French May Day." Debra strained her knuckles white just thinking about how clean she wanted her arms to look for the concert, not even the spooky blue crescent of an old bruise showing through.

Then the needle drew away with a final little drag of suction and the nurse said, "I don't expect to see this young lady for another three months now."

"Gee, hope you recognize me."

"Tell you what, I owe you a soda if I don't."

When she was gone, Mama said, "Maybe we ought to go with the long sleeves, just in case. Those French girls are wearing long sleeves now, aren't they?" She took a paper hospital gown off a stack on the counter and started drawing. First, a head with short, drippy curls, then the sleeves. She drew so fast it seemed she had Debra memorized, and knew by heart the things she had to hide.

"There. You want them raglan or leg o'mutton, like that?"

"Raglan," Debra said. "So I can pull them back and show everyone if I'm cured."

Debra got back to school just in time for music class, but Ms. Cybert was late. While the sixth graders waited, they duelled with xylophone sticks and scraped sandblocks against each others' arms. Stephanie sat alone at the piano wearing her Walkman, playing by ear. The song was "Material Girl" by a sexy singer called Madonna, and Debra had already messed up the lyrics in her mind.

"Well," Stephanie said, "did they say it's off?"

"For three months. Unless the tests are bad."

"Think they'll tell you about it if they are?"

Debra touched the Band-Aid on her arm. "They have to. 'Cuz then they have to give me more shots and transfusions and all."

"Yeah, grownups are like that. First off, they don't want to tell you where you came from. Then they never want to let you know what's going on."

"Not my mother," Debra said. "She's always giving me books and stuff."

"Yeah, your mother's different." Stephanie started playing the chorus again, but only with one hand. "Probably it's because of that loony place where she works."

"Who said the Institute's loony?"

Stephanie wriggled her shoulders and head in a slow, luxurious shimmy like Madonna's. "Don't look at me," she said. "I like loonies." Then she picked up her left hand and walked it down the far end of the piano, until Debra had to lean back to stay out of the way.

"Bravissimo," someone said.

Debra looked up at Ms. Cybert, who had one hand on the drawstring of her cape, the other hand on Stephanie's shoulder. Even though it was almost spring outside, Ms. Cybert looked like an advertisement for December with her green velvet cape and the silver eyeshadow streaked above and below each eye.

"Such spirit," she said. "If you can devote that much spirit to a populist jingle, just think what you'll do with a true *cri de coeur*.

"What's that?" Stephanie said.

"Stephanie, I need a little help from you. You know the 'Song of Joy' from Beethoven? Well, I really need my hands to conduct that particular straining and overstepping effect. You understand that, don't you? So I'd like you to do the honors for me, play the piano, if you would."

"The only thing is, I can't read notes."

"I'm sure you'll pick it up. Come on, Stephanie, this isn't very easy for me either."

She was squatting down by the piano bench now, with her cape pulled across her knees and over one arm. Like a statue holding its clothes on, Debra thought, but also like her mother folding sheets at home. Up close, Ms. Cybert's face looked too white in some places, too red in others, and there was an eyelash caught and half covered in makeup at the side of her nose.

"Ms. Cybert," Debra said, "can I turn pages for Stephanie at the May Fête?"

"Well, if she can't read—" Ms. Cybert flashed her silver finger-nails inside her hairdo and looked back at Debra. "Certainly, of course. Whatever the virtuoso says."

She signaled for them to move to their own seats, then stood up and arranged her cape on the lectern. Today she started class by ringing a triangle and singing questions about music and chords.

"What is a third?" she sang. "Can you give me a third?"

A third was two notes up from what Ms. Cybert was singing, which didn't make much sense and was almost as bad as long division. No wonder there was more laughing than singing, all in a different key.

"What's the difficulty here? You, Billy Carmichael, can you let me in on the source of your merriment?"

"Well, I ain't gonna sing it."

"That's fine. For this purpose, vulgar speech will do."

Billy pointed to the lectern and worked his face without laughing. "Matt says you was late because you was too busy out sucking people's blood."

Ms. Cybert set the triangle down. She felt along the buttons of her dress until she got to the belt. "Obviously, your friend is confused about the origins of the opera cloak. The two of you can come up and examine the question after class."

Debra tensed her fist as if for the nurse's needle and breathed in huge huffs of the tinny, chemical smell that was her now, but that didn't seem to come from any particular place when she went looking. Sick people weren't supposed to get mad, or, if they did, they didn't know the reason for it; they didn't have the concentration. But Debra was pretty sure how this went: she hated Billy for being so stupid and Ms. Cybert for letting him and Stephanie for talking about things she didn't know and playing the piano without really caring. At the same time, she hated not being able to act stupid or smart-alecky herself, to show off in some silly, comfortable way. And looking at her arm, most of all, she hated the clumsy bruise already budding below her skin, pushing up cloudy and purple.

After school, Debra called her mother at the Institute for Educational Change. She was supposed to do this every day, as soon as she got off the bus. Last summer and fall there had been a whole batch of child molestations, at least that was what her mother said, and so Debra just had to be sure to check in, that was all. When Debra thought about it, though, she wondered if it didn't have more to do with her leukemia. Maybe her mother was afraid she would collapse somewhere between the bus and the kitchen phone and crash into the stone flowerpots at the gate of Willow Park or cut her head on the tablesaw her stepfather kept pushed up under the front awning. Debra could never be sure, and didn't know if she wanted to be, so she didn't complain. She only kept her hand on the empty perfume bottle inside her bookbag as she walked up the exact middle of the drive, counted the steps she skipped over without breathing, then locked the deadbolt behind her and thought about the kind of cartoon where Bugs Bunny pants happily against a closed door, snickering into his hand until he looks up and sees the rabbit hunter coming out of the coat closet.

"You know, Mama," Debra said, "bruises are like snowflakes, and none of them are exactly the same. That's what our art teacher said. At least, she said the part about the snowflakes, and I made up the rest."

"Did you get a new bruise, pumpkin?"

"Well, I think so."

"That's all right. I know you want to look pretty for your program, but a little thing like that isn't going to make much difference in the end."

"It doesn't mean I'm sick again?"

"No, baby. Dr. Lane just called. He wanted to tell us as soon as possible. Your blood marrow's clean. It's a complete remission. So unwrinkle your pretty face, angel, and pick out something snazzy for us to wear to dinner."

"O.K.," Debra said. "If you want me to. Guess what? Stephanie's going to play the piano for the May Fête and I'm going to turn pages for her."

"That's wonderful, Debra, but I thought you'd be a little more excited over your news."

"Oh, I knew that would happen. Dr. Lane winked at me when you were putting on your jacket."

"All right. Well, do you have any homework?"

"Just long division."

"Try and get it done before I get home, O.K., child? We're going to be too busy stepping out later on."

"O.K., Mama. Bye."

"Goodbye. I love you, pumpkin. And I promise, we'll go someplace fun. It'll be almost as good as a birthday."

Debra hung up the phone and got a carton of yogurt out of the refrigerator—pineapple orange. She ate a spoonful and held it in her mouth as long as she could, until it soaked a tart flavor into her saliva. Then she untangled the phone cord. People were always fiddling with the phone cord.

When she sat down with the lapboard that she and her step-father had made out of leftover cedar from the lumberyard, it was already after four. She looked at the magazine pictures shellacked onto the wood and tried again to decide which lady was prettiest. The one in the striped sweater and tights had the best hair, very thick, and the color of Del Monte peaches. But the diamond lady had a better face. If you squinted your eyes, it was almost like Ms. Cybert's. This lady looked so serious about being beautiful that she made you believe it was the hardest and most scientific thing in the world, and that other accomplishments, such as math and social studies, were just silly pastimes for people who didn't know better.

People like Debra, she guessed. She slid her homework over the pictures and started into the first equation. They always started simple—a clean sinking into and slicing and diminishing, then moving out again to see what was left. But she had to do so much work in the margins that it got messy after a while. The numbers woozed into each other, getting longer instead of shorter, until she couldn't find her way back up the column anymore and turned dizzy and nauseous sideling her eyes between the remainder and the unfinished answer. Then, when she gave up and moved her pencil to the next bracket, she remembered that there was some-thing incredibly important back there at the beginning of the first problem, something she couldn't say the name of, and that it had to do with fear.

That night, after a big dinner at which her mother wore a yellow handkerchief dress and her stepfather told jokes to the waiter, Debra began to feel sick. It was just a lazy stomach pain at bedtime, but somewhere in the middle of the night it got active. It gripped and twisted her invisible organs out of the places she knew they ought to be. It made her dream of operating on herself, opening the abdomen like an overripe avocado, until she decided she'd rather just stay awake.

She pulled the comforter off her bed and went to lie on the bathroom floor, where the cool tile against her stomach distracted her from what was going on inside, and where the toilet was if she needed it. She imagined her mother coming in and feeling her forehead with chapped, fluttery fingers warm from sliding under her stepfather's pillow. But if her mother came, Debra would have to tell her how it felt. She'd have to describe and identify and mugshot the pain as if it were some criminal that Mama was after. And that would just make it worse. Sometimes she got confused when she was talking about her body, and wondered if she was lying. Was this worse or better than yesterday's pain and did it feel like it used to when she was first sick? She wasn't sure, and the faster she guessed, the more the pain shifted to become something totally new, dazzling and unexplorable.

When her mother did come in, it was basically morning and Debra was braiding fringes on the bathroom rug.

"Goodness, child, what's the matter?"

"I didn't feel like sleeping." Debra couldn't help it; she was glad her mother was there to ask questions and take over. "Mama, it hurts again. In my stomach."

"You know, baby, sometimes people get sick just from worrying too much."

"That's not it, Mama. There's something wrong."

"Now don't go thinking that yet. It could just be a reaction. They gave you an extra-big injection of vincristine, so you might get a stronger reaction. In fact, I'm sure that's what it is. I'll call Dr. Lane today at work." She touched Debra's hair, which was almost a regular length again, crisp and prickly over her ears. "Why don't you go in there and get your daddy to make you some half-and-half coffee? That should settle your stomach down a little."

"I'm not staying home from school," Debra said.

"Did I say for you to stay home?"

"Well, I'm just telling you."

In the kitchen, Debra's stepfather was making something with bananas. Peanut butter, bananas, fried egg, mayonnaise, tomato.

"Hey, punk," he said.

"Don't let me see that thing, I'm sick. What is it, anyway?"

"It's a breakfast sandwich. They got them at all the restaurants now. Only this one's fancier. This thing's a whole meal in one, breakfast on this end and dessert on this other." He started to take the sandwich apart again, to show her, then set it back on the paper plate. "Sorry. You're sick. Want some coffee?"

"Yes, please. So, are you gonna try to sell this thing to McDonald's or what?"

"No, this is just between you and me, sweetheart. I'll make you one sometime when you feel better."

Debra watched her handsome stepfather eating breakfast, then rubbing crumbs off the few slick hairs showing inside his open workshirt, and wondered if he thought anything like that was ever really going to happen.

At school, they were having music class every day this week, to get ready for the May Fête. Ms. Cybert seemed sorry about the day before, and either didn't wear any coat at all or took her cape off and hid it in the closet before the sixth grade got there. When they came in, she was playing a tape recorder, forwarding and reversing, trying to catch something in between. Her hair was riding over one shoulder, and when she turned around Debra saw that it was all tied off her face with a black, ruffly rag.

"Today," Ms. Cybert said, "you're going to hear a third. By that I mean it's not only going to enter your ear, but actually take up residence there."

"That sounds gross," Stephanie whispered. "Like that parasite movie we saw on Mindy's cable."

"That's not what she means," Debra said.

Ms. Cybert flicked on the tape recorder and played Hall and Oates's "I Can't Go for That," just the chorus. Then she turned it off.

"Now there's a third for you. In your own vocabulary."

"Man, that Daryl Hall guy's just a fairy," Billy said.

"No, actually he's fairly straight. I went out with his sound man several times, and he said it was just a vicious rumor started by a few ignorant, prepubescent boys. Now, are you ready to start rehearsal?"

Stephanie raised her hand. "Ms. Cybert, can we do this 'Song of Joy' song first and get it over with?"

"Well, I'd rather you didn't put it that way, but of course. Stephanie is going to provide us with accompaniment for Beethoven's choir piece."

Some people clapped, and Matt Berger said, "Go get 'em, baby."

Stephanie started toward the piano, then came back and pulled on the cuff button of Debra's sweater. "Come on, Deb. You're not going to make me go alone, are you?"

Stephanie didn't look particularly frightened, and Debra knew that she wasn't scared of Matt Berger, anyway. She had proven that on Valentine's Day, when she checked his mailbox every hour or so to make sure his cards from other girls didn't include sneaky presents that were just a little too good—full-size candy bars, wallet photos of rock stars, safety pins strung with colored beads and turned into "friendship pins." But even if Stephanie didn't actually need her, Debra still wanted to go. She wanted to sit at the front of the room with Stephanie and Ms. Cybert, not really helping them in any way, but connected to a feeling of being musical.

Debra barely looked away from Ms. Cybert while Stephanie was playing. The conductor's long arms drew out of her sleeves and stayed tight, like a dancer's, no matter how they switched and swayed. The "Song of Joy" was slow enough that Stephanie had time to try again when she hit the wrong pack of notes. But that didn't happen too often. And twice, Ms. Cybert made a signal especially for Debra, rolling her wrist and twisting her fingers one by one until Debra turned the page.

"A brave attempt," Ms. Cybert said, when the song was over. "Just a few mistakes, and I'm certain you'll correct them by the next performance. And Debra, right? Good work. Let me tell you, my own breakthrough came when I was serving as an understudy myself."

"Oh, I can't play," Debra said.

"Well, don't worry. You look as if you'll do something, anyway."

"Yes ma'am," Debra said. "I hope so." She went back to her seat and thought about what Ms. Cybert had said until she could remember it exactly, and imagined writing each letter in the air in front of her. Meanwhile, Ms. Cybert was telling the class about the rules of public performance, the intricacies of the half rest, the dangers of locking one's knees, and Debra started threading the message into the "Song of Joy," although the combination didn't seem quite right.

That afternoon when she was watching cartoons, Debra found a tangle in her hair. Daffy Duck was daring Bugs Bunny to step over the chalk line separating his side of the boat from the rabbit's, and Debra leaned back and pushed her hands into her curls, getting ready to laugh. But there was a twiny clot at the back of her head. Her fingers kept running to it all during Daffy's tirade, his attempts to build a barricade out of deck furniture, mop buckets, and rope. Debra separated the clot with her fingers, making two smaller tangles, then three. But she was pulling out a lot of hair that way. So she gave up and went into her mother's room for the tangle comb.

When she came back, they were showing another cartoon completely, the one with Sylvester and Tweety Bird. She sat down with her legs straddled out beside her and started combing. After she had narrowed the tangle to one wadded knot of hair, she felt around and noticed there wasn't much left on the sides. Then, slowly settling down to panic, she thought about what had happened to her hair before, about the bruises and vincristine. It couldn't be that now, especially with the May Fête coming tomorrow. She brought the comb out in front of her and saw that the whole tangle was caught in the tines, like a bunch of ratty, unravelling lace. Debra's legs started to hurt, with the fizzy pain that is supposed to be numbness, as if she had been sitting the same way for a long time. She could barely control them well enough to change her position, and when she did she felt them shaking, even though it wasn't enough to actually see.

By the time her mother came home from work, Debra was watching reruns, still combing out her hair, and making a circular pattern of curls on the carpet in front of her.

"Debra, honey," her mother said. She set a Rexall bag on the coffee table and then sat down in front of the television, sliding her arm up Debra's shoulder as she went. Her hand curved around Debra's neck like a collar, and the thumb rubbed against a nerve.

Yes, it happened, Debra was thinking, even if I did call you and even if you came home early. But she also knew that the only way she could possibly live now was by listening to her mother, telling her how it felt, concentrating on the meaning.

"Debra, it's all right, baby. I called Dr. Lane and he said you were having a reaction. Remember, he told us you could have a reaction, but we just got so excited we didn't even think about it."

"What about the May Fête, Mama? I've got to sit in front of everybody, I've got to turn the pages?"

"Now, Debra, you're going to be fine for your program. We'll get you one of those broad-brimmed, grown-up hats, or else I'll make you a cap to match your dress."

Debra touched the curls in front of her, rearranging their pattern. Then she realized she was doing something gross and spooky, like the dying girl in a book she'd read who cut off her curls and passed them around to whoever would take them—family, nurses, next-door neighbors, whoever. Debra imagined the adults hiding their gifts in plastic packets at the backs of kitchen drawers, or in shoeboxes at the tops of closets until the girl was safely dead. They only took the curls to make her happy, anyway, and just think of the germs. But the children kept their mementos handy. The children had different ideas. They tricked each other into seeing witch's blood at the tips of the pitch-black roots and set a few strands on the windowsill to attract vampires. They didn't forget the girl, but they kept changing her to fit every new game and monster movie.

Debra started to cry. She didn't want to be pitiful, but she didn't want to be scary either.

"Oh, Mama," she said. She pressed into her mother's cheek and smelt the flowers in her shampoo, the spice in her perfume, and the tense chalk of her makeup turning sharper as it got wet.

Her mother didn't say anything; she just rocked to the music of the commercial playing on the television behind her.

"O.K., Mama," Debra said, standing up, "I've got to call Stephanie now."

On Friday, in the coatroom, Debra told Stephanie what it felt like not to have any hair.

"Sort of itchy," she said. "And dizzy too, like there's nothing holding your brains down."

The coatroom was up the stairs from the library and opened onto the playground. It had the cold cement walls of a basement, printed over with graffiti: "Fuck Damn Shit." The words were written one on top of another, like a triple-layered equation. Back in the second grade, when Debra asked her mother what they meant, she said them all together, sure they were part of the same thing. And when she found out they weren't, she had been more disappointed than embarrassed.

Leaning against the wall under double rows of limp sweaters and windbreakers were the red wooden "Stop" paddles for the safety patrols. A broken slide projector sat in one corner. Debra used to have a game in the coatroom, she remembered. In the middle of winter, she would push into thick parkas as far as she could go and blink her eyes against their fur. When she came away, things would be a little blurry, and she would know that she had become frighteningly beautiful, that if she was careful it would last all day. Now she realized that she had been ridiculous, confusing the way she looked with the way she saw. But somehow, it still make a weird kind of sense to her.

"Are you going to get a wig?" Stephanie said.

"No, I'm not sure. My mother said we'd think about it. We never did last time because it was too hot. And now I guess it's going to be too hot again."

"You should make them let you try one. My mom says you can buy anything on trial now. Even a wig, she said."

"You told her?"

"Well, I have to tell her things like that or she doesn't let me stay in the kitchen and listen when her friends come over."

"Don't tell anybody else," Debra said.

"O.K., O.K. I'm not telling anything."

"'Cuz you know how they'll act." Debra found a groove in the wall behind her and drew her finger along it. "So, do you want to see?" A chill quivered between her shoulder blades: this was how Stephanie must feel when she did her shimmy and the jiggling ran all the way down to her hands on the piano. That was a reaction too, but no one had to call the doctor about it.

"Sure," Stephanie said. "I just thought it would be kind of crude to ask."

Debra untied her scarf and slid it slowly down the back of her neck, the way she had seen women doing in the movies.

"It's all right. You've still got some stuff on the sides. I bet I can tie it up so it shows, too."

"O.K., but wait a minute. I want to take a break." Debra leaned her head against the cold wall and where it touched her, a bright, numb relief broke over the itchy feeling in her scalp. She wanted to do this on the left side too; otherwise, she knew she'd feel lopsided all day. But she'd look pretty stupid turning around just for that.

She was trying to decide whether to do it anyway when the playground door opened and Ms. Cybert came in. Her silky dress was sticking to her legs, and the long braided tail of her belt was looped up into the stack of books in her arms. She looked toward Debra and Stephanie then moved back against the door and touched her hand to her collarbone.

"Ladies," she said, "are you prepared to face your audience?"

"Well, my brother can't come," Stephanie said. "So there's nothing to be scared about."

"Oh God." Ms Cybert started passing Stephanie thin paper music books, one at a time. "God, the second graders can't perform a Maypole dance. They can't even do the hokey pokey. They've got all the grace of a bassoon—or no, a cellist. One of those monkey women with legs like a treble clef." She stopped, then looked at Debra. "I've had bad experiences with cellists."

My hair, Debra thought.

"Maybe it would be better to have the first graders dance and the second graders sing. Those little urchins still have some infant sense of suppleness about them." Ms. Cybert was giving Debra books and sheet music now; they seemed to get thinner and more slippery as she got to the bottom of the stack. Debra reached for a song with a blue cover as it glided away. But she missed it and ended up looking at the pale little points of her teacher's sideburns instead, the two cracks in her lip where the orangey lipstick wouldn't stay.

"You remember how to file in, don't you, and that devious half rest in the Mozart? It's absolutely essential, remember, that you don't lock your knees. Only fainting can come of locking your knees. And, ladies, fainting is highly unprofessional."

"Jeez," Stephanie said, "it's not like we're going to be on television or anything. My mom will love it if somebody faints. She loves all that kind of thing."

"She appreciates the spectacle, then?"

"I guess," Stephanie said.

"Ah, there is something to be said for the spectacle. I fainted on the stage at one time. As a part of my role, you understand. That's one thing about opera—the sense of absolute precision in a diva as she breaks down. Those are all the best parts, you know. The fainting and the dying and the hallucinating. I love to sink my teeth into some really fine hallucinating."

"Like that loony business?" Stephanie said. "I can do some of that stuff." She let her eyeballs go loose and aimless inside her head and shook her hand in imaginary palsy.

"Gross," Debra said. She hated it when Stephanie made people their age look stupid in front of Ms. Cybert. But then, maybe that was the only way someone like that would notice them at all.

"A woman of sensibility, I see. I suggest that your friend perfect her instrumental ability before mounting the stage. What do you say?"

"I think so, too. I mean, Stephanie isn't very serious sometimes."

"Well, it takes a little of that to make an *artiste*. Please don't worry, you girls. We're going to give a grand performance. I can tell already." She took her books back and arranged them in a long, ridged stack sliding over one hip. Then, when she walked past, she tracked her finger around the cusp of Debra's ear. "You know, that isn't actually going to hurt your resonance any."

Debra pushed her scarf into the pocket of her jeans. "Sure, I know that," she said. Her heartbeat ran into her neck, and then to the queasy spot in her stomach where she had learned to measure things before she thought about them. Ms. Cybert wasn't going to take away her page-turning job because of the vincristine; she wasn't even going to tell her what kind of hat to wear to the concert. And it didn't look as if she cared much that Debra was almost bald, that she might throw up, or that she had a spooky, vampire-type disease everyone was afraid of. To Ms. Cybert, it all seemed as ordinary as a hard night of fainting at the opera, or a day of getting insulted by Billy Carmichael at school. But in another way, it wasn't ordinary at all. Because nothing Ms. Cybert did was ordinary. Even the blanks in a song had a special mood to them, and every note, no matter where it came from, had an equal chance at living the secret life of a parasite.

Debra had permission to go home with Stephanie after school, to eat refrigerator cookies and get ready for the May Fête. They walked the long way, past Matt Berger's and through the mall with the pink and green mannequins, then into a vacant lot of mulberry trees that led to Stephanie's backyard. In Stephanie's bedroom, Debra picked through the newer albums, smelling fresh print and plastic. Someday, they would make a perfume like this and she and Ms. Cybert would wear it constantly.

"This one is great," Stephanie said, pulling a long blue dress out of her closet. "This one shows my line."

"Your what?" Debra said, even though she knew that Stephanie believed it was possible to draw a convincing cleavage with eyebrow pencil. "Your mother's going to kill you."

"She'll just think I'm developing."

"Sure." Debra sat down on the far side of the bed. She didn't feel like Stephanie today. Her stomach wasn't actually hurting, but it seemed wobbly enough that she'd have to drink at least one cup of coffee before the concert. "I think I have to go home now. So I can decide if I'm going to be sick."

Stephanie let the dress slither down to the floor, and Debra watched it collapse over itself like a witch dissolving into a puddle of gauzy, pastel water.

"Hey, I'll wear this yellow one if you like it better."

"Stephanie, I don't feel good."

"Well, that's O.K.. We've got some stomach medicine and my mom can make this special kind of tea that helps you relax. Besides, you didn't even eat any cookies yet."

"Stephanie."

"Jeez, Deb, I know you're not that sick." She somersaulted over the bed and sat down next to Debra. "Maybe you just want to dance," she said.

"No, I mean it. I am."

So Stephanie got her mother up from the laundry room to take Debra home. When Mrs. Thorpe let her off at the gate to Willow Park, though, Debra was already feeling worse. She shouldn't have lied to Stephanie, because now it was all coming true. Her stomach jumped and jammed every time she stepped too hard on the pavement, and the itchy feeling in her scalp was scattering down her neck and shoulders into the long, unreachable span of her back. At home, her mother's car was there, and that wasn't a good sign either. Probably bad news. Probably something else Debra would have to learn the name of and learn to live with and then pretend to learn vague lessons from until she finally died, an incredibly wise child who couldn't do long division, and who never found out what it was supposed to prove.

Debra opened the screen door as quietly as she could, moving slowly so the aluminum didn't catch in the wind. Then she headed for the phone. She always called someone when she got home. Maybe she'd call Stephanie, tell her she was sorry, ask if they could spend the night together on Saturday. Debra didn't want to have to talk to her mother right away, or even any time soon.

But just before she made the turn into the kitchen, she heard her mother talking already.

"Well, Debra's all worked up," she said. "And that part couldn't please us more. It looks like you're doing a fine job up there." She moved in close enough to the doorway that Debra saw the pink tip of her elbow slipping out of her sleeve. So her mother was on the phone, leaning against the wall, probably, and curling the phone cord over her finger, loop by loop.

"But Ms. Cybert—I'm not sure if you know—Debra has leukemia. It's in remission now, but they had to give her some super chemotherapy before she went off the treatment, and she's having a reaction. She's having some hair loss. To tell you the truth, she's going bald. She's got this thin band of hair around the sides, like a little old man. Actually, she's taking it all right, but I'm worried about other people, and kids, you know. This did happen once before. You weren't teaching yet, though, and I didn't know how much you'd heard."

Debra felt a sudden confusion, the kind that came with vincristine. She could almost hear the weak blood slapping into her heart and sloshing through the arteries until it finally broke into her cheeks and forehead. She couldn't be mad; it was like remembering being mad, as if she had always known her mother would do something like this, and that she would hate her for it.

"So I just wanted you to know, in case anything was to happen. Because if you look at that child funny, she's going to notice it. She's that sharp. I guess I wanted to be sure you're in on everything. Thank you very much. And I'll be looking forward to your program."

She moved out of the doorway and clicked the phone off. But she didn't hang it up, because in a second or so it started the long, circular whine of a dial tone. Debra could just see her mother standing there with the receiver in the palm of her hand, trying to decide who to call. Hadn't she called enough, talked enough, told enough? The phone settled back into its cradle with a clattering sound and Debra uncurled her tongue. She couldn't believe her mother had changed her mind.

The sewing machine buzzed on, a rigid grumbling stirring up into a high, breathy whirr, and now Debra could do anything she wanted and no one would ever hear. She went back outside and sat on the front porch, pretending it was a sports-car and that Ms. Cybert was driving her to see the opera in Dallas, Texas. But it kept turning out that Mama was there too, calling from a drive-through window, making signs in the car behind them, waiting in a stained silk balcony to give them a copy of the words they never wanted to hear about anyway.

In theory, the May Fête went like this: the sixth graders strode onto the playground, very serious, singing the "Song of Joy." Then they did a few more songs and sat down in a row of chairs at the side of the stage. From there, the songs got giddier as the children got littler. There was a sugarplum song, a Maypole dance, a minuet of bees. After everyone was finished came Debra's favorite part of all. The sixth graders stood up, then the fifth graders. The sides of the stage moved. Now the whole school was in a series of inter-locking circles, twining together and apart. They did a few move-ments with their feet; they sang a song about the spring. Then the circles slipped, so they were one inside the next, ranging out to the merry-go-round on one side and the jungle gym on another. That was the moment, Debra decided, when she would disappear.

No ambulance, no I.V.; no blood, no scene. Just simple division, or maybe subtraction, the easiest kind. There wouldn't be any-thing for her mother to say about it. She'd just have to look at Ms. Cybert and nod.

At the bottom of the playground, Ms. Cybert was rolling the piano into position. Shoots of ribbon dripped and lifted from her waist. Something sparkled in her hair. Debra left her mother and stepfather talking to the minister's nephew over by the bike rack and ran all the way to the stage.

"Ms. Cybert, you don't have to worry. I'm fine. I'm really ready to perform."

"Then you're a bit beyond me," she said. But she was smiling and the dust of glitter from her hair seemed to spill over onto her eyelashes. "Why don't you sort out my music for me, Debra, so I can collect the cast."

She put a program and a stack of music on top of the piano and moved away, her ribbons tangling down to her ankles.

Then Stephanie came up, and Debra handed her the first song. "Nervous?" she said.

"Barely." Stephanie pulled down the front of her yellow dress, so Debra could see a tiny heart sticker where the breasts ought to begin. "For luck, you know. I wish I had a mole, though, like Madonna. You aren't mad, are you?"

"No, I just had a fight with my mother. Well, sort of."

"Oh, that can't last. She'll be waving and taking pictures any minute now."

"I guess," Debra said.

Ms. Cybert walked back to the piano again and kissed Stephanie on the cheek. "*Bonne chance.* Enthusiasm and dignity. Don't neglect your dignity, now." The wind swished a strand of hair into her mouth and she lifted it out with her little finger raised. Then she kissed Debra's cheek, leaving a thick mist of perfume in her nose, and moved up to the microphone.

The parents turned toward her, touching each other's elbows and switching their conversations to short, rugged whispers that eventually blended into silence. Debra saw her mother sitting in a metal chair near the front of the audience, twisting her fingers in her purse strap. She looked as if nothing had happened, her face flat and ironed open at the seams. But that was only because she didn't know. It was because she couldn't even guess what was going to happen.

"I'll play the wrong song if you give me a quarter," Stephanie said. "'Thriller' maybe, or 'Girls Just Wanna Have Fun.'"

Debra looked at Ms. Cybert's hands trembling on the music stand and heard the shimmer of her rings against metal.

"Just read the music," she said. "Aren't you supposed to know how to do that now?"

"Sure," Stephanie said. "If you hum a few bars." Then she began to play. The notes came in thin and slanted as the sixth graders walked up to the stage. But the sound was getting clearer all the time. Debra felt it edge into her cavities and flicker over the itchy spots on her scalp. She watched while different patterns glimmered in time on the back of Ms. Cybert's dress.

And it went on like that. Even when Debra and Stephanie stood up to go with the other sixth graders, and even when a little girl in the Maypole dance wouldn't give up her yellow streamer and stood there chewing on it instead.

Debra was still waiting for the finish, though. She checked the elastic under her hat and pushed some wrinkles in her tights back into the throat of her shoe. Then Ms. Cybert made the signal and everything changed. Debra was holding Stephanie's hand on one side, Billy Carmichael's on the other, and the circle was spinning so fast their bodies slanted outward on all the curves. The wider and tighter the circle moved, the more Debra knew it would break like elastic whenever someone stepped away. This must be Billy Carmichael's idea. He was the one pacing the whole ring. He wasn't even singing, and when Debra slowed down, he pressed their joined hands into her back so hard she could feel the weight of every knuckle.

But Debra didn't much care about that anymore. It was almost time now, anyway. She tried to find Ms. Cybert in the blur of circles and only saw her mother walking toward the stage. Past the flagpole, through the swings. With her jacket slicing open in the wind and her hair twisting out in thin, wavery strings behind her. If she gets any closer, Debra thought, I'll disappear.

She slipped her hand out of Stephanie's warm, wet fingers. She worked away from Billy's gritty palm. Then she was flinging free.

The fall wasn't what she expected: she flew further and hurt less. When she came to on the blacktop, she was laughing the ragged tune the wind knocked out of her as it went. I'll never stop laughing, she thought, I'll never catch my breath. Because above and all around her was her mother after all.

Mary Hood

AFTER MOORE

(from *The Georgia Review*)

I

Rhonda could divide her whole life into *before* and *after* Moore. She was fifteen when they met, and thirty now. She had gone to the Buckhorn Club with a carload of older friends and a fake I.D. in her pocket just in case. Moore, a manufacturer's rep, had been standing alone at the bar, thirtyish, glancing indifferently around, looking familiar. Her friends kept daring her, and after a few beers Rhonda threaded through the crowd to ask him:

"You think you're Ted Turner or something?"

It is true he cultivated the likeness, in style and posture, the neat silver-shot mustache, the careless curve of gold around his lean wrist, the insolence: his calculating, damn-all eyes focused always on the inner, driving dream. Because she had been searching so long for her mysteriously lost father, a trucker, she thought she preferred men rougher, blue collar, not white silk, monogrammed. For his part, he knew he was dancing with danger. Still, or perhaps because of that, Moore drew her to him, so close he could reach around her, slip his hands into the back pockets of her jeans, and ask: "You ever wear a dress, jailbait?" They were slow-dancing, legs between, not toe-to-toe.

"I take my pants off sometimes," Rhonda said. She was pretty fast for fifteen, but not fast enough. That was when and how it began, with her wanting someone, and him wanting anyone. Love was all they knew to call it.

"My problem is I'm a romantic," Moore said.

"I guess I still love him, but so what?" Rhonda told the counselor. They had sought professional help toward the bitter end. The family counselor listened and listened.

"I got married when I was fifteen," Rhonda explained. "A case of *had to*. . . . Three babies in five years, tell me what chance I had?" And Moore with such ingrained tastes and habits—sitting for barbershop shaves, manicures, spitshines on his Italian shoes. "What he paid out in tips would've kept all three babies in Pampers," Rhonda grieved, "except he didn't believe in throwaway diapers, said it was throwing away money." But he couldn't stand to be around when she laundered cloth diapers, either, and when it rained—before she bought her dryer at a yard sale—and she had to hang them indoors on strings all over the house, and the steam rose as she ironed them dry, Moore would leave. "He just doesn't have the stomach for baby business," Rhonda said.

Moore said, "I never hit her. If she says I did, she's lying."

"He had this *list*," she told the counselor. "A scorecard. All the women he's had." She found it the day Chip and Scott ran away.

The boys had made up their beds to look as though they were still asleep in them, body-shaping the pillows, arranging the sheets. They slipped out the window and dropped to the sour bare ground, not to be missed for hours. When Moore slept in on Saturdays, the duplex had to stay holy dark, Sabbath still, and no cartoons. "Boring," the boys remembered. Rhonda made sure there were always library books around, but Chip and Scott weren't readers then. They saw the window as a good way out. "We had a loose screen," Scott told the counselor.

"You've got a loose screw," Chip told Scott. He didn't see getting friendly with the counselor, who had classified him, already, as a "tough case." Chip lay low in his chair, legs spraddled, heels dug in, arms behind his head as he gazed at the ceiling tiles. He was the one most like Moore.

Corey said, "We had fun."

Scott said, "Not you. You were a baby in the crib. Just Chip and me."

Corey told the counselor, "Chip's the oldest."

"*Numero uno,*" Chip agreed. The boys were talking to the counselor on their own, by themselves. Rhonda and Moore sat in the waiting room.

"It wasn't *running away,*" Scott explained. "We were just goofing around."

Corey said, "I bet Mom yelled."

"Mom's okay," Scott said.

Corey agreed. "I like her *extremely.* I guess I love her."

Chip said, "Oh boy."

"Moore came after us," Scott said. It had been years but the shock and awe were still fresh.

"God yes," Chip said. "He gave us Sam Hell all the way home." And it is true that Moore had stripped off his belt and leathered their bare legs right up the stairs and into the apartment.

"It was summer," Scott said. "No Six Flags that year, no nothing."

"They thought you were kidnapped," Corey said, in that slow way he had, as though truth were a matter of diction. "Mom worries about dumb stuff," he told the counselor. "During tornado season she writes our names on our legs in Magic Marker . . ."

"And we have to wear seat belts," Scott added.

"And keep the car doors locked *at all times.*"

"That was because of Moore trying to snatch us that time and go to California, but that's okay now," Chip said. "He was just drunk."

"We call him Moore because that's his name," Corey explained. "He says, 'Is *Son* your name? Well *Daddy*'s not mine . . . '"

"He tells the waitresses we're his brothers," Chip said.

"He belted us because he thought we ripped off his wallet," Scott said. "That was why."

"Which we damn well did not," Chip pointed out.

Rhonda had found it in the laundry box, in Moore's jogging pants pocket, where he'd left it. "That's when it hit the fan," Rhonda said. She had looked through the contents, not spying, "just exercising a wifely prerogative," and behind the side window, with his driver's license and Honest Face, there had been the record of his conquests, a little book with names and dates.

"I was number seventy-eight," Rhonda said. Not the last one on the list by any means.

When the family counselor spoke to them one-on-one, they talked freely enough, but when they gathered as a group again, reconvening in the semicircled chairs, a cagey silence fell. The counselor, thus at bay, tested their solidarity, fired shots into it, harking for ricochet or echo. Were they closed against each other, or him? He left the room, to see. In the hall, he listened. There was nothing to overhear but their unbroken, patient, absolute silences, each with its own truth, as though they were dumb books on a shelf. He did not necessarily know how to open them, to read them to each other.

"It can't all be up to *me*," he warned, going back in, as they looked up, hoping it would be easy, or over soon.

II

Moore had said, "All right, then, let's split," more than once when the bills and grievances piled up on Rhonda's heart and she made suggestions. Moore called it "nagging." Sometimes Moore did leave them, not just on business. Perhaps after a fight, always after a payday. He'd be back, though, sooner or later.

"A man like Moore can be gone a week or so and then whistle on back home like he's been out for a haircut," Rhonda said. "In the meantime, he'll never stop to drop his lucky quarter into a phone and call collect to say he's still alive and itching." On a moment's notice he'd fly to Vegas, the Bahamas, Atlantic City, anywhere he could gamble. He never took his family.

"We'd cramp his style," Rhonda said. "He's the sort of man that needs more than one woman."

Moore had been the one to say, "Let's split, then," but in all those years Rhonda had been the one who had actually walked out with full intentions of never coming back. The first time had been early on, while Chip was still an only child, in that rocky beginning year, long before Rhonda discovered that she was number 78, Rosalind was number 122, and Moore was still counting. Rhonda took Chip and drove away, rode as far as she could till she ran out of gas. She had no money, and the only thing in her pocket besides Chip's pacifier was the fake I.D. she had used to get into the clubs.

Her learner's permit had expired while she was on the maternity ward.

When she had burned up all the gas, she nosed the coasting station wagon over the berm and into a ditch, and ran the battery down with the dome light and radio. This was a side road heading generally toward Alabama, and not much traffic passed. She told the ones who stopped she was fine, didn't need help. When things got dark and quiet, she and the baby slept. It was good weather that time, so they were fairly comfortable. By morning Moore had had the state patrol track them down. They had to be towed out.

"God, he loved that Volvo," Rhonda said.

The only other time she had left him she had learned better than to take his wheels. She walked, rolling Chip along in the stroller. Scott, baby number two, was due in three months. Rhonda headed for the church.

"You know, just to hide out," Rhonda explained, "till I could figure what to do next. The last place he'd look." She didn't count on its being locked. It was raining so she pushed the baby back on down the road to Starvin' Marvin's and bought a cup of coffee. She gave the baby her nondairy creamer, loaded her cup with sugar, and nursed the steam till the rain let up. Then she headed on home.

"Moore don't know about that time," Rhonda said. "He never even missed us."

She said, "Don't expect me to be fair. The kids love him. Ask them. They think he's Jesus Christ, Santa Claus, and Rambo all rolled into one. But you ask me, I'll give you an earful. I'll try for facts, but I can't help my feelings."

She said, "Between jobs he'd get so low he'd cry." Moore was always jumping to a better job, and when the glamour wore off, he'd jump again, sometimes with no place to land.

"I've only been fired three times for my temper," Moore said. "The real reason is I drink a little sometimes. But I never lost a client or a sale. When I did, I made it up on the next one. They've got no kick! Anywhere I go I can get a top job in one day. You kidding? My résumé's solid gold. People like me. They remember me. They trust me."

"He has a bad habit of talking up to his bosses," Rhonda said. "Says all men are created equal and he isn't in the goddamned Marines any more and don't have to call no S.O.B. *sir.*"

"I've got an 'attitude,'" Moore said.

One layoff with him home underfoot every day, Rhonda took up gardening. "I got a real kick out of digging in the dirt. Anything, just to stay out of his reach. If he wasn't yelling at me and the kids, he was wanting to talk, as in 'Lay down, I think I love you.' We didn't need any more rug rats!"

She made a beautiful garden that year. There was even time for a pumpkin vine to bear fruit. She trained it around a little cage of rabbit fence filled with zinnias. "Pretty as a quilt," she said. "I'd go out there and rake leaves, pull weeds, plant stuff for spring. . . . You have to look ahead, put out a little hope, even if you rent." They were always moving. They rented their furniture and TV.

"Someday I'm going to have my own place, great big yard. Put down roots a mile deep. My house is going to suffer, but that yard'll look like a dream come true. I'm tired of praising other women's glads!"

She and her babies would stay outdoors till moonlight, working, enjoying the air, steering clear of Moore's moods. She was still a teenager herself, more like their babysitter than their mother. They played in the leaves, piling them, jumping in, scattering them around by the armloads. "The way Moore spends money," Rhonda said. "Fast as he can rake it in."

He never did without anything nice he could owe for. "You've got to go into debt to get ahead," he'd tell Rhonda. But somehow they never could get enough ahead to put a down payment on a house of their own.

"According to *Woman's Day,*" Rhonda said, "what married couples argue about most is m-o-n-e-y." She had showed Moore that article about credit counseling, with the local phone number already looked up. He threw the magazine out the window.

"Not down, but *up,*" Rhonda explained. "I guess it's still on the roof, educating the pigeons."

But he did agree to open a savings account, salt a little away for the boys. "The school says they all test way above average and Scott's maybe a genius," Rhonda told the counselor. "I figure we owe them more than life. I *know* we do. What's life if there's no future in it? What did my parents ever hope for me?"

With the opening of the savings account, and the balance slowly growing, Rhonda had begun to feel that they were on their way. Then that fall the tax bill came.

"See, we rent," Rhonda told the counselor. "No property taxes on that. But here was this bill for taxes on a lot in Breezewater Estates! Waterfront high-dollar location." Rhonda couldn't believe it. Since it was near her birthday, she guessed that Moore had meant it to be a surprise. She didn't want to wait. "I tooled up that day, while the kids were still in school, just to sneak a peek. Wouldn't you?"

She drove along hoping for a shade tree or two. "An oak," she decided. "If there wasn't one, we'd plant an acorn. There was plenty of time for it to grow." But when she got there, there was no oak, just pines and a trailer. "Not a house trailer, but a little bitty camper," Rhonda said. No one was home. "But there was sexy laundry of the female persuasion dripping on the line," Rhonda said. Patio lamps shaped like ice-cream cones, a barbecue cooker on wheels, and a name on the mail in the mailbox: *Rosalind*.

"I won't say her last name," Rhonda said. "Why blame her? She'd be as shocked to learn about me as I was to learn about her."

Rhonda laughed. "I knew it wouldn't last either. Maybe not past first frost. That trailer had 'Summer Romance' and 'Temporary Insanity' and 'Repossess' written all over it."

Rosalind was Moore's 122nd true love.

"That's how Moore is," Rhonda said. "He can't help it."

She had driven straight home in her Fury, a rattling old clunker she never washed, believing that the dirt helped hold it together. "I could poke my finger through the rust," she said, "but not the mud." Moore hated the whole idea of that car. She had had to cut a few budgetary corners to achieve it—buying it from Moore's father at his auto-salvage yard—and from spare parts made its fenders whole again, though of unmatching colors. She paid cash, like any customer off the street.

"No favors," she told her father-in-law. "Except don't tell Moore."

For six months she kept the car a secret, parking it down the block. But when they moved away from there, she had to explain it to Moore when the car showed up on their new street. It wasn't the sort of car you can overlook. She told him his father had made her a deal on it, for two hundred dollars. Actually, she had paid three-fifty, but the extra had gone for transmission seals, retreads, and a new battery. The muffler was shot and the car blew smoke, rumbled and shook in idle, and when she gave it some gas, the U-joint clunked.

"You're a goddamn redneck," Moore had yelled, over the racket. "I don't want to see that car in my driveway!" He stood between her and his leased BMW.

"Like rust was contagious," Rhonda said.

All the way home from discovering Rosalind's little trailer Rhonda thought up ways to pay Moore back for the rotten surprise, for using up their savings to make another woman happy. She considered cutting off the sleeves of his cashmere sweaters, or filling his shoes with dog mess. He was particular about his shoes. . . . "He'll pay out more for one pair than he gives me for a week's groceries."

Moore said, "I'd rather go without lunch for a month than walk on crappy leather."

"He threw the slippers the boys bought him for Christmas in the fireplace. J.C. Penney, not junk! They burned. I couldn't even take them back for credit on our revolving charge," Rhonda said.

"In my line of life," Moore said, "you have to impress people into respecting you. I don't mean pimp flash. I mean class. What people can *see:* tailoring, jewelry, gloves, car. . . . Look at my hands, like a surgeon's. And I've got a great smile. A fair country voice too; I could've been a singer. I could've been a lot of things; that's why I can sell: I have sympathy. I'm a great listener."

Rhonda said, "I don't know why I wasted my breath arguing with him when he came home that night. And the funny thing is, we didn't really argue about Rosalind at all. We argued about money. So I guess *Woman's Day* is pretty much on the ball."

Moore had said, "That bank account was my money. I earned it."

Rhonda said, "I earned it too."

Moore said, "Housekeeping?" with a mean look around the

kitchen: greasy dishes piled in the cold suds, laundry heaped on the dining table for sorting, and no supper underway.

Thus the stage was set for the final argument, with shots fired.

III

Corey, their aim-to-please baby, the one they all called Mister Personality now he was nine, told the counselor, "Mom tried to kill Moore, so he left."

Chip said, "In your ear, Corey," but Corey didn't take the warning, just went right on, adding:

"It was Moore's gun. He had to buy another one. She stole it and kept it. It's on top of the refrigerator in the cake box."

"It's not loaded," Chip said.

"That's what Moore said," Scott pointed out. "Then pow! pow! pow!"

"She only fired twice," Chip said. He had watched, the bedroom door open a pajama button wide, his left eye taking it all in, from the first slug Rhonda fired into the shag rug between Moore's ankles to the way the taillights looked as Moore headed west.

"I probably shouldn't have drunk those three strawberry daiquiris made with Campbell's tomato soup," Rhonda said, with her wild, unrueful laugh, "but we were out of frozen strawberries." She was a good shot, even when hammered with vodka. That was exactly where she had aimed. She raised the gun a little, between Moore's knees and belt buckle. "Dead center," she warned. "Don't dare me."

When she and Moore had gone to the firing range so he could teach her how to handle a gun, her scores had been sharpshooter quality. His were not.

"An off day," he had said. "Too much caffeine." He didn't give up coffee, but he didn't take her there again either. It was the only thing in their life so far she had been better at than him. "Except holding a grudge," Moore said.

Moore never took her anywhere much after they were married. She was no asset, pregnant. Before, they had gone to clubs and races. He liked the horses, but he'd bet on anything running, walking, or flying, any sport, so long as there was action. He'd scratch up the cash to lay down even if he had to pawn something. When he'd win big, he'd spend big. "You've got to live up to your luck," Moore said. He didn't like anything cheap or secondhand.

"Like my car," Rhonda said. "I used up my Fury in the demolition derby, so I've got me a Heavy Chevy now, a Nova with a 355 engine. That's what I race. Moore's dad is helping me keep it tuned." She had only been stock-car racing a year, just since Moore left. She had found a job as a waitress at the VFW, working from two in the afternoon till one at night—"No way to keep my health," she agreed, "but I had bills to pay off." She had got them whittled down to five hundred dollars by hoarding her tips and with what she saved on rent by moving in with Moore's father, in the trailer at the junkyard. "It's easier on the boys, anyway," she said. "They can ride the bus to school, and I know there'll be someone there to meet them when they get home, even if I'm at work.

"What I really wanted to do," Rhonda said, "was drive an over-the-road truck. You know my daddy was a gear-jammer, and I'm still not satisfied with what I know about that story. I'm not even convinced he's dead." She thought he might be out there somewhere, and maybe she could find him, in the truck stops, rest areas, coffee shops. "I'd know him," she said. "Something like that, you know in your heart." In any other city she and Moore had ever traveled to, she had slipped away in cafés, gas stations, or motel lobbies to check the phone directory, furtively flipping through the pages, hoping for news. She wore that questing look on her face, always searching the crowds, every stranger a candidate. Moore didn't understand. He called it flirting. They had more than one fight about it.

"Can you picture it? *Him* jealous of *me*? Maybe I did a little shopping, but I never bought any. I'm no cheat," she said. "All I ever wanted was a man who'd be there for the kids, be a real daddy, not run out on me. And here I am living out my life like history repeating itself.

"So how can I go on the road, full time, with three kids to raise? I can't leave them—don't I know how that feels? They count plenty in my plans, and they know it." Her brother was in prison in Texas.

"Nine to life at Huntsville," she explained. "He's no letter writer." And her mother had dropped out of sight two marriages ago. With no family, and no diploma, she had chosen the best she could, and made the most of her chances. When she read that poster for the demolition derby out at the dirt track, prize purse of one thousand—"That's a one, followed by three zeroes," Rhonda marveled—she had decided to go for it.

Moore said, "I have a bad habit of not taking her seriously, you know? Like night school. She was all fired up over that, too, but she didn't stick with it. I thought racing would be the same way."

Rhonda had dropped out of night school, never getting even close to an equivalency diploma because she was so off and on about attendance. Moore didn't like watching the boys while she was gone, and there was no nursery at the school. The boys made him feel tied down, nervous, even if they slept through.

"I'd give them beer for supper," Rhonda said. The baby would take it right from the bottle and hope for seconds. "They were good babies," Rhonda said. "And they were *his,* but so far as I know, he never once changed a soak-ass diaper or cleaned up any puke but his own." Night school hadn't worked out.

"Nowadays, they let girls go back to high school when they get married. Regular classes, every day. I don't know if I would have, even if I could have. Maybe just gone back once to show my rings." It was Moore's first wife's diamond. "I knew I was number two, and that he had a past, but I thought I was woman enough to handle anything that came up. I don't mean that dirty. . . . Well, maybe. I was pretty cocky back then, before I knew he was keeping score."

She had painted her number—78—on the racer's door. "My first demolition derby was my last. I said to myself, 'Rhonda, why spend your life mostly in reverse, taking cheap shots and being blind-sided? That's too much like everyday life.' I decided right then I was going to race."

"It's just like Rhonda to think she can get ahead by going in circles," Moore said. "And my old man—Christ!—this is his second childhood."

Rhonda said, "Did he tell you that he thinks his daddy and I are a number? He came back from California and found that I was living there at the salvage yard and flung a fit."

"Did Rhonda tell you that she's living with my old man now?" Moore had returned home in a van. He drove it over to the auto salvage to ask his father if he could crash there a couple of days, "Just till I got back on my feet," Moore said. "The van's a home away from home, I just needed a water spigot to hook to and somewhere to plug in my extension cord. There they all were, one big happy family, churning out to see me like peasants around the Pope. Chip had grown. He was as tall as I am, and Corey wasn't sure if he knew me any more . . ."

Rhonda said, "He didn't have a word for me. He told his daddy, 'I was just going to plug into your outlet, to charge my batteries. God knows you've been doing a little plugging into mine.' He said it right in front of the boys!" Rhonda said, heating up all over again.

Moore's father said, trying to joke them past the awkward moment, but only making it worse, "She's got her pick of dozens of good-looking guys every night at work, why should she settle for a one-armed, gut-busted, short-peckered old-timer with a gap in his beard?" The gap came from a welding accident years before. Moore didn't stick around to listen to his father or Rhonda explain. He backed the van out and headed away, fast, taking the three boys with him.

"I saw those California plates vanishing down Dayton Road and all I could think was: *kidnapping*." She called the state patrol first, "and then every damn number in the world, and threw the book at him," Rhonda explained.

"She hoodooed me," Moore said. "I don't just mean the writ. She visits palm readers. She's put some sort of hex on my love life. I'm telling you, since that afternoon, nothing. As in, zero, *nada*. It's not just the equipment, it's the want-to. I'm seeing a doc. He says it's in my head, says if I lay off the booze and keep up my jogging program—"

"They got Moore back on the road at the wring-out clinic," Rhonda said. "He's looking one hundred percent better."

"—I'll be good as new in no time. I've just got to take it easy on myself for a while. Avoid challenging and competitive situations. I'm not even working as a rep any more. I'm a plain old nine-to-five jerk clerk for B. Dalton. Just till I get my feet back on the ground. Something's better than nothing. You'd be surprised at what-all you can learn from books. I'm reading more now than I

did in all my life before, a book a night. What else do I have to
do, you know?"

"He was gone a *year*," Rhonda said, "and he never sent back one
penny of child support, one birthday hello, one Merry Christmas.
I'm lucky his daddy helped us out, or we'd have been on food
stamps from day one." It was Moore's father she had called the
night of their battle when Rhonda fired those two shots, the first
one burning into the carpet and the second—because Rhonda's
attention wandered an instant before she pulled the trigger—
breaking the picture window and their lease. His father came right
over, asking no questions, taking no sides, with a stapler and a roll
of three-mil plastic garden mulch to tack over the empty window
frame. By then, Rhonda had thrown all of Moore's stuff out onto
the lawn and was praying for rain.

IV

"Moore's dad is so special," Rhonda said. "He loves the kids like
they were his own, and they get a kick out of him too. But I quit
going over there to see him when Moore was along. We'd go on
weekdays instead. Mainly, Moore just hated going, but he didn't
like it when we left him home, either. When he's ticked off like
that, it's a pain."

Moore liked things better than he found them at the salvage
yard. The junk dealer made jokes about Moore's exalted tastes,
saying things like, "You must've hatched from the wrong egg. If
we didn't favor, I'd say the hospital must've pulled a switch on us
as to babies, but they won't take you back now, so I guess we're
stuck." And he'd offer Moore a can of beer.

Moore always brought his own brand, imported. "Green-bottle
beer" is what Rhonda called it. He wouldn't drink Old Milwaukee.
"A pretty good brew if you ask me," Rhonda said.

Moore used the Old Milwaukee cans for target practice, out
behind the junkyard office. "All they're good for," he said.

"He'd have been a better shot if he'd have worn his glasses,"
Rhonda said, "but heaven forbid anyone seeing him in glasses!"

"Sure I wear a gun," Moore told the therapist he was seeing
about sexual dysfunction. "While I'm breathing I'm toting. It's

legal. I don't go around ventilating people. I just want a little respect, you know? Who's going to argue with a gun?"

Rhonda had hated it when Moore used to shoot up the beer cans in the junkyard. The way it sounded when he missed and the bullet shattered glass in one of the junked cars. The way Moore laughed. Rhonda wouldn't let the boys play outside when he was like that. She made them stay in, watching TV. Moore's father stationed himself at the door, apparently looking at the clouds, talking about the weather like he was a farmer. He had all sorts of instruments on his roof and kept records—wind speed, humidity, barometric pressure, records for high and low, precipitation—and called the television weathermen to correct them when they made a bad forecast. "It was his hobby," Rhonda said, "till he took up racing. He'd talk about clouds while Moore shot those cans through the heart like they were Commies. And the kids would have the TV going full blast. It was crazy. And his daddy just fretting, saying, 'Looks like a son of mine would have sense enough to come in out of the rain.'" Moore got as wild as the weather, sometimes, and he'd stand out in the open, defying the lightning and the kudzu. Every year the vines and weeds grew nearer, creeping over the acres toward the trailer on the hill, turning the pines into topiary jungles. On the junkyard's cyclone fence the boys had helped their grandfather spell out H U B C A P S in glittering wheelcovers, and on the pole by the office a weathered flag lifted and drooped in the breezes. This was the flag honoring Moore's brother, who was still listed officially as missing in action. It had, over the years, faded like their hopes.

"Moore and him were jarheads—"

"—leathernecks—"

"*Marines,*" the boys told the counselor.

"His name's on the wall—"

"—in Washington—"

"—D.C."

Moore's father still wore the Remember bracelet. "It's kind of late to start forgetting," he said.

When the boys would beg him to tell about the war, Moore wouldn't say much. He took them to any movie about Vietnam, though.

"We've seen *Rambo* twice, and we're going again," Corey said.
Scott said: "Moore says it's about time—"
"—about *damn* time—" Chip said.
"—we won that war."

Moore's mother had died, not suddenly, and too soon, shortly
after Moore and the Marines parted ways. She had, some said,
grieved herself into a state. She insisted to the last that she was
really ill. She consulted physicians and surgeons in clinic after
clinic about the pain. Finally, she found a surgeon who would
listen. "Tell us where it hurts and that's where we'll cut," he said.
She lay on the bed and wept, to be understood and taken seriously at last. Her continuing hospitalization and petition finally
convinced the Marines to release Moore, on a hardship. He was
supposed to be needed at the junkyard. In his fury at how she had
manipulated events, Moore hadn't even come home. The junkyard
to him was no future. Within two years she had died, her last
surgery—elective—being the removal of her navel, after which the
pain finally stopped, and so did she. Moore had married by then,
and he and his first wife Lana, the stewardess, were on a holiday
when the news came of his mother's death. He didn't fly back.
"So far as I know, he's never even been to her grave," Rhonda
said. "I ask him, 'You want me to run by there and put some
flowers or something?' He never did."
After Moore's mother died, Moore's father sold their house in
Paulding and moved into the little trailer on the hilltop at the
junkyard. He narrowed his interest in life to the weather and his
customers. He paid his bills and filed his taxes. He didn't look for
much more out of life. He had pretty well gone to seed when
Moore brought Rhonda by for the first time, just married.
Rhonda waded right in. "I'm gonna call you Daddy," she said,
"because I never had a real one." She hugged him fiercely, and
didn't shy away from his rough beard, his cud of tobacco, or the
stump of his left arm. He never would tell her how he lost it. "I'm
no hero," is all he'd say. He let her wonder, through all those
years—making her silly guesses, calling him in the middle of the
night when she thought of some new way it might have happened,
driving by in her ratty old car with the boys, teasing, joking, giving

him something to look forward to. Gradually he got interested in things again, like a candle that gutters and then steadies and burns tall. She had to remind him not to keep buying the boys bicycles for every birthday, spoiling them, quick to make them happy, generous with his time and his money. He had been so sure his usefulness was over, he took his second chance seriously.

"Second childhood, I'm telling you," Moore said. "A classic case. I thought when Mom cooled that was going to be the end of him. It was a real shock, you know, coming so soon after my brother bought it in Nam. We were in New Mexico when we heard she had died. Or maybe it was Brazil. Anyway, I wired roses. My mom loved roses. She's where I get my romantic side. Not from my old man, that's for damn sure. Hardy peasant stock."

"Moore's daddy stood by me through some rough times, I'll say that much," Rhonda told the counselor. "I never had to wonder if he'd show up. Like that night after Moore left us and went to California—"

"I wasn't having as much fun as she thought," Moore said. "It's dog-eat-dog out there."

"—and Corey had some kind of breathing attack and turned blue. I thought my baby was dead!" When she looked up to see who was coming so fast down the hall, praying it would be Moore—"though that would be a miracle," Rhonda said—that he had somehow got her frantic message and for once come running: it hadn't been Moore. It had been his father instead.

"I was glad to see him, but it wasn't the same, you know? I just bawled."

"Aw, hell, honey," he told her, "He'll be back. If he can't make it to the funeral, he's bound to send an armload of roses."

"Maybe, right then, I could have fallen for him, you know? For being there, and being strong, and laughing at heartache," Rhonda said. "But we didn't screw up a good thing. We're still friends, the way it ought to be. He's always been my friend, the only one I ever had, in my corner every round." And now on her team, as she raced.

"I like winning," she said. "The night I won my first race—not demolition derby, but out on the track, running against the others—maybe that was the best night of my life so far. Except the night Moore and I made Corey. I'll still have to call that one the best. He's the only one where it was love, not lust. I still feel good about him."

V

"They like Moore better than they do me," Rhonda said. "He can give them stuff—trail bikes, waterbeds, tapes. When they're fourteen, they can get him to go to court and ask for a modification in the custody. They can live with him full time. Chip's old enough now."

"The other day," Moore told the counselor, "Corey was dressing on the run, as usual, and as he passed I called him back. 'What's that written on your shirt?' He's always into something. He looked. 'Just my name,' he said, and headed on out the door . . ."

"His *name*," Moore said. "C-o-r-e-y." Moore shook his head. "I thought his name was spelled with a *K*! Can you believe it? He's ten years old, and I didn't even know how to spell his name. That's when it hit me. That's when I started thinking."

VI

"I'm pretty much self-contained," Moore said.

"He doesn't even have a permanent address!" Rhonda said. "He blew in from the West Coast in that van—"

"Listen," Moore said, "we're talking custom conversion here, not telephone-company surplus. I've sunk 23K in this buggy already." He had pictures of it, inside and out, to show to anyone who cared to see. "Take my word for it, the ladies looooove powder-blue shag."

"—with status plates: SEMPRFI—" Rhonda said.

"There are no ex-Marines," Moore said.

"—and a bumper sticker: *If this rig is rockin', don't bother knockin'*."

Chip said, "Corey thought that meant if the radio was playing too loud!"

"Why do grown-ups act that way?" Corey said.

VII

"You want to know something funny? Rhonda thinks Lana—my first wife—is still around . . . as in, 'not dead.' She thought—all those years—I was divorced."

Lana had died in a plane crash. Not even Moore's father knew much about Lana. She and Moore hadn't been married but a few months. They had been good months, though. They had known each other for about a year, had been flying on Lana's pass—"The airlines give great incentives"—as husband and wife, and they decided to make it official. They married on one of their trips, and it was on their honeymoon that word came of Moore's mother dying.

"I knew I wasn't a jinx or anything. It's luck, and being home wouldn't have saved my mom. But I really took it hard when Lana died. She begged me to go with her. She didn't want to fly that day. They called her to fill in for another stewardess. She went, of course. Part of the deal. Duty. She was a class act, head to heel. Natural blonde, a lady. She could blush, you know?

"I flipped my lucky quarter—go with her to Orlando or sleep in?—and I still don't know if I won, or lost.

"Don't tell Rhonda what I said about Lana's being dead. She thinks we're divorced. All those years we were married, I told Rhonda I had to pay seventy-five a week alimony. Great little alibi. Kept me in incidentals. I spread it around. I never saved a thing for myself. It all went. I blew Lana's insurance in one week at Vegas. Let me tell you, they're crooked as hell out there, luck doesn't enter into it."

After Lana died, Moore drifted. He didn't see his father again till he married Rhonda and brought her by the junkyard.

"I don't know why I did that," Moore said. "Like I was asking his blessing or something. Maybe I just wanted a witness, this time. Lana was like a dream. None of my family had ever met her. That's why when she died, I just said, 'It's over.' I didn't want any sympathy. I've got a strong mind. I can control my emotions. I'm no quiche-eater, no hugger. . . . I never told anyone, but I put Lana's ashes right there on my mother's grave. I went out there at night, there's no guard, it's just a walk-over. They'd have got along, if anyone could. Lana knew how to treat people. She was Playmate caliber."

After that, Moore didn't think he'd ever feel good again, or want to. "But a man has to get out, meet people, take an interest." Rhonda happened along at the right moment. "Bing-o," Moore said. "I'm not saying it was a case of something's better than nothing—I had my pick—but I'm not saying I didn't fall for her either. It was more a case of body than soul. She could be pretty cute.

"Whatever it was, it was no meeting of minds. It was a struggle all the way, to teach her anything about style. All we had in common at first was the kids. I took her to the museum once. So what did she ask the guide? *'Where's the clown paintings?'* And she laughed over Golden Books like she was a second-grader herself. She never got tired of reading stories to the boys. Said it would make them smarter."

"In my whole life, nobody ever read me a book," Rhonda said. "How much time does it take?"

"She saved Green Stamps for a year to get that damn serene picture, big as a coffee table—white horse, red barn, kids on a tire swing, ducks on a pond, daises, the whole deal. I wish you could see it! We were married—what, twelve, thirteen years?—"

"Fourteen years," Rhonda said. "We were together fourteen years."

"—and I couldn't teach her a thing."

VIII

"I learned how to fix appliances," Rhonda said.

She said, "I took remedial English my first course in night school. After that I picked small-appliance repair and automotive. I didn't tell Moore. I said I was flunking history. History couldn't teach me how to wind a watch, much less fix one. You can save a lot of money if you repair things yourself. The library has what they call trouble-shooter's guides. I'd look it up, order the parts, get whatever it was going again, and charge Moore what Sears would've charged me for a service call, thirty-five dollars for driving up in the yard! Not to mention labor. I fixed Moore's adding machine one time. Those guys make eighty-five dollars an hour . . .

"I learned all sorts of little tricks to help out our budget. Moore never suspected half of it. Including me doing his shirts laundry-style. He wanted them just so. But on hangers, not folded. But if he had wanted them folded on cardboard and in those little bags, I'd have figured a way. He never knew the difference. He paid me what the cleaners charge. What I saved like that—including laundry, couponing, repairs, and cigarettes—went into a special fund. He was always running out of cigarettes. He'd give me money and say, 'Rhonda, run to the store and get me some Kents.' I got to thinking. I started buying a pack ahead of time just to save me running to the store, besides which I didn't like him smoking— we'd made a New Year's resolution when I was pregnant with Corey that we'd both quit, and I did, but he didn't. I made him do his smoking outside, not in the house, and yet here I was hiding them for his convenience. What was in it for me? If I think long enough, I'll find an angle. After I wouldn't let him smoke in the house, he kept his cigarettes in the car. I started going out there and taking a pack from his carton, just one pack—and when he ran out, I'd sell it back to him! It all added up. I'm a patient person, generally.

"Anyhow, that's the way I saved enough for the encyclopedia set. I didn't order it right away. I went to the library and asked them which one was best, no doubt about it. It's a good thing I *am* a patient person; they aren't giving those *Britannicas* away. When they finally arrived, I told the boys, 'Anything you ever need to know, begin looking right here.' I told them, 'You won't hurt my feelings any if you wear these out.' They do pretty good about homework, but in the summers, forget it. Scott's the only book-worm I've got. He was reading me about the Appalachian Mountains while I ironed the other day. Did you know, as mountains go, they're *young?*

"I told Moore I won the encyclopedias at a raffle. 'Pearls before swine,' he said. But I could tell he was pleased. He respects knowledge a lot.

"He wanted me to learn. He bought me *The Joy of Cooking,* and that's serious cooking, you know? A page and a half just for pie crust! And what kind of weather is it, and all that hoodoo before you make a meringue. . . . He didn't think much of my cooking but I kept trying."

"If she ever loses the can opener she'll starve to death," Moore said.

"When Moore had clients over, everything had to be per-fect-o. We had honest-to-god butter and cloth napkins. Wine in little mugs on stalks, what-do-you-call-'ems? Goblets, yeah. I told Moore I wasn't going to wheel the food in under pan lids, like at the hospital, but everything else was just what he wanted. The night we got friendly and made Corey, I had cooked Christmas dinner for his crowd. And they didn't show up. Not one of them. Moore thought it was a reflection on him. I said, 'Invite someone else, look at all this food!'

"He said, 'Nobody else rates.' I said, 'How about your dad?' and he finally said okay and went on down to the Quik-Shop to use the pay phone. Ours was disconnected a lot. I had a system on how to pay the bills: rent, electric, water, car payment, Gulf, Visa. Phone was the last on my list, and some months, like when insurance came due, no way I could stretch income to cover outgo. That's why I got so upset at the fancy dress he bought me to wear for entertaining. There I was in that lah-de-dah deal—he wanted me to look high-dollar for his friends: 'No goddamn jeans,' he said—and I could've cried to think what-all he spent on it, and the food too. He went wild when he did the shopping. Anything he wanted, he'd reach for.

"That party dress was something else. I don't know what you call that kind of merchandise; I'm no lady. Light-colored stuff, nothing you'd choose for a funeral or anything. Maybe I could wear it to get married in again. There's just so much you can do in an outfit like that."

IX

"If she gets married again, I won't have to pay alimony, will I? I'm only pulling down minimum wage now," Moore said, "but still I'm saving some. That's better than I've ever done in my whole life. I figured it the other night at Gamblers Anonymous: in the twenty years I've been on my own, since the Marines, I've pissed away half a million dollars. That's conservative.

"Listen, since California, I've tried it all: I've been dried out, shrunk, reformed, recovered, Rolfed, revived, acupunctured, hypnotized, and chiropractically adjusted. I've knocked around some: look at me. And I was no Eagle Scout to begin with. The doctor says it's natural to slow down. . . . I just don't want to chase it much any more. I've got something else on my mind, believe it or not. I'm taking an evening course at the vocational school: blueprint reading. Look at my hands!

"Chip's already saying he's going in the Marines when he's seventeen if I'll sign for him. That'd kill Rhonda. She's been making plans since day one. She's such a piss-ant about money, but I have to hand it to her, she's never been lost a day in her life. She's got this inner map, and she knows which way is *ahead*.

"I was the first-born son, just like Chip, and I can see a lot of myself in him. He wants to be the leader, set the pace, push things right to the edge, and over. At that age, you don't think about death, or even getting old. I want to tell him things, but why should he listen? Did I? I left home on the run when I was seventeen, and never looked back. I guess I thought the clock would stand still if I kept moving.

"I'm not worrying about any of it. One day at a time and all that crap, you know?"

X

"I don't trust him, he's up to something," Rhonda told her Creative Divorce group. She and Moore had been officially divorced—"I've got it in writing," she said—for two months now, and he had completely dropped out of sight, paying child support on time, but not—as he had done before the final decree—driving by the house at all hours, or tailing her as she went to work or shopping, or calling to ask the boys if she was alone, or seeing someone else. "He was even hassling my boyfriend," Rhonda said, "the one who drives a dozer." Rhonda liked him a lot.

"Jake don't tell me how to drive or dress," she said. She was back on her feet again, had her own place—having moved out of the junkyard, living now in a rented cottage with Chip and Scott and Corey. "So far, Chip hasn't talked Moore into filing for custody," Rhonda said. "Things are going too smooth," Rhonda said. She didn't see Moore all summer. She raced well, and when she won the Enduro, she got her picture in the local paper. She clipped the article and sent it to Moore in care of his lawyer.

She had cried her eyeliner off. "I looked more like a loser than a winner, but they spelled my name right," she said. She used a red pen and circled the car's number—78—and wrote across the picture: BET ON ME!

"I don't know why I did that," Rhonda said.

Then Moore called her at work.

It was her busiest time of night, and she told them to tell him she couldn't leave her post. He called again, in an hour.

"What if I buy a house?" he said.

She said, "You never talked like that when we were married, don't bother now," and hung up. Hard.

Moore called again, in a couple of weeks. "I sold the van," he told her.

"To pay off gambling debts," Rhonda guessed, even though Moore swore he wasn't gambling any more, or drinking either. "He's definitely up to something."

Toward Halloween he drove over to the VFW in an old flatbed Ford.

"Used," Rhonda marveled. "Moore bought a used truck!"

"What if I *build* a house?" Moore said. His credit was still so bad, he couldn't find a bank willing to take a chance. By then, he had completed the blueprint course at Vo-Tech, and had ordered plans from Lowe's.

When she wouldn't talk to him about it, he said, "Just come on out to the parking lot and see . . ."

When she didn't even let him finish asking her, he yelled, "Just walk out to the parking lot, goddammit! I'm not asking you to go to North Carolina . . ." Heads turned, and Moore sat back down, his face in his hands.

He wouldn't leave. He took a booth and ordered supper and waited. He didn't eat much, Rhonda noticed. The boys told her he had an ulcer. He didn't look much different, only a little more silver-haired. He had a tan like he'd been working outdoors, and he was thin. "Wiry, not thin," she realized. He looked strong enough. She told her boss, as she left on break to go out with

Moore to the parking lot to see the truck, "If I'm not back here in five minutes, call the Law."

Moore was so proud of that Ford, Rhonda tried to be nice. Conversationally, she pointed out, "I don't get it. It's just an old truck, tilting over under a load of—"

"—cement bags. That's for the footers," Moore said. "I'm doing all the work myself." He had books and books on carpentry. He read late into the night, and dreamed about permits and codes.

"He's building a house," Rhonda told her boss when she went back to work. "Who's the lucky girl?" he asked. Everybody laughed. Rhonda hadn't kept much about her divorce a secret, including Moore's list. Everybody knew why her race car was number 78.

"I talk too much," Rhonda said, for the hundredth time.

"She was vaccinated with a phonograph needle," Moore used to say.

All that fall he worked on the house. His father helped too, in the evenings—not on weekends, when Rhonda needed him at the speedway. The boys were over there every afternoon now. They'd come home and report: "Roof's on." Or, "There's going to be a ceiling fan." Or, "You oughta see the fishing dock!"

Moore called her at work. She kept her phone unplugged at home, so she could sleep during the days. She had gotten used to nightshift hours, and didn't even mind sleeping in direct sunlight, but she couldn't stand noise. Moore told her, "Chip's getting pretty good with that drywall stuff, you oughta come see. . . ."

"Not now, not ever, not negotiable," Rhonda said.

"It's finished," Moore told her at Christmas.

"You bet," Rhonda said.

There was a party going on at the VFW, and she could hardly hear him on the phone. ". . . you always wanted," Moore was saying, when Rhonda hung up.

She told her boss as she went back to work, "What I always wanted wasn't much."

XI

Rhonda was five days away from marrying Jake—his mother had already taught her to crochet placemats left-handed—when Moore fell through the glass while recaulking the hall skylight. "If he'd just done it right the first time," Rhonda said.

Instead, she spent what would have been her wedding day at Tri-County Hospital, watching Moore breathe. He wasn't very good at it, but better than he had been at first, when they flew him in by Med-Evac, on life support. He lay unconscious in intensive care for three days, and the first thing he said when he woke was, "Don't tell my wife."

Rhonda, hearing that, drew her own conclusions as to what he had been dreaming about while in a coma.

After they moved Moore to a private room, Rhonda went back to work. Moore had a week to go before they could remove the stitches, and he was still in traction. Rhonda told her boss, with some satisfaction, "It'd tear the heart right out of your chest to see him like that."

As she went by the bulletin board after signing in, she ripped the wedding invitation for her and Jake from under its pushpins, and dropped it in the trash. The jukebox was playing "You're a Hard Dog to Keep under the Porch."

"I hate that tune," Rhonda said. Nobody laughed.

XII

To clean up the glass in Moore's hallway, Rhonda borrowed a pair of heavy leather work gloves from Jake. "Keep 'em," Jake said. It sounded final. Rhonda said, "I'll get back to you," but how could she mean it? She had the boys to see to, and work, and the racing season, just beginning. And there was Moore . . .

Nothing had been done at Moore's house to clean up after the accident. Rhonda and Moore's father managed to staple plastic over the skylight.

"Reminds me of old times," Rhonda said, thinking of the night she had run Moore off at gunpoint, and shot out the picture window in the duplex on Elm Terrace. Her laugh echoed hollow in Moore's empty rooms. Moore hadn't bought furniture yet. When

Rhonda turned the key and first looked in—she had not been out to see the house before—she said, "This place looks like 'early marriage.'" She was determined not to be impressed.

There was no way, that many days past its drying, to get all of Moore's blood off the hall floor. She scrubbed at it till her head ached and her hands trembled. Finally she stood up and said, "I've got a scatter rug that'll cover it," and added that to her list.

Rhonda felt funny just being there. Not because of the blood-stains on the floor—one handprint perfectly clear where he had lain broken—but rather on account of the house being built on that very lot where Moore had installed Rosalind in her little love-nest camper.

Rhonda took Moore's last two Tylenol. His medicine chest had only shaving supplies, a bottle of ulcer medication, and cold remedies. She drank from his glass. While she was waiting to feel better, she made his bed and hung up his clothes, checking out his closet as she did—hardly enough stuff to fill a suitcase—and examining the titles of his books—mostly paperbacks, mostly how-to's—and prowling shamelessly through the cabinets. She was amazed to see generic labels. Most of the kitchen drawers were empty, sweet-smelling new wood. She dampened a rag and wiped sawdust out of one. When she found his revolver, she spun the cylinder—it wasn't loaded—and put it back. She researched the garbage in the cans outside, marveling: "Even his Pepsi's decaffeinated."

She found not one drop of Southern Comfort, and no green bottles . . .

It had been the imported beer that finally told Rhonda where to look for Moore's paycheck, in the closing moments of their marriage, when he had countered her arguments about Rosalind by saying, "You're such a piss-ant accountant, you'll find this money in fifteen minutes. . . ." He endorsed and hid his whole paycheck. It was Rhonda's for the keeping if she could find it. He gave her a week, not fifteen minutes. "Seven days," he said.

Rhonda had torn the house apart. Not while Moore was home, watching, but during the days, while he was at work. Sometimes she felt that he could see her, frantic, down on her hands and knees, reaching under the sofa, standing on a chair to look on top of the hutch, probing with her flashlight under the kitchen sink, searching the shoebag, laundry box, flour and sugar canisters. She'd have the house put back together when he came home at night. He'd walk in and head for the refrigerator, stirring through the utensils drawer till he found the can opener, prying the cap off the beer and sighing after the first quenching. He never asked, "Did you find it?" and she never volunteered, "No, dammit," but he knew, by Wednesday, that she still hadn't lucked across it. She had to ask him for money for a loaf of bread and some milk. "For the boys."

"I gave you all I had," he said, with that smile she wanted, always, to slap off his face.

Thursdy night he brought three paper hats from the Varsity Drive-In. "For the boys." They loved those Varsity hot dogs, but Moore didn't bring any home, just the hats. "I had lunch there," he explained. "Hot dogs wouldn't have kept." Corey cried and had to be sent to bed. Moore was mean in little ways like that, when he had been drinking. And it occurred to Rhonda, on Friday, as her week was about up, that Moore might not even have hidden the check. He might have spent it all, and how would she ever know? It made her crazy to think that. She was rubbing lotion on the carpet burns on her knees—the "treasure hunt" had taken its toll on her nerves and flesh—when Moore drove home. She ran to the kitchen, and was washing dishes, when Moore strode by to get his beer. The rule was: Nobody messes with Moore till he gets his beer. "I don't want to be greeted by what broke, who died, or where the dog threw up," Moore always said. Driving the perimeter home left him jumpy. Sometimes he went jogging. This time he didn't. He said, after his first swallow, "The week's up."

Rhonda didn't even turn to look at him. What need? She could see his grinning reflection in the window. Before he tipped back his head to chug the last of the Heineken, he added, so smoothly she knew he had been pleasing himself thinking up the words all the miles home, "Since you haven't spent what I gave you last week, why should I give you any more?"

She said, "How do I know you even hid it?" He had lied before. Hadn't she looked everywhere? Turned the house upside down?

With the boys helping, like it was a game? Even behind the pictures on the walls, in the hems of the curtains, in the box of Tide . . .

"You always were a lazy slut," he said, laughing. He drained that bottle and reached for another—sixteen a night; he was just beginning. As he raised it to his lips, Rhonda figured out the hiding place. Just like that.

"That's when I knew," she said later. But she waited till Moore had padded into the living room and shoved his recliner back, staring at the world news through his toes, before she made sure.

She opened the door to the freezer compartment—it always needed defrosting, it was the job she hated most—and reached for his special beer mug. He had had a pair of them, so one could be in use, and one on ice, at all times. But she had broken one washing it, and after that, Moore said, "Hands off." He never drank from the bottle, always from that mug. "So why had he been pulling on the bottles all week?" Rhonda asked herself, just as she retrieved the answer from the frost. There it was: the endorsed check, dry and negotiable in a baggie. She took it out quick and banked it, with a little shiver, in her bra.

She needed time to think, to make plans. But he noticed, somehow, that the power balance had shifted. Maybe it was the way she unzipped her purse and slipped her car key off the larger ring, and into her pocket. She pretended she was getting a stick of gum. He couldn't have known better, she was so cool. She even turned and offered him a stick, the pack covering the palmed car key. Maybe it was her light-hearted laugh. He looked sharp. Something gave her away. He scrambled to his feet and headed for the kitchen, returning in a moment, incredulous. "You found it."

"You betcha," she said, patting her chest.

"Let me kiss it goodbye, then," he said, reaching for her with both hands.

That's when Rhonda hooked the gun from his armpit holster. Without yelling—the boys were working on homework in the next room—she warned, "Back off."

Moore grabbed her pocketbook and swung it at her, missing, but spilling the wallet and other stuff all over the rug. He snatched up her billfold and dumped it. Pennies rolled under the sofa. She put out her foot and stopped a quarter. By then he had torn her checks into confetti and tossed them at her, and was bending her credit cards into modern art. "Try making it without me," he said. He slapped at the gun. "It's not loaded," he said.

"That lie could cost you," she said, and fired right between his feet.

"If Chip hadn't opened the bedroom door there's no telling what might've happened next," Rhonda said, to no one in particular. She was sitting on the fishing dock, her feet dangling in the cool lake. She slipped her sneakers back on and started for the house. Moore's father was still on the ladder, stapling weatherstripping around the skylight.

"We'll just make it," she called up to him.

They headed back to town to meet the school bus.

"Do you realize," she said at the outskirts, "he's got nineteen windows needing curtains, plus that weird kitchen door?"

XIII

Of course, this thing led to that. That's how home improvements go. The counselor had warned them, even before they filed formally for divorce, that what can't be argued or bettered, in therapy, is indifference. "No use pretending it's over when it isn't," the counselor said.

"Or it ain't when it is," Rhonda pointed out.

Her lawyer, when she asked him about it, had said, "I've seen clients replaying their vows in candlelit churches the night before heading for divorce court in the morning. And I've seen newly divorced couples get back together before the ink dries on the final decree."

"Then they're fools," Rhonda said.

She said, "Not me, not for Moore."

"Something's different," Moore said, on homecoming, looking around, easing through the doorways on his crutches. Six more weeks in a walking cast, then therapy. "Then back to normal."

"God forbid," Rhonda said, when she heard that.

Those six weeks passed somehow. One Saturday Rhonda looked up on her final lap as she raced by in her Nova: Moore and the boys were in the stands, ketchup and chili on their identical T-shirts, red dust on their identical hats, waving mustardy hands, yelling, "Stand on it!" as she roared by. She didn't take the checkered flag, though. She finished third. Cooling off in the pits, she didn't even open the long florist's box Moore handed to her. She laid it on the fender, saying, uneagerly, "Roses."

"Did it ever occur to you—" Moore began.

By then, Corey had the ribbon off and was saying, "Look, Mom."

"I could hardly believe my eyes," Rhonda told her boss. "I could've puked."

It was Levolor blinds for that weird kitchen door, custom-made, custom-colored, with an airbrush painting on them of Rhonda's racer, a red Chevy with 78 on the door and a driver looking out, looking very much like Rhonda, giving the thumbs-up sign.

"Happy Mother's Day!" they said. Moore's father had the card. He'd sat on it, and it was pretty well bent, but its wishes were intact.

"At that point, there wasn't a thing I could do to stop it," Rhonda was telling the doctor. "I know it sounds crazy, but he should've started right then building another room on the house. It was just a matter of time." How could she explain it any better than that? Was it her fault? Her resolution had failed in a slow leak, not a dambreak, but still, the reservoir was empty. "Full circle," she said to the nurse, a fan of docudramas, who had no more sense than to ask, "Rape?"

Rhonda said, "The fortune teller swore my next husband's name would start with a J."

"Will it?"

"Yeah," Rhonda said. "Jerk."

When she came fuming back from the doctor's, her worst suspicion—pregnancy—confirmed, she told Moore, "I should've killed you when I had the chance."

Moore laughed. "You don't mean that," he said.

Andre Dubus

DRESSED LIKE SUMMER LEAVES

(from *The Sewanee Review*)

Mickey Dolan was eleven years old, walking up Main Street on a spring afternoon, wearing green camouflage trousers and T-shirt with a military web belt. The trousers had large pleated pockets at the front of his thighs; they closed with flaps, and his legs touched the spiral notebook in the left one, and the pen and pencil in the right one, where his coins shifted as he walked. He wore athletic socks and running shoes his mother bought him a week ago, after ten days of warm April, when she believed the winter was finally gone. He carried schoolbooks and a loose-leaf binder in his left hand, their weight swinging with his steps. He passed a fish market, a discount shoe store, a flower shop, then an alley, and he was abreast of Timmy's, a red wooden bar, when the door opened and a man came out. The man was in midstride but he turned his face and torso to look at Mickey, so that his lead foot came to the sidewalk pointing ahead, leaving him twisted to the right from the waist up. He shifted his foot toward Mickey, brought the other one near it, pulled the door shut, and bent at the waist, then straightened and lifted his arms in the air, his wrists limp, his palms toward the sidewalk.

"Charlie," the man said. "Long time no see." Quickly his hands descended and held Mickey's biceps. "Motherfuckers were no bigger than you. Some of them." His hands squeezed, and Mickey tightened his muscles. "Stronger, though. Doesn't matter though, right? If you can creep like a baby. Crawl like a snake. Be a tree; a vine. Quiet as air. Then *zap:* body bags. Short tour. Marine home for Christmas. Nothing but rice too."

The man wore cutoff jeans and old sneakers, white gone gray in streaks and smears, and a yellow tank shirt. On his belt at his right hip he wore a Buck folding knife in a sheath upside-down. Behind the knife a chain that looked like chrome hung from his belt and circled his hip to the rear, and Mickey knew it was attached to a wallet. The man was red from a new sunburn, and the hair on his arms and legs and above the shirt's low neck was blond, while the hair under his arms was light brown. He had a beard with a thick mustache that showed little of his upper lip: his beard was brown and slowly becoming sun-bleached, like the hair on his head, around a circle of bald red scalp; the hair was thick on the sides and back of his head, and grew close to his ears and beneath them. A pair of reflecting sunglasses with silver frames rested in front of the bald spot. On his right biceps he had a tattoo, and his eyes were blue, a blue that seemed to glare into focus on Mickey, and Mickey knew the source of the glare was the sour odor the man breathed into the warm exhaust-tinged air between them.

"What's up, anyways? No more school?" The man spread his arms, his eyes left Mickey's and moved skyward, then swept the street to Mickey's right and the buildings on the opposite side, then returned, sharper now, as though Mickey were a blurred television picture becoming clear, distinct. "Did July get here?"

"It's April."

"Ah: AWOL. Your old man'll kick your ass, right?"

"I just got out."

"Just got out." The man looked above Mickey again, his blue eyes roving, as though waiting for something to appear in the sky beyond low buildings, in the air above lines of slow cars. For the first time Mickey knew that the man was not tall; he had only seemed to be at first. His shoulders were broad and sloping, his chest wide and deep so the yellow tank shirt stretched across it, and his biceps swelled when he bent his arms, and sprang tautly when he straightened them; his belly was wide too, and protruded, but his chest was much wider and thicker. Mickey's eyes were level with the soft area just beneath the man's Adam's apple, the place that housed so much pain, where he had deeply pushed his finger against Frankie Archembault's windpipe last month when Frankie's headlock blurred his eyes with tears, and his face scraped the cold March earth. It was not a fight; Frankie simply got too rough, then released Mickey and rolled away, red-faced and gasping and rubbing his throat.

The man had lit a cigarette and was smoking it fast, looking at the cars passing; Mickey watched the side of his face. Below it, on the reddened bicep of his right arm that brought the cigarette to his mouth and down again, was the tattoo; and Mickey stared at it as he might at a dead animal, a road kill of something wild he had never seen alive, a fox or a fisher, with more than curiosity: fascination and a nuance of baseless horror. The Marine Corps globe and anchor were blue, and permanent as the man's flesh. Beneath the globe was an unfurled rectangular banner that appeared to flap gently in a soft breeze; between its borders, written in script that filled the banner, was *Semper Fidelis*. Under the banner were block letters: USMC. The man still gazed across the street, and Mickey stepped around him, between him and the bar, to walk up the street and over the bridge; he would stop and look down at the moving water and imagine salmon swimming upriver before he walked the final two miles, most of it uphill and steep, to the tree-shaded street and his home. But the man turned and held his shoulder. The hand did not tightly grip him; it was the man's quick movement that parted Mickey's lips with fear. They stood facing each other, Mickey's back to the door of the bar, and the man looked at his eyes then drew on his cigarette and flicked it up the sidewalk. Mickey watched it land. The hand was rubbing his shoulder.

"You just got out. Ah. So it's not July. Three fucking something o'clock in April. I believe I have missed a very important appointment." He withdrew his left hand from Mickey's shoulder and turned the wrist between their faces. "No watch, see? Can't wear a wristwatch. Get me the most expensive wristwatch in the world, I can't wear it. Agent Orange, man. I'm walking talking drinking fucking fighting Agent Orange. Know what I mean? My cock is lethal. I put on a watch, zap, it stops."

"You were a Marine?"

"Oh, yes. Oh, yes, Charlie. See?" He turned and flexed his right arm so the tattoo on muscles faced Mickey. "U S M C. Know what that means? Uncle Sam's Misguided Children. So fuck it, Charlie. Come on in."

"Where?"

"Where? The bar, man. Let's go. It's springtime in New England. Crocuses and other shit."

"I can't."

"What do you mean you can't? Charlie goes where Charlie wants to go. Ask anybody that was there." He lowered his face close to Mickey's, so Mickey could see only the mouth in the beard, the nose, the blue eyes that seemed to burn slowly, like a pilot light. His voice was low, conspiratorial: "There's another one in there. From Nam. First Air Cav. Pussies. Flying golf carts. Come on. We'll bust his balls."

"I can't go in a bar."

The man straightened, stood erectly, chest out and his stomach pulled in, his fists on his hips, and his face moved from left to right, his eyes intent, as though he were speaking to a group, and his voice was firm but without anger or threat, a voice of authority: "Charlie. You are allowed to enter a drinking establishment. Once therein you are allowed to drink nonalcoholic beverages. In this particular establishment there is pizza heated in a microwave. There are also bags of various foods, including potato chips, beer nuts, and nachos. There are also steamed hot dogs. But no damn rice, Charlie. After you, my man."

The left arm moved quickly as a jab past Mickey's face, and he flinched, then heard the doorknob turn, and the man's right hand touched the side of his waist, and turned him to face the door and gently pushed him out of the sun, into the long dark room. First he saw its lights: the yellow and red of a jukebox at the rear wall, and soft yellow lights above and behind the bar. Then he breathed its odors: alcohol and cigarette smoke and the vague and general one of a closed and occupied room, darkened on a spring afternoon. A man stood behind the bar. He glanced at them, then turned and faced the rear wall. Three men stood at the bar, neither together nor apart; between each of them was room for two more people, yet they looked at each other and talked. The hand was still on Mickey's back, guiding more than pushing, moving him to the near corner of the bar, close to the large window beside the door. Through the glass Mickey looked at the parked and moving cars in the light; he had been only paces from the window when the man had turned and held his shoulder. The pressure on his back stopped when Mickey's chest touched the bar, then the man stepped around its corner, rested his arms on the short leg of its L, his back to the window, so now he looked down the length of the bar at the faces and sides of the three men, and the bartender's back. There was a long space between Mickey and the first man to his left. He placed his books and binder in a stack on the bar and held its edge and looked at his face in the mirror, and his shirt like green leaves.

"Hey, Fletcher," the Marine said, "I thought you'd hit the deck. When old Charlie came walking in." Mickey looked to his left: the three faces turned to the man, and to him, two looking interested, amused, and the third leaned forward over the bar, looked past the one man separating him from Mickey, looked slowly at Mickey's pants and probably the web belt too and the T-shirt. The man's face was neither angry nor friendly—more like a professional ballplayer stepping to the plate, or a boxer ducking through the ropes into the ring. He had a brown handlebar mustache and hair that hung to his shoulders and moved, like a girl's, with his head. When his eyes rose from Mickey's clothing to his face, Mickey saw a glimmer of scorn; then the face showed nothing. Fletcher raised his beer mug to the man and, in a deep grating voice, said: "Body count, Duffy."

Then Fletcher looked ahead, at the bottles behind the bar, finished his half mug with two swallows, and pushed the mug toward the bartender, who turned now and took it and held it slanted under a tap. Mickey watched the rising foam.

Duffy. Somehow, knowing the man's name, or at least one of them, the first or last, made him less strange. He was Duffy and he was with men who knew him, and Mickey eased away from his first sight of the man who had stepped onto the sidewalk and held him, a man who had never existed until the moment Mickey drew near the door of Timmy's. Mickey looked down, saw a brass rail, and rested his right foot on it; he pushed his books between him and Duffy, and folded his arms on the bar.

"Hey, Al," Duffy said to the bartender. "You working, or what?"

The bartender was smoking a cigarette. He looked over his shoulder at Duffy.

"Who's the kid?"

"The kid? It's Charlie, man. Fletcher never saw one this close. That's why he's so fucking quiet. He's waiting for the choppers to come."

Then Duffy's hand was squeezing Mickey's throat: too suddenly, too tightly. Duffy leaned over the corner between them, his breath on Mickey's face, his eyes close to Mickey's, more threatening than the fingers and thumb pressing the sides of his throat. They seemed to look into his brain, and down into the depths of his heart, and to know him, all eleven years of him, and Mickey felt his being, and whatever strength it had, leaving him as if drawn through his eyes into Duffy's, and down into Duffy's body. The hand left his throat and patted his shoulder and Duffy was grinning.

"For Christ sake, Al, a rum-and-tonic. And a Coke for Charlie. And something to eat. Chips. And a hot dog. Want a hot dog, Charlie?"

"Mickey."

"What the fuck's a mickey?"

"My name."

"Oh, Jesus—your name."

Mickey watched Al make a rum-and-tonic and hold a glass of ice under the Coca-Cola tap.

"I never knew a Charlie named Mickey. So how come you're dressed up like a fucking jungle?"

Mickey shrugged. He did not move his eyes from Al, bringing the Coke and Duffy's drink and two paper cocktail napkins and the potato chips. He dropped the napkins in front of Mickey and Duffy, then placed the Coke on Mickey's napkin, and the potato chips beside it; then he held the drink on Duffy's napkin and said: "Three seventy-five."

"The tab, Al."

Al stood looking at Duffy, and holding the glass. He was taller than Duffy but not as broad, and he seemed to be the oldest man in the bar; but Mickey could not tell whether he was in his forties or fifties or even sixties. Nor could he guess the ages of the other men; he thought he could place them within a decade of their lives, but even about that he was uncertain. College boys seemed old to him. His father was forty-nine, yet his face appeared younger than any of these.

"Hey, Al. If you're going to hold it all day, bring me a straw so I can drink."

"Three seventy-five, Duffy."

"Ah. The gentleman wants cash, Charlie."

He took the chained wallet from his rear pocket, unfolded it, peered in at the bills, and laid four ones on the bar. Then he looked at Al, his unblinking eyes not angry, nearly as calm as his motions and posture and voice, but that light was in them again, and Mickey looked up at the sunglasses on Duffy's hair. Then he watched Al.

"Keep the change, Al. For your courtesy. Your generosity. Your general fucking outstanding attitude."

It seemed that Al had not heard him, and that nothing Mickey saw and felt between the two men was real. Al took the money, went to the cash register against the wall behind the center of the bar, and punched it open, its ringing the only sound in the room. He put the bills in a drawer, slid a quarter up from another one, and dropped it in a beer mug beside the register. It landed softly on dollar bills. Mickey looked at Al's back as he spread mustard on a bun, and with tongs took a frankfurter from the steamer, placed it on the bun, and brought it on a napkin to Mickey.

"Duffy." It was Fletcher, the man in the middle. "Don't touch the kid again."

Duffy smiled, nodded at him over his raised glass, then drank. He turned to Mickey, but his eyes were not truly focused on him; they seemed to be listening, waiting for Fletcher.

"Cavalry," he said. "Remember, Charlie Mickey? Fucking guys in blue coming over the hill and kicking shit out of Indians. Twentieth century gets here, they still got horses. No shit. Fucking officers with big boots. Riding crops. No way. Technology, man. Modern war. Bye-bye horsey. Tanks." He stood straight, folded his arms across his chest, and bobbed up and down, his arms rising and falling, and Mickey smiled, seeing Duffy in the turret of a tank, his sunglasses pushed-up goggles. "Which one was your old man in? World War II or—how did they put it?—the Korean conflict.

Conflict. I have conflict with cunts. Not a million fucking Chinese."

"He wasn't in either of them."

"What the fuck is he? A politician?"

"A landscaper. He's forty-nine. He was too young for those wars."

"Ah."

"He would have gone."

"How do you know? You were out drinking with him or something? When he found out they didn't let first graders join up?"

Mickey's mouth opened to exclaim surprise, but he did not speak: Duffy was drunk, perhaps even crazy, yet with no sign of calculation in his eyes he knew at once that Mickey's father was six when the Japanese bombed Pearl Harbor.

"He told me."

"He told you."

"That's right."

"And he was too old for Nam, right? No wonder he lets you wear that shit."

"I have to go."

"You didn't finish your hot dog. I buy you a hot dog and you don't even taste it."

Mickey lifted the hot dog with both hands, took a large bite, and looked above the bar as he chewed, at a painting high on the center of the wall. A woman lay on a couch, her eyes looking down at the bar. She was from another time, maybe even the last century. She was large and pretty, and he could see her cleavage and the sides of her breasts, and she wore a nightgown that opened up the middle but was closed.

"Duffy."

It was Fletcher, his voice low, perhaps even soft, for him; but it came to Mickey like the sound of a file on rough wood. Mickey was right about Duffy's eyes; they and his face turned to Fletcher, with the quickness of a man countering a striking fist. Mickey lowered his foot from the bar rail and stood balanced. He looked to his left at Al, his back against a shelf at the rear of the bar, his face as distant as though he listened to music. Then Mickey glanced at Fletcher and the men he stood between. Who were these men? Fathers? On a weekday afternoon, a day of work, drinking in a dark bar, the two whose names he had not heard talking past Fletcher about fishing, save when Duffy or Fletcher spoke. He looked at Duffy: his body was relaxed, his hands resting on either side of his drink on the bar. Now his body tautened out of its slump, and he lifted his glass and drank till only the lime wedge and ice touched his teeth; he swung the glass down hard on the bar and said: "Do it again, Al."

But as he pulled out his chained wallet and felt in it for bills and laid two on the bar, he was looking at Fletcher; and when Al brought the drink and took the money to the register and returned with coins, Duffy waved him away, never looking at him, and Al dropped the money into the mug, then moved to his left until he was close to Duffy, and stood with his hands at his sides. He did not lean against the shelf behind him, and he was gazing over Mickey's head. Mickey took a second bite of the hot dog; he could finish it with one more. Chewing the bun and mustard and meat that filled his mouth, he put his right hand on his stack of books. With his tongue he shifted bun and meat to his jaws.

"Fletcher," Duffy said.

Fletcher did not look at him.

"Hey, Fletcher. How many did you kill? Huh? How many kids? From your fucking choppers."

Now Fletcher looked at him. Mickey chewed and swallowed, and drank the last of his Coke; his mouth and throat were still dry and he chewed ice.

"You fuckers were better on horseback. Had to look at them." Duffy raised his tattooed arm and swung it in a downward arc, as though slashing with a saber. "Woosh. Whack. Cavalry killed them anyway. Look a Cheyenne kid in the face, then waste him. I'm talking Washita River, pal. Same shit. Maybe they had balls, though. What do you think, Fletcher? Does it take more balls to kill a kid while you're looking at him?"

Fletcher finished his beer, lowered it quietly to the bar, looked away from Duffy and slowly took a cigarette pack from his shirt pocket, shook one out, and lit it. He left the pack and lighter on the bar. Then he took off his wristwatch, slowly still, pulling the silver expansion band over his left hand. He placed the watch beside his cigarettes and lighter, drew on the cigarette, blew smoke straight over the bar, where he was staring; but Mickey knew from the set of his profiled face that his eyes were like Duffy's earlier: they waited. Duffy took the sunglasses from his hair and folded them, lenses up, on the bar.

"You drinking on time, Fletcher? The old lady got your balls in her purse? Only guys worse than you fuckers were pilots. Air Force the worst of all. Cocksucking bus drivers. Couldn't even see the fucking hootch. Just colors, man. Squares on Mother Earth. Drop their big load, go home, good dinner, get drunk. Piece of ass. If they could get it up. After getting off with their fucking bombs. Then nice bed, clean sheets, roof, walls. Windows. The whole shit. Go to sleep like they spent the day . . ." He glanced at Mickey, or his face shifted to Mickey's; his eyes were seeing something else. Then his voice was soft: a distant tenderness whose source was not Mickey, and Mickey knew it was not in the bar either. "Landscaping." Mickey put the last third of the hot dog into his mouth, and wished for a Coke to help him with it; he looked at Al, who was still gazing above his head so intently that Mickey nearly turned to look at the wall behind him. The other two men were silent. They drank, looked into their mugs, drank. When they emptied the mugs they did not ask for more, and Al did not move.

"All those fucking pilots," Duffy said, looking again down the bar at the side of Fletcher's face. "Navy, Marines. All the motherfuckers. Go out for a little drive on a sunny day. Barbecue some kids. Their mothers. Farmers about a hundred years old. Skinny old ladies even older. Fly back to the ship. Wardroom. Pat each other on the ass. Sleep. Children. Fletcher used to be a little boy. Al never was. But *I* was." His arms rose above his head, poised there, his fingers straight, his palms facing Fletcher. Then he shouted, slapping his palms hard on the bar, and Mickey jerked upright: "*Chil*dren, man. You never smelled a napalmed kid. You never even *saw* one, you chopper-bound son of a bitch."

Fletcher turned his body so he faced Duffy. "Take your shit out of here," he said. "God gave me one asshole. I don't need two."

"Fuck you. You never looked. You never saw shit."

"We came down. We got out. We did the job," Fletcher said.

"The *job*. Good word, for a pussy from the Air fucking *Cav*."

"There's a sergeant from the First Air Cav's about to kick your ass from here to the river."

"You better bring in help, pal. That's what you guys were good at. All wars . . ." Duffy drank, and Mickey watched his uptilted head, his moving throat, till his upper lip stopped the lime, and ice clicked on his teeth. Duffy held the glass in front of him, just above the bar, squeezing it; his fingertips were red. "All fucking wars should be fought on the ground. Man to man. Soldier to soldier. None of this flying shit. I've got dreams. Oh, yes, Charlie." But he did not look at Mickey. "I've got them. Because they won't go away."

Again, though Duffy looked at Fletcher, that distance was in his eyes, as if he stared at time itself: the past, the future; and Mickey remembered the tattoo, and looked at its edges he could see beyond Duffy's chest: the end of the eagle's left wing, a part of the globe, the hole for line at the anchor's end, and *lis* written on the fluttering banner. He could not see the block letters. "I tell them I'm wasted, gentlemen. The dreams: I tell them to fuck off. They can't live with Agent Orange. They just don't know it yet. But fucking pilots. In clean beds. Sleeping. Like dogs. Like little kids. Girls with the wedding cake. Put a piece under your pillow. Fuckers put dreams under their pillows. Slept on them. Without dreams too. Not nightmares. Charlie Mickey here, he thinks he's had nightmares. Shit. I ate chow with nightmares. Pilots dreamed of pussy. Railroad tracks on their collars. Gold oak leaves. Silver oak leaves. Silver eagles. Eight hours' sleep on the dreams of burning children."

"Jesus Christ. Al, will you shut off that shithead so we can drink in peace?"

Al neither looked nor moved.

"Duffy," Fletcher said. "What's this Agent Orange shit? At Khe San, for Christ sake. You never got near it."

"How do you know? How far did you walk in Nam, man? You rode taxis, that's all. Did you sit on your helmet, man? Or did your old lady already have your balls stateside?"

"I hear you didn't do much walking at Khe San."

"We took some hills."

"Yeah? What did you do with them?"

"Gave them back. That's what it was about. You'd know that if you were a grunt."

"I heard you assholes never dug in up there," Fletcher said.

"Deep enough to hold water."

"And your shit."

Duffy stepped back once from the bar. He was holding the glass and the ice slid in it, but he held it loosely now, the blood receding from his fingertips.

"You want to smell some grunt shit, Fletcher? Come over here. We'll see what a load of yours smells like."

"That's it," Al said, and moved toward Duffy as he threw the glass. Mickey heard it strike and break and felt a piece of ice miss his face and cool drops hitting it. Fletcher was pressing a hand to his forehead, and a thin line of blood dripped from under his fingers to his eyebrow, where it stayed. Then Fletcher was coming, not running, not even walking fast; but coming with his chin lowered, his arms at his sides, and his hands closed to fists. Mickey swept his books toward him, was gripping them to carry, when two hands slapped his chest so hard he would have fallen if the hands had not held his collar. He was aware of Fletcher coming from his left, and of Duffy's face; and the moment would not pass, would not become the next one, and the ones afterward, the ones that would get him home. Then Duffy's two fists, bunching the shirt at its collar, jerked downward and Mickey's chest was bare. He had sleeves still, and the shirt's back and part of its collar. But the shirt was gone.

"Fucking little asshole. You want jungle? Take your fucking jungle, Charlie."

With both hands Duffy shoved his chest, and Mickey went backward, his feet off the floor, then on it, trying to stop his motion, his arms reaching out for balance, waving in the air as he struck the wall, slid down it, and was sitting on the floor. Through the pain in his head he saw Duffy and Fletcher. He could see only Fletcher's back, and his arms swinging, and his head jerking when Duffy hit him.

Al had gone to the far end of the bar, to Mickey's left, and through the opening there, and was striding, nearly running, past the nameless two men who stood watching Duffy and Fletcher. Mickey tried to stand, to push himself up with the palms of his hands. Beneath the pain moving through his head from the rear of his skull, he felt the faint nausea, the weakened legs, of shock. He turned on his side on the floor, then onto his belly, and bent his legs, and with them and his hands and arms he pushed himself up and stood. He was facing the wall. He turned and saw Al holding Duffy from behind, Al's hands clasped in front of Duffy's chest, and Mickey saw the swelling of muscles in Duffy's twisting, pulling arms, and Al's reddened face and gritted teeth, and Fletcher's back and lowered head and shoulders turning with each blow to Duffy's body and bleeding, cursing face.

Mickey's weakness and nausea were now gone. He was too near the door to run to it; in two steps he had his hand on its knob and remembered his books and binder. They were on the bar, or they had fallen to the floor when Duffy grabbed him. He opened the door, and in the sunlight he still did not run; yet his breath was deep and quick. Walking slowly toward the bridge, he looked down at his pale chest, and the one long piece of shirt hanging before his right leg, moving with it, blending with the colors of his pants. He would never wear the pants again, and he wished they were torn too. He wanted to walk home that way—like a tattered soldier.

Vicki Covington

MAGNOLIA

(from *The New Yorker*)

The reason I drive this blue Mercedes is because my baby son, Jackie, gave it to me. Jackie used to be a preacher. Now he teaches college in west Florida. He has a sailboat, cars, and a second wife with natural-blond hair. He was born during the Depression and needs his toys. My older two hate to hear that—they think I indulge Jackie. "Born during the Depression," they mock. Jackie almost lost his life in a boating accident after he got divorced and left the church. But that's another story.

Saturday is my day to take Mrs. Fraley to buy groceries. She's my age, but I call her Mrs. Fraley because I work as a waitress for her son at the restaurant. A family restaurant is a nice thing to have. I wait tables on Sundays for the church people. It makes for a busy weekend, since I take Mrs. Fraley to buy groceries on Saturdays. I am the only one my age who can still drive. It's a blessing I don't take lightly. God moves in mysterious ways, as witnessed by Jackie giving me this car. At first, I was thinking of all that money that might have gone to the poor. I see now that this car is a vehicle of God that carries old people to grocery stores.

Right as I was leaving to get Mrs. Fraley last Saturday, the phone rang. It wasn't Mrs. Fraley. It was Lila, calling from the nursing home.

"Come get me," she said.

"What's wrong?"

"Something needs to be done."

"What is it, Lila?"

"I'll tell you when you get here."

So I went to the garage and cranked up the car. I decided to see about Lila before going to get Mrs. Fraley. The nursing home is just a few minutes away.

The place is new. Lila's son put her there after she started behaving oddly. When I got there, I went straight to Lila's room. She was standing by a bureau doing her hair.

"Well, forevermore!" I declared.

"What?"

"Oh, Lila."

"What?" She pouted, knowing what I was talking about. She was wearing a light-green evening dress. Lila's got balls of fat in places. The dress made her look like a bunch of big grapes. "The ladies' auxiliary sent used clothes."

Why don't they sort through them, I wondered. Sending an evening gown to an old lady isn't funny.

I led her by the elbow down the hall past wheelchairs, old people, and struggling plants. We sat by a Coke machine.

"I want my car," she said.

"No, Lila. Ben said no car."

Ben is her son. He told me not to let Lila have her car. "She'll wreck it," he said. It's a Plymouth.

"Take me to my house. I just want to see if it's still there."

"I'm sure it's there, Lila."

"Take me."

"Well, it's my day to get Mrs. Fraley," I said.

"Take me to the car first."

"No. We'll have to get Mrs. Fraley first."

"Then you'll take me?"

I stared at her.

"I'd do it for you," she said. Her eyes were the color of weak tea.

Lila and I have the same birthday. We graduated from high school together in 1923. She married Hal Ray. I married Scotty. Hal Ray was an ordinary man. Scotty was a drunk. He was born in England, and his family crossed over when he was a baby. Scotty was a tiny man. His eyes were very blue. Jackie asked me once if his daddy was a good lover. My older two would never ask a question like that.

I steered Lila to the nurses' station and checked her out till lunch. Then we went to get Mrs. Fraley. On the way, Lila dabbed her face with a violet handkerchief.

"Why are you crying, Lila?"

"Hal Ray."

"Don't cry, Lila."

Hal Ray died several years ago. There are two kinds of widows: those who go on living and those who don't. Maybe I was lucky to have lost Scotty when I was fifty—young enough to keep going. My older two knew him for a drunk. Jackie believes he was only misunderstood. I'm the only one with the real story. It begins with the fact that I loved Scotty. What kind of woman can love a drunk? I slept with that question for years.

We drove to Mrs. Fraley's. She was standing on the porch, clutching her black patent-leather purse. Mrs. Fraley's hair is like cotton balls.

"Who's with you?" she called, holding the wrought-iron rail, taking the steps with care.

"Lila."

I held Mrs. Fraley's hand as she settled into the back seat.

"Thanks, sugar."

"Pleasant day," I said.

"That's right, sugar."

"Lila needed to get out, didn't you Lila?"

"We're going to get my car," Lila said to Mrs. Fraley.

"O.K., sugar."

"First we're going to the grocery store," I reminded Lila. "To do Mrs. Fraley's shopping."

"Don't mind me," Mrs. Fraley said. "We can do Lila's business first if needs be."

I glanced at Mrs. Fraley through the rearview mirror. Her eyes sparkled as she looked out the window.

"Daffodils," she said.

"My car's parked in the back yard," Lila said.

"O.K."

"Ben parked it there."

"How is Ben?" Mrs. Fraley asked. "And your grandbabies?"

"My grandbabies are at Auburn."

"That's good, sugar. What're they studying?"

"Ben shouldn't have parked the car in the yard."

"Ben knows what's best," I said to Lila.

"What if somebody stole it?"

"We'll take care of it."

"Have they put pets in your home?" Mrs. Fraley asked her.

"The grass will die under the car," Lila said.

"Mrs. Fraley asked you a question, Lila."

"That's O.K., sugar. I was just wondering if they got pets at her home. They're putting them in the homes. It's good therapy."

"It's an idea," I said. "Wouldn't you like a puppy, Lila?"

Suddenly Lila turned to face Mrs. Fraley in the back seat. "The reason I got on this dress is because the auxiliary sent it."

"It's right pretty," Mrs. Fraley said.

Lila turned back around. "I'm worried," she said.

"We'll be there directly."

Lila jiggled her car keys between her breasts.

"Well, forevermore," I said.

"What?"

"You need a purse."

"Hal Ray told me this is the safest place for keys."

"Well, he was right about that," Mrs. Fraley said.

I pulled the car into the parking lot and helped Mrs. Fraley heave herself from the back seat. She took a grocery list from her purse. Her sparkly eyes were bright as ever. I squeezed her hand, thinking what a great morning it was to be alive.

When Scotty died, I had no place to go. We never had a home in the true sense of the word. We moved here and there. Scotty got us a little service station. It wasn't much of a family business—just one pump—but it belonged to us. The only thing we ever owned except for a cow. My older two helped pump gas. Scotty sat in back and drank with his friends. Jackie was only a baby. Lila and Hal Ray let me live in a garage apartment behind their house after Scotty died. I cried a lot. After a few months, Lila began calling my older two. "You've got to do something about your mother," she told them. My older two, to this day, hold it against Lila that she had this attitude. I started working for Mrs. Fraley's son at the restaurant after a year.

"Oh, I look a fright," Lila said as we pulled into her driveway.

"Nobody's caring, sug," Mrs. Fraley said.

"Your ice cream will melt," Lila said to her.

"I didn't buy ice cream, sugar. Here, have one of these," Mrs. Fraley said, holding out a handful of lemon drops.

"Look," Lila said. "It's there."

Her old Plymouth stood amidst spring weeds. I helped Lila from the car. Mrs. Fraley wanted to stay in back with her lemon drops and grocery sacks.

Lila walked to her Plymouth, unlocked it, and sat in the driver's seat. "Please, just let me sit here."

"Don't crank it."

Lila stared ahead to the pasture behind her house. I walked around the place. The nandinas had grown tall and branched haphazardly onto the porch. Lila's home was always freshly painted when Hal Ray was alive. It was a perfect white box. In the spring, butterflies danced along the hedge.

I heard the old Plymouth start up. Lila made it roar.

"Roll down the window." I motioned to her.

She did.

"I'm going to drive it," she said.

"No, you're not."

"Just to the corner and back."

"No. Ben said no."

Lila clutched the steering wheel and gazed ahead to the pasture with those watery brown eyes of hers.

"Give me the keys, Lila."

Obediently, she turned off the ignition. "Let me sit here," she said.

I took her keys and walked across the weedy lawn to what was left of the garage apartment where I lived after Scotty died. I peered in. It was empty. It was a mess of cobwebs. I went to the fence and looked into the pasture. When I lived here, Lila and Hal Ray had a horse. The horse was a friend to me. I gave him apples and sugar from my hand. All I felt was that horse's tongue; the rest of life was numb. Scotty had been a drunk, but in the winter his body was warm in bed—even though I didn't touch it. Scotty smiled at me—even though he didn't speak. His blue eyes were like mute friends to me. The smell of liquor was a kind of perfume that dabbed me. Don't get me wrong—I hated it. But misery becomes an animal that lives in your house. It rubs your legs, crawls into your lap, sheds itself in summer all over your pillow and hands. And when it dies, you miss its claws. That's why I was numb. But the horse nudged me. In the morning, I looked at that horse and thought, This horse is brown; its tongue is like sandpaper. Hearing it neigh, I knew I still had ears. We shared the apples. I wore the same dress every day. It was the color of chocolate. Lila believed I was going crazy because of this. "Your mother won't change clothes," she'd tell my older two. The truth was I liked that dress. It was almost the same color as the horse. I'd stand in the pasture and look up. The land was flat and made the sky a big blue dome over me. I knew I was one solitary woman on this earth.

Death knocked Scotty's feet from under him. We'd been standing in front of Jackie's place in Florida, and a neighbor had taken a snapshot of Scotty with Jackie's kids. Scotty dropped to the grass, knees buckling like he'd been shot. That's how a heart attack works. Jackie held him. Later, we went through his wallet. It was empty. We kept hoping for a keepsake—something to save, a memory—but it was empty. It was good that Lila had the garage apartment. Hal Ray brought me hot meals. I had a bed, a rocker, a thermometer that hung over the sink. It had a rainbow above the hundred-degree mark. Lila was like a bumblebee—always darting all over the place, bringing ladies from the church, praying for me, baking me pies, trying to cheer me. I was Lila's project, her charity work. She felt that being married to a drunk had tainted and scarred my character. Oh, my older two hated that. The desire to both thank her and forgive her daily is a blessing I don't take lightly.

I shuffled through the dandelions in Lila's pasture. It's so futile trying to dig this type weed up, once it's deep. I wonder why people try. The sky promised only blue for the day. It was no secret spring was coming. Daffodils dotted the land, and specks of gold grew up the forsythia fingers.

I went back to Lila's car. "Come on, let's go, Lila," I said.

"I don't want to leave."

I opened the Plymouth door and took her hand. Like a fretful child she accepted. "Let's don't go yet."

"Mrs. Fraley might be getting annoyed," I reminded her.

I led her leisurely over the property, past the place where she once planted pansies this time of year. Nut grass grew over the rocks that had formed a square garden.

"Tell Ben to take me out of that home."

"He will when you're better."

"I want to come home."

"It'd be hard keeping up the yard."

"Listen," she said, stomping her foot. "I'm going for a ride in my car."

"No."

"I want my keys."

"There's no place for you to go."

"I'm going to the corner and back."

"No."

"I'm getting a lawyer."

"Ben owns the car, Lila."

"I'm calling a lawyer. I know one."

"It's no use fussing over this. Nothing will change."

Suddenly she took my wrist and jerked it hard, causing the keys to spring loose. When I bent to pick them up, she stepped on my fingers. I winced. I held the keys tight. Lila grabbed my hand, trying to pry my fingers. Her nails were hard as weapons. They dug into my skin.

We stood there. Gradually, Lila's hands went soft. I glanced over to where Mrs. Fraley sat in my back seat sucking a lemon drop, content. Side by side, Lila and I ambled over to her magnolia tree, where a mockingbird was perched. "Let's sit a minute," I said.

In order to make the magnolia a shade tree, you have to cut the lowest branches when it's young. You do this once a season. If you're smart, you do it in December so you'll have green on your table at Christmas when the family sits to carve a turkey. You decorate in this way. It is natural and festive. Magnolia leaves are not delicate. They only grow strong and handsome. Scotty and I helped Lila and Hal Ray plant this tree. It didn't bloom for many years.

John William Corrington

HEROIC MEASURES/VITAL SIGNS

(from *The Southern Review*)

When the call from the state police came, Rawls had just handed over the keys of a new Buick Electra to Mr. and Mrs. Miley, who had come down from Plain Dealing to pick it up. He stood out on the hot concrete smiling and waving as they drove away, the old man veering a little as he moved the car slowly out onto Highway 80, trying to get used to the steering while his wife leaned toward him, surely telling him to be careful, to watch where he was going, as she had for over forty years, no matter what car they had owned.

Rawls was still watching them as they turned west and seemed to vanish into the white glaring path of the afternoon sun as surely as if they had suddenly run into a snowfield. Then he stood there watching nothing at all until Mildred called him on the loudspeaker, telling him he should pick up line four.

He shivered as he passed from the moist heat outside into the air-conditioning that was always set too high in the showroom and the tiny offices. Then he picked up the phone. For some reason, he paused before he spoke. There was that odd hollow sound that one ordinarily hears only when the call comes from some other place. Rawls rarely got long-distance calls, and none had done him any good.

This one was worse than all the others. Trooper Peterson from

Minden was calling. Was he the father of Doreen Rawls? Rawls paused for a split second as if he had been asked to admit to an offense, as if his answer might involve him in something he wanted no part of. He had felt that way about Doreen for a long time. He was sorry and he wished he felt differently but that was how he felt and it was useless to try to feel some other way. Yes, he said when the fraction of a second had passed. Yes I am. What's happened?

What happened was that there had been an accident. A number of young people had been driving at high speed on the highway just west of Minden. The van had left the road and plunged into one of the abandoned gravel pits filled with water near the city. Passersby had tried to rescue them, but only Doreen had been pulled out. Trooper Peterson had six other calls to make, and as bad as this one might seem the others were worse. As for Doreen, she had been under the water quite a while before someone had managed to break open the rear door with a prise bar and pull her out. She had received emergency treatment in Minden, but the Parish Hospital was not equipped for medical problems of her sort, and an ambulance was taking her back to Shreveport. Did Mr. Rawls know where the Physicians and Surgeons Hospital was located? Yes. At the corner of Line Avenue and Jordan Street. Right. They should be arriving in less than an hour. If there were other close kin, Mr. Rawls should notify them. The doctors in Minden seemed unwilling to hazard a prognosis regarding Doreen Rawls. Was there anything else, the trooper wanted to know. Anything he could do? No, Rawls told him. Nothing he could think of.

Rawls put down the phone then, taking care to set it right in its cradle. No one on the floor appreciated a line sounding busy during the summer selling season. The sales manager liked to point out that sometimes that first contact over the phone brought them in, and if they didn't come in, you sure as hell couldn't sell them, could you?

He walked slowly over to the salesmen's lounge and drew a cup of coffee out of the urn. But when he touched it to his lips, he didn't want it. It was black and bitter and cold. It tasted like dying. He stood with the plastic cup in his hand as if he couldn't decide what to do next. He was still standing there when Malik, the sales manager, came up to him.

—It's terrible, Malik said, fishing out one of his most somber expressions and fitting it to his dark face. Malik was a Lebanese or a Syrian or something. He was a master of internal disguise, able on an instant's notice to rummage in the grab bag of feelings and moods he had brought with him in his blood from that hot archaic distant land, to find the one most suitable to the moment, to the American situation he found himself in.

—Listen, you go on, he was saying. —Nobody can work with something like that hanging over him. —If the Lawsons come in for the LeSabre, I'll take care of them. It'll be your sale.

Rawls nodded, realizing that Mildred had been listening in on the line while he was talking to Trooper Peterson. It was not that she was a snitch for the company or passing on private conversations to Malik. No, it was that Mildred had no life of her own. She listened in on calls when they sounded tense or spicy or important. Just to take a silent part in them. She rarely told anyone what she had heard. So far as Rawls could recall, only once before had she told Malik what she had heard. One of the salesmen, Crawford, had gotten a call from his wife, who told him she had taken an overdose of sleeping pills. Good, Crawford had told her. That's the best news I've had in years. Go lie down. Don't call anybody else. Mildred had told Malik, who had donned a ferocious expression, something from the old days in the mountains in whatever Middle Eastern country he had come from. He had told Crawford to phone the emergency squad, then go home and see to his wife. Not on your life, Crawford had said. She wants to go, she can go. What do you think? Dying's a big deal? It's not. It's not anything at all. If she doesn't kill herself, she's going to kill me. Christ, if she could, she'd kill all of us. Rawls remembered Malik standing there, Mildred, like a wraith, almost out of sight back near her desk. Both of them had looked at Crawford without speaking, and after a while the silence seemed to work upon him what Malik's words had not. He had shrugged and turned and left. He had never come back. Not even to pick up his last small commission check and his expenses. Someone said Crawford and his wife had moved to Gladewater, that he had gotten out of cars and was assistant manager in a hardware store. As far as anyone knew, the wife was all right. But then, Rawls remembered thinking, maybe she had been all right all along. Maybe she hadn't even taken the pills. Maybe it was some kind of a thing that Crawford and his wife did from time to time. Maybe it happened whenever she wanted to move on.

—They're good customers, Malik was saying. Rawls tried to pay attention to him. —They'll understand. A family emergency. I'll check them out in the car. It's your sale. Everybody knows. They all understand. You go on over to P & S.

Rawls looked around. The other salesmen, the ones who were not working a customer, were watching Malik and him. Over there, standing by her desk, Mildred was watching, no determinate expression on her face. As if she were waiting for something more to happen. As if, perhaps, she was expecting Rawls to break down and cry, leaning forward on Malik's shoulder, sobbing about his only child, his little girl.

Malik licked his lips, his eyes still on Rawls. He was waiting for Rawls to say something. It seemed something needed to be said, but Rawls stood in silence.

—I mean it, Malik said again, as if to fill the void or prompt Rawls into speech. —I mean it. We all understand.

Rawls took Malik's word for that. Still, it seemed amazing if it was true. If Malik understood, and the Lawsons were going to understand, and Mildred and all the other salesmen understood, why couldn't he understand? It was not that he doubted they understood. People seem to understand a great deal that Rawls could not understand. Or perhaps what he did not understand was what they meant when they said they understood. Probably it was some kind of convention. It didn't mean that anyone actually grasped a situation, could place themselves within it, live it for a little while on their own. It must mean that they knew such a situation existed, and that it conformed in some fashion to circumstances not so out of the ordinary as to require lengthy explanation.

Something resembling panic seemed to crouch in Malik's eyes. He could not look away from Rawls. As if he suspected that in his silence Rawls was kneading the loss, the desolation of his daughter's condition, and might, at any moment, launch himself in blind

and purposeless vengeance against any fixture of the world standing nearby.

—You go on now, Malik said, and Rawls found himself turning,
walking through the electric eye controlling the main door that
led outside into the August heat.

Out there, the sun stood halfway down the sky, but the concrete
pavement seemed to waver, and the roofs and hoods of the ranks
of parked cars waiting to be sold shimmered and eddied as if their
blazing metal were melting, subliming away under the sun.

Rawls looked up to the sky. There were no clouds at all. No
hope of an afternoon shower to break the heat and soften the
evening. The sky was a delicate azure with a great bronze ball
standing in its center. As he looked across the concrete toward his
own car, the heat rising from the pavement bent the very space
between, making it seem that the car was moving away from him
even as he walked toward it. As if in strange evocation of Zeno's
hapless arrow, Rawls was walking toward a vehicle poised at a
horizon the distance to which would never lessen, never close, no
matter how rapidly he moved, how earnestly he sought to reach
his goal.

Of course it was only a trick of the light, but when he stopped
beside his auto and reached out to open the door, the shock of the
hot metal on his hand brought him back to what other people
understood as reality. He opened the windows quickly, gingerly,
and then stood outside a while longer to let the heat inside come
down to a temperature he could bear.

As he cranked the engine and started off, the air-conditioning
unit on his demonstrator began blasting at him. At first the air was
warm and humid but the fan was on high and in a moment or two
Rawls found himself chilled by the jets of cold air playing across
his cotton jacket and soaked shirt.

Rawls did not find it necessary to think as he drove across the
Texas Street Bridge toward the P & S Hospital. He was not given
to thinking in a discursive mode. What happened in his mind,
aside from those moments when he had to calculate the price of
an automobile or the difference between a new car and a trade-in,
had nothing to do with thinking. What went on within him was
play of images. Just now he was remembering a garden he had
seen somewhere long ago. Incredible flowers, large and colorful,

carefully tended. Someone had gone to great pains with the garden, spent much time with it. Perhaps hundreds of people over hundreds of years had tended to it. Standing in the midst of that garden, it was impossible to see the end of it. He had not the least idea when or where he had seen the garden. Perhaps he had never seen it at all. Sometimes he imagined things. Not thoughts or ideas. Simply images.

The garden seemed to eddy and swirl like the air above the hot concrete back at the dealership and then it dissolved and he could not remember it any longer. There remained no more in his mind than the abstract category of Garden. As if, moment to moment, there was no permanent Rawls, only that one who remembered a thing and then another who remembered something else. The Rawls who recalled the garden had gone on now.

What he should be thinking of was Doreen. He had not seen his daughter in almost two years. She was going to college, when last he had heard, at LSU-Shreveport. Even though they lived in the same town, they never saw one another. There was no reason that they should. No reason to pretend that the tenuous bond of blood somehow stapled them together. Each month, when he paid his other bills, his utilities and his rent, he made out a check to Doreen and mailed it to the last address he had for her. Some post office box number at the university. He was sure she received the checks. Each month they would return to him endorsed in a wide thin spidery hand he did not recognize but assumed belonged to his daughter. Those checks going out, returning with her name scrawled on the back, were the sole nexus between them.

It had been that way since the divorce. Since Rawls and her mother had parted and gone their own ways almost two and a half years ago. Not because Doreen loved her mother and despised him for deserting her or causing her great pain, neither of which was true. More nearly because the parting gave her something like an excuse to be rid of them both.

The truth was, Rawls and his daughter had not gotten on. Sometime during her adolescence whatever binds father and daughter together had failed them. There had been no argument, no ugly scene. No confrontation at all. They had just gone away from one another. He could remember when Doreen was very small and ran around the house like a small bright puppy, poking here and there, propelling herself into his lap at inopportune moments. He had pretended to be a pony for her, and a dog and a camel. Rawls smiled then, recalling the menagerie of creatures he had found within himself for her sake, into which his tiny daughter had transformed him.

Just then he realized that he was very hot again. The airconditioner was blowing, but it seemed to do no good. It was as if he were in the depths of a jungle. Sweat poured down through his thin hair, down his face, especially from his eyes. Then he realized that it was because he was sitting in his car with the windows up and the motor turned off. He was parked in front of a rundown bar on Louisiana Avenue. He could not remember pulling in or cutting off his motor. He could not even remember wanting a drink. But he got out of the car and started toward the scarred wooden door as if behind it lay the end of a pilgrimage. He knew that above him, were he but to lift his eyes, the tall hospital building reared like an outsized tombstone behind the jumble of buildings that housed a gift shop, a convenience store, a karate training institute, and the bar.

It occurred to Rawls that he disliked hospitals. Nothing good happened in them. No, that was wrong. He knew better. People got born in them. People who would otherwise die were saved in them. Why would he have thought to think that nothing good happened in hospitals? New life and life saved was good. Everyone understood that.

He stepped inside the door thinking that perhaps everyone's understanding about hospitals was like their understanding of his present situation. Another convention, another attitude. No, he kept being wrong. Perhaps it was the phone call from the trooper. The good is a situation everyone has agreed to evaluate that way. The birth of a child *is* good; the death of a murderer or rapist *is* good. It is the same with the bad. No one goes around inventing goods and bads for himself. You can't live that way. Situations become imponderable if you don't take them as they are given.

The bar was dark and quiet. There was a blur behind it which, as his eyes became accustomed to the subdued light, took on the form of a tall lengthy mirror framed on every side by dozens of bottles. The stools in front of the imitation mahogany bar were all empty. One woman was sitting in a booth. He squinted and found himself in the distant mirror. Tall, thin, reddish hair, shoulders sloping and with no reasonable hope of ever straightening up again. He considered that his own presence seemed of no account to him. He did not despise himself or walk about weighed down with some unspecified subterranean guilt. He was simply indifferent to himself. He would not miss himself if he were to find one morning that he was not there. Which thought he recognized obscurely as being absurd. He sat down on a stool too small for him and asked the bartender who had materialized out of the gloom for a double shot of sour mash. Rawls almost laughed aloud as it occurred to him that he did indeed value his presence when there was good whiskey to be drunk. He spoke to the bartender again and asked for a beer with his whiskey. A draft would be fine. Brand names meant nothing to him, especially now. He was drinking to quell the tightness he had felt inside since the call from Trooper Peterson, since Malik had come up to him and used him to show the depth and quality of his fellow-feeling. He thought he would have another couple of drinks and then find the pay phone and call his former wife, Delphine. Any way it went, he had that to do. He would as soon not do it. He didn't want to do it, because he did not like talking to Delphine anymore now than when they were married. But it was no big thing, not some kind of dread that clutched him. Two more fast shots of whatever kind of sour mash this was would make the call inconsequential. Still, he wondered if he was obliged to go to the hospital first and find out what he could about Doreen before he made the call. Maybe he had ought to do it that way. After all, you don't just call a woman and tell her her little girl is in the hospital after being underwater for a long time, and that, No, you don't know a thing more because it was hot on the way to the hospital and you stopped off for a drink or two. Delphine would not understand that. She understood almost nothing, and she would not understand that. Which struck Rawls as strange, since he *did* understand it. He tossed down the whiskey, chased it with beer, and gestured for another round. It was no convention this time. He would do better with a couple of drinks. He would not say something strange to the doctor or start in to tell how he had been a llama once for Doreen. With a pillow for a saddle. He would simply stand there wearing a pleasant expression and listen to whatever the doctor had to say and respond as ap-

propriately as he could. He would likely even be able to avoid the
questions that were flooding across the surface of his mind in a
thin depthless stream, too attenuated to fix themselves in words
just yet.

He finished the second whiskey and curled a finger at the bartender for a third. This would do it. He was cooler now and feeling
better than all right. Whatever they told him, he would just listen
and say nothing. He would not mention the old scruffy stuffed
animals that lay in a heap on the daybed on the back porch of the
house he still occupied, where Doreen had grown up, where he
had once been married. The puppy was named Jiggs, the snake
Olaf, the frog Feed. Don't ask why. Doreen named them and loved
them and played with them and then one day went on, leaving
them behind. He should have thrown them away. He had not
gotten around to it. Not in several years. Situations drift, he considered. One day you feel strongly about something, another day
the feeling is barely perceptible. But you average. You can always
average. More or less, one thing taken with another, you love your
wife and your child more than you don't. Moreover, there is the
relationship itself to take into account. If it is your father or your
son, your wife or your daughter, ordinarily you will not want that
connection broken. You do not lose a relationship if you can avoid
it. Someone had said, You Are What You Eat. No, most of what
we eat turns to shit. We are our connections, our relationships.
Whether we like them or not. Rawls had learned that long ago.

He had never enjoyed selling cars. But he seemed to be very
good at it. People coming to the dealership liked him and trusted
him. They believed for some reason that he would be honest with
them, that he wished them well. Mildred, who handled the switch-
board, thought she understood. It's the way you smile, she had
told him. That little smile that says, Look, this is the Great American Game. But I don't take it seriously. I leave that to the rest of
them who think that one day they'll own a place like this and
smoke big cigars smuggled in from Cuba. Me? I'm just like you.
Making a living, trying to have a good day. Make me an offer. I
might take it.

Rawls had smiled at that. The truth was that he was honest. Not
out of some moralistic vision taught or discovered, but because it
was difficult and demanding to lie and misrepresent what he sold,

and because he did not have enough imagination to create alternative realities. He was not clever and it did not bother him that he was not. He had become a master of the soft sell, simply standing with a customer and looking over the auto that he had examined a thousand times before, without praise or condemnation. Rawls could answer all their questions, quote facts and figures, compare costs. But for the rest it seemed to him that he served like that mirror behind the bar. He reflected the customer's appetites, his dubieties, his desires, his concerns. When he was talking to Rawls, the customer might as well be talking to himself. But that was what customers wanted. They did not want to be pushed or discouraged. You sold cars by becoming part of the customer's situation, by standing in the customer and becoming part of his own interior monologue. That is what a relation means, Rawls thought. That is how you sell things. If the buyer and the seller cease to be two, become one, then the transaction is with oneself. A transaction with oneself is usually a safe transaction. One sells what one wishes to buy; one buys what the seller fancies.

—What do you think, a customer would ask quietly, intensely.

—I don't know, Rawls would answer with equal seriousness. He couldn't know. The customer didn't know yet. —I think . . .

—Yes, the customer would say, and continue looking, thinking, shopping, selling one car or another to Rawls and to himself. When the customer was done, Rawls would let him know.

—Don't you reckon . . .

—Uh-huh. That damn tan one with the white top.

—I believe so.

He was on his third double when he noticed the illuminated beer sign hung before the mirror back of the bar. It was an old sign. Busch Bavarian. Rawls did not know whether that brand was being brewed any longer. Once it had been popular throughout the South, but it seemed that no one ordered it anymore. The sign was brilliantly colored. Almost abstract mountain peaks stood gleaming in sunlight with a clear stream sluicing down through a deep gorge between the mountains. The thin rill of water was actually clear plastic tubing behind which some kind of oil roiled and turned slowly, poor imitation of bright water, filled with bubbles. The oil did not flow as water does. It probably never had even when the sign was new. The effect was as if, amidst the sketchy clefts and shadowed slabs of granite, the water was falling down from high above in slow motion. Because the chill stream appeared to flow, to tumble laboriously over the crudely colored rocks and boulders and down to some green plain of reality out of sight beneath the bottom of the sign. Down there, the mirror took up where the sluggish stream of fraudulent water ceased.

In the mirror, he could see his face reflected. His eyes looked dark, ringed. It looked as if he had forgotten to shave this morning. He was without expression, a mirror reflecting a mirror. Doreen, in a fit of spite and anger, had once told him that he wasn't in it, that you couldn't watch and listen all your life and still be in it. She had said he was out of it and somehow when she said it, he had understood what she meant beyond the silly argot phrases cribbed from her young crowd.

He looked back to the slowly racing, somnolent stream of plastic water tumbling in endless cycle through the beer sign. He watched it then for a long time and it seemed after a while that the water took on some character of reality, that he could almost hear it buffeting the rocks, feel that cold distant wind that must surely blow down from the mist-muffled slopes above. The wind coursed through his body like a god no one had told him of. The water flowed in his veins and his head, worn and craggy, jutted up into the clouds where the pale sun gave weak pastel light but no warmth at all. Up there, the clouds moved slowly with great measure across the azure canopy of the sky, and the meaning of their staid configurations was to stand in the stead of that which was not to be seen, conditionless, which did not change at all. As a mirror remains unchanged despite the endless nervous play of shadows across its face.

Rawls tore his eyes from the sign and found that his brief concentration on it had once more made the bar seem even darker than it was. No, that was not right. The bar was as dark as it was. The change was in himself. Except that mirrors do not change. They tell the truth unless they are warped or broken. He could see the blur of the bartender far down the length of the bar. He seemed to be talking to someone who had come in and was sitting on a stool. He could see nothing beyond. He took out a bill, squinted at it, decided that it was sufficient, and set it down beside his empty glass. He felt much better now. He felt better than he had in a long time. But as he turned on the stool to step down, vertigo seemed to flow over him like that gelatinous oil pretending to be water in the sign, almost carried him off the stool. He reached behind him and took hold of the edge of the bar. His fingers pressed into the bland plastic as if they were caught in the minute crevices of a mountain ledge, holding him from the abyss below. He was all right after a moment. Not all right enough to stand and stride through the door, outside into the heat. But drawn back from that sickening moment in which the liquor's pleasure seemed to melt into dread. Then he realized that it was not the whiskey. It was that now he would have to go to the hospital. It was time he went there. By any measure of time, the ambulance must have arrived long ago. It was like a summons to jury duty or a parking ticket. It was a situation. You could not choose what you would do because if you did not do what people do, what everyone does, the situation would only thicken, change from a general situation of the kind in which everyone finds himself from time to time into one specific to you. To be safely out of things, you are obliged to do what everyone does, whatever is conventionally done. Ordinarily, you are called on to do no more, and then you are, in one way or another, sooner or later, relieved of the situation.

Rawls wondered if that was what Doreen had meant. Was it because he always did what was required so that he would have to do no more that made her say he was not in it? He recalled that before she became involved with people in saffron robes, she had belonged to some youth group at the college. She had talked a great deal about commitment then. At the very first, he had supposed for some reason that she was referring to the legal process by which people bereft of their senses or out of control might be placed in mental institutions by their relations. She had spoken of the need for commitment and he had agreed, saying it seemed many people might be better off in an asylum than on the streets. Doreen had stared at him in anger when she realized what he was saying. That was not what she had meant, and he knew it.

He had been surprised by her vehemence. No, he had not known it. If he had, he would have responded otherwise. When he realized that by commitment Doreen meant the investment of all one's emotion in some cause or task or idea, Rawls was still not sure what the fuss was about. Such an investment itself seemed evidence of derangement. Thus to be committed suggested the need for commitment.

Delphine, his wife, had shaken her head with an ugly laugh. Not because she had any belief in what Doreen was committed to at the moment—something faintly comic like pouring pig blood into government records of some kind—but because by then she missed no chance to sneer at Rawls. No ally was so base, no notion so grotesque that Delphine would not rally to it to take sides against him.

It did not bother him. By then, he could hardly remember a time when he had cared what Delphine thought, or whether she was even there with her puling and complaints about the money he brought home. Thus it had not bothered him when she moved out, either. She had gone to stay in an apartment with Doreen, mixed with her friends, and listened to their latest commitments without comprehension, without interest, happy simply to be included in something intense and strongly felt—whether it meant anything or not.

Before she left, Delphine had told him, in a moment of subdued rancor, that life had not turned out at all as she had hoped. It had all gone utterly wrong somehow. She had intimated that, in some way she could not quite grasp, the failure of her hopes had to do with him. Rawls had not taken what she said to heart. He had found over the years that there was no real relation between the words Delphine spoke and any other object or activity in the world. The words were more in the way of a report on the weather in her soul: dry, bleak, a permanent harsh fetid wind blowing over lifeless sexual soil, broken spiritual slate, fractured emotional gravel. The last thing Delphine had said before she left was that she had come to see that she required some kind of commitment in her life. Rawls had said nothing, thinking that Delphine seemed likely to have her requirement fulfilled. One way or another.

He felt better then. The vertigo had passed. He could see again in the vast gloom of the bar and made his way to the door. Outside, the heat was still there in its imponderability, its stark presence. He strode through it to his car as if he were pressing against waves in a shallow inland sea. When he started to get into the car, an eddy of superheated air flowed around him like a whisper from

Delphine's mind, its current making him pause. He reached over, started the engine, and turned on the air conditioner. After a moment, he climbed inside and shut the door as the heat fell away and he found himself in the mountains again. It did not matter that he could not see them as he had in that chipped beer sign in the bar. They were there, and he stood among the juts and dips of dark rock, looking down to the streambed filled with coarse gravel. Just above, the snowfield began, its edges frayed and melted like old lace, tiny streams of chill blue water dripping and spilling down to stone worn smooth that had not been dry in a thousand millennia.

The field rose on a steep incline upward into thick clouds. There was a faint drizzle, and the misty rain fell, pocking the stream that flowed by carrying away the melt from the edge of the snow. The clouds above were low and thick, almost of a piece with the dense mist that seemed to be gathering around him there, swirling over the boulders, soothing the broken heavy spears of granite where ice rested slim and transparent in cracks and breaks. It seemed to be twilight there, but he was certain it was not, because now and then the clouds and mist seemed to thin, and he could see a slash of lighter sky above, against which the rocks stood in silent frozen definition.

Rawls came to himself then, started the car, and eased out into the street. Traffic was light, and in a few minutes he pulled into the multistoried structure where visitors to the Physicians and Surgeons Hospital parked. The walls and pillars of the garage were of cast concrete. Those rough surfaces, that irregular stoic density fascinated Rawls. His car turned and turned, circling upward, passing row after row of parked empty cars. He did not need to watch the shadowed path before him. It was enough to keep his eyes on those pillars which seemed to march out ahead of him, appearing and disappearing. At last he reached the roof level of the garage where the pillars fell away and the tall azure sky appeared again, faded by the bronze sun. He sat there for a moment, his eyes becoming once more accustomed to light as they had become accustomed to the dark. It was as if he had trekked through a deep forest of dead barkless pale trees up into the tendentious light to see that razor-sharp line of demarcation between enduring concrete below that measured its life in ages, and the distant sky arrayed with clouds that were never—even for a moment—quite the same. He was not thinking of his daughter then, but of the wandering fish in his aquarium at home as they passed through the column of air bubbles rising from the vent in the helmet of a tiny toy diver down below. Insouciant, incurious, rapt in their sinuous filmy cosmos, they swam indifferent to the surface of the water above whence dwelled That One who sent food, whose electricity maintained the weather and light of their world.

The elevator from the roof of the garage was cool and almost dark, one of the lights in the ceiling broken. The elevator car was not air-conditioned, but the journey seemed breezy, chilled, as if on its way downward it passed through the heart of an icy mountain. Of course, he thought, the way down and the way up were one and the same. Rawls could hear a small fan humming up above the dented dirty translucent plastic grille. The sound pulsed louder, softer. He found himself betrayed into its rhythm. Then he realized that he had reached the ground, the elevator had stopped and the door was open. A woman stood facing him out in the corridor. When he became conscious of her, it seemed that she had been watching for him, waiting for a long time. He smiled and stepped past her, hearing the sound of the fan's single syllable fading in the distance.

There was a sign indicating the route to follow to the emergency room. He did not expect Doreen to be there, but someone could tell him something. If you were patient and in no hurry to find out, there was always, sooner or later, someone who knew something. He turned a corner and almost ran into a gurney being propelled along the corridor with an old man on it. A tall black orderly was pushing, and a thin Asian girl held aloft a bottle of fluid that flowed down into the old man's arm through a clear plastic tube that reminded Rawls of the sign in the bar. Perhaps they were sending chill mountain water into the old man's veins. Maybe he was being prepared rather than healed. Nothing wrong with that. Death should not be a surprise, it should be a reward. Rawls frowned. Why would he think that? Did that make any sense? Surely he would not say it to anyone. It sounded like something Crawford might have said. No one would understand. Rawls didn't understand it himself.

The girl at the emergency desk was perspiring, her hair in her eyes behind thick glasses, and it seemed to take her some while to understand what Rawls was asking her. Then, after fumbling with some papers that appeared to have nothing to do with his question, she nodded.

—Three-eighty-four, she said.

—Three-eighty-four?

—Yeah . . . Three Eight Four.

Up once more in a different elevator but still the same, and along a corridor so brightly lit that Rawls squinted as he walked, glancing at each room number posted on a dark plastic plaque on the wall beside the door even though he knew the room he sought must still be yards away. He looked down the hallway and saw a small knot of people outside a door. He increased his stride, supposing that it might be the room where they had put Doreen. Maybe the state trooper was still there. Maybe a number of doctors. It could be Delphine. He should have phoned Delphine. As he neared the group of people, he realized that he was smiling, approaching them as if they were all looking at a new station wagon. He tried to erase the smile because he was sure it did not suit the situation, but it was no use. The harder he tried to pull his face into a decent sobriety, the wider the smile became. It was as if the smile were some sort of visitation from which there was no escape. It was then that he realized he was drunk. Not to the point of illness or even disequilibrium, but distinctly, notably drunk. His feelings, his attitudes were not his. They belonged to some other, some inhabitant of the distillation. That one would guide him, speak for him. Rawls need say nothing. That other would defend him. It was a great release—no, relief.

—Would you be Mr. Rawls? someone said.

—Uh . . .

The man was bald in front with hair down to his collar in back. He wore a white coat and stood just inside a door on the far side of the corridor from the group toward which Rawls had been moving.

—Yes . . . I'm . . .

—Sanbourne, Basil Sanbourne. Your daughter . . .

—They called . . . the trooper said . . .

—It's bad, Mr. Rawls. Very very bad . . .

—That's what the . . .

—I've been waiting because someone who has legal authority . . .

—. . . grown girl . . .

—In cases like this . . .

—. . . mother . . . ?

—Not yet. It seems she went to Dallas for the weekend. The
people at her ashram . . .

—?

—The lady on the phone told me it was a communal . . .

—All right, yes . . .

—So it seems you . . .

—Well . . .

—We're using heroic measures, Mr. Rawls. Dora's vital
signs . . .

—Doreen. That's good. Whatever you can . . .

—Yes, well . . . There's no easy pleasant way to put it. The EEG
is flat, utterly flat . . .

—Uh . . .

—She was underwater too long. If it had been an icy stream, a
cold mountain river . . .

Rawls shook his head. His eyes had passed Dr. Sanbourne's
glistening head and fixed on the room beyond. He could see only
the foot of the bed, but there seemed to come from within a thin
steady stream of chill air, as if they were preserving great blocks of
ice inside.

—. . . brain-dead is what the journalists call it. You see . . .

—How long will she stay that way, Rawls asked, astonished at
his own words. —You see, she failed the ninth grade. She was
never any good at . . .

Dr. Sanbourne was staring at him in abject astonishment. Rawls
could feel that unnatural smile creeping back over his face. He
turned half away. He didn't want to prejudice Doreen's case, whatever that might mean.

—I'm afraid I haven't made myself . . .

—Yes, you have. Can I see her?

—Of course, but it might be better if you gave me permission
to have an authorization typed up. These things are still terribly
troublesome. The courts are medieval about . . .

—I'd like to see her.

Dr. Sanbourne shrugged his narrow shoulders, moved aside, and gestured Rawls into the room. If he had been ashamed of stopping for the liquor before, he was not then.

A brief glance revealed her lying under a blue light in what seemed an inordinately small bed. The rest of the room appeared to be filled with machines of a kind Rawls could not hope to understand. Some looked like stereo receivers, covered with controls and small indicators. Bells and whistles, one of the salesmen at the Sound City franchise called them. They could sell a stereo to a hi-fi addict even though they made little difference to the music. Others had the appearance of the instruments used back in the service department to check out electrical systems, timing, fuel efficiency. He saw what had to be some kind of oscilloscope on which the heartbeat and other vital signs were displayed. He recognized the device because he had seen it on one of the soap operas the salesmen tended to watch on dead afternoons. It, in turn, reminded him of the display of an electronic game in an arcade when it was not in use, the tiny signal bouncing aimlessly from one side of the screen to the other as if bodiless contenders funded with infinite patience were engaged in endless play. That smile tugged at the lower half of Rawls's face and he made no effort to erase it. He contemplated the ambit of the electric signal that represented Doreen's heartbeat for a long time.

Then he turned back toward his daughter. Her arms lay on the sheet, and they were covered, rather entwined in coils of plastic tubing, clear and flexible, and curls of insulated wire. Her eyes were open, and her forehead was covered with small plastic cups or patches with wires running over to one of the machines. An oxygen tube was taped to her nose, and her mouth stood slightly open. The blue light seemed somehow to heighten the emptiness of her stare, the isolation of her situation—the situation which Malik had told him everyone understood.

Rawls stepped closer to the bed, but nothing changed with the shortening of perspective. The light above the bed made it seem that her face was blue with cold, as if the chill of the room might be emanating from her rather than from the necessity of keeping the room temperature low because of the sensitivity of the equipment. He started to touch her, but something stopped him. At first, he thought it was that primordial horror of the dead or dying, of those who have ceased to be actors, subjects in the texture of the world and have been reduced to the status of objects. Then he realized it arose more surely from his memory of Doreen's contempt, hatred, for him. Whatever she had felt, it had not invited his touch, and somehow even in her present situation, he did not want to violate her feelings.

—You're a real idiot, she had said. —You just stand there with that goddamned silly smile and let the world roll past, no—roll over you.

—I don't manage the world. I'm just . . . here.

—Bet your ass you don't. It's bad enough as it is. God, what would a world you put together be like?

—I don't know. I never thought about it. It doesn't matter. Maybe there wouldn't be any people in it.

—Right on. Empty, cold, vacant. Nothing in it at all.

—Dogs . . .

—What?

—Dogs. And frogs. Birds, flowers, rivers, mountains, ponies, camels . . .

He remembered going on and on enumerating the items his world would contain, speaking faster and faster, louder to be heard over Doreen's contemptuous reply—compulsively, as if establishing in final and ultimate defense of himself a world constructed of words that reverberated and vanished as quickly as they were enunciated.

She had left then, with some caustic remark he did not hear because even as she walked out of the house with what she wanted to take along stuffed in a Pan Am travel bag, he was still talking, still naming entities.

—. . . rocks, clouds, baboons, vines, llamas, every kind of tree there is, and some new kinds I'd invent.

He had stopped then, his eyes on the door as he heard her climb into the Chevrolet demo he had bought her the previous year and drive away. The fish were swimming in the tank, fluttering up toward the surface as they sensed his presence. —. . . and fish, he remembered saying, almost shouting after her.

He found himself sitting in a metal chair beside the bed then, his hand reaching out gingerly, almost touching hers. There was a smear of dried mud on her wrist. It must have come from the accident, he thought, and the rill of cold water at his feet, flowing through broken stone and earth, shimmered under the pale sun, its light sifted blue haze through the branches of larch trees above. Someone in a white woolen poncho or cloak squatted near a tiny fire.

But Rawls's eyes refocused, and the fire was only one of the lights on the control panel of a machine pulsing and humming, involved in some portion of the heroic measures Dr. Sanbourne had mentioned.

When Doreen had left that night, when she had been gone a few minutes, he remembered, he had found himself close to tears. There was no explanation for it. What would happen if people burst into tears every time another person went away? Was this a situation that other people could easily understand? He had doubted it, but how was he to know?

Now his eyes found the spirals of transparent tubing circling her arms. A clear liquid slowly rolled down from a suspended bottle above. A needle carried it into Doreen's arm. Rawls wondered if it was chill, pure, if it usurped the heart's useless warmth and freed one of the clinging infestations of flesh and blood that never proved true, never outlasted a season or two.

He shivered at the thought and closed his eyes. There, on the inside of his lids, the scene arose again. It must be early morning and the air was chill, vacant. He almost expected to see a camel or a llama. The wind sounded from high above, and the water running downward barely rustled in its rocky channels. The fire was small, and the one robed or cloaked seemed to be staring into it from within a hood that obscured the face. Rawls tried to call out, but found he had no voice; tried to move toward the fire, but found he was not in that place at all, simply an observer, out of it, watching with his eyes closed, able to see not only that single one outlined vaguely in the mist against the dark cramped piled rock, but the sweep of the snowfield as it reared itself painfully above the tree line into the distant sky. Up there, snow was falling, softly at first, then furiously farther up until such puny landmarks as might distinguish one sector from another were obscured by its endless effortless falling.

He must have remained that way for a long time, because when he opened his eyes again, he found that his neck and shoulders were tight and painful, as if he had slept the night through in the cold room, in that unpadded upright chair. Doreen had not changed in any way. It was as if she had become part of an environment, her changes marked with the geological torpor that lifted mountain ranges, scooped out the deepest ocean, then wore them down and filled it up again. He wondered if there was time for her, in that place where she was. Was she, brain-dead as Dr. Sanbourne had said, already in some paradise of hippies and freaks, tripping on whatever equivalent of drugs and random thought we discover upon putting this life aside? Or was she trapped in some limbo beyond this living, yet not far enough?

Not that Rawls believed in anything. He neither did nor did not. If you asked him if he believed in an afterlife, he would have smiled and said nothing. If you had asked him if he did not believe, he would have said nothing. If you asked him if he did and did not believe, he would have maintained that smile which might signify wisdom or foolery. And said nothing.

He stood up and stretched, his glance passing over the machines without interest. There could be no question about it. The room was cold. Now and again, he could feel a breeze stirred up somehow pass over him. That explained the stiffness in his neck and shoulder.

When he had worked the stiffness out, he realized that he had no idea what he should do next. The whiskey had begun to wear off, and there was an emptiness in the pit of his stomach. If he was hungry, he couldn't tell it. But he felt something ought to be done, that he should change the situation. Not by some great act or decision. Not that at all. Rather he should move or go out into the hall or perhaps leave the place altogether, come back later.

He had thought that by sitting with her for a while, he would somehow be able to find Doreen amidst the shambles left there in the bed by the accident. But that was no good. He would have done as well to sit by a stone and ask it for its provenance. Sooner or later, the doctor was going to come and ask again, go through his explanation once more. Rawls had no idea what to say. It would be easy to tell him to do what he thought best, but Dr. Sanbourne did not inspire such confidence, and Doreen, always one to speak up for herself, was going to give him no help at all.

—Harry . . .

He did not turn at first. His eyes were fixed on the blue light or the white light or whatever color it was that shone down on Doreen's face, and he had almost slipped back once more to that cleft in the rocks at the foot of the bed. But the voice broke him away, and finally, with something like a touch of sadness, he wheeled around. It was Delphine.

Not that he would have known by looking at her. He had recognized the voice when it broke in to his thinking. She was dressed in what appeared to be cast-offs from a dance team that might have prospered in the 1920s. There was some kind of fillet around her hair and the folds of the ocher robe fell all the way to the floor. Now that he thought of it, no one could have ever danced in such a thing. She looked more like a myopic fortune-teller: Madame Lasagna Knows All Tells All. Actually, she knew very little, Rawls thought, his smile reawakening, but whatever she did know she had told over and over again.

—That's our little girl there, Delphine mumbled. It seemed there were tears on her plump cheeks. She looked healthy enough. Perhaps she had even lost a few pounds at the ashram.

—Yes, Rawls said, not looking back at Doreen, since he was sure she had not changed.

—Oh, God, how did it happen?

Rawls started to tell her what Trooper Peterson had told him, then he realized that the question was rhetorical. Either she had already been told or she didn't care.

—What are we going to do?

Rawls did not even think to answer that, since whatever was to be done would go forward without advice from him. He frowned then as he noticed for the first time that the hallway outside the room seemed filled with new people, all of them looking strange in much the same way as Delphine. One of them, a small man in a saffron toga who seemed either unaware or unconcerned that he looked like a damned fool, stepped forward. He had a small scraggly moustache and a goatee that contained no more than a dozen loose hairs. Rawls got the impression that he was the leader of the pack.

—There's no one in there, Delphine. You know that.

—What, Delphine asked, her expression at once becoming studious. As if the man in the toga was calling her to an overpowering effort of thought.

—That bed is vacant. Your little girl is gone.

Delphine stood frowning, caught in the midst of some great effort for a moment.

—Right, she said at last. —I see that.

—There's no one there, the small man said. —I think we should go and do japa.

The others behind him heard, and began repeating, Japa, Japa, Japa.

For a moment it seemed to Rawls that Delphine had something other in mind, but at last she nodded.

—All right, she said.

The small man glanced at Rawls. He smiled broadly. Rawls didn't smile back. The small man looked like a faggot. Perhaps one could be a faggot and still prosper in an ashram.

—The doctors say they need the bed, the small man in the toga said. —They want to take Doreen's earthly sheath away.

—What, Delphine said. —I don't understand that.

The small man looked at the others behind him with an expression that suggested he had endured much from Delphine. Rawls thought he could understand that. But it didn't matter.

—They want you to sign something. Come sign it.

—All right, Delphine said. —If you say so. Will it be all right for her?

—It will be just fine; the small man told her.

Rawls felt his head pulled back just then. He turned away from the others and stepped back into the room where the snow was falling fast now, covering the bed, covering the chairs and the scarred linoleum floor, building up so rapidly that he was amazed that no one had noticed. It was deathly cold there, and the walls had fallen away and he could see in their place jutting ribs of dark stone fading as the snow fell.

The figure in the hood was beginning to climb, reaching out thin arms and clawed hands to take hold of the rock, to pull itself upward onto the base of the snowfield. The angle of ascent was steep and Rawls found himself flooded with vertigo, unable to understand how he managed to remain there above the field, disembodied, watching the other begin to press upward into the darkness, into the falling snow.

—Delphine, are you coming? She's gone. She's not there.

Rawls frowned, brushed the snow away from his hair, his cheeks.

—Yes she is, he said. —She's not gone yet.

The small bald man stared at him.

—Who is this, Delphine?

—Harry, my . . . He's Doreen's daddy.

The man fluttered his hands and gave Rawls the kind of smile one reserves for children. —You see, he said, half to Delphine, half to Rawls,—the bodily existence has ceased. Your little girl is carrying out her struggle . . . on a higher plane.

Rawls squinted. The cloaked figure lost its grip on a ledge of iced basalt and rolled down the snowy incline until another outcropping of rock brought it up short. The figure rose to its knees, its covered head bent forward. Rawls felt an unutterable sadness, a distant chill compassion for it. The time and space lost would have to be regained.

—She's still here, Rawls said.

The small man raised his eyebrows. Obviously Rawls either wasn't listening, or he was simply too stupid to understand.

—The doctor told me that . . .

—The doctor doesn't know anything. She's still here.

The small man shrugged. —Let's go, Delphine. We should get this over with. If you sign the form, they can ignore him and . . .

Rawls felt his smile returning and saw his hands reaching out, grabbing the neck of the small man's saffron robe, throwing him out into the hall. He staggered across into the door opposite and sat down on the floor looking bewildered.

—Shit, Delphine said. —You know who that is?

—No.

—Sri Lingananda . . . Spiritual Director of the Dammapuka ashrama. . .

Rawls ignored her and was about to push her out of the room too so that he could close the door when Dr. Sanbourne and a security guard shoved past her into the room.

—I'm going to have to ask you to leave, Mr. Rawls, Dr. Sanbourne bleated. —We can't have this kind of . . .

Rawls moved back from him, and Dr. Sanbourne nodded to the security guard. The guard, no more than twenty or twenty-one, with a thin strengthless moustache and a look of something close to terror in his eyes, reached for Rawls's arm. Just then, the small man, Sri Lingananda, pressed forward.

—I want him arrested. I'll lodge charges . . .

Rawls caught the security guard off balance, spun him around, and lifted his gun from its holster. He hit the guard behind his right ear and was surprised and pleased to see him wilt and fall to the floor much as Rawls had seen it happen time after time on television. Then he aimed the gun carefully at Sri Lingananda and pulled the trigger once.

The bullet caught the small man squarely in the right eye. Even as the impact lifted him up and backwards into the hall once more, tissue and bone spraying the others waiting there, Rawls noted the terminal expression of utter and unrelieved astonishment on Sri Lingananda's ruined face.

Dr. Sanbourne and Delphine pushed their way into the shrieking mob in the corridor, and almost before Rawls could grasp it, the hallway was vacant, silent.

Rawls took the security guard and set him in one of the chairs beside the array of machinery near Doreen's bed. He could not tell for certain whether the guard was still alive or not. One last glance into the corridor assured him as to Sri Lingananda's condition. The small bald man lay in a creeping enlarging pool of dark blood, his robe in disarray, one sandal off, his feet looking dusty and incongruous caught up in the twisted saffron fabric.

He heard people running, the squawk of a portable police radio down the hall, so he pushed the room door closed and began to pile things in front of it. There was a large piece of equipment that looked like a generator on a pushcart that he moved first. Then another cart with an array of small boxes that seemed not to be functioning at all. Probably they were there so that they could be charged for, despite the fact that they were unnecessary. Mildred had told him and the other salesmen that a hospital in Louisville, Kentucky, had done that when her sister had had a stroke. Finally, he moved the security guard, chair and all, to support the two carts, and knelt down to tie the guard tightly to his chair with the power cords of the unused machinery.

Then it was done, and Rawls shivered in the chill half-light, the snow beginning to settle on the shoulders of his sport jacket, in his hair, his eyebrows. He drew his chair up beside Doreen's bed again and sat down. He could hear the water flowing, the wind sobbing across the icy rocks and flat planes of the snowfield above. Something had changed with her. She did not have the look of one dead, brain-dead or otherwise. Her cheeks were flushed with life as if she had been—or was even now—undergoing some great exertion. Rawls heard her breathe deeply of the pure chill oxygen being pumped into her lungs. Now the snow had covered the blanket on her bed, fallen lightly on her dark hair. Somehow the stream had diverted itself and ran clear and cold over the brown scuffed shoes of the unconscious security guard, up around his ankles, his white athletic socks.

Behind Doreen's bed, he could see the snowfield canted upward into the thick obscuring mist. Wind was catching the mist, creating eddies in it, breaking it up, whirling it back together ceaselessly in one new form after another. Rawls turned slowly in a full circle, realizing that nothing was as it had been before. The room, the machine, the distant sounds of police planning some desperate sally to capture the madman—all were fading. He sensed that he had never been so cold before, the sharp angular wind blowing from every point of the compass, cutting through his thin cotton jacket as if he were naked. Yet in some way he could not understand, the cold did not trouble him. He found himself preferring this comforting bone-deep chill to the fetid heat outside—or inside, or wherever it had been as he drove into the parking garage past ranks of ancient pillars which as it turned out were the trunks of immense larch trees, their branches bent under the weight of falling snow, growing out of cold moist soil that had been worn by the ages off the obtuse angles of dark granite beside the stream that now ran out into the hall where the wind ruffled its swift surface, where the snow fell and melted and became nothing more than more water in the stream.

The figure in the white cloak had regained its position on the dark rocks at the edge of the snowfield. Now it stepped carefully, avoiding the slick sheaths of crumbling ice wedded here and there to the stone. One step into the clotted snow, then another. Then one more. Perhaps the cloak was a bedsheet, Rawls thought. Close to where the bed had been, there was only the small shimmering fire. When he extended hands that were not there, he could feel no heat. It must be some other kind of fire.

As he watched, the mist, the low clouds began to waver and dissipate. The cloaked figure was moving upward now, slowly but confidently. It was as if the very passage of the figure divided and dissolved the thick vapor, and in another moment or two Rawls began to see light up there ahead of the stooped straining climber. Down below, in the shadow of the boulders where the edge of the field melted and melted forever, the fire flickered, faded, unfueled.

When the sun first broke through, it was sudden, overpowering. One moment the mist was still swirling. The next it was gone, the immense stretch of the snowfield exposed as it towered up into the pale yellow light. Then the thick clouds began to go, to fade under the strict unqualified glare. Rawls moved up through the thick branches of the larches, their shabby textured perduring trunks, then the delicate architecture of their needles, finally the trees themselves melding, amalgamating into the depthless dark granite below. The sound of the water, the final flicker of the fire whispered away and all that remained of his vision focused on that distant cloaked or sheeted figure moving up the incline of the snowfield that revealed itself to stretch up the slope of a mountain or glacier so enormous that no end could be seen of it in any direction at all.

The sky above, midnight blue, joined the expanse of the snow at each point of the horizon so that the world itself was fractured into a field of darkness and one of light, soundless, motionless— except for that tiny figure still barely distinguishable upon the bright sparkling surface of the snow against which Rawls had to squint. Just then it seemed the figure turned and looked backward for a moment, but he could not be sure and at that great distance it hardly mattered. Whoever it was, if it was anyone, was unrecognizable and even as Rawls watched, something like tears forced out of his eyes by the glaring flared reflections from the receding field, the figure seemed to melt, merge with the undifferentiated white of the snow and was visible no longer.

—I understand, Rawls whispered as he heard the security guard moan, returning to what he probably thought was consciousness.

Rosanne Coggeshall

PETER THE ROCK

(from *The Southern Review*)

I began having them when I was quite young. Mother didn't believe me and neither did Nettie Lee, my best friend by marriage (her big brother was married to my cousin Rosa and Nettie used to come over to the house with Aunt Pal on Sunday afternoons in the summertime and on Wednesdays just before prayer meeting). Nettie always said I was storying but I wasn't. The first one I didn't even tell Mother about. I must have been three or four and I was lying in the big bed upstairs in Grandmama's room, the bed she'd died in. It was a four-poster mahogany bed and the posts were bigger around than I was. It was so high up off the floor we used to play house under it and that night Mama had fenced me in with three or four huge pillows from the room across the hall.

I'd not been able to sleep, I remember, and I was playing a game with myself called drakes and duckers in which I tried to make up three songs that had identical first lines, all with the words drake and ducker in them. It was a game I taught myself when I was about two years old. Some of the songs were funny and I still can remember them: "Drake and ducker, drake and ducker, what a mighty little trucker, / Comes and goes on my shirttail, comes and goes like a sack of mail." That sort of thing. Well, this particular night I was lying awake between the mountainous pillows and Something or Someone, I should say, took my hand. It was a truly wondrous feeling. I wasn't, at the time, upset or anything; I mean before I felt His hand. I wasn't frightened or unhappy or lonely or anything. I was just singing my song and suddenly out of no-where my hand's being held. That's what made it, makes it so much better than most stories like this; see, there was no reason for this thing, the visitation or whatever you want to call it. I always call it, to myself only, Vision Number One. But, I guess, it wasn't really a vision. I didn't see anything. I just felt. It was surely nothing like Vision Number Two.

I was six when the second one happened. I remember I was six because it was just before we started to school and Nettie was over the day after with her new lunch pail and I was so impressed by the design her mother had drawn on the plastic cover: a rhinoceros with a baby rhinoceros on his back. Below it her mother had en-titled her drawing, printing in fine red letters, "Kanger." Nettie was justly proud of the pail and I remember being jealous and wanting to fill it with broken doll legs but then I decided to tell her about my vision to compensate for the gap I felt inside me. I took her out to the back barn behind the yellow rosebush and made her sit down on an old tractor tire Papa had left lying around since the spring before.

"Nettie," I said, "I saw Him last night."

"Saw who? Lester?"

Lester was a little red-headed boy I used to sit behind in Sunday school and talk to Nettie about in an amorous fashion.

"No, dummy. Not Lester. *Him*."

Nettie, who was quickly bored in those days, began to break up straw and drop it into her lunch pail. She glared at me but she didn't say anything else; it was as if she had told herself she would only ask me "who" a certain number of times, the number that day being one.

"I saw Peter."

Nettie sighed, and breathed afterward, "Peter who, dummy yourself?"

"Peter the Rock, like in the Bible."

I was a little overcome. These things are not easy to talk about now, and back then, ten years ago, when my vocabulary and my verbal powers were even smaller, it was no easy trick to try to explain what I'd seen. I was also, even then, aware of a little guilt feeling; I wasn't altogether sure these things should be talked about. It seemed almost like a betrayal of some kind, as if the vision was something Peter might want me to keep to myself. Still, the lunch pail was too much and I just kept on telling.

"See, I was out back at the swings," I told Nettie. "It was just dark and the sky was kind of graying and yellowing at the same time over where the sun had disappeared. I was staring at it, kind of just talking to myself when I saw Him. He was wearing a blue suit. Not like the ones they wear in the Bible, but a furry one. Kind of like winter pajamas, with zippers up the front of the coat and the front of the legs of the pants. It was neat. I watched Him come toward me out of the woods and He sort of glowed. Not really glowed like sparklers or anything but glowed like a candle just burned out. Sort of an afterward glow."

I can't remember my exact words to Nettie but the story went on something like this for a time. I told about Peter's shoes, which were sneakers, also a heavenly blue color and laced up to midthigh. He wore an aviator scarf of bright rose which hung rather rakishly from his throat and blew in the breeze.

Nettie wasn't having any of it, I could tell from the first. She continued to load her pail with straws and let her long yellow hair fall to the sides of her face and stay there so that I couldn't see her expression. After my first extended pause, which was, I can remember, a long time coming, she looked up at me with something close to a scowl and said, "How you know it was Peter anyway?"

I gasped. It was the best part of the story and I'd forgotten to tell her.

"See, Nettie," I said, "He walked up to me in this pretty suit with zippers and this scarf and I knew He was from the old timey times because He had long hair and a beard—and not like hippies or anything; it was different, it was smoother and not scruffy. So I expected He was from Bible times. Even though the suit was so strange. He came up to me and I was kind of sore afraid and He took me by both my hands and said, 'Lo, I am Peter, the Rock.' Then He took my hands and made me unzip the front of his coat and sure enough He was rock on the inside. Cold and gray and hard. His pants legs too He made me unzip and I touched the rock under them. I am still pretty afraid. And I didn't know what to say; but His hands were different—not like rock at all—they were soft and people-colored and they were very gentle with me."

Nettie was shaking her head, whispering to herself.

I said, "What? What are you saying?"

And she said out loud, "You crazy, Berry. You crazy as that wall-eye cow Mama's got shut in the barn back home."

About that time Aunt Pal came out and called us; she'd been looking for Nettie everywhere she said, and she was getting mad. I told Nettie good-bye and I stayed out by the barn and played around with the straw. I was halfway hoping Peter would come back. The experience the night before had frightened me at first, but Peter had stuck around for a few minutes letting me feel His rock chest and legs and then talking to me a little about faith and about how I could stand on His shoulders or even on His belly if ever the going got too rough; it turned out to be real nice for me.

I went in the house after He left (He just kind of went away; I guess He disappeared; but I just remember that after about three or four minutes He was gone) and had some apple cider and gingerbread with Mama in the kitchen. I didn't say anything to her about the vision. Somehow I didn't want to talk about it then. The only reason I'd really brought it up that evening with Nettie was that I was annoyed with her for being so uppity about her lunch pail. And even then, like I was saying earlier, I knew I was wrong, that, even if I had to tell about seeing Peter, I should have a better reason than that. He didn't come back that night and Nettie and I didn't speak of Him again. Not for a long time. Because the next time Peter showed up I was almost nine and it was nearly Christmas and this time the encounter was totally different.

I'd just been through a pretty excruciating experience. We'd had to sing in church that night, the junior choir that is, and that meant Nettie, too. It was about three or four days before Christmas. Nettie was standing beside me and we were both wearing the little purple robes the junior choir wore, with the collars made out of pink velvet. Right in the middle of Brahms' Lullaby she jerked my scarf loose and whispered in my ear, in a singsong voice in tune to the music: "Your mama's gonna have a baby, your mama's gonna have a baby."

I stopped singing and stared at her. There was no reason that I knew of that Nettie would tell me a story about my mother like that; anyway, I always believed Nettie; I sensed even then she didn't have the imaginative ability of even an occasional liar. So I believed her right away and I felt as if my stomach had caved in. I had been an only child for nearly nine years and I liked my status quite a bit. I sometimes had worried that there might be a younger brother or sister, especially when my friends' mothers had had babies, but I'd never let myself really go all the way and imagine such a catastrophe.

That night in church I didn't sing anymore, nor did I say anything to Nettie afterward. Even on the car ride back to the house, while Mama and Papa told me how pretty I looked and how well I sang, I was as quiet as I could be. I didn't care to say anything because my throat felt as though if I let one word out it would unstopper a rush of crying. I went directly to my room and when I'd put on my pajamas and gotten into bed Mama came in to tell me good-night and she asked me if anything was wrong. I shook my head but I was already taking note of her broadening lap and the way her skirt poked out just a little too much in the front. I let her kiss me and turn out the light and I was just tuning up for a big cry all by myself when Peter the Rock appeared in the rocker beside my bed.

This time He was wearing a green robe, like in the Bible, and I felt a little more secure that it was really He. He had a necklacelike string around His neck with a diamond-shaped rock on the end. He took my hands again and told me not to be distressed, that the Master loved little children all the same, and that my parents would still love me as much when the baby boy was born (He did that; he told me Albert would be a boy). He offered me His shoulders and His stomach again to stand on and let me touch the hard stoniness of His flesh before He once again took His mysterious leave. I never did cry that night. After Peter left I felt all warm inside and I went right to sleep.

Peter was right; at least He was almost right. After Albert was born in June, I only felt a little jealous; only on the first night Mama was home from the hospital when she let the baby sleep in her room. That night I remember wishing for Peter to come back but He didn't. I'd devised months before some compensation for His absence, however. Because He came so infrequently I felt like I wanted something to keep with me always to remind me of Him and I'd found the perfect keepsake talisman. I had been down playing in Mert's Creek and I found a rock in the shape of a small loaf of bread. Somehow I associated this with the Bible story of the loaves and the fishes in which I then figured Peter as playing a prominent part, and I kept the rock with me from then on, in the pocket of my pants. I always insisted on wearing jeans or shorts or pedal pushers after that because I had to have pockets. So that night after Mama and the new baby Albert had gone to bed, I went into my own room and sat on the comforter on my bed and just held onto my rock. Sometimes when I felt particularly bad I rubbed it on my shin and arms and face: it was cool and soothing and made me feel calm.

Albert grew quickly and Peter did not come again until he was nearly two years old. This time He came at an appropriate time again; appropriate to those who think visions have some kind of connection with everyday occurrences, that is. I mean, I was upset that night and in sore need of some kind of consolation. Albert had wet my bicycle seat while I held him on it and I had gotten angry and fussed at him which made Mama come out and scold me. I had been hot and tired (it was in July, I think) and I'd gotten so upset with Mama for raising her voice to me that I'd ripped Albert's little shirt off of him and thrown it at her. This produced more upsetting reactions: Mama tried to spank me and I ran away.

I was too old for such behavior, I knew even then, but I ran back to the barn and I hid. Mama didn't follow me because Albert was crying and because she was not really a violent woman and probably cooled down immediately after I disappeared.

But I didn't cool down. I stayed in the barn and seethed. I remember I kept repeating, "And he wee-weed where I have to sit and she didn't even spank him."

Albert had been without rubber pants and the results of his accident were no small rivulets, but a veritable overwash. I stalked around the barn kicking bales of cotton and crying to myself. Finally I stuck my hands in my pockets in a furious gesture of defeat (it was so furious my pants slipped down two notches) and I felt my Peterrock. I grasped and held onto it and then I took it out and rubbed it across my tear-hot face. Then Peter was there suddenly.

This time he was dressed in a business suit, like the one Daddy wore when he went to church or to the Lions' banquets. He had a vest on and everything. At first he didn't touch me or speak or anything and I just kind of stood there, still breathing heavily from crying, and watched Him. Then He pushed over a bale of cotton really easylike (He was awfully strong) and started to unbind the fasteners. It scared me because my immediate thought was that He'd leave it all messed up and that Daddy would find it and blame me. But he only unloosed the top binder and then He pulled out some snatches of cotton. He was doing all this silently and I was just standing there watching.

He took the cotton and with a lightning-quick motion of His hands He produced a handkerchief, a large white handkerchief which, though it was roughly woven, was soft and symmetrical. This He handed to me. I accepted it wordlessly and continued to stare at Him as He zipped the cotton bale closed and pushed it upright.

He then turned to me and said: "You have the loaf rock which is a sign of me. Now you have the veil in which to cloak it. Keep them with you always. I am ever near if you flail or waver; I will provide succor and support. You may stand upon me and my memory. Lo, do not weep or be disgruntled."

Then He took my hand again and thrust it into his vest and I felt the hard, reassuring mettle of the rock. And then He was gone.

That was the first vision I told Mama about and the second one I told Nettie about. I had the handkerchief and somehow that visible sign of what had happened to me made me think that it was all right to share my experience. But I was wrong. Mama thought I was sick, that I'd cried myself into a fret about Albert and had imagined the whole thing.

"Berry," she said to me, "you've not seen Peter or any man made out of rock; you're just so keyed up about Albert you're imagining all kinds of things. You want attention, baby, and that's just natural. But you don't have to make things up. I love you and I'm sorry Albert wet your seat but I washed it off; it's fine now."

I didn't tell Mama about my other visions because I had no proof, and I also had a vague notion she might be upset with me for withholding such information from her, but I did show her the handkerchief. I said to her in a high voice, "But look, Mama, the handkerchief. How you 'spect I got that if Peter didn't give it to me? And I did, I touched His stomach and it was made of rock and He said He would be with me whenever I got upset or scared or anything like that."

"Berry, Berry," Mama shook her head. "You're nearly eleven years old. You've got to calm your dreaming self down. That handkerchief. Where did you get it? It looks like an old one of Grandmama's. Did you find it in the attic?"

I argued some more with her, but with a sinking feeling inside. I didn't show her my Peterrock for fear she'd laugh or make fun. Finally, Mama just took me by the arms and kind of gave me a playful shake and told me to go upstairs and take a bath because I'd gotten dirty in the barn.

I was pretty disappointed that Mama hadn't believed me so I decided to call up Nettie and tell her about Peter. I'd not mentioned Him to her except that time over five years before because I figured she wouldn't believe me. When I phoned her, however, I changed my mind; I had my handkerchief out before me on the table and I thought to myself if I was going to tell her I'd have to show her that, and so I invited her to come over to play in the morning and told her I had something big to tell her.

That night I had trouble sleeping and when I finally did get to sleep I dreamed about Peter. He was in the barn, and the barn and the cotton bales and the baler and the tractor and everything else in the barn was gray, made of rock. Peter was standing astride two bales of cotton and singing a little song that went to the tune of the "Battle Hymn of the Rupublic." The first line of it stuck with me and I remember it to this day. "Mine feet have passed the missiles of the tumor of the Lord." I remember that in the dream He just stood there singing (and the song went on, though I don't remember the words) and swaying back and forth. I wasn't in the dream but it seems to me that then I thought that it was an awfully long dream and when I woke up I felt sad because it had been so nice to see Peter for so long and to hear Him singing. He had a very pretty, deep voice.

That morning when Nettie came over she really gave me a shock. She was wearing a low cut T-shirt and I could see that she wore a bra beneath it. I'd never really thought of wearing a bra; I really had no need for it (not that Nettie did) and I'd somehow reasoned that girls didn't get them until they were at least eighteen or so. I wasn't really a backwards child, I just had other things on my mind. So when I saw Nettie's newly enhanced figure I was startled and distracted from my mission. It took some playing around and talking (I didn't mention the bra) until I felt comfortable enough to mention Peter and the handkerchief.

"Look, Nettie," I said. We were out back in the hammock and the sun was hot; we'd been talking about going swimming and I began to feel a little bit desperate. I wanted to tell her before we got too far in time away from the event for it to lose its forcefulness. "Look, Nettie. Look at this handkerchief." I held it out to her.

She took it and folded it up and unfolded it and turned it over and over in her hands. "So?" Her yellow hair was pushed back and her eyes looked vaguely impatient.

"He gave it to me." Somehow I expected her to remember who "He" was.

"He who?" It was almost like a replay of our six-year-old exchange.

"He—Peter the Rock."

"Peter the *who?*"

It was suddenly clear to me that Nettie had completely forgotten my account of my second vision and I decided not to remind her; I simply outlined the happening of the night before for her in great detail, de-emphasizing of course my own babyish behavior before Peter's appearance.

"The only rocks you saw last night was in your own head if you happened to see a mirror." Nettie got up and stretched. "You sure have some 'magination, Berry. Peter the Rock, sure. That's your grandmama's hanky, for sure. Come on, let's go down to the creek. Maybe we'll see Lester and Wild Bill. We can swim, too, but I can't get my top wet."

I knew she wanted me to ask why but I wasn't going to. I started to insist again on repeating my story, but Nettie had already moved away from the hammock and was heading in the direction of the creek. I looked at my handkerchief and then took the Peter-rock and wrapped it up and put them both back into my pocket. Then I followed Nettie and we did see Lester and Wild Bill at the creek; and Nettie did get her top wet; and there was much teasing by the boys of Nettie for wearing a bra and of me for not wearing one; and by the time we got back to the house for lunch I was so distraught that I'd almost forgotten about Vision Number Four.

Nettie stayed over after lunch and after we'd been playing cas-

sino for about an hour I started to think about Peter again and I
said to her, "He's come four times, now."

"Who?" Nettie looked at me, with her pale eyebrows raised.

"Peter. Like I told you. Peter the Rock."

"Oh, come on, Berry. You ain't seen no man made out of rock.
Peter in the Bible wasn't made out of rock, anyway. That was just
a name Jesus gave him. Like your name's Elizabeth and we call you
Berry because you liked blackberries so much when you was little.
Peter used to build things with rocks. So Jesus called him the rock."

"That's not the way it goes," I was sure and my voice was steady.
"It was to signalize something. To signalize Him standing upon
the ground upon which the church was built. He was too made
out of rock. Or at least He is now. Maybe in His transgression He
was turned."

My vocabulary was a little deficient then; but the startling thing
to me was what Nettie said about Peter's not being made of rock
in the Bible. That had never occurred to me. That night after she
left I took out my white Holy Bible, King James Version, and tried
to find everything I could about Peter. All I could find were two
books called First and Second Peter and there were no rocks in
them that I could see. I decided that maybe I'd been right when
I'd told Nettie that in His transgression (I mean transcension)
He'd been made literally to be rock. That made sense to me then;
and I determined to ask Him the next time He appeared to me.

Which happened pretty soon afterward. I was having a bad summer and I spent a lot of time fooling around with my rock and
handkerchief. Somehow I think I might have happened on a way
to summon Peter; at least it seemed so for that short period of
time. He came to me twice in the next month, in August. Once
after Albert had fallen and knocked out his baby tooth, his front
tooth; he bled an awful lot and Mama was real upset and I was
frightened and upset too. I went out to the barn after they'd taken
the baby to the dentist and had my rock and handkerchief out
when Peter showed up.

He was wearing a yellow shirt and gray pants and saddle oxfords. He sat down beside me, Indian style, on the ground and
looked at me and said, "Lo, Berry. You are in distress. Do not
waver or wander. I am here. I am the rock of Christ and I will
support you in His name."

With this outright mention of Jesus, the first such in my encounters with Peter, I became confused. I looked at Him and said, "Where is Jesus?"

Peter shook his head slowly and then took my hand. "He's in Tucson this afternoon; a woman lost her favorite son. But I am of Him and for Him and I can give you anything you might need. Albert's all right. He'll be snaggle-toothed for six years but it will not be painful. Lo, do not be afraid."

I started to ask Him about His rockness but I stopped. He had picked up my handkerchief and was brushing His sleeve with it.

"What are you doing?" I asked Him. It was really the first time I'd felt anywhere near relaxed with Him.

"I'm leaving you some of my essence," he said. "My dust will succor you if you breathe in."

Then He was gone.

But He was back again inside a week. Daddy had been in an accident on his way home from work and the doctor had come and everything. It wasn't serious but everyone was upset and Mama had been angry at me since I'd told her about my latest vision and she'd fussed at me for being silly. She was still somewhat put out a week later and with the news about Daddy (he'd hit his knee on the inside of the car when he swerved to miss a cow—it was chipped, it turned out) and her being so agitated and Albert with his little gap mouth, I was feeling pretty nervous, so I went out along the north fence to where the cows were and sat down on a baler that someone had left there. Again, I took out my rock and handkerchief and again Peter came to me. He had on his green robe again and I must say when He wore that I felt most easy with Him.

He took my hand immediately and said in His soft voice: "Berry, Berry. Accidents are trials of God and soon over. Your father is blessed; he only has a minor injury; do not be waylayed or forlorn. You are in my care. Lo, believe in me and you will be succored." For the first time I scraped up nerve enough to address Peter directly with the question about His essence.

"Peter," I said, a little nervous about calling Him by His first name because he was so much older but I felt that if I called Him Peter the Rock that would be too awkward; "Peter," I said, "how come Your stomach and legs're made out of rock?"

He squeezed my hand: "That is to reassure you, Berry. That is to convince you that I am steadfast and solid in my vows to you. It means simply that I can be depended upon. That I will not waver or wishwash in my service to you. That you can stand upon me, just as Christ has chosen me because of my steadfastness to be the site upon which he builds his church."

Then Peter stood up and walked away from me a little. "I have something now to tell you." He turned when He spoke to me. "Do not let it upset or disturb you. It has to do with my rockness." He came back toward me and then He knelt beside me. "The time has come when I must leave you."

I gasped a little and held on to the sleeve of His robe.

"No," he said. "Do not be alarmed. I must go to Voswell, North Dakota, to be the site of a church of Christ. He needs me to stand for him. He needs me to build upon. These things happen periodically. I may be back very soon. Or it may be years. It depends on the congregation."

I was very disturbed. That summer, seeing Peter so often, I'd come to depend on Him and the thought of having no hope of a return visit from Him almost overpowered me. He took my handkerchief and brushed it over His arms and legs and face. Then He gave it to me and said, "Keep this in remembrance of me, Berry. Think of me if you're distressed. I will be with you in spirit if not in body. I will return when and if I can."

I stayed there after He left and held the handkerchief. I was close to crying but I tried to be brave and to think about Him and feel His presence even though He was no longer there. It worked and it continued to work all through the rest of that summer. I never said another word to Nettie or to Mama. I kept the handkerchief and rock with me always; even when I wore a dress I carried a little cloth purse in which I kept them securely wrapped.

Peter didn't come back. I got a bra the next November and after that there was junior high and Nettie and I drifted apart and I became an assistant librarian and started reading all of the time. I read a lot of books about the Bible and some about visions, the ones I could find in the school library, which were not many. One called *The Visions of Mary Lucas* in which Christ appeared to a small girl in New Zealand in a flash of light and color after which she fell into a coma, and one called *Matthew's Vision,* which was, I'm sure, fiction. It was a children's book and Matthew was a little boy who saw angels in cupcakes and popsicles only. His whole psyche was attuned to colorful small food objects, it seemed to me. He played like any normal child until he was at a birthday party or at some celebration in summer at which popsicles were served; then, "Lo, he saw angels."

No matter what I read, however, nothing could convince me that I'd imagined my visions. I kept my handkerchief with me and even when I came here to college I packed it first of all. It's not in the least bit worn out. It hasn't been washed yet either, so it's a bit dingy but I did have it dry-cleaned two or three times. Somehow I thought that the dry-cleaning process might not disturb the Peter particles left on the cloth.

I've been here at Galbraith for three semesters. I do very well in English and in French; my English teacher says that she admires my "way with words." I always felt as if I owe something to Peter about the way in which I express myself. Somehow when I felt His presence, when He was with me and afterward, when He left and I'd think of Him, words just came easier.

Robert Boswell

EDWARD AND JILL

(from *The Georgia Review*)

EDWARD'S STORY

I've done everything a man can do to make a good home. Nobody cares about that. It's the few times I've slipped that people focus on. So be it. I've borne that burden a long time.

I met Jennetta in the fall of 1966, the last year I lived in Kentucky except for the summer of '68, which I don't count. She was the waitress at Hale's Café, a little burger and barbecue place near the school. I'd eat there with one of the teachers or a problem student, with Jill for that matter—school cafeteria food is nothing to dedicate yourself to. Hale's was nearby and good.

I flirted with her. Everybody did. It was friendly and harmless. It was *Southern*. And she was pretty. Beautiful is a better word for what she was. I'm trying to be honest. Her hair was dark, a natural dark. She wasn't tall but had that compact sexiness some women have. Yes, large breasts. Yes, blue eyes. She had all of that, and none of it meant a thing.

One day late in October I was there with Del Went, a fifth grade teacher, for lunch. I went there near every day, but this was the day that mattered. Keep in mind that by December our youngest, Cassie, was having breathing fits, and by January I was teaching in Arizona.

Del and I sat in a booth. There were a few other people there—I can't remember everything, but we were the only ones in that booth and the only ones who matter to the story. Except Jennetta, of course.

Del was a wolf. That's what we called them back then, men that prowled the whole time for women to take to bed. To put it bluntly. Sitting in Hale's, waiting for Jennetta to come take our order, we talked about sex. It was what Del always wanted to talk about. A lot of men are like that, and sometimes you just have to put up with them.

"For me," he said, "it's always a letdown. I get to thinking about a woman, get her image inside my mind, and I got to fuck her. Most times I do. By the time I get it in her though, hell. Then it comes back to me that a fuck is a fuck, and that's it."

"That's too bad," I said, acting interested, when the truth was he didn't have any right to think he could talk to me like that. I was the principal of the school. I had authority. Everyone knew I didn't go for that kind of talk, but sometimes you've just got to sit through it, even though the truth is you don't want to hear it.

"It's not like that for you?" he said. "The hell it's not. You're no different from me, I bet. You ever had a fuck that really made you happy?"

"Truth is," I said as Jennetta came near us, "I never had one that *didn't*."

I thought that would shut him up, at least make him move on to a new subject, but no luck.

Jennetta was wearing a short skirt with a red-and-white plaid apron. I can see that skirt and apron right now as clearly as I can see my hands. I remember that apron better than I remember her face. How do you account for that?

"What can I get for you two?" she said.

"This man says he's never had a woman who didn't make him happy," Del said to her.

I could have hit him.

"Can you believe that?" he said, and then he laughed.

"You shut your mouth," I said. "Don't pay any attention to him." I looked up to Jennetta and smiled.

She nodded, rolled her eyes a little as if to say she knew how Del was. Then she said something that changed both our lives.

"I could make you unhappy," she said.

It was as if a plug came loose inside me. I became giddy, although I tried not to let on, but my sentences came out chopped and stupid. "I want a barbecue toast," I said, immediately wanting to laugh and say, "*On* toast," but she didn't react and . . . and what? I fell in love? I was infatuated? The label you lend to it doesn't much matter. That moment was profound.

Years later I would go to bed with a girl, a high-school girl in one of my classes, because she made that moment come real to me again. That's later, but I wanted to mention it now because it all ties in. That's not making an excuse. I don't have an excuse for any of it.

I started going to the café without anyone else. It was still harmless. After all, even if I'd wanted more (and I didn't), my in-laws lived right across the street, just up the hill.

We'd talk. I could tell she liked me. God knows I should have left it alone, but I couldn't. I discovered that she had next to nobody in the café around nine-thirty—breakfast crowd was gone, lunch group not there yet. I started going then.

One day in November, I came at nine-thirty (I'd tell my secretary I was taking an early lunch so I could patrol during the school lunch period—a principal of a small school can do almost anything), and there was no one there but her. She had a barbecue sandwich on toast ready for me. I sat at the counter, but she walked right past me, put it on one side of a booth, and sat on the other. I joined her.

"You shouldn't eat the same lunch every day. Your stomach will get bored. We have a wide menu. You like tuna fish? Egg salad? You don't look like a burger man."

Was that flirting? I thought it was, but I can't say exactly why. "I guess I'd like whatever you make." That *was* flirting.

"Lydia makes the barbecue. She's back there now mixing up new sauce."

A warning of sorts, I thought, to let me know we weren't totally alone. Then I said something strange. It just popped into my head.

"You ever heard a duck when it's been shot? I'm talking about a duck flying overhead and you're out hunting. You ever heard one when it's hit?"

She bit her upper lip, maybe trying to figure how to take this new line of talk. I didn't know where it was leading either.

"I used to hunt with my daddy," she said. *Daddy* sounds to me now like an affectation, but I was just getting to know her then. "It sounds," she stretched out the vowels, "like someone laughing while he's being strangled."

She was thinking about the quacking gaggle of a hit duck; I was thinking about the sound of the air through the feathers as it plummeted. I'd never heard anything that sounded like what she described, but what I said next wasn't a lie anyway. It was the truth because I didn't know it was coming.

"That sound went off inside me the other day, talking to you, something wild. Strange."

That sounds corny, stupid. It always does when you try to speak the truth and have to lie to do it, but Jennetta could tell I meant it. She nodded at me, slow and real, without any of her put-on. We sat that way for a while, and she said, "Tell me about your kids."

Every day I saw her and we talked. About my family. About hers. About Jill, and I never said one word against her. About her ex-husband, a bluegrass banjo picker who used to dance naked in the kitchen, then one day turned mean on her for no good reason. Some days we didn't seem to talk about anything, but the time flew. After a month of talking every day, during school, before, after, we talked about going to bed together.

I told her I couldn't.

If I had a Bible here I'd swear on it. I said no.

Two weeks before the end of the semester, Jill came back from Paducah with Cassie on a vaporizer. We had to move or Cassie would be sick all the time. I had known this was coming but hadn't admitted it to myself. Jennetta and I had talked about it. I couldn't put the move off any longer. I made some calls and found a job in Arizona starting in January. Only after I was sure I was leaving, only after I knew that I'd be a thousand miles away and she knew it too, did I make love with Jennetta.

Once.

In a motel in Paducah. One time. On a single bed in a room that smelled of rust and mildew. I never even kissed her on any other occasion. As God is my witness.

The day I arrived in Arizona, there were four letters waiting for me at the school. They had no return address on the envelope, but I knew who they were from. She has written me every day since then. She could wait, she said. I wrote back to her regularly for a while. I told her I would never leave Jill. She said she could wait.

We moved back to Kentucky the next summer. I hadn't liked Arizona—there was no one to talk to, and the desert was nothing but empty. Cassie was better by then. I thought she'd grown out of it, the way kids do, but I was wrong. We only stayed the summer back East, living with Jill's sister Hannah up the hill from the café. I looked down there, across the highway, every day. I could see her move up and down the fry counter, in and out between the tables. She worked double shifts, wanting to be there when I came down.

I never did, although each day I was there I considered it. She never made any attempt to contact me. I had come the thousand miles; I reasoned that she should come the rest of the way.

How could she have? That one summer was the only time I didn't get letters from her. She had no place to send them. She wrote anyway. Once I saw her from the hill sitting in a booth, bent over the table, writing. When we settled again in Arizona, the letters all arrived. They were full of patience and love. I don't write her much anymore, not as much as I should. Her letters arrive at school every day. I don't read them. Occasionally, I do. As far as I can see, I ruined her life.

Sometimes I wonder why. Why she decided I was the one, why she has held on so long to so little. Much as I'd like to think otherwise, I know I'm just another man. Nothing went on in that single bed in Paducah that wasn't going on in a million other beds between two million other strangers. I asked her once, on a post-card, *Why me? Why do you love me?* I got a letter from her a couple of days later, the shortest letter she ever sent me. *Just because,* she said.

The high school girl—a senior and eighteen, or God knows what would have happened—came to my room one day after class sat in a desk in the front row, and said she needed some make-up work to raise her grade. I checked through my grade book.

"You're getting an *A*," I told her.

"Then I need something to lower it," she said.

I laughed and it sounded like I was strangling. I was already lost at that point.

She was a child. I have weaknesses.

We went to bed several times. Many times. She let a friend know. It got around the school. I probably would have lost my job, my wife. They switched me to Driver's Ed., a class that teaches itself. I should thank them for it.

And Jill never said word one, except to let me know she knew. I should thank her too. I should tell you how I've loved her day in and day out for thirty years, how she's loved me, how we fell in love and married and had a baby boy that everyone in Ballard County envied. Charley, a boy so beautiful and full of promise that parents were pushing daughters on him in kindergarten. No one wants to hear about those happy years. No one wants to hear about a good man being good. It's the failings people want to hear.

So be it.

JILL'S STORY

Until I saw May sitting alone at a picnic table, I thought everyone at the Tarrs' hamburger party was grotesque. Most of them were teachers—it was a teachers' function—and they knew about Edward's affair with a student. The affair was over and no one was talking about it, but they knew, and their knowledge made them grotesque. Those who weren't teachers, the spouses and dates of teachers and administrators, were just as bad. I could read the sentences on their lips: "Which one is she? The poor woman."

Mrs. Tarr, who threw the party, was vice-principal. Later that year she would die in an airplane. On her way to Hawaii with her husband, she would fall asleep and never wake. A heart attack, they said. I wondered if a bad dream had stopped her heart. A terribly bad dream.

Eva Horne was there with one of the new teachers. A woman older than I was, she dressed and acted like a tramp—or worse, like a teasing teenager. She came to the party in a low-cut blouse and miniskirt. Later, of course, we would become almost related.

May was also the girlfriend of a teacher, one of the young teachers. She had been a student of Edward's some time back, then worked for over a year with me in the real estate office as a receptionist. After she left I lost track of her until I heard about the accident, a head-on collision. The other driver and his passengers had been killed. May had gone into a coma, was kept alive mechanically; then, miraculously, after a month she came out of it. I hadn't seen her since she came out. It hadn't been long.

Her hair was very short and splotchy. Her scalp, ice-white, showed through in places, but there were no visible scars. She had a large, pretty face. She had been plump, that sexy kind of plump that some men love. But she had lost weight.

"May," I said, as I walked to the picnic table, "you look wonderful."

She smiled at me and tilted her head. "I wondered if that was you," she said. She was wearing a mauve dress with little frills on the short sleeves and around her waist. It seemed to fit her funny. A size too large, I imagined, since she had lost so much weight.

She stood uncertainly, like a child trying to be proper. I hugged her. "You're so skinny," I said. In her ear I whispered, "It's so good to see you here. I didn't think there would be anyone worth talking to."

She giggled and sat on the picnic bench. "That's a good one," she said.

While she'd worked in the office, we'd been friends—lunches, a drink at five. She had been infatuated with our son Charley, but I had discouraged her from seeing him. Charley wasn't always kind to the girls he dated. He had a meanness in him, and his girlfriends had to bear some of it, as did any of us who cared about him. Later, I told her to call him, thinking she would be good for him and that she was strong enough to deal with any of his doings.

I took her hand. Her arms were very thin. "We were all so worried," I said. "I'm happy you're all right."

"That's what Mother told me," she said, grinning and half shaking her head. "It's so funny. Everyone worrying."

I waited, thinking she would explain why that was funny, but she didn't. Instead she began playing with the napkin dispenser, the squeeze bottles of mustard and mayonnaise, the tall glass bottle of Heinz ketchup. Her fingernails were purple. To match the dress I guessed.

"You really do look wonderful," I said.

"That's what everyone says."

What I wanted to ask her was what it was like to be gone like that, to be almost dead. I assumed she didn't have any recall, but I wondered if it might be like a dream where you remember nothing at first but later see a kite or the vapor of a jet and little parts of the dream come back to you.

She touched me on the arm. "Should we eat now?" she said. Her voice was low and serious.

I smiled at her seriousness. Mrs. Tarr had made little menus and run off copies on the school mimeo. There were several ways to order a hamburger. Burger à la Tarr came with soy sauce. The nuclear burger was smothered in mushrooms. There were a number of other cutesy possibilities.

May held her menu close to her face, her purple fingernails lining the sides. Finally I said, "I think the mushroom burger sounds good."

She dropped the mimeoed sheet, obviously relieved. "I'll have that, too."

This was the first moment I wondered whether she was damaged in some way. I wondered if she could read.

Mrs. Tarr came by, overdressed in a white blouse and skirt already spattered with hamburger grease. "You two gals ready to order," she said, acting like a waitress in a greasy spoon.

May picked up the squeeze bottle of mustard, began fiddling with it, staring at the table. I felt, suddenly, that I needed to cover for her. "Well, ma'am," I said. "We girls'll have us two mushroom burgers."

"That's a good one," May said, laughing.

"Two nuke burgers for the sassy gals," Mrs. Tarr said, and she shoved her short pencil behind her ear.

"She's so funny," May said as Mrs. Tarr walked away. She set the yellow squeeze bottle of mustard down, touched the white squeeze bottle of mayonnaise, then brought the ketchup bottle close to her face. "When did they start putting ketchup in glass bottles?" she said, laughing again. "What will they think of next?"

The tenderness I felt at that moment was large enough to provide for the rest of the party members. I forgave them their knowledge, their grotesqueness.

I put my hand on May's. "Do you remember me, May?"

"Oh, of course," she said, and began turning the ketchup bottle in her hands, looking at the table.

"I have a terrible memory myself for some things." I smiled and she gave me a sidelong glance. "It's Jill Warren. We worked together for a while at a real estate office. You were the best receptionist we ever had. Well, one of the best." I didn't want to be condescending, although I felt it was probably too late to worry about that.

May leaned forward, her voice low and serious again, "Did I like that?"

I nodded. "For a while. I think you got bored with it."

She smiled. "I'm like that, aren't I?"

At that moment I remembered the dream I'd had a few nights before, and I decided to tell May about it. I probably remembered it because I wanted to ask her about the coma, wondering if a memory of being in the coma would come back to her as a dream does. But what I had observed was that she was trying to recover her life, trying to retrieve little bits of her history.

In the dream I was an adult in the farmhouse where I grew up. I had just wakened, naked under a heavy white sheet. There was a bloodstain on the bottom sheet. I looked closer. The stain was a family crest. I knew, in the way one knows in dreams, that generations of my blood had marked these sheets in just this way. The crest was a buzzard with a long crooked neck and great wings. The claws of the buzzard held an enormous diamond and a steering wheel.

Then I was in the kitchen, heating water for coffee. The room was just as it had been when I was a child: white stove with curled feet, faded yellow wallpaper, hardwood floors that would be a selling point now. I began wondering, in the dream, whether the child I had been would care for the adult I had become. At that point, a girl walked into the kitchen. I realized instantly, with that recognition that marks dreaming, that the girl was me as a child. I became nervous, intimidated by the bone-thin child, me at twelve, with dark hair and a patient smile.

Steam curled off the pan of water. The girl approached me, her eyes twisted around my body. "Let me drink coffee with you?" she asked.

I realized that she would like me if I let her drink coffee. It was that simple. Children don't judge in much deeper ways than that. I nodded to her, watched her swirl milk in her coffee to dilute the bitterness. I took mine black. We drank. She stared at my breasts. "These will be yours," I told her. She giggled.

Then our mother came in. I realized we'd been waiting for her. She told us our father was all right. This was news we were hoping to hear. I, as a little girl, ran to her. She swung me in an arc around her chest. I, as a woman, nodded in silence, approving.

May listened intently to my recollection of the dream. "I remember my dreams," she said. "Last night I was in a toolshed. There were two hammers and a rake."

Mrs. Tarr brought us our burgers. The black mushrooms oozed over the sides. She had dropped the waitress pretense. "Enjoy," she said to May. She set my paper plate in front of me and stooped to whisper in my ear. "You're holding up well," she said.

If I hadn't just spoken with May, I would have slapped her. "That's a good one," I said.

May stared at her mushroom burger. After Mrs. Tarr left, she said, "Do I like this?"

I laughed. "Maybe," I said. "Try it."

We ate slowly. I told her about the lunches we used to have when we worked together. "Was I there?" she asked. I nodded and continued. Some of the others had begun dancing on the Tarrs' patio. Edward was dancing with Eva, very close. He was drunk and liked to dance. Normally, I wouldn't have been annoyed, but with the affair unspoken on everyone's lips, I was angry.

Eva yelled to be heard over the music. "My best position is first base," she called out to a teacher dancing next to them. He was putting together a summer softball team. I had already passed on that opportunity. "Edward here," she yelled, "has gotten to first base with me already." All the dancers laughed.

"We've got a first baseman—first-base *person*—my wife," the softball coach pointed to the woman he was dancing with. "What's your second-best position?"

Eva smiled. "The missionary position." The dancers laughed again. The music stopped. "I know what Edward's position is." They kept dancing without music. "I won't say, but his number should be 69." Edward smiled but tried to step away from her. Most of the party had crowded around and was laughing. "This team might be a little old for him, though," she said. The laughter stopped. "I hear he likes to practice his positions with a younger crowd." She ran her finger under his chin. "My Brenda has heard that he has a big bat and swings from the hip."

May laughed. Everyone else was quiet, dead quiet. Edward pulled away from her. "Come on, Ed," she said. She grabbed his arm but he yanked it away, pushing through the crowd. "I need a pinch hitter," Eva said and opened her arms.

May laughed again. "She's so funny," May said.

Then something extraordinary happened: I laughed with her. Just me and May. I was happy that Edward was already around the corner of the house. He would have thought I was laughing at him. I don't know how I would have survived that moment if I hadn't started laughing with May.

Mrs. Tarr put on some more music. People started moving, talking. I stood and May stood with me. She followed me around the corner of the yard to the fence gate. "Oh, you're leaving," she said. I kissed her on the cheek.

"Can you remember anything, May? From being in the coma?"

She shook her head. "I can't remember a thing," she said. "I can't remember your name."

"It's Jill," I said. "I'm your friend."

"I can't remember the funniest things," she said. I swung open the gate. "I can't remember sex. Oh, I know how you do it, but there was some other part. There used to be more to it." The space between the Tarrs' house and their neighbors' was narrow and shady; a single shaft of light shone on the yellow stucco beside us. "It's like I'm in a whole new world," she said, and we touched hands.

I looked up and down the street for Edward, then walked to the car. He was in the front seat, lying flat, undetectable until I was right on top of the car. He sat up when I got in. "I hate that woman," he said. I started the car and drove us home.

He was quiet and restless at home. He yelled at Charley to turn down the television. Charley, of course, turned it up. Edward stormed around the house, finally deciding to go to bed at eight.

I was sitting at the kitchen table, drinking tea. Charley joined me. He pointed with his thumb toward our bedroom. "What's with him?" he said.

"He had a bad time at the party," I said.

Charley nodded. He seemed concerned about his father, a begrudging concern, but real nonetheless. I realized I was concerned too. "Something awful happened," I said.

I told Charley the story. He knew about Edward's affair, everyone at the high school did, so I was sure someone had told him. But my acknowledging that he knew, acknowledging that my husband had an affair with a high school girl, was a bit of intimacy that was rare between Charley and me. I told him the whole story and I felt close to my son.

The following weekend Charley had a date with Brenda Horne. When he saw how much it upset his father, he began seeing only her. Within a few months, she was pregnant, and they were engaged. I guess he really did fall in love with her. I'm sure of it. But if I hadn't sold out my husband in order to have a moment of intimacy with my son, it never would have happened. Maybe none of the things that followed would have come about.

I forgave Edward his trespasses.

Years later, after Charley's short marriage and long divorce, after the ugly fights he had with his father and the stupidly cruel things he said, our love for him grew crooked and bitter as a root. When he left town and disappeared from our lives, when I knew he was really gone, I felt just the way that May had felt in the narrow space between the suburban houses, between the laughter of the party and the sunlit street where my husband hid in our station wagon: I was entering a new world. It was sad and frightening, but full of possibility. And it became intoxicating. I discovered a world full of things I could give up. Then I knew what Charley had been looking for: a clean start. And only then did I know how much he must have hated himself and us.

I gave up the past. I gave up my oldest son. I started anew, and I felt *lucky*.

May was not so lucky in her new world. The teacher who took her to the party, a man everyone admired for sticking with her through her recovery, turned out to be an awful man, or maybe just typical. God, I don't know. When they pumped May's stomach, they came up with almost a pint of semen. She didn't know how many men there had been. She couldn't remember. And all I could think of was her saying, "Do I like this? Do I like this?"

James Gordon Bennett

DEPENDENTS

(from *The Virginia Quarterly Review*)

"Get real," Cora says when I ask her how long she thinks Dad will stay in the BOQ. "Just lighten up, will you?" and she smacks the page down on her movie magazine.

One of my father's black MPs is substitute bus driver this morning. You can already see waves over the macadam so he keeps the door open, which my sister says is against military regulations. As soon as we're past the guard hut, he switches on his portable radio, which Cora whispers "qualifies for an Article 15."

It's a half hour from the proving ground to Yuma Grammar and mostly the enlisted kids do their homework. Except Jeffrey Orr, who Cora claims is "narcoleptic." Last month when he fell into the aisle and knocked himself unconscious, our regular driver, Corporal Greenspun, had to race back to the dispensary, and we were an hour late for school. Now everyone tries to get Jeffrey to take an aisle seat.

The only other officer's kid is Evelyn Pallas who no one sits next to. Cora says it's because she "wears the old man's rank on her sleeve." Colonel Pallas is CO. Still, I believe Evelyn is in love with me even though we've never sat next to each other on the bus.

When we pass the giant saguaro with all the bullet holes in it, I ask Cora what a "philander" is.

"Philanderer, knucklehead. Give me a break, for chrissake."

Cora will be salutatorian of her eighth grade class ("Only because Sheila Haggar gets credit for crap like Home Ec."). She is an expert on all crossword puzzles. "Your sister is precocious," my mother will say to me. "She is also given to moods. *Nota beta.*" When I tell this to Cora, she makes her favorite snorting sound through her nose. "What Mother meant was *nota bene.*"

But right now my sister is more interested in movie stars than crossword puzzles. Last year, she tied for runner-up in our newspaper's Oscar Awards Night Contest ("Big deal, a crummy *Yuma Gazette* T-shirt"). This year she will win ("Because I'm *sick* of finishing second"). The grand prize is again a week for two at the luxurious Riviera Hotel, air fare included, only one entry per family permitted. Cora jots notes to herself in the margins of her magazines. Whenever an Oscar nominee gets mentioned, she underlines it in red felt tip. "It's all political," she says, uncapping her pen. "You have to know who's in and who's out. Or whether the vote's going to get split. Or whether they want to give it to a musical two years in a row. In other words, too complicated to explain to you."

Cora's too busy to play "ridiculous children's games." So when I see my first road runner of the morning, I don't bother to shout "beep-beep" before anyone else on the bus. Even though Beth Sibula and I are tied in points this week.

My mother says "things will work out" and that I'm not to "take the cares of the world" on my "young shoulders." Cora says I should "hang loose" or I'm going to have an ulcer before I can shave. "Besides," she says, "it's not the first time Daddy's been in the doghouse." But this time is different, I think. This time my father is a philanderer.

The public school where I am in the sixth grade is not, according to my sister, "academically sound." The best teachers come from the proving ground and leave when their husbands are transferred. Many of my classmates are mestizos who live in adobes and go to school barefoot even in the winter. They have black, shiny hair and brown teeth, and always smile when they try to speak English. They are friendly and seem happy but will never, Cora says, graduate.

When I get to home room today, Miss Clark is wearing her red Chinese dress. The one with the slit up the side and the same one my father saw her in at PTA. Afterward he joked with my mother that he regretted more than ever having gone to parochial school.

My mother nodded at me and said that I could "relax." My father wouldn't be missing any more parent-teacher meetings.

Cora says that Miss Clark is a "tease" and that she's been "egging on some hick rancher for months." But whenever I see her in the cafeteria, she is always eating alone. My home room teacher thinks I will make "an excellent college student someday." In the meantime, she wants me to try to "interact" a little more. To get outside and "mix" with the other boys and girls. But during recess I prefer to sit on the swings and talk to Miss Clark, who, like me, chooses to keep to herself.

This afternoon, when I point this out to her, she tilts the swing back and smiles crookedly. Her hands are raised overhead to grip the chains, and her bare knees locked to brace her feet in the sand. Under her arms, a thin crescent darkens her oriental dress. In class, while we write our composition papers, Miss Clark manicures her nails. She studies them with eyes slightly crossed, flicking the file as if salting her food. Outside, in the bright sunlight, she squints, making it seem when she talks to me to be concentrating fiercely. And I can pretend to be her rancher. Cora, who misses nothing, is the first to suspect this ("Just watch she doesn't string you along like her lonesome cowboy").

"Well, young man," Miss Clark says finally, bending her knees to allow the swing to carry her forward, "then we must both come out of our shells."

When she says "young man," my chest prickles the same way it does whenever the bus hits a road runner.

Saturday my father arrives to pick up my mother. Somebody big is coming through, and there's to be a color guard reception at the officers' club. As provost marshal, my father is required to wear his dress uniform even when the guest is a civilian.

"Must be hot stuff," Cora says, tapping the ribbons over his pocket. "Pop's all dolled up."

There are six oak-leaf clusters, two of the Purple Heart. But the Silver Star with its tiny metal v is my personal favorite. And the most important because it is first on the top row. I no longer ask my father how he earned it. He would only tell me once again how an Italian peddler had charged him a thousand lira. And that had he not run out of them five minutes before, it could have been the Medal of Honor. When I was a boy, my mother frowned upon his "filling the child's head with nonsense." I would repeat the tales at school and they would come back to her through the parents of my classmates. That my father's master parachute wings were won at a carnival in Chicopee, Massachusetts. That the scars on his knees only looked like shrapnel wounds. He had, in fact, accidentally knelt on a red-ant hill while on a picnic with "your mother."

My father has not been by in three days, and the hothouse tomatoes he set out on the window sill are now ripe.

"Look at that baby," he says, palming the biggest one admiringly. "Cora, le sel."

My sister hands him the shaker, wagging her head. "You get that on you, mister, your ass is grass."

But my father slices the large tomato in half and jabs the salt shaker at it repeatedly. "I get one seed on me," he says, thrusting his square chin forward, "I take it out on your hide."

But the juice only dribbles a little down his chin and he slurps it up with his tongue.

"Our role model," Cora says to me.

Although my sister tries not to show it, she is excited to have my father back. She has spent the morning straightening her room and tells him now that it is "ready for inspection." But before he can get up from the table, my mother is standing in the kitchen door.

"Hello, Major."

At first, I hadn't recognized her voice. It seemed deeper, almost hoarse. And it's the first time I've ever heard her call my father by his rank.

"Come for your tomato?"

Even Cora laughs at this.

My father scrapes his chair back. "I guess we'd better march," he says, clearing his throat. He seems as startled by my mother's presence as I am. Something more than her voice has changed.

"You can check out the room when you come back," my sister says and hands him his braided service cap. "Assuming you do come back."

When my father glances sheepishly at my mother, she rolls her eyes to the ceiling. "Your daughter, Provost."

As soon as the Fairlane backs out onto Truscott Circle, Cora is pounding me on the shoulder.

"Could you believe that getup? Un-be-*liev*-able!" my sister smacks her forehead with her palm. "Where did I see it? Give me a second." She closes her eyes dramatically. "It's coming. Uno momento. I see it. I got it." She graps my wrist and drags me into the living room. "Sit." And she pushes me back onto the couch. "Remain seated."

I watch her race back down the hall.

"Mom looks as good as a spit shine," Cora calls out to me from her room. "That Kraut won't know what hit her."

My sister claims "the other woman" is "some German war bride," the wife of one of my father's young lieutenants. "Dad's partial to the Dietrich type. What can you do?"

My sister wanders back down the hall, flipping through an old issue of *Modern Screen*. "If it's not in here," she says without looking up, "then it's. . . ." But she's found it. "There," and she smacks the page triumphantly, thrusting it before me. "Who's that remind you of?"

I study the black-and-white picture of a woman standing beside a large canopied bed. She's wearing only a slip and has one arm over her head, gripping the wooden post.

"Jesus," Cora says, snapping the magazine out of my hands. "It's Liz Taylor. *Butterfield Eight*? Best actress nomination?"

But all we get at the post theater are Westerns and James Bond.

"Mom's vamping him," Cora says, more to herself than to me. "Obvious to everyone, of course, except a certain airhead sibling."

But the contest entry form has to be postmarked by midnight tonight, and she retreats to her room with her felt tip pen.

In the carport, I unzip Dad's golf bag and scoop out a half dozen balls. He keeps two sand wedges, and I take the older, scratched one.

The parade field is just up the block, and I wear my nylon parachute cap. It's probably close to a hundred out. This is supposed to be a big proving ground, but I've never seen a rocket fired yet. Mostly they test out experimental equipment. Like this cap my Dad brought home. Somebody from Quartermaster claims it's the original "prototype." That it cost a couple million dollars to develop. When I told my father that my Little League cap was more comfortable, he said I was what made "America strong" and that I didn't have to worry about ever getting drafted.

Even on the parade field you have to keep your eyes open. Last month, my father's first sergeant killed a sidewinder in his daughter's sandbox. Every other dog you see around here has a limp. "They want to test something useful," Cora likes to say, "why don't they test one of those neutron bombs on all the snakes? They're not supposed to hurt buildings. We could all go to Vegas for a few weeks, government expense."

I try to remember to keep my elbow stiff on the backswing. There's enough room to hit a driver, but it's too hot to do much walking. Every other week my father lets me tag along with his foursome. I'll hold the flag or replace divots. He didn't mention anything about tomorrow though. So I guess it's off. Lots of times when he goes fishing or hunting, he'll bring me, and I'll be the only kid. Even though some of his buddies have sons my own age. But I didn't ask him about Sunday. He doesn't have to think about me all the time.

The ball makes a little puff of dust where it lands and you can't take your eye off the spot or you'll lose it. But when I see Evelyn Pallas crossing the parade field toward me, I forget about the ball. She's a year ahead of me and runs the relay on the girls' track team. I've seen her in her gym shorts and spike shoes out practicing on the cinder track.

Her younger brother trails behind her, tossing a play parachute into the air. She suddenly stops and points at the ground.

"Got it," she calls out to me.

I wave the club and pick up the other ball. I don't want to risk sculling it. While they wait for me, her little brother wraps the handkerchief tightly about the rock and hurls it toward the road. But it doesn't open.

Evelyn stands with her hands on her hips like a runner. She's slightly taller than me but still has a flat chest. We both watch her brother stretch his arm out behind him like a javelin thrower. He makes a grunting sound, heaving the rock with all his might. But the handkerchief comes down again without opening.

"What's that—a nine iron?" Evelyn asks me.

I raise the club for her to see. "A sand wedge."

"Then that was a pretty good hit."

Evelyn's mother, Cora says, is an alcoholic, "par excellence." According to my sister, Mrs. Pallas "tools around half the time drunk as a skunk." Last month, for instance, one of the MPs had to tow the colonel's staff car over to the motor pool. "She hopped a curb and took out a fire hydrant." Cora said. "But get this. She told Dad she was only trying to get a pizza home before it cooled off."

"I guess everybody's over at the reception," Evelyn says, taking the club from me.

She nods at the ground and I drop one of the balls at her feet. In the distance, her brother stops to watch her take several practice swings. She bends both elbows the way girls do but I don't say anything.

"Your mom and dad go together?" she asks finally.

Cora says that it's always going to be news when "the goddamn provost marshal's living in the BOQ."

"Yes."

She swats at the ball but it only skitters off to the right.

"You probably think track's pretty stupid for a girl, don't you?" I watch her squat down to scoop some sand into a small mound. "Well, it doesn't matter. I'm good at it."

Looking up at me, she snaps her fingers, and I hand her the second ball. "I should tell you what my mother said about your father." She balances the ball on top of the mound. "It's rich."

Her brother yells something to her, but Evelyn ignores him.

"She said your father knows how to wear a pith helmet."

This time she hits the ball more solidly, and it sails high over her brother's head.

"I hate this place," Evelyn says, shading her eyes. "I'd like to know what they think they're proving. I've never even seen a stupid rocket go off."

Later Cora and I talk my mother into letting us see *Dirty Harry* at the post theater. Even though the proving ground is several hundred miles square, you can walk to everything on the base in ten minutes.

"Mom's a wreck," my sister says as soon as we're out of the house. "That stupid Kraut was at the reception."

It's already dark enough out to see a few stars. And in another hour or so you'll be able to hear the coyotes. They like to wander down for any scraps they can dig out of the mess hall cans.

"Dad introduced them," Cora is saying. "So now they're supposed to go over for drinks. That lieutenant must be a total idiot. Mom's ready to shoot him."

I find the Dipper and then the North Star. "The lieutenant?"

My sister glances past me at the canal across the road. It's stagnant and thick with algae, and her lip appears to curl up at its smell. "Daddy, moron."

There's a long line at the theater, and Cora spots one of her friends farther up near the ticket window.

"Every man for himself," she says and is gone.

But ten minutes later, Sergeant Shuman sticks his head out of the double glass doors to the theater.

"Sorry, folks. All sold out."

They'll have a second "special showing" at ten if we want to buy our tickets now. "Make my day," someone shouts from the back of the line, but only a few people give up their places.

I don't much feel like a movie anyway so I'm not real disappointed. There's a National Geographic Special on at eight about the Arctic. Or I could just read.

All the street lights flicker on ahead of me like new, bright stars. And it's dark enough now to see satellites. I take the long way home, past Evelyn Pallas's street. She said as "Dependents" we could use the driving range at night. For fifty cents split a large bucket of practice balls. Because she's athletic, she'd probably learn to keep her elbow stiff.

But then suddenly I'm sitting in the road, a metal pole only inches from my bloodied nose. The pavement is still warm from the heat of the day, and I want only to stay seated. To stand I must grip the stop sign before me. And then I understand that it's what I had walked into.

At home, my mother puts me to bed. She's wrapped several crushed ice cubes in a facecloth.

"Miss Clark says you're preoccupied," she says, pressing the facecloth to my burning forehead. "That you daydream in class."

We both listen to the coyotes howling outside.

Usually, for something like this, she will say, "Like father like son." But tonight she doesn't.

Some time later, I'm awakened briefly by the voices of my sister and mother in the kitchen. The hushed, adult tone seems intended to exclude me. And then it's Cora, I think, who is crying. Or perhaps my mother. In the dark, it becomes impossible to distinguish between them.

I had been dreaming of the Arctic and of playing golf with Evelyn Pallas in the snow. There it's as flat and bare as the proving ground, and each ball we hit hangs in the air like a miniature moon. "Don't even bother to look," Evelyn remarks, dressed in her track suit and spiked running shoes. "You're not going to find anything."

I slide up against the headboard, shielding my eyes from the overhead light.

"Honey, you want to get up?"

It's my mother. And then Cora is standing in the doorway. Both of them still dressed.

"Too bad you're not on the ballot," my sister is saying. "This is Oscar-winning stuff."

My mother angrily whips the blanket from my legs, leaving only the sheet to cover me. "Watch the mouth, young lady." But then just as abruptly her voice is gentle and coaxing. "Put your clothes on, sweetheart. I need you for something."

As soon as she leaves the room, Cora crosses her arms as if to mimic my mother's stance.

"Don't let them give her a breathalizer," she whispers.

My mother waits for me in the car, the engine already idling.

"You feel all right?" she asks, reaching over to touch the Band-Aid on my forehead. But before I can answer, she shoves the gearshift forcefully into reverse.

Cora comes out to the carport to shout, "Headlights," but my mother purposely ignores her. With the abrupt dip at the end of the driveway, the tail pipe scrapes the gutter.

I know where we are going. My father has taken the staff car. Now my mother will retrieve him from the duplex over on Stillwell Avenue. Cora has pointed out the flat-roofed house to me from the school bus. "Mata Hari's place," she said and then fogged the window to trace a skull and bones. Even though Cora is older, my mother brings me instead because I am the male.

"You don't want the wrong impression here," she begins, gazing straight ahead. It's the same blank look she has after an hour of ironing my father's khaki uniforms. "Your sister can get a little carried away. Right now she's upset with your father. And she's probably said some things to you."

I crack my window slightly. At night the cooler air conceals the rancid smell of the canals.

"He just wants his men to like him," my mother is saying. "But sometimes the social drinking can get out of hand." She glances over at me as if to be certain that I've not fallen back asleep. "We both know when to let Cora go in one ear and out the other."

My mother's voice grows sullen as we move out of the senior grade housing and into the low, flat duplexes of the junior officers. I recognize the tone. It is the same one Cora uses whenever she believes things have gone "beyond brother's feeble limits."

"You may have your father's coloring," my mother says as if I have just contradicted her wilfully, "but you've damn well got my eyes."

She concentrates on the straight, flat road ahead but occasionally jerks the steering wheel sharply to keep from crossing the center line.

"I know what you're thinking," she says without looking over at me. "But I'm not."

Last year her license was suspended for six months when she accidentally drove the station wagon into the canal. It was late, and she had taken the turn off MacArthur Boulevard in third instead of second. The judge advocate told her she was lucky she hadn't drowned and then put her on probation for an additional six months. "Mom got off light," Cora told me afterwards, "mostly because Dad has the goods on guess-who's sixteen-year-old." The judge's daughter had been caught laminating fake IDs for the PX.

My father's familiar green staff car is parked in the double driveway of the duplex, and on seeing it, my mother pulls up too close to the curb, squealing the tires. She leaves the engine on, looking first into the rearview mirror to wet down her eyebrows and then at me.

"Your head must be pounding," she says and hooks her warm hand around my neck to draw me towards her. "I won't be a minute, sweetie. Then we can all go home."

There's rum on her breath. Cora had fixed her piña coladas in the blender ("Half a dozen minimum").

"I hate him," I say, but my voice catches, garbling my words.

"What?" My mother grabs my wrist when I try to open the door. "Sweetheart, you just sit and listen to the radio. I won't be a minute." And then as if she'd finally been able to decipher my sentence, she smoothes the wet hair back from my forehead. "Your father's the bravest soldier in the army, honey. This doesn't mean anything next to that."

Cora likes to say that "Mom's your basic 'take-orders' kind of housewife." But even my sister knows better than to break the Rule. We are never to "bad-mouth" our father in her presence. Never.

I slump down in the front seat and watch my mother, one shoulder lower than the other, walk up the yellow patch of lawn as if trying to get to the front of a moving bus. Her toes point, like my sister's, slightly out. Cora says that my father does not love her anymore. That the lieutenant's wife is "built like a tank" and that "Dad wants to get back into artillery."

When at last the screen door is pushed open several inches, my mother steps back out of the way as if to accept the invitation to come in. Instead, she waits until my father joins her on the porch, wearing civilian clothes and holding a glass in his hand. I turn off the radio but their voices are too low to hear. In a minute, my father has disappeared back inside the house and the lieutenant and his wife replace him, framed in the light of the door. The lieutenant's wife is nearly as tall as her husband. And I think of Miss Clark standing in line at the cafeteria, the heads of her students barely to her shoulders. They are both smiling, talking to my mother as if still trying to win her inside. But she does not uncross her arms until my father reappears, this time wearing his leather aviator jacket.

At the driveway, he turns to wave good-night to the couple, who have come out onto the porch holding hands. But my mother does not turn or wave or say another word to my father. She walks instead ahead of him past the staff car and around the lieutenant's MG.

As soon as she is back in the driver's seat, my mother pats me twice on the knee and tells me "Never marry a WAC." But then she tries to turn the key in the ignition even though the engine is already on. When the gears grind, she snaps her hand back as if from a hot stove.

"I know what you're thinking," she says to me.

My father ambles up alongside the car, stooping so that his chin rests on my open window. "Hey, buddy," and he taps his forehead with one finger. "You been backtalking the old lady?"

My mother looks coolly. "Step away you don't want any major toes flattened."

My father's tanned face shines in the dark. He grins happily, his straight, even teeth those of a movie star.

"Sure you don't want to come in?" he asks my mother. "They're right nice people."

"Don't patronize me," she answers sharply. "That's your son sitting there."

My father reaches in to grip my shoulder. "Then maybe I ought to invite him in. What do you say, soldier? You want to show your mother how to be sociable?"

He squeezes my arm as if to gain attention but I haven't taken my eyes off him. I have never seen my father smile this way before. My heart is racing even faster than with Evelyn Pallas this afternoon.

"Don't you ask him that," my mother says. "Don't you ask him anything."

Over my father's shoulder I can see the lieutenant and his wife still waiting on the porch. She wears high heels and appears as tall and slender as Miss Clark. They shift their weight from one foot to the other in the cool night air. But they cannot close the door on us.

"No," my father says resignedly and takes a single duck step back from the car. "He's a momma's boy, all right."

But before I can even turn to see her, my mother has flung her door open and is shouting over the hood.

"What did you say, mister? What the hell did you say?"

I twist in the seat as she flashes by the rear window. But by the time I unlock my own door, my father is grasping both her wrists, dancing away from her furious kicks.

"You bastard!" she is screaming. "You conceited, lousy bastard!"

The lieutenant trots down the driveway but stops respectfully at the mailbox.

"Sir?"

His wife has stayed on the porch, one hand at her mouth.

"Sir?" he repeats but then looks away helplessly.

My ears still ring from the stop sign and I cover them with my hands. As if in pantomime my mother attempts to wrench free until my father trips over the embedded sprinkler head and they both drop to their knees in the scorched grass.

"Don't you come home," my mother says, her face only inches from my father's. "You don't live there anymore, mister."

"Fine," he says, wishing only to calm her. "Fine. Let's just go home."

But he does not follow her across the lawn.

When she staggers around the car, my mother glares at me menacingly.

"And the kids are mine," she shouts, closing her eyes as if to steady herself. "Mine."

Back again in the front seat, my mother rests her forehead on the steering wheel.

"I could drive," I say even though I've never gone farther than the driveway.

But she lifts her head tiredly. "I'll get us there, sweetheart."

And she does, but not without first backing into the lieutenant's mailbox, crushing the little red metal flag.

At the house, my mother pours herself the rest of the piña colada mix from the blender and goes to bed, locking the door after her. It is what she does whenever my father is left to sleep alone on the couch.

Cora tiptoes down the hall to peek into my room.

"Any stabbings?"

But I pretend to be asleep.

"Military life," my sister says, easing the door shut behind her. She sits cross-legged on the throw rug beside my bed. "The civilian population doesn't know the half of it."

Over her head, I can just make out the different model airplanes suspended by fishing wire from the ceiling. Several of the real ones my father has jumped from on maneuvers. Once, when I asked him how it felt to fall all that way before his chute opened, he said he'd be able to explain it better when I was a little older and "maybe had a sweetheart like Miss Clark."

"Don't take it too hard," Cora advises me, kneeling beside my bed now. "They'll kiss and make up. Mom's not going to let him rot in the BOQ." When my sister stands up, she tries to touch the damp pillow case so that I don't notice. "Listen, you're just an army brat. You don't know the whole story yet."

At the door, she whispers that if she wins the contest, she'll think about taking me along. "Who knows, Vegas might be good for you. Give you a shot at the big picture."

But, in fact, Cora does not win the Second Annual Oscar Awards Night competition. An unemployed typesetter who once worked at the newspaper does. "Mostly they were just wild guesses," he tells the reporter from the *Yuma Gazette*. "Half the pictures I didn't even see." My sister's letter to the editor, in which she demands an "entire revamping of the contest rules," is never published. That summer, I see Evelyn Pallas break her ankle in a practice relay race. She trips on the baton dropped by her team-mate. "No big deal," she confesses to me afterward. "We're getting out of here anyway. Pop got passed over for his star." By then my father has received his orders to Sasebo, Japan. But Miss Clark leaves before any of us. She is fired by the school board two weeks into the new term. Cora claims the vice-principal found her in the teachers' lounge smoking a joint. "But dig this," my sister adds, "she was standing in front of the floor fan in her slip."

I would like to learn how to speak Japanese. They seem to be a very polite people. And I think I would get along with them. "Even if they do only come up to your knee," Cora says. But my mother does not want to "drag the rest of us over there." And at night you can hear her arguing bitterly with my father. On the bus today Cora sits beside me without having been told to. It is the first time she seems to consider anything I ask her seriously. But when I wonder what makes army families any different from the rest, she peels her thumbnail back so far that the skin bleeds. "Mom keeps us stateside," my sister says, scanning the desert as if for a road runner, "you can kiss our platoon leader sayonara. *Nota bene.*"

BIOGRAPHICAL NOTES

Luke Whisnant, a native North Carolinian, received his MFA degree in 1982 from Washington University in St. Louis. He teaches now in the writing program at East Carolina University and has published fiction and poetry in various magazines and journals. This is his second appearance in *New Stories from the South.*

Robert Taylor, Jr., an Oklahoman by birth and a Tennesseean by heritage and inclination, currently lives in "pleasant exile" in Pennsylvania, where he teaches at Bucknell and co-edits the literary journal, *West Branch.* He is the author of *Loving Belle Starr,* a collection of stories, and *Fiddle and Bow,* a novel (Algonquin, 1984 and 1985).

Marly Swick doesn't claim any regional allegiance. She was born in Indianapolis, but lived there only two weeks. Because of her father's job with General Motors, the family moved repeatedly throughout her childhood—the longest stop was two years in Atlanta. She lives now in Iowa and has published other stories in *Redbook, The Iowa Review,* and *The North American Review.*

Lee Smith grew up in Grundy, Virginia, and graduated from St. Catherine's School in Richmond and from Hollins College. She lives now in Chapel Hill, North Carolina, and teaches at North Carolina State University, where she is Director of the Creative Writing Program. Her most recent novel is *Family Linen.*

Bob Shacochis's collection of stories, *Easy in the Islands,* won an American Book Award in 1985 and his first novel, *Swimming in the Volcano,* is soon to be released. He is a native of Virginia and a former Peace Corps volunteer. His stories have appeared in many magazines.

Peggy Payne writes both fiction and nonfiction. Her articles have appeared in *The New York Times, McCall's,* and *Family Circle* among others, and her travel writing has taken her to more than twenty-five countries. Her fiction has been syndicated by PEN and included in the North Carolina anthology, *Cardinal.* A North Carolina native, she lives now in Chatham County, North Carolina.

Lewis Nordan, a native of Itta Bena, Mississippi, is assistant professor of creative writing at the University of Pittsburgh. His stories have appeared in *The Greensboro Review, Harper's, Playgirl, Redbook,* and *The Southern Review* and have been collected in two volumes, *Welcome to the Arrow-Catcher Fair* and *The All-Girl Football Team* (LSU Press, 1983 and 1986).

Trudy Lewis was born in Oklahoma, but grew up in Belleview, Nebraska. She holds an undergraduate degree from The University of Tulsa and a masters degree from Vanderbilt University. At present, she is completing her MFA at the University of North Carolina at Greensboro.

Mary Hood lives near Woodstock, Georgia. She is the author of two collections of stories. The first, *How Far She Went,* is now available in Avon paperback, and the second, *Venus Is Blue,* was published last year by Tichnor and Fields.

Andre Dubus was born in Lake Charles, Louisiana, but feels his real home town is Lafayette, where he attended the Cathedral School from third grade to twelfth. He has four grown children and, with his wife Peggy Rambach, two young daughters. They live in Harverill, Massachusetts. His latest book is *The Last Worthless Evening,* four novellas and two stories (David Godine, 1986).

Vicki Covington was born in 1952 in Birmingham, Alabama, and has lived there all her life. Her work has appeared in *The New Yorker, Ascent, Southern Humanities Review,* and *The Louisville Review.* She received a PEN Syndicated Fiction Project Award in 1986.

John William Corrington of Shreveport, Louisiana, is a lawyer, scholar, and writer. He and his wife, Joyce, are at present living in Los Angeles, where they are working as Producer–Head Writers for the television show "Superior Court." His most recent novels are *So Small a Carnival, A Project Named Desire, A Civil Death* (with Joyce Corrington), and *All My Trials* (two short novels).

Rosanne Coggeshall was born in Florence, South Carolina, grew up in Hartsville and Darlington, South Carolina, and lives now in Fincastle, Virginia. She has had stories in several magazines, including *Epoch, Iowa Review,* and the *South Carolina Review,* and her story, "Lamb Says," was reprinted in *The Best American Short Stories* 1982. Her second book of poetry, *Traffic, with Ghosts,* was published by Houghton Mifflin in 1984.

Robert Boswell grew up in Wickliffe, Kentucky, on the Mississippi River. His collection of stories, *Dancing in the Movies,* won the 1985 Iowa School of Letters Award for Short Fiction and his second book, *Crooked Hearts,* will be published by Knopf this year. He teaches writing at Northwestern University in Evanston, Illinois, where he lives with his wife, Antonya Nelson.

James Gordon Bennett "was born jaundiced and an Army brat" at Ft. Bragg, North Carolina. He attended Johns Hopkins and Stanford, and teaches in the writing program at Louisiana State University in Baton Rouge. His stories have appeared in many magazines and literary quarterlies including *The Antioch Review, Quarterly West,* and *Western Humanities Review.*

Shannon Ravenel, the editor, was born and raised in the Carolinas—Charlotte, Greenville, Camden, and Charleston. After graduating from Hollins College, she went to work in publishing. For the last ten years, she has served as Annual Editor of *The Best American Short Stories* series and, for the last five, as Senior Editor of Algonquin Books of Chapel Hill. She lives in St. Louis with her husband, Dale Purves, and their two daughters.